LIBBY FLATS

Libby Flats

THE LONGEST JOURNEYS LEAD BACK TO YOURSELF

Alan O'Hashi

Boulder Community Media

Contents

Dedication

Libby Flats is dedicated to my parents, Becca and Gary Steiner, and their friends, Avery Meadows and Jack Middleton.

I finished editing Dad's book in 2007. It's about how my mother held her small group of University of Wyoming friends together and reunited with them 40 years later. Dad granted me an editorial license, and I added my perspectives. That was cathartic.

I've journeyed through life, leaving my past acquaintances in the dust, thinking they were useless to me as I clawed my way to the top but made it as far as the middle. I realized they wouldn't be there for me when I slid back down to the bottom, which is when I appreciated Mom's efforts to force me to be more accepting and less self-absorbed.

There's always time for a fresh start. What occurred to me was that my negative traits rose to the surface when I complained and bitched. I tended to categorize my experiences as various levels of bad. I had forgotten what Grandma Sally had always said, "Experiences are neither happy nor gloomy. They just are."

The book is also dedicated to the 26 writers who regularly attended the Shut Up & Write writing group I started on ZOOM during the COVID-19 pandemic.

During those sessions, I wrote outlines for three *Libby Flats* book sequels. I collaborated on a screenplay that was optioned and wouldn't have been completed had it not been for the accountability that came from writing in the company of others.

Thanks to Laramie artist and climber Joe Arnold for his assistance with the Medicine Bow and Grand Teton climbing sequences and to

Bill Edwards for his insights about working as a teenager outfitting mountaineering school students.

Elizabeth Steiner - E.S.
Boulder, Colorado
September 7, 2023

1

Sunrise

October 2, 2006—7:27 a.m. MDT: The ear-piercing tinkle of a delicate china teacup and saucer shattering on the hardwood floor echoed into the kitchen.

"ELIZABETH!" Her father wailed in shock as he stood at the threshold of her mother's bedroom door of the Blue Sky Village cohousing community condominium.

Elizabeth strode quickly into the room.

"She fell out of bed and banged her head," Gary Steiner said of his wife, Becca. There was a pool of blood on the floor that oozed from the forehead wound she sustained from hitting the corner of the steel frame.

Elizabeth checked for a pulse and took a deep breath upon seeing her mother's glazed-over eyes.

"Her heart stopped," she said as tears welled up in her eyes. Elizabeth's life experiences with her mom, spanning 38 years, rapidly passed through her mind as she sprang into action. She rolled her mother over and tilted back her head. Elizabeth used her finger to clear her airway of sputum and stomach contents.

"Dad, your handkerchief."

She completed 30 compressions and exhaled two breaths through the hanky.

Her father grabbed the phone off the floor.

"Sunrise Health Care Center," the dispatcher answered.

"My wife fell out of bed. Elizabeth started CPR."

He let out a deep sigh.

"Her morning nurse should be on the way."

"You know the place? Blue Sky Village? We're upstairs in 1501, the orange door."

"Thanks for the reminder, Mr. Steiner. I'll call 911."

****

There was a knock. The shift nurse entered the unlocked door and headed straight to the bedroom.

"She wasn't responsive," Elizabeth panted. She had been at it for 38 minutes and was exhausted.

The nurse squeezed her shoulder.

"That's enough."

Elizabeth finished the last round of compressions and toppled over.

An ambulance and fire truck pulled up in the alley, their lights flashing. The community Caring and Sharing Committee members gathered at the bottom of the stairs as two EMTs and a firefighter bound up the outer stairs.

The nurse checked for vital signs.

"Time of death, 8:37 a.m. My boss will call the coroner. I'm very sorry."

The nurse looked up at the medical crew while checking the "Natural Causes" box on the incident form.

"She's staying here for the time being."

"Sounds good. We're parked in the back doing our paperwork if you need anything."

"I think we have this under control, guys."

****

Gary Steiner plopped down on the bentwood chair and dropped his head as his eyes welled up with tears. Still catching her breath,

Elizabeth sat cross-legged and deep in thought beside her father. Tears again flowed down her cheek. She covered her mom, Becca, with the sky-blue wool blanket Becca dragged to the floor.

"Bad things always happen when I'm around. I don't think we would have ever finished our talk, anyway. Elizabeth took a deep breath with sadness and took her mother's hand. "I wonder if you'd still be alive if it weren't for me."

"You had nothing to do with this. The outcome could have been different had we made other choices."

"Like What? Me not being born? Well, maybe that wouldn't have been so bad."

"She had a big family surprise to tell you about."

"I don't need any more surprises."

"You think you're in the dark? I don't know anything about it, either. Even if I did, someone would have to remind me. She was so eager for you to come home."

"Maybe I should have waited a couple more days."

"Remember Grandma Sally's advice."

"I know. 'Things happen, neither good nor bad. They just happen.'"

"You can help us get organized. Help me notify people."

"During our knock-down-drag-out, Mom mentioned your friends Jack and Avery. I've met Avery."

"Avery's a good egg. Jack? Me, the odd leg in his love triangle? Never thought it possible."

"What are you talking about?"

"We don't talk about Jack, that self-centered bastard. Present company excluded."

"Gee, thanks, Dad."

"Forty years ago, we all made a promise because of Jack. I don't know if I can fulfill our pact." Gary's eyes grew big, and his fists clenched.

Gary knelt beside Becca, took a deep breath, and stroked her cheek. We had a good run, you and me. You were one helluva woman."

"I wish I would have been a better daughter."

2

Tommy Lasorda

20 Days earlier–2:36 p.m. MDT: Gary and Becca Steiner were moving from their upstairs bedroom in their cohousing community condo to the downstairs guest room, where it would be easier for Becca to get around.

"Relapse? I call it a temporary setback," said Becca. "I'm perfectly capable of handling the stairs. Becca lay in the hospital bed in the first-floor guest bedroom.

Gary was moving into his office. Both rooms adjoined the downstairs bathroom.

"Couldn't you have hired a moving company?" Becca asked, fidgeting around, trying to sit on the edge of her bed.

"The neighbors have been good about helping," Gary said patiently. "We don't have that much to haul."

The biggest chore was carrying down their clothes. Becca used the top two guest room dresser drawers, and Gary placed his clothes in the bottom two. He slept on the futon in his office.

"Careful with your typewriter. The last thing we need is another invalid around here," warned Becca.

He awkwardly grasped the 30-pound manual Olympia and carefully descended the stairs. It was an Army-green monstrosity, and if dropped from one of the helicopters that evacuated Gary from his missions in Southeast Asia, the bomb could have handily taken out a Commie machine gun nest.

"Glad they caught your lymphoma early. If what they say is true, you'll be back on your feet in no time."

"Who's 'they?' Where'd you hear that, from Dr. Search Engine?"

"Virtual docs have more time to tend to their patients."

"Can you get my pills? Riley will be by later to help. I want to stay on schedule."

"Why aren't you going to the clinic?" Gary handed Becca an amber bottle from the nightstand.

"What would be worse? You driving me 25 miles and forgetting where we're going or waiting for the nurse to show up? It's not the usual, but good enough for now."

"True' dat."

Gary fetched Becca a glass of water before going to his office and continuing his writing project.

"Click Clack Click Clack…!"

"How do you expect me to be half miserable with your writing racket and that 'DING' at the end of every line?" Becca yelled, scrunching up her face and covering her ears. "Move your typing table to the living room. When can we get back upstairs?"

"Patience, patient!" Gary bellowed back.

"R iii PPPPP"

"SCREECH!"

After he yanked the page out of the carriage, Gary grabbed the bentwood chair and sat at Becca's bedside while waving the paper in front of her face.

Gary straightened out the hand-woven sky-blue blanket covering her legs.

"Would you mind? I meant for you to move yourself out now! At least fix that squeaky caster. The last thing I need is to lose my hearing."

"Page 382. The End!" Gary exclaimed, taking her hand as if they were prancing around the room."

Becca grabbed the remote from her abdomen and elevated the bed to its full and upright, locked position.

"I have my little Blue Sky Village celebration party script project to write until this medicine fogs my brain."

"You're a workaholic. Why not let Susan take over? She thrives on being in charge. You won't get better as long as you keep up this pace."

"One thing I learned from your mom on the ranch is to treat people like horses. Make them think it's their idea, 'Oh, Susan. You'll be such a terrific producer of our 10th-anniversary celebration.'"

"Celebration? Yeah, right, Becca."

It's very romantic. I'll edit my book. You finish your script. To-gether, we can write like the wind."

Gary located a manila envelope on Becca's bedstand and pulled out a stack of hand-written pages.

"Here's your latest draft. Who's gonna be your director?"

"*Blue Sky Village 10th Anniversary*," she read from the title sheet. "How about Skorsburg directing?" Becca snidely retorted.

"He's due for a box office blockbuster." Gary wandered back to his typewriter.

"You always walk away from me when we're having a conversation."

"I'm listening."

"... and Morgan Stanford catering craft services on set."

"She needs something to do now that she's out of the slammer."

"Maybe she'll write a new book, *Morgan Stanford's Prisoner Pamper-ing*," Becca joked. "I haven't heard back from Paula Peters."

"Ha! She's so vain. You didn't say anything about her." Gary rolled his eyes while paraphrasing her hit single, supposedly about her ill-fated romance with singer-turned-actor Roscoe Tanner. "You've been working on that script for five years.

"This is a great opportunity for the cohousers to learn from our experiences."

"I have a few war stories in my book based on the goings-on here. It's all about community." He leafed through Becca's notes. "Okay, let's see here. 'INT. COMMON HOUSE - AFTERNOON.' I see you called out music. *There's Nothin' You Can Do.* Roscoe Tanner's best. Your favorite song from the *Our Conference* movie," Gary said, changing the subject. "When are you telling our daughter about all this fun?"

"Elizabeth is on 'need to know' status. She thinks she has it all figured out. We've always let her do her own thing. Doesn't like to talk to me," Becca said with a yawn.

"Face it. You're the one who thrives on creating conflicts," observed Gary.

"She'll be here in a flash once I tell her that all will be forgiven if she can pry Morgan Stanford away from her restaurant in New Orleans."

"As if she'll believe that. It's going to be one rousing release party for your book heading to the publisher and a community celebration, Gary, my precious. Ten years in the making. I can't believe we've lived at Blue Sky Village since the start."

"More like a 'relief' party. Much has happened during the past five years," said Gary, pointing to the intravenous (IV) line taped to Becca's wrist.

Becca had wrapped her once wavy, shoulder-length brunette tresses with a Los Angeles Dodgers rally handkerchief.

"Your circumstances were different in '01. There's no better time than now. You still have that 1981 scarf from Dodger Stadium?"

"Thanks to your press pass, we were one of the first through the turnstiles, and what a World Series souvenir!" Becca responded.

"I don't know why you keep wearing that thing. It was the strike-shortened season," Gary reminded her of his bias about why the Dodgers beat the Yankees. "A baseball history asterisk. It was hard to write those stories. So much for working vacations. They're stressful!"

"What do you mean 'asterisk'? A championship is a championship," Becca shot back. "Tommy Lasorda out-coached Bob Lemon in Game 6. The Yankees take out Tommy John in the 4th with it all tied up at 1-1? Give me a break! We play the Cubbies tomorrow. Hand me the sports section. See here? What's today, Tuesday? It's next week. Here it is."

"We don't get the Baseball TV channel. Email the Community Activity bunch. They'll put it on the calendar," Gary suggested. "Can I get you a different do-rag? The one from Wrigley Field?"

"How about you reserve the TV room? That committee will never get around to it ... and no, I don't need a different Do-Rag." Becca splattered the sports section on the floor. "'Do-Rag,' what a funny word. Did you know Ethiopian kings wore them?"

"Always the cultural anthropologist."

Gary held up the water pitcher.

"Yes, please. I get dehydrated."

Becca picked up a framed black-and-white photo on the end table next to her bed of three smiling young men surrounding a younger version of herself with long, windswept hair in front of a vast panoramic scene.

"Hard to believe I pioneered out West. I wonder how things would have turned out had I stayed in Jersey."

"'No matter where you run, there you are," observed Gary.

"... and since when did you become such a Yankees fan? Our friend Jackie must have rubbed off on you more than you realize."

3

Cherry Ridge

It wasn't until I sorted through Mom's stuff and met her friends that I learned much about her background. As a child, she was withdrawn and quiet but rebellious. I took after her in those ways. My mission was to do anything contrary to what I was asked. Mom's self-isolation was a throwback to her parents pushing her to conform to societal norms. Like Mom, I needed a fresh start, but I wasn't ready for it to begin with a family emergency. E.S.

******

The warm light under the tree canopy was a lovely accent to the clear blue skies of Cherry Ridge. Mid-century Modern societal formalities from the 1950s and 1960s kept Becca Pembroke in New Jersey until she was in high school. She was supposed to marry a successful local fellow, settle down, and spend her spare time dusting the knickknacks.

About as far as she ventured was to Cape May in the southern part of the state, where her father substituted in the pulpit a few times a year.

Becca often stayed behind because she didn't like the feel of big-city crowds, nor was she particularly fond of the shore. When she did tag along, it was because she talked her father, Pastor Jere, into wandering the Boardwalk in Atlantic City, where they shared a "Famous Jersey

Pork Roll Sandwich" at Piggy's, one of those short-order walk-up booths specializing in greasy gut bombs.

She liked to watch the cook prepare the sizzling delight. Her mother, Mary, turned up her nose at the thought of pork roll. That was a small but yet another source of conflict she had with her down-to-earth husband and daughter.

****

Mary was the Cherry Ridge Historical Society president. The group had monthly meetings, sometimes at members' homes but more often at the museum. It wasn't technically a museum.

A wealthy benefactor donated an old house that was converted into a small exhibit space. It was more like a repository where families in town brought old stuff gathering dust in the attic. The collection was notable for a local museum, considering everything on the East Coast was old. George Washington slept everywhere.

The Pembrokes were middle class. Jere was the latest Congregational Church minister and was a very practical sort compared to Mary, who dreamed of living a more opulent lifestyle. She ascended the Historical Society hierarchy to rub elbows with the Cherry Ridge rich and famous, including Fred Middleton, the wealthiest man in town.

"Becca? Time to get ready," Mary commanded.

"I have a riding lesson," a reluctant Becca deflected.

"We'll be finished with the decorating by then."

Becca's favorite time at the museum was helping to set up for the winter holidays, which spanned Thanksgiving through Christmas and New Year's Day. She was fascinated by the displays of festive trees adorned with old blown glass ornaments. The Society volunteers decked the museum halls with wooden, plastic, large, and small Nativity scenes.

Holidays or not, her favorite attraction was the cast iron Trick Dog bank on the front counter. It featured a clown with a red, bulbous nose holding a hoop for the dog to jump through.

Before heading out with her mother, Becca scrounged under the living room couch cushions in search of small change. She'd always find a few cents. Her Uncle Stanley had coins jingling in his pocket. A few leaked out when he came over for coffee after the 11 o'clock service.

She would place a penny in the sitting dog's mouth and then push down a small lever. A spring-loaded hammer propelled the coin through the hoop and into a barrel with a dull clunk. The bank was the source of endless entertainment and countless smiles. The few found coins Becca fed into the bank were her donations to the Historical Society.

Occasionally, a penny would miss the mark and fly onto the oak plank floor. Becca would always let them be. Her theory was that if everyone picked up all the coins they dropped, there would be no lucky money for others to find, like Uncle Stanley's good luck coins under the divan cushions.

"Do you want one of those?" a voice murmured behind her.

It was her classmate, Jack Middleton. His grandfather was the church minister before her father was confirmed. Becca loaded another penny into the bank and let it fly.

"If you gave me one of these banks, I would have no reason to visit the museum."

"I'll grab five bucks from my dad's emergency cash if you come to the church Christmas party with me."

"You steal money from your dad?"

"He should hide it better. Got time for a soda?"

"I wish I did. I'm helping set up the Christmas display."

Becca turned back to the counter.

"I asked your mom. She gave you permission to go with me. Wouldn't that be better than being bored with the other grownups?"

"Little old lady gossip fascinates me," Becca retorted as she walked to the prehistoric artifact display in the next room, where she gazed into the glass case and imagined what it was like to grow up in a Lenni-Lenape tribal family.

There were several Native American tribes in New Jersey. She was most interested in learning about the Lenni-Lenape who lived near

Cherry Ridge in wigwam villages, where they raised corn, hunted, and fished.

Then there were the tribal tattoos. The library books provided no information about the designs. At the summer Vacation Bible School church bazaar, Becca set up a booth where she painted kids' faces, mostly with her favorite turtle designs.

Becca's mom and Jack entered with armloads of boxes filled with tinsel and Christmas tree lights.

"Why don't you do the Society a favor? Help Jack carry more decorations from the basement. The Holiday Open House is next week."

Becca had a mind of her own. Conforming to East Coast social norms was also challenging as she grew older.

"Help your mother and be more interested in the history of New Jersey people. Those Indians and their prehistoric rocks are meaningless in this day and age."

"What are you talking about? Cherry Ridge wouldn't exist if it weren't for the Native Americans. Who helped the starving boat passengers, your ancestors? The Lenni-Lenape guided George Washington, Mom."

"Native Americans? We're 'Native Americans.' I want you to be more interested in historic New Jersey people. Your people. You will follow me and join the Sisterhood of the American Revolution."

Mary's pathway to membership wasn't obvious. She was always at the library looking up "American Patriots," hoping to find a long-lost relative who at least held the door open once for Patrick Henry.

Being a preacher's daughter had its challenges for Becca. She chose to be alone to avoid her mother's never-ending mission to fix her up with Jack.

"You're both solid Congregationalists. He comes from money. I wish you'd stay away from those rowdy friends of yours."

"Why won't you let me have a life?"

"Bring them with you to youth fellowship. They could stand to be around some better people like Jack."

"Nobody likes him."

"The Middletons are our closest friends. Dad has his job because of them. Be more grateful."

"Jackie and his dad are so phony. Have you noticed that Mr. Middleton never stops smiling? If he ever dropped a suitcase filled with the family gold bricks on his toes, he'd still wear an ear-to-ear grin."

****

Late one Friday night in the spring of 1960, when Becca was a sophomore in high school, she and three friends were caught drinking and driving. It wasn't the best idea to speed around the access circle in front of the school, honking the horn. The commotion woke up two cops parked across the street.

That stunt got her kicked out of school for the spring semester.

"What were you thinking? Getting expelled is worse for us. How can I face the Historical Society? Everyone will think about you and not hear your father's sermon."

She was grounded and forbidden from messing around with her working-class pals. Becca moped around the house all summer and not looking forward to school.

4

Albert Park

September 13, 2006–3:39 p.m. MDT: Gary and Becca were founding members of the Blue Sky Village cohousing community. They moved from Laramie to Boulder in 1996 when Becca took a new job at the University of Colorado (CU) Anthropology Department.

The Steiners lived in one of 32 condos in a newly developing area of Boulder. They didn't realize that the bonds they formed with their neighbors would continue after the paint colors were selected, the garden's layout was determined, and everyone unloaded their boxes.

Blue Sky Village reminded Becca of the welcoming Cherry Ridge neighborhood where she grew up, and families were acquainted because the kids knew each other since they all attended the same school.

In response to Becca's illness in 2001, the community formed a Caring and Sharing Committee to support one another.

"The neighbors are driving me crazy. I'm getting tired of all the attention. They keep bringing over covered dishes."

"Quit changing the subject. Forget the neighbors. When are you going to tell that daughter of ours?"

"The less she knows, the better. Tell Susan we appreciate their gestures. We can't eat that much tuna casserole. Why don't you send an email asking for unprepared food like canned goods or frozen stuff? I don't want them to think I'm another Albert Park."

Their downstairs neighbor was on his deathbed in May and snapped out of it.

"Albert was in total denial. Lost weight, dragged around, got worse and worse ..."

"... then was flipping pancakes on the fourth of July. Didn't skip a beat. It must have been that good-luck plug-in aluminum griddle. It reminds me of my mom's breakfasts at the ranch."

Gary retrieved the plastic mug from Becca's latest hospital stay.

"Can you add a few ice cubes? Those blueberries and strawberries made for some colorful flapjacks. The impromptu get-togethers are what community is about."

"Don't forget Albert's 49-star flag to honor the day."

"Asking for help is one thing I learned. I'm no Albert. No sitting around waiting for the phone to ring or hoping you people will help. I presume you're stepping up?"

"You know where my wallet is!" Gary walked back into the room. "You don't have to yell. We cohousers are quiet and serene."

"Tell that to Sandra and Felix."

"By the way, you have permission to smother me with this pillow if I get too annoying."

Gary returned with the mug filled with ice. She fetched the remote next to her and lowered the bed's height.

"Can you drop the railing? I'll need to get up for a stretch. You're in charge of calling our daughter. I'd appreciate a little fuss from her."

Gary fiddled with the latches.

"The neighbors will think we're rejecting their goodwill. Especially Susan."

"Oh, let them be. They're trying to be helpful. Susan bugs me. We have Fort Chambers and Caesar salad in common. She gives me her anchovies. Those make her meddling tolerable.

"Remember to ask her to help with the party production," reminded Gary. "She doesn't need you to figure it out."

"Maybe someone else will get sick. Divert her attention."

"How about this? Why don't we sponsor a dinner?" Gary suggested. "We'll cater the potluck with the extra food. One thing I learned from the ranch is not to throw away leftovers."

"Do a reading from that book of yours. They like hearing community war stories." Becca banged on the railing. Gary folded it down without too much damage. "Read them the part about the infamous St. Patrick's Day party."

"Felix rigging up the ice machine to spit out green cubes. What a mess. Lucky for us, he stuck with the oboe. We sopped up the water with those white table covers. They're still tinted green," recalled Gary as Becca swung herself around.

"A constant reminder! The mess turned out for the best for the Maintenance Committee. It was the first time the refrigerator was pulled out from the wall in eight years. How nobody noticed those fossilized rodent parts will be a Blue Sky legend."

Gary helped her slip a pair of rubber clogs over her stocking feet.

"Watching Felix and Sandra scramble around during that mini-flood reminded me of my first summer at your ranch—the time your freaked-out mom chased the mice around the kitchen. We could have killed each other with those big blades as if we had a chance to whack off their tails," Becca recalled. Your mom was a good role model for an old-fashioned East Coaster like me."

"Old fashioned? Based on what you've told me about your mom, it doesn't surprise me that I was never invited to visit the middle-of-nowhere New Jersey. No wonder you didn't like it back there. You were an untamed horse."

Gary steadied Becca's walker in front of her.

"Middle-of-nowhere Wyoming will spoil a girl. YOUR mom didn't take crap from anybody. It's funny how life plays out."

"Speaking of untamed horses, am I calling that wild one of ours?" Gary asked.

"I knew you'd come up with a great idea like that!"

5

Yankee Stadium

When I moved from Wyoming after high school graduation, I was out of touch with my parents, forgetting their lives had moved forward and weren't frozen in time. I was relieved to get away from my control-freak mother. I watched her bring the best out in others while she ignored me. I didn't figure that out until I learned more about my parents and their friends. Over the years, I gathered a few hints. One of my chores as a kid was to keep the Calamity Club garage straightened up. When I first met their friend, Jack, I learned that the coveted junk stacked in the back corner belonged to him. I've always wondered what was so precious in those boxes and suitcases. E.S.

****

The Middleton family were 17th-century immigrants from Great Britain. Cherry Ridge was founded as a religious colony by several families from Connecticut who acquired land from the indigenous people.

Jacob Middleton was the Cherry Ridge Congregational Church minister. His stay-at-home wife, Millie, kept up the house where they lived a modest lifestyle.

The couple had a son named Frederick in 1917. Being associated with the Congregationalists throughout his childhood took its toll on young Fred.

"Sit still. Your father's giving his sermon," Millie scolded with a whisper during a church service. "Set a good example for the other boys."

After the youth fellowship group that afternoon, a girl slugged him in the cheek because she couldn't take his teasing.

"Freddie's a sissy! Can't take it, Wimpy?" chided his churchmates.

****

Despite driving a junk car and never buying new clothes, Jacob always had the money for Yankees tickets. His dad dragged Fred, when he was 10, to a few baseball games in the Bronx, including the decisive fourth game of the 1927 World Series.

"Babe Ruth just smacked another one out of the park! Second of the game!" Jacob exclaimed over the roar of the crowd. "Son, this is history in the making!"

"Can we go now?" a bored Fred asked.

As Fred grew older, he became more self-absorbed and rebellious and didn't enjoy the teamwork of sports. Jacob and Millie thought more money would translate into obedience.

"We'll increase your allowance if you quit acting out in church."

Instead, it translated into extortion.

"Invite me over for your party. I'll bring my electric train set."

****

Jacob graduated from Princeton, where he studied engineering. He took a few seminary classes, became a self-taught preacher, and was confirmed as the Cherry Ridge Congregational Church pastor in 1920. It was Fred's destiny to continue the Middleton Ivy League legacy. He earned a degree in business and landed a steady job as the Cherry Ridge State Bank Vice President right out of college.

Fred made good money and married his high school crush. The timing was right to have children. The couple had one son they named after Grandpa Jacob. As a kid, everyone called him "Jack" to avoid confusion.

Fred was overworked and didn't spend much time with his son. Grandpa Jacob kept mud in the cracks as best he could when it came to being a positive influence. Although he didn't have the weekends off, Jacob spent time with his grandson on Sunday afternoons fishing on Stony Pond or otherwise expanding his horizon.

"I took your dad to watch the Yankees when he was about your age. He wasn't interested in men wearing funny hats running around a park. I hope you'll be the next Yankees fan. It'll skip a generation!"

During the summer of 1952, Jacob and Jack rode the subway into New York City to Yankee Stadium. On their way home, Grandpa treated him to an egg cream at the Dugout Soda Shoppe near the subway station in the Bronx, where he spent his allowance on his first baseball cards. He sorted out all the Yankees from each pack, especially "The Mick"—Mickey Mantle—heir to centerfield when Joe DiMaggio retired.

Jack was hooked on baseball. Each card had a colorized black-and-white portrait of a player on the front. The backs had trivial baseball facts like each player's batting record. Jack was a math whiz like his dad, and baseball statistics fascinated him.

Most of his classmates were Dodgers fans. He had no trouble trading Andy Pafko and Pee Wee Reese or dreaded Jackie Robinson to his friends for more Yankees cards like Ralph Houk, Yogi Berra, and The Mick.

Grandpa Jacob encouraged frugality and gave Jack three nickels for his allowance.

"Remember, save some, spend some, give some away. Your mom would have approved of this."

Jack heeded his grandfather's conditions.

During the summer, he and his pals met at the Cherry Ridge Ideal Drug Store, where they bought up the red, green, and white wax packs with five cards and a stick of pink bubble gum for a nickel.

Jack shuffled through the rectangular wax pack display box, hoping his lucky touch would choose one with five Yankees.

He saved the second nickel for bribery and kept the third in a coffee can.

Most of his trading buddies despised the Yankees and were more than willing to dump them.

"Who do you want for that Mickey Mantle?" Jack asked as he sorted out his latest acquisitions.

"How about Minnie Minoso and Eddie Robinson," a Chicago White Sox collector responded.

"Done."

Some kids kept their cards bound by rubber bands stuck in their pants pockets. Jack nested the Yankees in one pocket and the rest in the other.

He organized his cards by player and team in a White Owl cigar box by meticulously cutting cardboard dividers to keep his prized possessions in alphabetical order. This allowed quick access if one of his friends wanted to trade for a particular player.

While it didn't cross Jack's mind, the rest of the world wondered how a mild-mannered Congregational minister could afford an extravagance like two season tickets for the Yankees.

Nobody knew until Jacob's death that when Universal Lights and Electric was founded in 1892, he worked as an electrical engineer and, as part of his income, was an early stockholder in the utility. The power company weathered the Great Depression. Between 1932 and 1954, the share price rose an astounding 24,000 percent.

Pastor Jacob took his frugal influences on his son and grandson to the grave. When Fred signed the inheritance papers, he quit his bank job and became a full-time philanthropist.

Despite his flamboyance, Fred remembered his father's advice while administering the Middleton fortune by spending some on the latest luxuries, saving some for Jack's future, and giving lots away to curry favor from the good people in Cherry Ridge.

Fred became a prominent member of the Cherry Ridge community. He was the local Country Club president and the New Jersey chair of the March of Dimes.

Jack was an outgoing boy groomed by his father to take over and manage the Middleton Family Trust. Coming from one of the wealthiest families in town, Jack was a good match for Becca Pembroke, so thought her mother.

6

Tarzan

September 16, 2006—11:03 a.m. MDT: Elizabeth was restless and paced around her third-floor apartment in Metairie, a suburb of New Orleans (NOLA). She wasn't used to having so much extra time on her hands. She wandered to the balcony overlooking the Gulf of Mexico and soaked in the sun as the sea breeze blew through her flowing locks.

"Can't complain about the view. Beats the aroma of beer bottles tossed into the dumpsters."

Elizabeth kept the TV picture in the background, with the sound turned down. She wasn't much of a soap opera fan and spent hours clicking through the channels and ending back on cable news.

"Terrorists held a news conference and called President George W. Bush names. More on that, and a story about a service dog in Nebraska that likes to bite men on meth when we return."

"Slow news day."

When Elizabeth first moved to Louisiana, she thought living in the French Quarter would be relaxed during Mardi Gras, except that every night was Fat Tuesday on Bourbon Street and fun while it lasted.

Elizabeth came to her senses about Mardi Gras hedonism. She no longer partied like she was 25 after learning about the underpaid workers in China who made the countless strands of beads consumed and discarded during the worldwide Carnival season.

The sun above the Gulf of Mexico glistened off her collection of gold, purple, and green beaded necklaces tossed by bacchanalians during past Mardi Gras parades that she draped over the wrought-iron balcony spikes as mementos of her past life.

"If those beads could talk, I'd have to pay them off so they'd keep quiet."

Her new place was quieter, considering no bottles were clanking into the dumpsters below.

"Too bad Katrina washed away the giant trees in the courtyard," she thought while fidgeting on her balcony.

Her unemployment benefits and savings were a safety net that allowed her to pursue creative entrepreneurship as a screenwriter.

"I have several projects in various stages of development," was her stock response to questions raised while milling around at networking arts and cultural events.

Being a starving writer occupied her time as she continued looking for full-time work. The gulf breeze was distracting as she sat at a table on the deck and flipped through booklets and brochures about the Louisiana Film Office. Despite a rich film history beginning with *Tarzan of the Apes* in 1917, the latter-day Bayou State film industry was in its infancy.

Elizabeth daydreamed about producing a movie, motivating her to finish the screenplay she had been writing during her NOLA tenure. Her phone went off. She checked the caller ID.

"This is Elizabeth."

"I'm surprised you picked up on a Saturday. What's the latest? How's your movie coming along?" her father asked.

"Between reporting to the unemployment office and qualifying for food stamps, I managed to get the first draft done. I don't have much hope it will go any further. I can't get anyone to read it. You and Mom okay?"

"Mostly," he paused. "Your mother. Doctor says she has a mild case of lymphoma."

"What do you mean, 'mild?' She went into remission five years ago after she had radiation and chemo."

"I heard it's not as bad this go around. She'll be back to full speed in no time."

"Why didn't you call sooner?"

"We've called several times. You never answer. Your mom wanted me to try. I forgot until now when I was thinking about it. My memory isn't as good as it was."

"What do you mean 'forgot?'" an exasperated Elizabeth asked.

"I didn't want you to worry. Complicate things more. You two fight so much. I don't want to get in the middle."

Gary motioned for Becca to pick up the extension phone by her TV chair.

"Elizabeth, I assume you'll be coming home? I have a surprise for you."

"Oh, good. You tell Dad. He can tell me." Elizabeth listened indignantly. "… The job hunt? I'm about ready to give up. Don't worry about me."

"I thought the movie business in Louisiana looked promising."

"Well, everything looks good on paper. I'm living at the film office. Can't get a foothold. I'm not from around here. Plus, it's a man's world."

"Forget those 'old boys.' You're an intelligent, independent woman. Why don't you come home? Get here next week. It's a short drive."

"I don't get a choice? Put Dad back on."

"The film industry is the next big thing in Wyoming," Gary encouraged. "Stay at the Calamity Club until you find something. A big movie was shot up by Sheridan."

"You don't have to keep telling me. I'm impulsively calculated. Moving from one place to another hotel job is one thing. Abandoning what little security I have to be a writer?"

"Keep the faith, Elizabeth. It's the perfect time to make a move."

"I have faith until my luck and money run out." Elizabeth picked up her copy of *Hollywood Now* magazine. She scanned a story about *The Stallion*, based on the novel by Marion Mason. The film featured country music legend Roscoe Tanner.

"Maybe *The Stallion* is a turning point. I've met Roscoe. It's a thought."

****

Elizabeth weighed her options over the weekend. She rehearsed lines she wanted to convey to her mom about reconciliation and mustered up the courage to call.

"Mom? Are you okay?"

"I don't mind being caged up. The neighbors are good about stopping by. How about you come back and keep writing? You still have nursing in your back pocket."

"I don't want to work for other people again. The world belongs to the younger generation. Dad talked me into jumping off the creative cliff."

"You're still the younger generation. In Boulder, you can't swing your yoga mat around without whacking into someone claiming to be a screenwriter. Is moving a good idea?

"Who said anything about me moving?"

"Do you know how long it took for your father to earn enough as a reporter to make the hours worthwhile?" Elizabeth half-listened and plopped down on the couch. "You've carved out a niche for yourself in the hotel business. Whatever it is you do, keep doing it. You'll be stuck if you don't settle down, especially since you move around so much. If you start over from scratch, you'll be unemployable."

None of the empathetic lines Elizabeth rehearsed fit in with the conversation.

"I can take care of myself. Make my own choices. We have different views of the world. No matter how hard you wish, I won't change."

"If you were more open, you'd find your mother to be a very sensitive one. I don't like to outguess you with irritating questions. Why don't you take an interest in what I'm doing?"

"I've read your book. I did find it interesting that some cultural rituals have broken down because of climate change. Maybe I'll write a movie script about it. Why can't you lay off? I'm not like you. My life plan is not to have a plan, and I don't need the world to be different, although I wish there were no more Mardi Gras beads. I'm enjoying life as it comes to me."

"I'm not taking your guff. When will you be home? Here I am, sick again. YOU owe your life to ME, young lady. Don't forget that."

Becca placed her palm on her forehead and took a deep breath.

"Oh, you're playing the guilt card. Good for you. You're the one who made the lousy choices. It's not my fault," Elizabeth argued back.

Gary took the phone back from Becca.

"Let us know your plans."

Elizabeth hung up.

****

On Monday, she made an impulsive call to the Wyoming State Film Office in Cheyenne. The Director encouraged her to make the move back home. Elizabeth asked if there were any jobs in the film office.

"Not right at the moment. We may be hiring if the legislature approves our funding request. We're a small staff right now. We transferred existing employees from other divisions. We want to set up field operations. Didn't you say you have roots in Lander? We're planning an office there."

Elizabeth entered her name into the film office service provider database.

"If I'm one of the three writers, and the other two are high school students, either they don't know what they're doing, or it's going to be a breeze."

As much as Elizabeth didn't like to face it, whatever happened in her life was set up by the situations she experienced. She was upwardly mobile and had a knack for landing in places where good things could happen. Changing jobs every few years fit her need for instability.

Elizabeth relied on the writing skills she picked up from her parents to research local trivia. She included those tidbits in her responses to proposals for organizations and people planning their meetings and weddings at the Triumph Hotel.

Even though she despised working vacations as a kid, combining work with leisure turned out well for her when she entered the labor force. Elizabeth attained Premiere Platinum Plus airline mileage status, meaning she hadn't paid for plane tickets, hotel rooms, and car rentals for her entire adult life.

She didn't think twice about spur-of-the-moment road trips. Her journey to check on her mother in Boulder would be no exception. She had a half-packed bag ready to go.

7

Quiver Mountain Ranch

I had little idea what was happening with my parents since I was so absorbed with my life uncertainty. Over the years, I was more successful in learning second-hand information about Dad because I kept in closer touch with Grandma Sally. Mom's parents were self-consumed and aloof. Grandma Mary was upset about Watergate. Grandpa Jere was always on church business. They assumed their daughter would stay out of trouble until she didn't. Mom vicariously lived her ideal childhood through me. The jury is still out on that. E.S.

****

Becca had moped around the house most of the spring after being expelled during the 1961 spring semester.

"You're bored? Tired of Cherry Ridge? You want to get a life of your own? How about spending the summer in Wyoming?"

Becca's mom flipped open a brochure about the Equality State that one of her friends at the museum handed her. The Wyoming option had Becca jazzed up. She couldn't get her bags packed fast enough.

In early June, Becca started her three-day train ride on a commuter line to Penn Station. She boarded the Lakeshore Limited to Chicago, then the California Zephyr to Rawlins, where she transferred to the northbound Blue Zenith bus.

The howl of the air brakes startled Becca awake. She was one of three passengers who got off in Lander at the Wind River Mill parking area. The driver unloaded her luggage. Becca struggled with both hands to carry her bags to the bench near the front door. She tipped her head back and breathed the dry Wyoming air warmed by the brighter-than-Jersey sunshine.

"Rebecca?" A voice from behind startled her awake. "Looking for the Quiver Mountain Ranch? Sally Steiner, here."

Becca's crossed feet, propped on her suitcase, dropped to the ground. Her sneakers created a cloud of dust.

"Figured this wiry thing must be you! It'll be good to have another woman around."

"Call me Becca. I'm named after my great-great-great grandmother."

"That's a lot of 'greats.' You go way back."

"Family lore. True or not, I always felt like we had a connection."

Becca pulled out an old tin-type image from her small suitcase.

"You look like her."

"So I've heard."

Sally untied the black riding helmet, strapped on the suitcase handle, and placed it on Becca's head. Sally motioned with her solid, sinewy arms for Becca to get off her duff. With her work-worn hands, she hoisted the enormous suitcase into the bed of her truck parked in the gravel lot.

"I have to pick up a few things." Sally tossed Becca's small vanity case that bounced off a hay bale onto the truck bed. "Let's get you outfitted."

Becca searched through her purse to be sure the money her mom had given her was still in the envelope.

"Keep your cash. Part of your board includes work clothes. I doubt you brought anything good for ranching."

A cowbell on the mill store door announced their entry.

"Hey, Sally. Is this your new hand?"

"Becca Pembroke, meet Lloyd White. We go way back. He worked at the Eagle Crest Ranch, where I grew up. Lloyd took over for me here at the Mill when I quit to manage the Quiver Mountain." Sally turned back to Lloyd. "We'll need a few of the basics."

"She's a lanky one. We don't have many small sizes. You may have to get her coveralls at Berwin's."

"Two pair of these." Sally and Becca looked through the gloves on the pegboard display rack. "We'll break you in easy."

"That's $27.50 on your account, including the chicken feed."

Lloyd rang up the sale. Becca sneezed and coughed as she walked by the grain bins.

"Different pollen and dust here. You'll get used to it."

Lloyd carried out a 50-pound feed bag and dropped it in the truck bed.

"Welcome to Wyoming!"

Becca opened the faded-green Ford truck door and climbed to the bench seat.

"How was your trip out?" Sally asked through the passenger side window while giving it a good slam that echoed through the hollow door panel.

"The train ride was long. The bus ride seemed twice as long."

Becca pushed down the door lock.

"No need for that. Someone might have to move the truck."

Sally pushed the ignition button until the engine turned over. The pickup bounced down the street. They finished shopping, stopped for a snack at the Railway Cafe, and headed to the Quiver Mountain Ranch.

"You'll do some cooking. We feed anywhere from 30 to 40 men, so I hope you know a little about the kitchen. Between the chores, you'll look after my son, Billy. His older brother will help you with him. Gary's about your age."

Becca sniffled into a tissue she pulled from the box, sliding around on the dash.

"The boys I know in Jersey are big pains. My mom wasn't much in the kitchen. About all I learned was how to boil canned chicken noodle soup. I burned that once."

"I'll show you how to make the noodles and butcher the chickens. This truck ride is your orientation."

******

Billy had trouble adjusting to junior high school. Becca was patient and helped him with his studies. He took an immediate liking to her.

When she wasn't tending to Billy, Sally allowed her to join the ranch crew. During the haying season, one of her jobs was threading spools of twine into the hay baler. How it all worked seemed like magic.

The cut hay dried out for a few days before the driver hooked up the baler to the tractor, navigated over the rows of alfalfa, raked the cuttings into the machine, and then regurgitated rectangular bales bound with twine.

When she wasn't helping Sally, she drove the truck that pulled the baling wagon. Other times, she helped load the bales.

In Wyoming, farmers cut the alfalfa twice during the summer. If the rain was right, there was sometimes a third cutting. The hay was high-quality, rich in nitrogen, and always won a ribbon at the Wyoming State Winter Fair.

Becca befriended all the other hands. She was younger than most of the guys and gained their respect when she showed she could keep up with them.

Sally picked out a horse for Becca. She and her mount were a good team for jumping over the makeshift steeplechase barriers in the corral.

During her off time, Becca stuffed her folded-over Dodgers cap into her back pocket before donning the black equestrian helmet she hauled from the Stony Pond Stables near her home in Cherry Ridge. Her headwear was the subject of many smart-aleck remarks from her fellow ranch hands.

"I'm not a cowgirl. I'm a rider. A steeplechaser."

******

One day, the tractor driver noticed the bales were no longer landing on the wagon bed. A worker had twisted an ankle, stumbling through a rut in the main alfalfa field.

"Hey!"

The driver put on the brakes, hopped down, and sprinted back to his crew. He nearly stumbled as his work boots caught on the dry hay stubble.

Another of the hands ran back to the adjoining pasture, hopped on his horse, and lumbered over the dusty road back to the ranch house. The horse hadn't yet stopped when the frantic fellow dismounted and hopped up the three steps in a single bound. The screen door slammed behind him.

Becca and Billy were in the kitchen preparing lunch.

"Call someone," gasped the disheveled worker. He explained the situation to Becca.

She untied her apron and handed it to Billy.

"Keep tearing the lettuce. Get your mom when it's time to slice up the brisket." Becca unhooked her helmet and riding gloves that hung by the back door. "Tell her I rode out to the big field."

She ran to the stable, saddled her horse, and took off as Sally entered the kitchen. Billy told his mom what happened. Sally soon arrived at the accident site in her pickup and helped get the injured crew member back to the main ranch house.

"You should have fetched me. Now you're showing off!"

Becca had something to prove. She had a way with the young gelding, a natural steeplechaser. The accident was a test for free-spirited Becca and her frisky mount that vaulted the fence into the big pasture.

Sally and her husband, Marvin Collins, worked with Becca and her mount for barrel racing. Racers trained their horses to gallop and tightly cut around two 55-gallon drums.

She recorded the fastest time and won a buckle at the July 4th Fremont County Settler Days Rodeo. Nobody knew who she was, nor anything about the horse during the pre-event gymkhana betting, except for Sally and Marvin. They cleaned up when Becca won the top prize.

Not bad for a Jersey girl.

******

Becca had a competitive spirit and worked hard to excel. There was no TV on the ranch, and the radio reception was staticky at best, so there were no sports to watch or hear. Barrel racing and pickup baseball games were her recreational distractions.

Becca surprised her fellow workers with her glove and bat when she took to the field for baseball games in the most level pasture. A ball that disappeared into a prairie dog burrow was deemed a ground-rule double.

There were few athletic opportunities for girls in Wyoming and maybe fewer in New Jersey. Becca was the sole girl who took to the sandlot with the neighborhood boys in Cherry Ridge.

She grew up a Dodgers fan and wore her well-worn blue cap with a white felt "B" on the front despite not forgiving Branch Rickey for moving her team from Brooklyn to Los Angeles in 1957.

She learned that sportsmanship rules didn't apply to her hero, Jackie Robinson, the first African American Negro Leaguer. Rickey signed him to a contract with the Brooklyn Dodgers in 1947 amid the racist attitudes of his teammates on and off the field and by the fans.

Despite his mistreatment, Robinson excelled on the field. She listened intently to the 1955 World Series on the radio. The Dodgers defeated the wretched New York Yankees. She was disappointed in the decisive seventh game when Manager Walter Alston benched Robinson.

When Becca was a team captain, she always picked the kids who were overlooked and gave them a chance to play. Nobody questioned her swagger because she could keep up with the boys in all aspects of the game played on the Garden Valley School playground.

She was tall compared to the other kids and liked to play 1st base because she could catch the high and wide throws, which were most of them. Her athleticism made her Sunday school friend, Jack, jealous. If you've seen one average boy try to play shortstop, you've seen them all.

"Hey, batta, batta." Becca made infield chatter from her position between 1st and 2nd base. She bent over in anticipation of the pitch. "C'mon, swing the bat, Jackie Boy!"

He frowned at Becca and took the second pitch in a row, adjusted his Yankees cap, and tapped his bat in the dust before digging into the back of the batter's box, thinking he would be the one to break Babe Ruth's single-season home run record.

He swung hard on the pitch with a grunt and topped the ball toward the pitcher. Becca charged forward like a lightning bolt, bare-handed the dribbler, and tossed it to the pitcher covering first, getting Jack by a mile.

"Lucky play. You don't get to call me Jackie. He's your hero, not mine," he uttered as he trotted past Becca.

"Get over yourself. It's just a game."

"Yeah? Maybe for you."

The boys quit making fun of her about the time she smacked a home run ball into Mr. Becker's backyard, except for Jack.

****

Between baseball on the Quiver Mountain Ranch prairie and barrel racing at the Lander rodeo arena, Becca spent much of her time wandering the Quiver Mountain Ranch with Billy and Gary, exploring for teepee rings and petroglyphs.

Then there were the crew meetings. Her job was to warm up the coffee cups every morning after breakfast when the cowboys were given their daily assignments. Becca didn't mind the meetings because she learned about ranching by being around the conversation.

8

Sandra & Felix

September 18, 2006—5:28 p.m. MDT: Living in a cohousing community was a very supportive place for older people. The downside of collaboration was the meetings. Becca was accustomed to them because she had sat through them her entire life, at church in New Jersey, on the ranch in Wyoming, and as a college professor. Gary had lots of news meetings at the Laramie newspaper. Those experiences readied them to live at Blue Sky Village.

Villagers joined committees to handle the day-to-day operations. They reported on the third Monday at an all-community meeting in the Common House dining room. Most everyone showed up to get updates about the condo association, gossip about who's been neglecting their duties, and why people always brought the same thing to potluck dinner.

Gary tipped back in his desk chair, deep in thought. He pulled a full-color computer printout from a drawer and showed Becca.

"Check this out. I don't know when they're unveiling it."

"We do have some creative people here. Such colorful designs. I'll add something one of these days. I have to support Susan and her little time capsule project."

"Our 10th-anniversary hallmark event is happening because of you! Act surprised."

Gary tacked the print on the wall behind the dresser.

"Thanks to my stodgy mother, I know how to pretend like I'm surprised."

"Speaking of surprise, did your mother ever call you back?"

Gary rummaged through his dresser drawer and pulled out a gray sweatshirt.

"I don't think she cares. 'You'll either get well or you won't,' she said last time. I've tried calling her place for the past few weeks." Becca got off the bed and positioned herself in her walker. "I doubt she got my messages. They're so understaffed."

"Here it is 40 years later. I've never met your Mom. Careful!" Becca's walker rolled unsteadily with wheeled front legs and back feet shod with old tennis balls. "Lift up that contraption when you walk so you don't catch on the carpet edge. "Maybe one day, your Mom will pound on the door. Surprise us both."

Gary zipped up his hoodie, and they made the short walk to the elevator. He held the first-floor door while Becca negotiated her walker out of the elevator car and across the wooden floor into the meeting area.

Harold was the community meeting facilitator. Fifty-six residents sat on dining room chairs in two concentric circles.

"Before we begin, I want to check in with the Steiners. Welcome!"

"Thanks, Harold. We can't stay long. We appreciate all the CARE packages you've dropped off. Becca and I want to have a special dinner on Thursday rather than Sunday and serve up the casseroles and desserts."

"Any excuse for a party. Are there any problems with changing the Sunday community dinner to Thursday?"

Felix raised his hand.

"The food won't keep until Sunday? Sandra and I have a schedule. Thursday doesn't work for us."

Felix was the guy who flooded the Common House with green water during the St. Patrick's Day party.

"Becca and I aren't dessert eaters. We would hate for the pie you and Sandra dropped by to go to waste. Life is uncertain, as Becca can attest. Eat dessert first! We'll fix you two a plate and put it in the fridge."

Felix and Sandra could be counted on to be the community nay-sayers. It was always something with those two. They had a knack for creating problems and leaving the pieces for others to pick up. The tinted green tablecloths were evidence of that.

"Any other concerns? Any issues?" Harold closed the discussion. Felix and Sandra looked down at the floor with their arms crossed. "Hearing no objections, it's the consensus of Blue Sky Village to accept the Steiners' invitation."

Becca waved her hand.

"Gary showed me the first draft of his book. He'll do a reading as the live entertainment. Lots of good stories. There's never a dull moment at Blue Sky Village. The names are changed, of course, to protect the guilty."

"All right. We're all looking forward to an action-packed evening. The community dinner is changed to Thursday." Harold confirmed the consensus. "Is there anything else?"

"Thanks for being flexible," Becca added. "Now I have to get Gary HIS medication. We gave Albert our vote for any other decisions tonight."

Albert waved the hard copy proxy form to the crowd.

"The next item of business is picking the facilitator for next month."

As Harold moved the meeting along, Gary had another thought.

"I think some of you know our daughter. Elizabeth will be arriving sometime within the next week or so. She'll be here when she gets here. Just a heads up if you see a stranger around."

They excused themselves from the meeting.

"I'm surprised Felix and Sandra didn't complain about your part in the 10th-anniversary event in the Common House."

"We'll see if they said anything important enough to make the meeting minutes. It won't be anything worse than the green flood!"

"Why did you mention our flighty daughter? I doubt she'll make it."

"The likelihood of her coming here is greater if I say it and get the intention out there."

"Get real. Elizabeth never picks up when I call. She screens."

"Don't use the landline. I'll get with her when our plans are set. If there's no schedule, there's no telling when she'll get organized. YOU call. She's your daughter."

"Elizabeth drives me crazy. Talk to me, damn it! I'm your mother."

9

Laramie Daily Press

I was around adults for much of my childhood and grew up fast. My parents didn't know how to relate to me since I learned to blend in with their crowds. I was dragged to their workplaces and left to entertain myself under their not-so-watchful eyes because my overworked parents couldn't afford babysitters. I became less reliant on them because I figured life out independently, having met their colleagues who opened my eyes to the world. As my parents aged, they wanted to be more reliant on me. E.S.

****

On July 16, 1979, Elizabeth walked three blocks to the *Laramie Daily Press* offices from East Elementary School, where she attended the school-sponsored summer camp. Even in a smaller market, publishing a newspaper was a 24-hour business. She liked spending time at her dad's work.

Gary climbed his way up the ranks and was a co-publisher. Regardless of position, everyone in the editorial department had to do some reporting. It was a rarity if he could break away at 6:00 p.m. Sometimes, quitting time was as late as 10:00 p.m. when he had to cover city council meetings every other Tuesday.

The University of Wyoming (UW) didn't allow children to be brought to the office except during emergency situations. Becca's hours were regular. When Gary worked late, she stopped by to pick up Elizabeth.

"How was camp, Elizabeth?" Gary asked.

"Today, we took a field trip to the senior center and helped serve sandwiches. Do you need me to sort out old papers or anything around here?"

"Big news. A big tornado touched down in Cheyenne and blew through the north side of town. Sit here. A fifth grader should learn how to type."

He showed Elizabeth to the pool typewriters.

"Can you two drive over to Cheyenne and see what's happening with the tornado?" Gary pulled a $20 bill from his wallet. "Here are a few bucks for gas and food. Get plenty of 'people angles.'"

Elizabeth sat in front of one of the Olympia Were AG Wilhelmsha-ven SG-1 typewriters. She scrolled a piece of paper into the roller and began typing when her dad walked up behind her.

"It's the same one I have at home." Gary pulled up an office chair next to her. "It's been borrowed from the UW journalism department since I was news editor at the *Cowboy Weekly*. I think it's the John Deere of typewriters. Straighten out your paper like this. Pull this lever. It releases the roller. There, now it's straighter."

Elizabeth tried it.

"To keep your lines of words the same. Move this little gizmo to set the margins."

Gary slid the left and right stops at about one inch from each edge of the sheet. Elizabeth gave it a try.

"This little thing lets you set the rows between lines. In the news-paper business, we use double spacing. Write a story about the latest at East Elementary summer camp."

Elizabeth had a greater interest in nonfiction than fiction. Her pri-mary reading books were fictional accounts of a brother, sister, their parents, a dog, and a cat. She couldn't figure out the story plots. The characters had no arc. Had she been able to read the encyclopedia or almanac, she would have become a better reader.

She was excited about the nonfiction challenge posed to her by her father. Gary returned to his office when he saw George Tiller behind the front counter.

He owned the biggest insurance company in town and was the paper's biggest advertiser. His son was the high school football team's star quarterback.

"George. Please. I'm a little scattered. Did you hear about the tornado in Cheyenne?" Gary motioned for him to sit.

"This is the first I've heard. If you're too busy now ..."

"Our coverage is under control. What's on your mind?"

"There were a bunch of kids having fun after the homecoming game. My son's been recruited by Nebraska and Wyoming. We don't need that kind of publicity."

The sports editor treated the kid in print like he was writing a *Sports Today* tabloid exposé about fur coat-clad tight-end Freddie Rayburn, the third-round draft pick for the Mile High Miners, having too much fun at the infamous Squirrel's Cage Lounge on Morris Street, so named after Esther Hobart Morris of South Pass City, the first justice of the peace in the United States.

****

Elizabeth was seated a little too low to strike the keys properly. Two laid-back reporters on break placed an oversized dictionary under her tush, raising her to a more comfortable typing level. She positioned the paper at the top of the page. She thought for a moment, then hunted and pecked a headline. Black ink pressed the page as the keys struck the new ribbon with a pop. It let off a petroleum by-product aroma.

"DANNY DAVIS GETS SNAIL PRIZE

"Danny Davis sits next to me in class. Today, he chased me around the playground at recess. The principal made him stand against the fence until the bell rang. He thinks he is very cool because he was the student of the month, and now he is the snail of the month. Why is it the snail? Danny is slow and had to hide inside his shell when he got in trouble."

Gary's meeting ended.

"Thanks for your concern, George. I'll have my sports editor write a positive story about your son getting a full ride to South Dakota Technical College."

"You know, Gary, have you thought about comprehensive coverage on that Scout of yours? They don't make 'em like that anymore."

"I'll give you a call."

Gary walked George to the door and then checked on Elizabeth.

She always spoke her mind, which caused strain on her parents. Her father read the story, leaned over, and repositioned the paper.

"When you write stories about others, you have to take responsibility for your words."

Under the title, he typed, "By Elizabeth Steiner."

****

Elizabeth went outside to look around the neighborhood. The two laid-back reporters stood against the building in the alley behind the offices. The guy had one knee bent and his crepe Chuka boot sole flat against the brick wall.

"You don't have to write anything about the tornado?" asked Elizabeth.

"The real news gets covered by the old guys. If a Laramie person was killed, I'll write the obit. What are you doing here? School get out early? I like your hair. We must go to the same salon," the young woman reporter observed and then exhaled a puff of marijuana smoke.

She had on a pair of those giant round tortoiseshell framed glasses like the ones Roberta Williams wore in *Dames*, which won "Best Picture" in 1975. She passed the joint to her colleague.

"I like your jumper. My mom has one. It's kind of peach-ish," Elizabeth said, exchanging compliments.

The young woman reporter feigned a hand-on-the-hip modeling pose.

"We should talk more, Elizabeth."

The guy reporter pinched off the ash and dropped the roach into his shirt pocket.

"Marijuana will damage your brain," Elizabeth warned.

"Didn't I read that Rosalynn Carter said it's okay if we don't inhale? Go back inside, little lady."

"Lay off, jerk," his colleague retorted.

He looked like a newspaper reporter with his light brown plaid shirt and a loosened blue necktie knotted with a half-Windsor.

"I saw you typing up something."

"It's about the bully in my class."

Elizabeth leaned up against the wall.

"Was he like my bully reporter friend here? We feminists need to stick together," the young woman reporter encouraged. "I hope he's not your boyfriend. Boys like this fellow get away with bullying until they are grownups. Pick nice boys. People don't change no matter how hard you wish them to change. Don't fall for their tricks."

"My bully had to stand against the fence."

Elizabeth was attracted to the young woman reporter who took such an interest in her.

"Served him right. We should be taking over. Who started the Vietnam War? Men. Who broke into the Democratic National Headquarters? Men. Who runs this newspaper? Your dad."

"I agree with you on that. Reporters keep this place going. And we edit our own stories. We write more than twenty-five cents worth of news so your dad can rub shoulders with the Chamber of Commerce."

Elizabeth felt uncomfortable when she realized this was her first conversation with older people.

"I think I'll go in now. My mom is picking me up."

The two reporters had a few more minutes on break. Elizabeth found her way back into the office. She sniffed her shirt sleeve to be sure it hadn't absorbed any of the pungent smell of smoldering weed. Elizabeth didn't want to get the reporters in trouble, not to mention what her mother might say if she reeked of reefer.

******

Her mom's crowd was different. All of Becca's colleagues were heady academics. They talked about their research papers and campus politics. It was a volatile workplace. There was a constant turnover of younger professors since the tenured faculty members weren't going anywhere. Even though Becca was on a tenure track, she kept getting passed over for the Department Head job, which was frustrating.

UW anthropology professors were a white wine crowd. At one holiday party hosted in the Arts & Sciences College Dean's spacious home, one of the graduate students, also bored, came into the den.

"What are you doing out here?"

The grad student fluffed out her skirt and sat in the big, overstuffed chair by the glowing fireplace next to Elizabeth.

"Waiting for my dad to pick me up. He had to work late."

Elizabeth flipped through a back issue of *Scientific World* magazine.

"Tired of listening to arguments about how much tribesmen eat compared to the baskets of crops they harvest?" asked the sarcastic grad student as she searched through her purse for a tube of lipstick with a small oblong mirror clipped to it. She checked if there were any smudges from snacking on the appetizers. "I get tired of anthropology small talk."

"You don't live with it every day and all night. I guess some of it is kind of interesting. We're going to take pictures of dancers on the Wind River Reservation. If I beg hard enough, maybe we'll go to Yellowstone."

Elizabeth set her magazine down and extended her arms to feel the heat.

"You smell nice."

"It's Cactus Blossom," the grad student said with a smile. "Anyway, my mom does the same thing. She calls them 'working vacations.' The best thing about turning 18 was that I didn't have to go along with her. Ever hear of 'latch-key' kids? I was one of those. I was pretty much left on my own after school. Lucky for my mom, I liked to stay inside and read. She's still in Brooklyn and out of my hair."

"Your parents must be divorced."

"My dad lives in Uganda. He works for a United Nations organization and feeds poor people there. Of course, there are lots of poor people, so he has to work all the time. One day, I'll figure out a project. Go visit him. He's in Kampala."

"A working vacation? It would have been hard to stay with him when your mom was busy."

Elizabeth reached for her small plate, stabbed a celery stick into a pitted black olive, and crunched off the end like a Tootsie Pop.

"Do you have roots in New England? We used to have celery and olives at Thanksgiving." The grad student poked a celery stick into the olive hole. "I learned in one of my classes that celery was discovered in 1779. It was a delicacy. Then, canned olives from California were shipped to the East. My dissertation is about how culture patterns have changed because of better transportation."

"My mom is from New Jersey. Is that New England?"

Elizabeth stabbed another olive.

"No, I think New Jersey is New Jersey."

"Can you go to Uganda for Thanksgiving?"

"There's no Thanksgiving in Uganda, so he'd be working, anyway. I can't afford to go there unless a grant paid for it."

The grad student swirled her wine glass.

"Unless I get a better offer, I'll pop in on my mom. She has a new boyfriend. Kind of an idiot. My cousin's there if my mom gets too annoying or if the idiot tries to put the moves on me."

Elizabeth sniffed the air.

"It's a white wine, *Pouilly-Fuissé*. Very pricey. I like the 'nose.'"

"Pooweefoosay, you say?"

"The department springs for it."

Elizabeth, out of curiosity, pointed to the center of her face.

"The 'nose,' the aroma. Suppose you want to look like you know what you're doing. You do this. Stick your nose in the glass. Take a good whiff. Then say something like 'very rose-like, oaky with a hint of tangerine.' Then take a sip and do this."

She swished the wine around her mouth and swallowed without dribbling.

"I went with my mom on one of her working vacations to wine country in Upstate New York. Some vineyards have tastings. The *sommeliers* give out sips of any wine they make. Instead of swallowing, you spit your wine and saliva into a spittoon."

"Gross."

"I worked for a fancy hotel in New York City. I was older than you. It was my first job. I pretended I was a *sommelier* when I wasn't a busboy. Nobody was the wiser."

"Busgirl?"

Elizabeth took the grad student's glass.

"Back then, everything was named for males. Same as now." The grad student looked around to be sure Professor Steiner wasn't nearby. "We just celebrated the bicentennial. After 203 years, you'd think there'd be more changes."

"That's messed up."

Elizabeth swirled the glass, causing the wine legs to stream down the inside walls of the glass.

"I helped set up the important banquets. In New York, everything is important. We cleared off all the tables. There was always leftover wine." The grad student reached for her glass. Elizabeth held tight. "When we were done, we downed some of the open bottles. I developed a taste for the *Pouilly*. I've liked it ever since I was a teenager."

"Hard work?"

"I don't know if the job was hard. Even doing what I did was good. It gave me an appreciation for jerks at a young age. It was after school. I could pick my shifts since it was filling in for the full-time workers. I also worked in the kitchen. Learned how to cook from being around food."

"My mom pushes me in all directions. She wants me to get married." Elizabeth checked to be sure her mother wasn't watching and took a sniff. "I detect a hint of dandelion." She took a sip, swished, swallowed, and then coughed from the burn of alcohol.

"The *Pouilly* is a little dry. You're a quick study!" The grad student handed Elizabeth a cocktail napkin.

"You should be grateful you have two parents. They do the best they can," Elizabeth said, struggling to get out her words.

"You got your whole life to figure things out. When you're old enough, pick a job with the least amount of responsibility and pays the most money! Pick good friends. Your life doesn't count until you get into high school. Experience as much as you can when you're young. The stakes are lower. I've always appreciated my dysfunctional childhood."

"I can relate. Mom doesn't like that I treat everyone as equals."

"So you're the ringleader. My mom didn't like my choice of friends, either. 'I don't know their parents.' She would warn me, 'You might start drinking.' A lot of good that did. I don't want to be a bad influence on you. I'm in line to be your mom's lead research assistant. If you tell her about our conversation, I'll deny it."

"We have the 'Pact of *Pouilly*.'"

****

Gary and Becca cajoled Elizabeth to be something she wasn't. She was tallish and a pretty good athlete but didn't have the discipline to play team sports. Regardless, her dad pushed her to play basketball and volleyball. Her mother encouraged her to do anything that would keep her out of trouble.

Elizabeth's claim to fame was juvenile delinquency. In her sophomore year, the girl with the locker beside her squealed to the principal about the marijuana stash she saw in Elizabeth's backpack. The police tossed the contents of her locker all over the hallway.

****

"Anthropology Department, can I help you?"

The assistant was on her computer with one window with attendance records and a second where she placed the two of diamonds on the three clubs and won the game. Nobody would notice her slacking because classes were in session.

"Is my mom there?" Elizabeth asked with a shake in her voice.

"She gets out in 10 minutes."

"I'll call back."

Elizabeth hung up the phone at the Laramie Police Department. She waited a few minutes before trying again.

"Mom? Don't get mad." Elizabeth's voice uneasily grasped for words. "I'm at the police station."

"Are you okay?"

"Yeah, considering I thought I'd be sitting with drunks and prostitutes getting booked, like on TV."

"Have you talked to your dad?"

"Since the principal didn't hear back from either of you, the police detained me. If I called you, the principal wouldn't press charges."

"Press charges?"

Becca hung up and called the high school principal.

****

"You shouldn't be surprised, Mrs. Steiner. Elizabeth and her gang like getting caught. They own their behaviors. Showing off their power. It's a pack mentality."

Becca let down her guard.

"There are no gangs in Laramie. She's standing her ground. Maybe a little rebellious, but weren't we all?"

This latest episode turned out relatively okay for Elizabeth, considering possession of marijuana was a felony. She didn't tell her parents that the principal sentenced her to detention. Not too bad, considering her mother was kicked out of high school for drinking.

Elizabeth often thought about her conversation with the grad student at her mom's office party and the *Daily Press* newspaper reporter and didn't regret having too much fun.

"I thought you went early for history club meetings. Why didn't you tell us you were in detention?" asked Becca.

She told her dad she had to stay after school to work on the school newspaper staff.

"Elizabeth, you're grounded for the rest of the year," Gary commanded.

"Sheesh. Do you know how hard it was to make up those stories? I don't think I could do anything to keep you two happy."

Based on what Elizabeth knew of her friends and the alcoholism that ran in some of their families, her parents and the rest of the world would be more empathetic if they followed the Alcoholics Anonymous 12 steps to recovery all the time, especially number 9, around acceptance and forgiveness.

"If you're not going to play sports, do something to stay out of trouble your last two years," Gary advised. "Take a typing class."

Elizabeth ended up joining the school newspaper staff. Her rowdy friends criticized her for being too much of an intellectual.

"Forget writing," Becca countered. "Go to Southeast in Cheyenne for the nursing program. Next year, take some biology classes."

Elizabeth flipped through the community college brochure. She followed her mother's wishes and signed up for several science classes as a junior. Not to keep her mom happy, but Elizabeth did well in advanced biology. She enjoyed the course and kept that to herself.

10

Jack Middleton

September 19, 2006—7:15 p.m. MDT: The Steiners took a detour on their way home from the community meeting. They checked out the 10th-anniversary time capsule in the Art Room. Gary took the cap off a felt-tipped pen, drew a circle with four quadrants, and filled each with different colors as his contribution to the work. Becca picked up a piece of blue construction paper and scissors. She cut a geometric figure the same shape as the one in the middle of her wool blanket.

"This is very nice. It's a tribute to cohousing, the Blue Sky Village Alumni celebration. I wonder how my opening event will go over."

"Everyone likes you. You're a connector."

"Sometimes, I wonder if it's worth it. This place can be a pain sometimes. Can't complain. I'm glad this is my home base. Beats a nursing home." Becca glued her paper medallion down on the masterwork. "I hope you put this piece of art into your book. It's part poetry, part collage, part painting."

"Maybe the publisher will use it for the cover."

Becca nearly nodded off mid-stride on their walk home, even though she was breathing supplemental oxygen tethered to a green cylinder in a zippered black nylon bag hanging from the front of her walker.

Keeping the air hose from getting entangled with the handbrakes and her wrist was a nuisance. The Sunrise Health Care Center arranged for an oxygen concentrator the size of a small refrigerator.

The air pump gurgled through the aerator like a giant aquarium. Gary hid the machine in the closet to muffle the bubbling drone. The noises were better than dragging around a green oxygen bottle the size of a torpedo on a wheeled cart.

"If you'd slow down, the doctor says you won't need the supplemental oxygen."

****

The morning temperature was in the low 60s. Gary escorted Becca downstairs for their morning walk. Becca's two strolls around the community courtyard, once in the morning and again in the afternoon, were her only regular exercise. The weather would soon be turning cold. She wasn't too excited about the prospects of bundling up for a stumble over the packed snow on the sidewalk.

"Hey, you two. You took off just in the nick of time." Harold was in the fireplace nook, working on a 1,000-piece jigsaw puzzle. "We didn't get out of there until 9:30."

"What was the hot topic?" Becca asked while shifting around the pieces, trying to find one to finish out the border.

"Oh, you know our usual suspects," Harold responded in reference to Sandra and Felix.

Harold returned to his morning brain stimulation. Becca and Gary strolled outside. The morning was sunny, and they paused to soak in a few rays.

****

Upon their return, Gary poured them a glass of vegetable juice. Becca picked up her phone and called Elizabeth.

"Unless this is a life-threatening emergency, you know what to do."
"BEEP!"

"It's Mom checking when you're heading home. I'll keep trying. Change your message. Someone's liable to call 911!" On the other end, Elizabeth stared at her cellphone screen, flashing with her mom's number, trying to get through. "I should have used the landline."

Gary handed her the juice glass.

"Will it take long to prepare for your big show?"

"It's a reading. I don't have to memorize anything." He flipped through his three-hole-punched manuscript, organized with sticky note tabs in a black binder. "I'll tell the story about you getting lost hiking around the ranch with my little brother."

"That's your version. Billy knew where we were. I panicked when you made me find the way back." Becca was defensive, with a grin on her face. "Why don't you read the part about how you tried to kick me out of my car at Libby Flats?"

"Seems to me it was the other way around."

"Ha! You should be happy to know that story didn't make it into the draft."

"Good. Now, I won't have to explain it to anyone."

"Relax. Take a nap. Is there anything I can get? Coffee? Tea? Tylenol?"

Gary rattled the amber plastic vial with prescription-grade acetaminophen with codeine. Becca jabbed her thumb into the air.

"Make it a double."

Becca popped a pill, and Gary jacked up the morphine control module. The pump regulated the dosage, so there was no way for her to get too much of the opioid into her system.

"Settle down, and you can do away with these drugs."

"I might as well live it up!"

"Do you want to get out of those clothes?" Gary asked as Becca closed her eyes.

"I'm an anthropologist. I can sleep standing up. I don't want to feel like I'm sick in bed. Did you remember to call Avery? Did you tell Jack?"

"Who cares about that piece of crap, Middleton?" Gary scolded as he walked out of the room.

"It's been 40 years. Get over yourself. How I let myself get mixed up with you and Jackie, I'll never know," groaned Becca. "Maybe the good Reverend and Avery can referee."

"You don't piss off anyone. If you didn't lead Middleton on, we'd be better off," Gary scolded, poking his head around the bathroom door frame.

"You two were very obedient," said Becca. "I had Avery to be my go-between. Being bedridden at home is a good time to ponder life. I have some thinking to do if you don't mind."

Gary wandered out to the living room out of earshot and turned on the TV.

******

Becca sneaked the phone out from under the covers and dialed 411. The operator answered.

"Do you have a listing for Jack Middleton in Laramie, Wyoming?"

"Not Laramie. I do in Centennial. Would you like the number, or I can connect you for a dollar and add the fee to your next bill?"

"Just a minute." Becca climbed into the walker with the phone in one hand and about flew over the top when the tennis balls caught the edge of the carpet. "Damnit." She rolled to the kitchen and found a pen in the junk drawer. "Okay, I can write."

"Are you okay, ma'am?"

"It's nothing."

"Please hold."

The operator connected Becca to a recording.

"The number is 307-555-5487. Please make a note of it. Goodbye."

Becca hung up and dialed.

"Beep, Beep, Beep."

"The number you have reached is no longer in service. Calls are now being accepted at 307-765-6068. If you believe you have reached this recording in error, please dial the operator or try your call again."

"Old Stage Stop. What do you want?"

The gruff voice took Becca aback.

"Uh, is this 307-765-6068? I was told I could reach Jack Middleton at this number. You have phone manners worse than my daughter."

"If that son of a bitch shows his face around here again, it will be the last time." There was indistinguishable conversation amid the background noise. The bartender clanked dirty glasses while he talked. "Does your daughter have a room full of drunken pool shooters and poker players yelling at the top of their lungs?"

"Oh, my. We're talking about the same Jack Middleton?" There was more bar noise. "Are you there? Jack was a friend of mine. I haven't seen him since college. I want to catch up."

"Yeah, sorry, it's busy tonight. Are you part of the SOB's fan club? The other night, a guy called looking for him. What happened? Did he steal your purse? Middleton lives somewhere above Turquoise Lake. Okay, good luck!"

The bartender hung up and got back to his patrons. "Three of a kind beats two pair! It's Jacks or better to open! A pair of Jacks to start the betting, moron!"

11

Lake Marie Lodge

I spent a lot of time with my parents growing up and put up with Mom mixing her business with pleasure. I should have thought back to our family trek to Lake Marie Lodge after my high school graduation. That year, Halley's Comet flew by and should have brought enough good luck to last me for a while. My luck was bad luck. E.S.

******

Elizabeth was done with the boredom of high school and had theoretically become a bona fide adult after her high school graduation in 1986. It was time to celebrate. Summer school was in full swing. Becca taught a class in cultural ecology.

"Why don't you come along? You can finish whatever you're doing at the campground," encouraged Gary. "You usually can't wait for this trip."

"I can either get ready to go or go. I can't do both. I have papers to grade. Elizabeth, I'm happy for you. You're flying out of the nest."

"Mom, how much time will it take to grade 10 papers? I want to share this, especially with you. You beg me to get ready. This is my parole party. I'm released from Laramie High School prison. The Fuji Café?"

"All right, all right. Let me put on some better shoes."

Becca was the last to load into their Sherman tank size 1980 International Harvester Scout. Four-wheel drive was good in snow and overkill in the summer. Gary learned to drive an earlier model while growing up on his ranch.

Becca stalled around and made a second trip into the house because she forgot her pack of multiple-colored felt-tip pens for grading papers.

"Dad, remember to stop at Libby Flats. It's such a clear day. It's tradition!" demanded Elizabeth.

They drove up Wyoming Highway 130, known to the locals as the Snowy Range Road. Elizabeth sat in the middle of the front bench seat because she liked to be in charge of the music. She fiddled with the tuner and settled on the Laramie rock-and-roll station.

"Why don't we sit here quietly?" Becca reached over and clicked off *Wanting More Passion* by Thomas Williams in the middle of the refrain about spontaneous lovemaking. "Maybe have some conversation for a change. Are you sure we have time for Libby Flats? I want to get these papers graded."

Around the next curve, Gary waited for two bicyclists whizzing down the hill before creeping his rig into the scenic overlook parking lot.

"Mom, we aren't on a schedule. The sky is bluer than blue!"

Elizabeth unbuckled her lap belt.

"Some days, this is a place I like to visit alone." Becca stayed behind. "I don't need another negative experience here, and I don't need reminders."

Gary pulled on his black Laramie Mountaineering cap stuck between the dash and the windshield.

Elizabeth charged up the stone steps to the observation deck and gazed around the landscape with her dad.

"One of these days, I want to live in Colorado. Climb Long's Peak."

She stood on the circular platform and looked through the brass tube that pointed to various landmarks.

"Maybe someday. If anyone saw my car with green and white plates, we'd be viewed as traitors."

"Who said anything about us moving? Besides, you tell me about some 'Pact' you have about Wyoming."

Elizabeth flipped her hair away from her face, which wavered in the wind,

"Not just Wyoming, this place. Libby Flats. We'll explain it to you when you're older!"

"You keep saying that. I'm a high school graduate!"

After the obligatory stop, Elizabeth bounded down the steps to the parking area. The Scout in low gear chugged a few more miles to the Lake Marie Lodge campground. Gary pulled into his usual site next to the lake, number 37.

"We're scrambling up the boulders. Traversing the snowfield. Then glissading down."

Elizabeth held up her ice ax.

"You play through your mind how to slow yourself with that thing. The snow's wet, so it should dig in pretty well," warned Becca.

They gathered their hiking stuff. Becca waited in the Scout until the commotion died down.

"I'll be with you in spirit."

Parking by the lake wasn't the best place for Becca to concentrate. She had trouble holding the papers, flapping in the ever-present breeze sweeping across the water. Elizabeth helped her mom pick up a few rocks to hold down the stack of school assignments.

Elizabeth and her father cut across the campground to approach the boulder field. About halfway up, Gary steadied himself with his ice ax. He stepped on a slick spot in the shadow of a large boulder, and his feet slipped from under him. The day pack filled with lunch and water bottles made him top-heavy. Then gravity took over. Gary went down fast and tumbled out of control, hitting large fallen rocks and stopping between two giant boulders.

"Dad!"

Elizabeth scrambled down to her father. Her heart raced. When Elizabeth peered down at him, Gary was coherent, with a gash on his head and a scuffed-up face.

"Where's my cap?" Gary squinted as the sun shined onto his face and glistened off the blood, free-flowing from the head wounds over his face.

"Take these." Elizabeth handed him a small pack of Kleenex.

"Wait a minute." He awkwardly removed one arm from under the backpack strap. "It's my shoulder." Elizabeth helped him with the other strap and set the pack aside as Gary sat up. "Not as bad as it looks!" He pulled out a tissue, then another, and wiped off the blood the best he could.

A frantic Elizabeth scrambled back to the campground.

"It's Dad!"

Elizabeth was out of breath by the time she arrived at the campsite.

"He fell. Banged his head."

Becca placed a rock on her work and twisted her legs out from the wooden picnic table.

"The last thing he needs is another brain injury."

Elizabeth led the way. Gary crawled to the top of a flat rock. Becca carried the pack, steadied Gary to the campground without further incident, and loaded up. Becca folded down the back seat where Gary lay flat in the Scout cargo area.

The drive to the hospital took forever. Becca took the straight shot down Nellie Tayloe Ross Boulevard and hit every red light through town to the hospital emergency room parking lot. They waited for what seemed to be an eternity in the ER reception area. Head wounds were a low priority when it came to patient triage.

"Elizabeth, wait here with your father."

Becca walked around the corner to the pay phone. She located a number in the Yellow Pages, plugged a dime into the coin slot, and dialed.

"Fuji Café," There was quite a bit of background noise. "Who's hungry?"

Becca grimaced when the phone receiver on the other end made a big clunk from being dropped on the counter.

"Hello, Tak? It's Becca Steiner. I have to cancel our reservation."

"Okay, if you change your mind, we'll make room for you. Is that all?"

"Lemme think ..."

She hung up and returned to the ER waiting area.

"Head injuries should be an emergency," Gary impatiently uttered as Becca returned.

The nurse called his name and assisted him into a wheelchair and through the double doors.

"The last time this happened was 19 years ago. Do you think his concussion will be worse?" asked Becca.

"Brain trauma is tricky. It depends on the person," explained the ER doc before turning to Gary. "Now, you pay attention. Call me if your headache worsens. Get plenty of rest, no TV, no movies, no caffeine. You sprained your shoulder and should stabilize your arm in a sling. If you need anything more than Tylenol, call me." The doctor handed him some samples.

"Are they poisonous?" Gary asked with a grin, referring to the Chicago Tylenol murders in 1982.

****

On their way home, Becca stopped in front of the Fuji Café.

"Becca! We weren't expecting you for another hour," said Jennifer at the end of the counter, tending the cash register. "We have some very good specials tonight."

"I talked to Tak."

Becca waved at him as he cleared one of the back booths.

"Oh, this is yours. $21.85." Jennifer handed over a brown paper bag. "What happened?"

"Gary wasn't paying attention!"

Becca was stoic as she searched through her wallet, whipped out a twenty and a ten, and slapped them down on the counter. Jennifer dug through the cash drawer.

"Keep it for someone who comes up short."

Becca checked the white cartons with "Fuji Café, Laramie, Wyoming" printed in red that were packed and marked with egg foo young, chop suey, pork noodles, and steamed rice.

"Tell Gary to get well soon. Thanks!" Jennifer yelled out at Becca as she opened the door and hurried back to the Scout.

She tapped on the back seat window. Elizabeth rolled it down and was handed the bag through the rear seat window.

"Dad ends up in the emergency room, and you order dinner?"

"Happy graduation. No sense disappointing everyone today."

"Mom? What were you saying before about negative experiences?"

****

After the Lake Marie tumble, although Gary took every precaution, his cognition wasn't as sharp as needed for newspaper interviews and writing complicated news stories. He had more trouble matching his brain to his words.

He also experienced chronic fatigue. Gary was old school and wrote in longhand or composed on a manual typewriter. It turned out that analog writing slowed down his creativity, so his thoughts better coincided with his fingers typing or scrawling words onto sheets of paper.

12

Susan & Harold

September 20, 2006—2:15 p.m. MDT: Gary was antsy awaiting his Thursday night speaking gig. One more day to hurry up and wait. He took the afternoon to rehearse his community dinner reading. He rehearsed in front of the mirror, mouthing his manuscript to himself one more time. There was a pounding on the door. Gary walked into the living room and greeted Susan and Harold.

"Hey, you two. Thanks for helping out." Gary showed his neighbors into the house. They stopped by to empty the refrigerator of all the leftovers and haul the food down for the special dinner. "Good idea to get all this downstairs today. No sense rushing around tomorrow."

"Did you have time to see the Activity Committee's project set up in the Art Room?" Susan asked as she opened the refrigerator. "I added three small items to the time capsule. I thought I should do something extra. It's a fitting tribute to Blue Sky Village. Becca is so creative. Do you think it would be all right if I popped in to say 'hello?' I know the community would love to get a report. Me being her best friend and all."

"Thanks for the offer. I don't think she's in the mood to talk with anyone right now. I think she might be napping."

Harold retrieved more food from the refrigerator and lined up the covered dishes on the center island.

"Do you think Becca will make it to the dinner?"

Harold's forearms trembled when he cross-stacked dishes of lasagne and baked chicken thighs on his forearms.

"She may make an appearance. Been a little loopy."

Gary helped stabilize the load as Harold backed out of the condo.

"Is there anything special you or Becca want me to do, or should I say the Caring and Sharing Committee?"

"I don't think so. I've been rehearsing my book reading. You can't help with that."

"What's your book about, or is it a secret?"

"No secret. It's based on my childhood on a ranch, and here we are at Blue Sky Village after a strange sequence of life's ups and downs. You and Harold may be included in a paragraph or two."

"Turning points are in the eye of the beholder," mused Harold. "Good stories have happy endings, according to my kid, the screenwriter."

Susan sorted out the rest of the potluck items from the fridge.

"If it's okay, I asked some people from the local Justice Society to attend. They are very interested in your story."

"Invite 100 of your closest friends as long as they bring whiskey. I may need it. My brain isn't what it once was."

"What about Becca?"

"She may join in the fun. If I cave, she can pinch-hit for me. Since college, she's been researching the Mountain Shoshone up in the Big Horns, the Sheepeaters. Becca was involved in an expedition to return a ram's horn bow that was in a museum collection."

"They ate sheep? In the mountains?"

"You know, the ram, like the CSU [Colorado State University] mascot?" Gary did his best to explain how the tribal hunters took ram horns and made recurve bows out of them. "In 1998, Becca co-presented a paper about the relationship of the Mountain Shoshone with the Anazasi people."

"I've heard of Anazasi. They lived in cave dwellings in southwest Colorado."

"In the 1920s, a ram's horn bow was excavated from a tomb near Mess Verde."

"The National Park by Durango," responded Susan.

"This one was covered with gold foil tooled by the Aztecs. Ask her. She doesn't like to talk about it. Maybe she'll tell the story at the dinner. It was a harrowing experience."

"A bow made in Wyoming gilded in Mexico ends up in Colorado? Must be a good story."

"That's an understatement."

Susan delivered the last Cherry Coke Jell-O salad dish to the Common House. Becca made her way to the kitchen when she heard Susan close the door.

******

"Is the coast clear? Since when am I giving a talk about the chaotic symposium in Puerto Vallarta? I'm still looking over my shoulder after that. No, thank you."

"Bad memories? Maybe you'll want to wait until your friend Jack gets here. I'm sure he'll stir up some doozies."

"Get back to your rehearsing."

13

St. Alban's Rectory - Lander

Mom has been fascinated by native cultures since her childhood in New Jersey. She didn't say much about how her early days in Wyoming reinforced those interests. She didn't talk much with her parents. I doubt they knew she drove herself five hours to visit Grandma Sally for school and personal business. I didn't speak with my parents much, either, and didn't clear anything with them. I had no reason to return home after leaving Laramie in my rearview mirror. E.S.

****

Becca had taken a break from her summer classes in 1966 to visit the Quiver Mountain Ranch. Sally invited her back to help her prepare for the annual Rocky Mountain Cattlemen's Association barbecue in Lander. Becca always jumped at the chance to get back to ranch work.

Sally was in the back adjusting the garden hose when she heard a car bounce up the access road. The familiar red Ford Falcon pulled up in front. Becca exited her vehicle and walked up the porch steps. Sally swung open the screen door that slammed behind her.

"Welcome, Stranger. I see that Red Bird of yours is still alive and flapping."

"I didn't hear or feel any knockin' or squawkin' on my way up." Becca plopped on the wicker chair. "My saddle is more comfortable than any car seat."

"I'll have Marvin take a look to be sure she's roadworthy. Do you see much of that son of mine?"

"We had a class together. He's okay."

"That boy of mine should have stuck at home. We could use his young back. You tell him his brother needs him."

"We don't have a chance to talk much. I think he had a rough time in Vietnam. He spends his spare time with his nose in a book or at a typewriter. Avery Meadows from Jackson was in the class, too." Sally was momentarily perplexed. "Remember the Piedmont Mountaineering School on the west edge of the ranch? Avery was the instructor?"

"Now I remember. When I was growing up, the cowboys at the Eagle Crest Ranch rodeoed in Jackson. We stayed at the Moose Paddle Inn. Mrs. Meadows gave us a good rate. For the life of me, I don't know what she saw in that husband of hers. Probably met Avery when we were young and didn't know it."

"Your big picnic is tomorrow. Friday night? What are we waiting for?"

Sally dry-rubbed the meat in preparation while Billy was charged with getting the smoker ready.

"I'll put the briskets in the slow cooker outside. Put on your apron."

"We have to mix up some potato salad. My macaroni hamburger soup's always a hit. There's no need to cook anything separate for the men." Sally stood up and held open the screen door for Becca. "They have the day off to go to the picnic in Lander. A few of them will help us carry everything."

Sally walked out to the root cellar for the potatoes and the chicken coop for some eggs. The screen door slammed behind her.

"Did you get my letter? I know you're connected around here." Becca poked around the fridge for the condiments. "Can you put me in touch with someone who would know about the Arapaho ceremonial things in museums?"

"Look no further." Sally turned up the heat. She placed the potatoes in a big pot of water and the eggs in a medium saucepan. "We should meet Reverend Perez. Before moving here, he worked for the Pojoaque Pueblo and the Navajo."

"I'm working with some of the anthropology grad students. For starters, we want to inventory Arapaho and Shoshone artifacts in museum collections," Becca explained about the two tribes that share and jointly manage the Wind River Reservation.

"The ranch is partly tribal land."

Becca brought out the cutting boards from the cupboard next to the sink and vegetable knives from the knife block by the mixer, where they've been for generations.

"I don't get in to see Pedro much anymore. This would be a good excuse to drop by. I know some about what's around the ranch. He'd have more ideas."

"I can stay over. I hope we can set up a time with Reverend Perez."

The two cooks chopped up onion and celery to make a mass quantity of potato salad in a large white-speckled blue enameled metal bowl.

"Several nomadic tribes came through these parts. This is traditional Shoshone land." Sally stuck a fork into a few potatoes to check if they were tender enough. "Gary's dad, Clyde, too bad you didn't know him. Anyway, before we got married, he used to take me to the far edges of the place."

"Remember? You made Gary show Billy and me around. Those rides are why I decided to study anthropology."

Sally retrieved a bison skull from the front room.

"We found this at the bottom of a small canyon. It was a buffalo jump."

Sally held the bulky artwork and leaned it against the kitchen counter wall. Becca examined the black, yellow, and red designs painted on the skull.

"It's signed. The artist?"

"Leonard White. He's Lloyd's boy."

"I met Lloyd my first day."

The conversation was distracting since they had to rinse off their hands. There was no telling what critters might lurk in the ancient skull.

"Leonard's pretty good with paint. I traded him a Pendleton for the skull. Lloyd returned the blanket to me as a wedding present when Marvin and I got hitched."

"I like the detail. Speaking of art, when can we set up a time to meet with Reverend Perez?"

Becca used a pair of potholders printed with "Shop at Berwin's" to pour the spuds into a giant colander over the sink.

"The phones are out. I go to town on Saturday morning. We'll drop by the rectory." Sally ran cold water through the colander. "You're staying the night? Help me get the dinner ready for the boys. Leftover stew. It'll be like old times."

"Old times? I've been helping you since I've been in college!"

Becca and Sally finished preparing the side dishes.

******

As usual, the Cattlemen's BBQ was a huge success. It began at noon and ended when nothing remained. Clean-up was a snap. The following morning, a few ranch hands helped by washing the pots and pans from the big wingding.

Becca and Sally pulled up in front of St. Alban's Episcopalian Rectory in Lander.

"My dad arranged for me to move into a basement apartment here when I transferred to Lander High."

The two got out of the Falcon and strolled up the walk. Sally rattled the screen door.

"What a surprise. Hello, Sally. Come in, have a seat anywhere. Excuse the grubby work shirt. I was out back watering."

Reverend Perez removed his reading glasses perched on the end of his nose and stuck them in his shirt pocket.

"We thought you might be saying grace at the barbecue last night. We didn't know if you'd be around," Sally recalled.

Sally and Becca walked up the two steps and into the front room while Reverend Perez held open the door.

"Oh, I don't have anywhere to go. Yesterday's picnic? It was the Presbyterians' turn for the prayer duties." He picked up the Lander newspaper on the easy chair and reassembled the sections before sitting down. Becca and Sally sat on the red leather couch. The frame was constructed from finished knotty pine logs. "What's on your mind?"

"Pedro, meet Becca Pembroke. She's an anthropologist and interested in the tribal things at St. Alban's."

"I was helping Sally cook for the big barbecue. I thought I'd catch two birds with one piece of bread."

"We've met. I remember a Christmas dinner your senior year in high school."

"That was the first Christmas Gary wasn't home," lamented Sally.

"How can I help young lady?"

"I want to learn from you. My anthropology department is cataloging tribal items in museums. Some of my classmates are checking with the State Museum in Cheyenne and the Western Historical Center in Cody. Finding out what might be around here would be a good start."

"We have a small exhibit at the Mission. More like a lighted storage area where we display a handful of artifacts. The Arapaho elders are compiling a list and recording stories."

"I know the collections manager at the Lander Settler Museum. Alison Robbins can tell you about an Arapaho headdress there."

"Terrific! Professor Wolfe or a grad student will be in touch."

"Have you considered looking at your project from a wider societal perspective? I studied sociology. Anthropologists look at culture from a micro level. I view the stories of all the items as snapshots of cultures as they once were and how they fit into contemporary society. Maybe 'big-picture' interconnections are why I became a priest."

"That's why I want to write down the stories."

"What else, Becca? Do you have time to meet at the Settler Museum? We can go there now."

"Not this trip. I have plenty to share with Dr. Wolfe."

"I hope to see you in church soon, Sally. You're welcome here anytime. It's been a while since you stayed in the basement apartment. Speaking of Alison Robbins, she's living there now."

Reverend Perez walked his guests to the door.

14

Nurse Riley Connors

September 21, 2006—5:10 p.m. MDT: Gary took a break from his third and fourth final rehearsals because he didn't want to over-prepare his book reading.

"I don't know why I'm wasting so much time on this. It's taking away from time I should be paying attention to your needs," Gary said to Becca.

"I appreciate you being so conscientious."

He paused to decide what to wear, not that it mattered.

"What do you think? I don't want to overdo it."

"You think every day is T-shirt and shorts weather." Becca noticed Gary's toothpick legs extending from his forest green twill carpenter shorts. "Have you called Elizabeth?"

"That's your department."

"She never picks up when I call."

"Use my phone. The bait and switch."

"Put on some long pants and button-down shirt."

Becca sat up, wearing her street clothes.

"You want me to dress in my formal wear?" Gary changed into his lone pair of gray slacks, held by a cowhide western-style belt with "Chief" tooled on the back. "Don't call me 'Chief.'"

That was in reference to his informal *Adventures of Superman* title based on *Daily Planet* Editor-in-Chief Perry White.

"Is that the only shirt you have?"

"I wear it once a year."

"Well, the Cheyenne Stampede will soon be upon us," Becca reminded.

"Not until July. I'll put in for credentials. There are references to the Stampede in my book. I want to refresh my memory about my 'views from behind the chutes.'" Gary was hooked on Wrangler Press Association media passes. "You know I never miss a chance to hang out with my cronies."

"It is the 21st century. I can hear it now. 'I remember when newspapers were printed on paper.'"

"Every summer, we all toss ten bucks into a hat. Last one standing takes it all."

"Elizabeth's retirement fund."

"Journalism's a thing of the past. At least we can talk about typewriters and the smell of ink. There's always cold beer in the press trailer and small talking with people from around the world."

"That's your excuse to call Elizabeth. Set up an interview."

He snapped his re-re-re-gifted buckle onto the belt. Nobody knew anything about the red, black, and white beaded abstract design, a genuine work of art made from tiny cut beads.

The first owner was his cousin, Bobby Smithee. The Lander Lounge paid him with the ornate buckle and matching bolo tie set for playing a small gig. He couldn't share the trades with the bass player and drummer, so he returned them to Gary as a birthday gift.

Gary then presented the set to Reverend Perez after his and Becca's wedding at the Episcopal church in Laramie. He accepted the beaded gifts with gratitude before handing them back because he didn't take any payment for his services.

He pulled on a pair of tan, scuffed-up Acme western boots.

"Those pants are a little short for the heel. I doubt any of these flatlanders will notice." Becca motioned him to come over. "Remember to call your daughter. Don't ask. Tell her to come home. You're always too accommodating."

"And you're not? We wouldn't be here if you hadn't been so pushy."

"That's not what happened, and things worked out pretty well if you ask me. Offer her that fancy buckle and bolo tie. They're early 1900s. The smoked leather is also ancient."

"That's not a big enough bribe. All she has to do is ask. For that matter, she doesn't have to ask. I'll try her when the community dinner is over."

"You clean up pretty well."

"…and Halloween is coming up. Are you going to be okay? I'll be about an hour. I don't have to do this. Everyone will understand. You'll be by yourself. Why don't you call Elizabeth while I'm downstairs?"

"Maybe. I'm good. I may make an appearance. You never know."

Becca puckered up. Gary gave her a peck, then dropped the bed railing.

"Just in case."

He picked up his manuscript and walked toward the door. On second thought, he returned to the bedroom and retrieved the matching bolo tie. He modeled it, and Becca gave the "thumbs up."

"*biixoo3e3en*," Becca demurred in Arapaho.

He blew back a kiss.

"You're now multi-lingual?"

"Give me some credit. We, anthropologists, are pretty good listeners." Becca rolled her eyes and laughed. "*houhou!*"

"Thanks, and I love you, too. Come on down if you're up to it." Gary took a breath. "I'm not looking forward to facing the neighbors."

"I know. I'm tired of the endless doting. We can't be ungrateful for their support. Caring and Sharing? Remember to microwave Sandra's chicken. It's generally undercooked. Big-time indigestion is the last thing we need."

"Most times, it's pretty good around here. Beats a nursing home with no relatives around. At least I have a daughter to complain about."

Nonetheless, Becca accepted the attention with good graces. Others in her situation had insurance benefits or were well enough off to move into long-term care facilities or assisted living homes.

Becca's illness in their midst was a cue for the community members to think about their mortality.

"Don't we have other things to worry about besides what to plant in the garden or whose turn it is to lock up the Common House?" Becca was the neighbor who brought up a reality check about the gorilla in the room since she was the gorilla. "We talk around our fears of aging. How about next month, we write our obituaries?"

"I'll teach a class. Obits were my specialty," said Gary. "It was the only time most people made it in the paper."

It was challenging for the accommodating residents to change their self-interested perspectives. Their excellent collaborative work was nullified by attempts to get the others to become rule enforcers.

"Why would a community of senior citizens want to snitch on their neighbors for missing a few meetings or forgetting to unload the dishwasher?"

"I don't think we're supposed to call ourselves 'senior citizens' anymore."

"Are we the only ones who complain about the Older Americans around here?"

"Enough cohousing blather."

"Get down there before all the food gets too old and cold!"

Gary summoned the elevator. It dropped to the first floor. When the door opened, he entered the dining room, where his neighbors mobbed him, even Felix and Sandra. He led the crowd into the dining room.

"Thanks to Susan and Harold, the potluck dinner items are organized by courses," said Gary as the potluck buffet line formed. He sat at the back table, reviewing his notes for the fifth time.

****

Becca sat on the edge of her electric hospital bed, which was taller than her regular one. She pulled on her soft slipper socks, stepped down using a small stool, settled into her walker, and picked up the photograph on the nightstand taken during her college days.

"Oh, shit."

With one hand on the walker, Becca floundered mid-stride. The front wheels rolled faster on the kitchen floor, and the picture frame flew out of her hand.

"THUD, CRASH, TINKLE!"

After hearing the noise through the ceiling, everyone at the party below suddenly became quiet. Gary didn't wait for the elevator. He ran out the back door and scampered up the steps, two at a time.

Becca was sprawled out on the floor next to the walker.

"Will I ever play the violin again?" Becca muttered to Gary.

"Riley told you those are no good, even with the rubber grips."

"Hospital socks are comfy, but they do make me look sick."

Becca wiggled her toes, covered by the pink anklets.

"What were you doing carrying that photo?"

Gary moved the stool over so Becca could push up to her knees. He helped her up to the walker, and she scooted to her chair.

"It was that picture's fault! I was gonna clean the glass!"

She struggled into the comfy seat in front of the TV.

"That's a Riley job."

"I can still take care of myself." Becca was out of breath. Gary greeted a few of his concerned neighbors at their front door. "Nothing to see here, folks."

The neighbors cleared out. Gary lingered and helped Becca place the oxygen cannula tube around her head.

"I can do the reading another time. The main thing was to get rid of all the food."

"Go!"

Gary returned to the potluck. Becca made her way to the freezer, dug out a bag of frozen peas, and banged it on the counter. She returned to her chair, held the makeshift cold pack on her head, and made a phone call.

"Sunrise Health Care Center after-hours. Do you have an emergency?" asked the operator.

"It's Becca Steiner. I fell. My head's spinning, and it's not from the morphine. Can my nurse stop by sooner?"

"Okay, Mrs. Steiner. I see Nurse Connors is stopping by in a couple of hours. I'll make a note about your accident. Have a good evening."

It was close to 8:00 p.m. when there was a knock on the door.

"Is it my favorite nurse?"

Riley entered the living room, where Becca sat in her TV chair, holding the cold bag of peas on her banged-up head.

"I've been your only nurse. Now, what did you get yourself into? Other than clonking your noggin, how are you feeling?"

Riley pulled out a blood pressure cuff from a black leather bag.

"153 over 72. A little high. Not emergency level."

"Did you see my skid marks?" Becca readjusted the cold pack on her head. "Not the most relaxing visit to the kitchen."

"Have you weighed yourself lately? You're looking thin."

"High blood pressure isn't an emergency. I've lost 10 pounds downing high-protein drinks. That's an emergency. I'm 5'8" and 125. That's all dead weight hitting the deck."

"You have to eat more solid food. How's the pain tonight?"

Riley handed Becca a pain range chart from mild to severe.

"No diff. I'd say between six and seven, not counting my headache."

Becca frowned as she rotated her neck, trying to get some relief.

"I'm not crazy about changing your pain meds. Let's keep you on the ibuprofen. The acetaminophen. You call if anything changes."

"Would you mind sweeping up the glass?"

Nurse Riley retrieved the photo and frame from the kitchen.

"A few memories I could live without."

****

Gary finished up his reading and helped the kitchen patrol. He rode up the elevator with Susan and Harold.

"I hope Becca's okay," consoled Susan.

"Bruised ego more than anything. Her nurse is good about keeping her calmed down."

Gary and Harold shook hands. The three went their separate ways.

Gary plopped on the couch.

"Did you scare Riley off?"

"At least until next time."

"Enough excitement for now. This should be a wake-up call for you to slow down!"

"Slow down? Why not live it up!"

"Okay, then why don't you live it up and head down to Looziana? Tell your daughter about what you and that focus group found out. I don't even know!"

"I want to keep it between Elizabeth and me."

"I'm happy to convey a message."

"That's the problem. I've leaned on you too much to be my go-between. You never get it right, anyway."

"Fly out within the next few days. Help her get organized. Drive back together. It'll be good to spend some 'buddy' time together. Like that road movie when the two friends let loose."

"'Buddies?' I don't know if I could carry on a conversation. I can't relate to anything she says. I'd drive us off a cliff!"

There was no telling what could happen on an airplane, followed by a road trip through the middle of nowhere. The following day, Becca consulted with her medical team and Nurse Riley. All agreed that she should stay home.

"Whew," sighed Becca.

15

The Saddle Horn

When I graduated high school, my parents thought I was still a kid. All my time around their friends set me up to deal with coworkers twice my age. Halley's Comet flew by in '86 and was supposed to bring good fortune. On the flipside, the Space Shuttle Challenger exploded in January. Then, in April, the Chernobyl nuclear reactor melted down in Ukraine. Despite the bad luck in the world, I was let off the hook as a felon. Everything in life is relative. E.S.

******

Elizabeth's most challenging class was physics, which she had put off until her senior year. She and a lab partner conducted experiments like determining the acceleration of different objects dropped from various heights. It was very frustrating because they kept getting different results. The teacher let the seniors slide by making lab attendance optional as long as they passed the weekly quizzes.

Driver's Education was the other class that gave her fits.

"I don't have time to do a traffic safety project. It's my last semester."

Elizabeth only had a learner's permit because her parents didn't want to teach her how to drive. They thought she should be taught by an expert, who was also the track coach.

"You had all semester to get something completed."

Her teacher cut her some slack and gave her a solid D. It didn't matter because Southeast Community College, 45 miles from Laramie, over Sherman Hill, had already accepted her. There was very little academic pressure since the college took anyone who applied.

Even though her parents had too much fun when they were in college, they were relieved that Elizabeth graduated with an overall C+ average, pretty good for a juvenile delinquent.

Then, there was her disastrous high school graduation ceremony.

"I'm making a statement, Mom."

"Tell me why going naked under your gown is a statement? You're the only one who'll know ... and me!"

"What are you going to do about it?"

"At least wear a pair of shoes. Not sneakers!"

****

An Associate degree would be good enough for now. Getting her feet wet at a community college meant no SAT or ACT admission testing was required. Elizabeth could enroll as an upperclassman if she later attended a four-year school. Her parents agreed to pay for her room and tuition. She was on her own for books and spending money.

The Saddle Horn Inn was a big hotel and conference center on the outskirts of Cheyenne. Gary knew the owner's son, John Hyatt, from their time at UW.

"Hello, Hyatt. It's Steiner."

"Steiner! What an unexpected call. How are you and Becca?"

John signed a paper handed to him by his assistant.

"Let me put you on speaker."

"She's good. I'm calling about my daughter, Elizabeth. She's going to Southeast in the fall."

"What? She's not going to UW?"

"She wants out of her mother's hair. Do you have anything for her?"

"We're always looking for summer help. Let me get with the Food Services Manager to be sure he has a spot. There's plenty of time. I don't foresee a problem. Does she have any experience?"

"She didn't work at all during high school. This will be her first go at it."

"I'll watch after her. Let's say she's hired unless you hear from me otherwise. Have her stop by. Talk directly to me. Will you and Becca be in Cheyenne anytime soon? I'll buy dinner."

"We'll help Elizabeth with her move so when school lets out."

"Does she need a place to stay? We have a few long-term rentals for railroaders. I could trade that out for some of her pay."

"One of Becca's colleagues is renting her a basement apartment near Holliday Park. If that doesn't work out, I'll stay in touch."

"What about wheels? I'm selling my son's egg beater Vega."

"I got a good deal on an '80 Pinto hatchback."

"I imagine so. Aren't they time bombs on wheels?"

"I found one that was fixed up after the recall."

The repair was a plastic barrier the company installed between the rear axle and the gas tank. The fuel filler tube was lengthened so it wouldn't break loose.

"I'm less worried about her car blowing up and more concerned about minimizing her winter driving over the Hill."

Interstate 80 extended from Washington, D.C., to Sacramento and was completed in 1986. The drive was usually a straight shot except for the 10 miles of wind and blizzards between the 8,000 ft Sherman Hill summit and Veedauwoo.

"I guarantee you she won't be driving to Laramie much. Working here is addictive. She'll meet some interesting people. Give me a call, and we can set something up for dinner. I want to show off our three new dining rooms."

"She's kind of a free spirit like her mother."

"Don't worry about it. She'll be a good fit. Compared to some of the riff-raff I have around here, how bad could she be?"

****

Southeast was one of six community colleges in Wyoming. They were like an extension of high school because most students lived at home. Older nontraditional students had families and little interest in student life. Occasional socializing happened in the student lounge connected to the library.

Elizabeth was one of a handful of traditional students who lived independently. Since she didn't have any classmates in town, her part-time job at the Saddle Horn was a valuable distraction. Elizabeth got to know the other employees. It was the first time she'd spent much time with adults other than her parents.

"Have you ever been to the Cheyenne Cowboy Stampede?" one of the other prep cooks asked.

"I've been with my dad. He gets press passes."

The prep cook motioned for Elizabeth to join him on a smoke break outside the back entrance.

"When's your next shift?"

He opened the aqua cigarette pack from the bottom corner, shook out a menthol, and offered it to Elizabeth as she shook her head, "No thanks."

"That's upside down?"

"Keeps the filters clean."

"Mr. Hyatt told me the Stampede tips are pretty good. I can cut my afternoon classes on Friday."

"Clock in early. We can get set up in the big ballroom. We'll work the night show when we're done in the kitchen. Pull a double. To-morrow's Saturday. Lots of action."

"I'm not old enough."

"Don't worry about it. All we do is set up and haul booze from the basement to the bars. Nobody checks nobody during Stampede week."

Elizabeth could roll those big round tables and set them up single-handedly to maximize the crowd size while still meeting the fire codes in case of an emergency.

That afternoon, her parents stopped by for dinner on their way home from the afternoon rodeo.

"You look great in those Western duds. Who would have thought Elizabeth Steiner would be caught wearing boots and a Stetson?"

"It's a knock-off Stetson from the carnival rip-off market."

"Dad taking me to shoot pictures over the chutes during Wild West Days must have rubbed off."

"Back then, you wanted to break horses like your mom. Why aren't you in class?"

"I'm setting up for the big show tonight, Dad."

"Are you learning anything?"

"School's school. Here? I've learned how to bake meatloaf for the coffee shop and chicken *cordon bleu* for the dining rooms at the same time. We serve the same salads, vegetables, and potatoes. The difference? Coffee shop customers eat with one fork."

"Who's playing tonight? Anyone we know? I think our press passes should be good."

"Bobby Smithee and the Barnstormers. You should stick around."

Nursing schmursing.

16

Phil Perkins

September 23, 2006—2:07 p.m. CDT: Gary tidied up the house while Becca was getting ready to attend the meeting she set up with Phil Perkins from Eco-Haven Events. His company was organizing the Blue Sky Village 10th anniversary celebration. Becca wanted Phil's help to fill in a few holes in the script she'd been writing.

The Steiner's next-door neighbor, Susan, paced back and forth, waiting for Phil, who soon struggled up the sidewalk, toting a large folded-up cardboard box shrink-wrapped in cellophane under his armpit.

"I have a meeting?" Phil quietly said as the glass door opened.

"Susan Butler. The community put me in charge of this little project."

She led Phil to the Art Room, where he slid his package onto a long folding table.

"As you requested, I recommend this. Some assembly required. Batteries not included." Phil ripped off the wrapper and crinkled it up. "We've never done an event like yours."

"Who knew a corrugated cardboard box could have so many folds, flaps, and slots?" Phil said while he and Susan put on the finishing touches.

"It's a time capsule of sorts. Everyone will be contributing a little something. Becca is writing the script for the opening event she's producing. We're 10 years and counting."

"It's amazing that your entire neighborhood organized everything. What is this place? Blue Sky Village is a nice Boulderish name."

"The Arapaho used to live around here before they were exiled to Wyoming and Oklahoma. They refer to themselves as the Blue Sky people. The original idea was to use the Arapaho words, *hinono eino*. We figured the average American couldn't say it, let alone spell it. So, we settled on Blue Sky Village."

"When the Steiners joined, they knew about the Arapaho connection to Boulder. Gary is from Wyoming. Becca's an anthropologist. She's been involved with Native American projects since college. They insisted we honor the tribal presence."

"I heard about the Arapahos being around here when I first came to Boulder. Eco-Haven helped plan an event for a family east of town. They said the Army built a fort on their property in the 1860s. I read in the paper about a group called the Social Justice Society raising awareness about it."

"I'm part of Justice Society. So's my husband. The U.S. Army trained Boulder volunteer soldiers there."

"The family ordered a cake in the shape of Fort Chambers. Kinda spooky."

"Our higher purpose is saving the world. Returning the fort to the Arapaho is a Blue Sky Village project."

"Good luck with that. Your little village reminds me of my college days."

"Before anyone moved in, we were in the planning stages for two years. The Steiners drove down from Laramie once a month for the organizational meetings."

"Talk about dedication. I hope it's been worth it."

"That's nothing. Harold and I phoned in from California. We flew to Boulder for community planning activities. One time, when we arrived, the planning committee changed the date and forgot to tell us. Buried message on the answering machine."

"I went to a small college. We had an open area like this in the dorm basement," recalled Phil. "It had a kitchen, a ping-pong table, a TV room."

"We call it the Common House. It's like your dorm, except the average age here is 71, not 21," said Susan. "When we were first getting the community organized, we were 63 total strangers from all over the place. Many of us don't have family around. We thought living together would be a good alternative. We all watch out for each other. No keggers, though."

"So, you all must own your condos? My parents are looking for community housing. I gather you all help run the place, like managing the compost bin?"

"We downsized from a big place between Ventura and Santa Barbara. Colorado's not perfect, especially the weather. I don't miss cleaning a big house. Harold would rather watch the Rockies play the Dodgers than mow the yard. We kicked our kid out of the nest some time ago. We're all getting crotchety and into doing our own thing. Not the best for working together."

"It seems you're with it enough to plan this gig."

"I'd say parties are our strong point, but we need professional expertise from you, Phil," Susan explained. "It's been a good diversion from the work. Maintaining this place is getting to be a challenge. I used to be on the Gardening Committee. Last summer, I couldn't bend over to pick weeds. I water but can't do any planting. We sit in meetings and figure out how to boss around our contractors and whether or not we need a property manager."

"My uncle wants my folks to move to Arizona. 'We don't play golf,' my dad says. I'll mention 'cohousing.' Speaking of cakes, do you need any referrals for catering? Photography?"

"Good questions for the Steiners. While we're at it, let me call up there." Susan walked over to the intercom and punched in 1501. "Gary? The Eco-Haven guy is here."

"Who?" a staticky voice from the intercom answered.

"The EVENT PLANNER," Susan slowly enunciated.

"We'll be down."

"That'll save me a stop. I know Becca had some questions about the 'run-of-show.'"

"Before I forget, there's a condo coming up for sale. We can put you on the notification list. Same email address?"

******

The elevator door opened.

"Gary Steiner." He and Phil shook hands. "Meet Becca. I think she's the one who first called you."

"Nice to put a face to the voice. You'll have to tell me about the Arapaho and Fort Chambers."

"Susan is on top of all that," mentioned Becca. "I have a few questions about organizing the Common House and the best seating arrangement. I want to be sure everyone can see the program."

The meeting was short. Becca and Gary returned home. When she found her chair and untangled herself from the vinyl tube behind her neck, she inserted the cannula prongs into her nostrils before turning on the oxygen. She sorted through a pile of papers and found the manila folder under last month's *Boulder Seniors Today* magazine on the end table.

17

Triumph Hotel

My parents had their own lives. Their day-to-day decisions had nothing to do with me. Nor did I want them to know about what was happening in my life. I was out of touch and let too much time lapse between calls and visits, thinking I'd never have to deal with my parents' life events. It was hard talking on the phone, let alone popping in for a visit. Maybe that was why I moved around so much and developed only superficial relationships. Upward mobility was part of the hotel business, which fit into my restless behavior. E.S.

****

Elizabeth was under the impression that the 1988 family trip to California was her community college graduation present. In reality, her mom wanted to visit Uncle Frank Pembroke about an academic paper they were writing. Everyone knew Frank as a shirt-tail relative and called him Uncle.

Frank was also one of Becca's high school classmates in New Jersey and became one of her colleagues. He and his now ex-wife moved to Santa Monica when UCLA hired him after he received his Ph.D. in Meso-American history from Rutgers.

Frank had arranged for a nice room at the Triumph Hotel on Ocean Avenue. On the last day of the family visit, Elizabeth noticed a sign above the coffee station advertising for an Assistant Catering Manager.

"I can do that," thought Elizabeth.

She backtracked to the Food Services Office and filled out the paperwork.

Uncle Frank invited everyone to a picnic later in the afternoon.

"I applied for a job in the hotel catering office," Elizabeth announced as Uncle Frank flipped the steaks on his backyard grill.

"You did what?" queried her mother, who overheard from the picnic table.

"I'm being independent. You told me to use my people skills. Develop a work ethic."

"Be eager and personable in Laramie, not California!"

"As I recall, your mother sent you to Wyoming to find yourself," Uncle Frank reminded Becca. "You couldn't wait to get out of Jersey. Elizabeth will be fine."

"Thanks, Uncle."

"First job?"

"Second, sort of. I worked part-time at the Saddle Horn. It's a big hotel in Cheyenne."

"Even better! That's fantastic! I'll put in a good word for you with the hotel manager. How much you liked the room."

"... and the sweet rolls!" added Elizabeth.

"You can stay with us until you get settled. My youngest has been hounding me to let her spend more time with her mother. You can stay in her room. We'll work something out."

******

Elizabeth had an interview the following day, if you want to call it that. The Catering Manager looked over her application form.

"I see you know the restaurant business. You mentioned that you're in town for vacation. When can you start?"

Her new job entailed developing menus, pricing options, and handling logistics for each gig. Situating the tables around a banquet room was second nature to her. She knew how to cram too many people into a small space.

"I'll be in Mexico and Guatemala for a month," said Uncle Frank. "You'll have the place to yourself."

While her parents returned to Laramie, Elizabeth settled in with her Santa Monica relatives until she could find her own apartment. She enjoyed the big city and developed a social life in California that was far different from what she had expected.

The hotel chain transferred Elizabeth from Santa Monica to Denver. When her parents relocated to Boulder, she moved again to Atlantic City in 1996. She stayed put until after 9/11 when she was sent to NOLA in 2002. Three years later, Hurricane Katrina made landfall.

****

As her luck would have it, the swanky Triumph Hotel chain kept Elizabeth on staff after Katrina to make a desperate effort to entice visitors to the property.

"Seventeen years. So much for loyalty," Elizabeth thought as she read the sticky note on her desk phone informing her she was laid off from her Vice President of Sales job.

Her live-in companion, the Banquet Manager at the same hotel, was fired and moved back to Dallas. There wasn't much romance, but having half the rent covered was helpful.

Elizabeth gained personal satisfaction by trying to transform her suitors. She'd become bored and move on to the next dating project. Talking shop was the main thing she and her latest accomplice in life had in common. Otherwise, she grew tired of gathering dirty clothes off the floor and picking hair from the bathtub drain.

She was obsessed with her work. Talking about her previous jobs bound what few relationships she had together, friendly or otherwise. Her small talk became tiring for everyone around her, including her mother, who had no interest in hearing about sales increasing by 57 percent or the server dropping a tray of rubber chicken dinners over a movie studio executive, who had it coming.

Unemployment benefits of $250 a week and her savings allowed Elizabeth to stay afloat as she put full-time effort into being around the film industry.

"Do something you didn't because you were tied to a mundane job," her employment counselor advised. Elizabeth had to report to the Workforce NOLA office weekly with the list of jobs she sought and the retraining classes she attended. "This is the perfect time to chase your dreams. If you don't have dreams, they will never come true."

****

In 2004, two years after it was established, the Louisiana Film Commission held a national conference at Elizabeth's hotel.

"Richard Johnson. I lead our Production Division," he said with a deep Southern drawl. "You certainly dress like a professional. Very impressive."

Elizabeth was a tall, lithe tomboy like her mother. Her hotel manager uniform was a silk blouse and a bowtie under a blazer worn with pants and comfortable black or navy pumps.

"Are the facilities working for you?" asked Elizabeth when she made her rounds through the meeting spaces.

"Everything's been great! Haven't I seen you around the office lately?"

"I've been spending some time there. I'm working on a film *noir* screenplay set in Baton Rouge."

"We've been looking for a crime-drama story."

"It's more of a rom-com with a criminal twist. Imagine *Love Happens* meets *Murder in Maine* meets *Long Shot*."

"I like your idea. We can work with it. Why don't you call my assistant and schedule a time to drop by on Monday? We can talk about developing your idea into a concept."

"Do you have any women in your office I could meet?"

"We've been looking for some fresh talent. Add some highlights to those long brunette locks. Your high cheekbones give you a classic look. Have you thought about being on the other side of the camera? We brought along a make-up artist. He can make those big brown eyes more alluring. And your lips ..."

"I don't even wear Chapstick."

"If you can, bring me your script. I'll read through it before the conference ends."

"I'll make an appointment at your office."

****

When there were meetings in town, Elizabeth's days were long. She went to her office, kicked off her shoes, and poured a shot of Jim Beam into a hotel water glass from the bottle in her desk drawer when her Palm Treo buzzed in her jacket pocket.

"It's the kitchen. I just took a room service for room 720. Can you take it up?"

"Why can't one of the bussers deliver it?"

"We're kind of tied up with the big banquet, and I'm short two. Besides, you always say you know all the jobs and can do anything in our job descriptions to be sure we're not trying to fool you."

"You're holding me hostage."

She downed her drink, picked up the order, wheeled the room service cart while steadying the bud vase with a yellow rose to the elevator, and pounded on the door.

"What a surprise! Y'all tell your dispatcher I appreciate her having you personally deliver my order." He scribbled his name on the check and added a $100 tip.

It was the Louisiana Film Commission executive wearing a Triumph Hotel bathrobe and terrycloth slippers.

"Boy, what a long day. Did you remember to bring your screenplay?" he asked while uncovering the plate of crackers and caviar. "I have a camera set up in the other room for a table read."

"Ya know, I didn't." Elizabeth grabbed the liter bottle of Moet by the neck from the ice bucket. Her towering presence overwhelmed her stalker as she approached him, tapping the bottle on her palm. Maybe it's time for you to take a dip in your jacuzzi." She flipped on the switch.

"We're consenting adults here," the executive pleaded while undoing the belt securing his robe. Elizabeth glanced at his portly waist with a smirk.

"Well, Mr. Johnson, or can I call you Dick. I'm happy the Louisiana Film Commission likes our hotel." Elizabeth rested the bottle on her shoulder like a baseball bat.

"Get real. Roberta Williams had to start someplace, young lady."

Elizabeth tossed the champagne bottle into the bubbly tub.

"We hope you'll consider us for your future meetings. Maybe I'll cross paths with Roberta someday. I just loved her in *Dames*. She's had a great career thanks to you."

She swiped her index finger into the caviar and licked it off. Before taking the check from the cart, Elizabeth changed the tip amount to $500 and backed toward the door.

"If you want to get anywhere in this business, wear a skirt, you arrogant bitch."

******

After her layoff, she had more spare time and joined the NOLA Film Society and didn't spend as much time at the state film office.

She towered over many of the over-dressed southern ingenues, who carried around file folders with their headshots and artist statements at networking events.

Her timing was right. Elizabeth liked being on the ground floor when presented with growth opportunities, giving her the flexibility to make the job her own. This time, though, she felt stuck in the basement unless she slept her way to the penthouse.

A temp agency found her work as an assistant manager at the Sleep Cheap Suites by the airport. The hotel paid her under the table so she could keep most of her unemployment benefits. She worked the night shift, which gave her plenty of downtime to work on her story ideas.

During the day, she spent at least six hours every morning working on her film script. In the back of her mind, Elizabeth was unsure why she was spending so much time writing stories with little or no chance of being made in Louisiana.

"Just what I need right now," Elizabeth thought as she flipped through her credit card bills and collection demands. "'You should have listened to me. 'Settle down and have kids.' I can hear it now."

18

Cameron & Miguel

September 28, 2006—6:17 p.m. CDT: Elizabeth was in no rush for this Boulder visit and plotted a back road route from Metairie to avoid traffic.

"Why am I dreading this?" Elizabeth slammed shut the cargo hatch on her white Subaru Forester before pulling out from in front of her apartment building. The parking garage was still closed because of flood damage. "It's always the same. We fight and apologize. Time passes until the cycle repeats. Maybe things will change. I can be an optimist, can't I?"

When she made Texas, the expansive landscape transitioned to rolling hills sprinkled with scrubby oak stands. Elizabeth looked through her address book. "I could use a little attention and a bucket of money about now."

She approached Dallas and decided it wasn't worth the brain damage she would experience putting up with her ex's doting and arrogantly wealthy parents.

"I'm not that bad off."

It was dusk when Elizabeth saw a Sleep Cheap Suites sign that rose above the highway as she approached the Ennis exit.

"I should at least give them a little business for keeping me afloat the last few months," she thought as she pulled off the interstate. "My kind of place."

The fluorescent lights in the lobby cast a bluish glow that reflected off the artificial Ficus tree. While waiting for the clerk, Elizabeth read through the tourist information in the rack by the front desk. The desk clerk finished up her paperwork.

"I see you're an employee at our New Orleans property. That's a 10 percent discount."

"I'm a temp."

"No matter, if you were full time it would be 20 percent."

Elizabeth signed her registration form and saw a poster on the wall.

"National Polka Festival? Czechoslovakian heritage event?"

"Yeah. Over Memorial Day. It's the biggest attraction in town."

"Too bad I missed it. Sounds like good story fodder.

"Your employee discount plus the coupon on page 38 in the magazine over there will let you 'Sleep Cheap.' It's good on holidays. The biggest sponsor is Carl's."

"Sounds like a deal."

"This is good for $3 off at any downtown merchant."

The clerk handed Elizabeth a round wooden disc.

She found her room, unloaded her Forester, and then drove into Ennis for a bite. On a Thursday, she found easy parking in front of Carl's Czech Café. When Elizabeth walked into the place, her presence turned a few heads.

"Sit anywhere. There's no menu. The specials are on the board." The server resumed her chat with one of the regular customers. "I'll drop my car off tomorrow. Thanks for fitting me in. I can't bum rides from my dad forever."

Elizabeth stared out the window at the empty small-town Main Street. There was no shortage of things for her to think about.

"At least everything is collapsing in on me at the same time," she thought, oblivious to the server setting down a glass of water.

"Welcome to Carl's. I'm Cameron. Have you decided? I see you're from Louisiana."

"I had to stop and support the Polka Festival."

"Nobody comes to Ennis on purpose."

"Passing through. Visiting my folks in Colorado. Haven't seen them in a while."

"At least you get to take a vacation to visit family."

"Listen, if I want a vacation, my mom is the last person I'd want to see."

"Sounds more like work. All my people are here. We're all polka dancers. I'm about ready to dance my way out of here."

"And go where? It's tough to break into new towns."

"I should be happy with what I have here. I can dream."

"It's good to have family around, annoying or not."

"They can get irritating. 'You should get with that Kelly Hajek,' Mom says. I suppose she's looking out for my best interest."

"Sometimes I wish I wasn't so independent. I'm driving 1,300 miles and not looking forward to getting reacquainted. Your mom may get on your nerves. At least you don't have to deal with the perfect storm swamping your boat."

"You must have left home when you were young. As much as I complain about it, I'm glad I've stayed put in little ol' Ennis. I can't imagine having to constantly catch up with family happenings. It's not like life would have stood still waiting for me."

"I'm starting to figure that out. I'll try the Early Bird Special."

"We offer the same things every day. Early Bird, Late Bird. My dad says nobody will notice. Large portions. Two cabbage rolls, a sausage, and boiled potatoes. Dessert's a blueberry *pierogi* smothered with a whipped cream and sour cream topping."

"I could use a big pile of comfort food."

"I like the food here. Probably too much. I could stand to stay away from the leftover *pierogi*!"

"Lately, I'm the opposite. Not much appetite," said Elizabeth

"You look like you could use a few more *pierogi*. I was as thin as you when my mom was sick last year. Another reason I've stayed in Ennis. I don't recommend high stress as the best way to lose weight."

The last customer paid. Cameron flipped the welcome sign to "Closed, Come Again" on the front door window. Elizabeth savored her first full-fledged Eastern European meal.

"How was everything? By the end of the day, the cabbage rolls get better with age." Cameron pointed to a photo of Czech food on the wall. "We call them *holubky*."

"I like the spiciness. What do you do for the wrappers? Steam a whole head of cabbage?"

Elizabeth wiped her plate clean with the last bite of bread.

"Yeah, all this is easy to make. Just time-consuming. If you cook like me, very cluttered counter. You haven't touched your *pierogi*."

"When I was coming up with menus for the hotel, one of the appetizer options was *pierogi*." Elizabeth sprinkled a little sugar from the dispenser onto her dessert. "Yours looked fried."

"Steamed and pan-fried. Not as greasy."

"Pretty good. Not too sweet. Seems like all cultures have their turnovers. When I was a kid, my favorite Chinese food was crab and cream cheese wontons."

Cameron handed Elizabeth the check.

"No rush."

Elizabeth let her food settle and slipped a twenty and the discount disc under her plate.

"We don't get many of these during the off-season."

"Tell Carl the special was very special."

"Carl? He was my great-grandfather. My dad runs the place now." Cameron waved to Elizabeth as she made her way out the door. "Have a good visit with your parents. They're all you got. You can't trade them for new ones."

Elizabeth didn't sleep well, partially due to a case of *holubky* indigestion. In the morning, she stumbled to the lobby for a coffee and a hard-boiled egg from the motel's basic continental breakfast.

****

On her way north, Elizabeth made a gas stop at the Deli & Hardware Store, 60 miles from Oklahoma City. She was enticed by a "Ten Cent per Gallon Discount" sign and pulled into the filling station.

"Full service, what a luxury, Miguel Rookham!"

She pointed at his plastic name tag. He unscrewed the gas cap and flipped on the pump. Miguel practically had to get down on one knee to speak through the car window.

"Can you pop the hood?" Miguel asked as he tossed aside his ponytail, which was tied back with a beaded turtle barrette.

He searched around for the dipstick.

"I like clean engines."

He inspected the oil level, showed her the dipstick, and wiped it on a red shop cloth.

"Almost half a quart low. You'll be okay for a few hundred miles. Bring it in for a full oil change when you get a chance."

"What qualifies for 10 percent off?" Elizabeth hollered out the window as Miguel replaced the dipstick.

"Do you have an ID card from any tribe?"

"The dog ate my ID?"

"Nice try! You get credit if you did any time on the Rez?"

"My mom helped the Arapahos in Wyoming locate ceremonial things in museums."

"That's a good thing." Miguel lowered the hood. "Study your history. Check out the Sand Creek Massacre site. It's on your way."

"I went to a powwow once when I was a kid. Didn't get what it was about. My grandmother has a ranch near Lander."

"I know Lander. A bunch of us are saving up to drive there next July 4th for the rodeo and powwow. I hope Bobby Smithee is playing. He's always at the Lander Lounge. I'm a fancy dancer and a team roper. Was your powwow at Fort Washakie?"

"It was a memorial for someone at Ethete. I didn't want to go. What's a 12-year-old city kid know, anyway? Bobby Smithee? He's my dad's cousin. The last time I saw him was when I booked him and the Barnstormers at my hotel in New Jersey. It was right after the Bull City Rodeo."

"There's a rodeo in New Jersey? My family is originally from New Jersey," said Miguel.

He wiped his burly hands on the cloth before poking it back into his jeans hip pocket.

"Ever make it back there?" Elizabeth asked.

"Nah, bad memories."

"That sounds like my mom's story. I was in Atlantic City for a few years. Bobby was a victim of circumstances when he opened for Rosco Tanner. That was the worst gig I ever booked. What a jerk, that Tanner. At the last minute, he demanded sliced kiwis and peeled grapes."

"What's a kiwi? Lighten up. Isn't your job the care and feeding of entertainers?"

"My assistant had to drive to Issacton. Canned kiwis are mushy and too sweet. Before having to deal with Tanner, I had a big fight with my mother over the phone. I should have hung up on her."

"But then you wouldn't have this story to tell. You didn't have any fun at Ethete? Powwows are a blast."

"It was a trip for my dad's work. He was the editor of the Laramie paper. My parents dragged me along to the powwow opening ceremony. Some big shot was in town."

"In my house, it's better to obey."

Miguel topped off the half-empty reservoir with clear blue windshield wiper fluid.

"It's never too late. I'm getting to be middle-aged." Miguel gently closed the hood. "I thought about my regrets the other night. It was powerful."

"Regrets are all I've been thinking about. You sound like my Grandma Sally."

"What came to me?" Miguel surmised. "Just let the world unfold. One man's failure is another man's opportunity. Edison didn't invent the lightbulb. The guy before him did. He just improved on it."

"Where'd you learn that?"

"Public TV. It's the only channel I get. You know, Edison is from New Jersey."

"So he says. Revisionist American history. My mom, the anthropologist, says Tom's mother was from a small town in Mexico. She married a miner."

"What?"

"Yeah. When she was at a conference in Mexico, she came across a museum exhibit in Sombrerete, Zacatecas."

"No tellin' what I might learn at the gas pumps," said Miguel. "Are you heading to Wyoming?"

"Colorado. My mom teaches at CU in Boulder." Elizabeth fumbled through her purse, looking for her billfold. "She's not so good about talking."

"Stay over. Stop at my uncle's this afternoon for a sweat. You're invited. Kin is important. Maybe it's you who didn't want to do any talking."

Miguel pointed to the gas pump.

"It's $35.10. Make it $30 with the discount."

"I have the ten cents."

Elizabeth had a big smile on her face and shook his hand. "*houhou.*"

"There's hope for you yet! Where'd you learn how to talk Arapaho?"

"I'm from Wyoming. A little native speak rubs off on everyone. Plus, my mom's been studying tribal stuff her entire life."

Elizabeth turned the ignition switch.

"Oh, it's called the Grand Entry, not the opening ceremony. All the dancers enter the powwow arbor before everything begins."

"Thanks for the culture lesson. Thinking back, it was never for vacation whenever we traveled. Even this trip is 'work.' Dealing with my parents is harder than work. I complain. I want this to be a carefree visit. They're good people. I'll never admit that!"

"If you want 'carefree,' stay away from your family. Don't be disappointed if there's no time to do your own thing."

"Funny. I was just thinking about that."

"Life is short. Do you think I dreamed of pumping gas? Your parents took an interest in you. Maybe they were a good influence more than you realize."

Miguel noticed stubborn bug remains and squeegeed them off the windshield with extra elbow grease.

"Is there a place where I can get lunch?"

"Inside. Today is Tuesday. Special on Turtle Tacos."

He tapped on the Forester roof, signaling Elizabeth to pull out from the pump and move to the front of the tribal convenience store.

19

Wind River Mill

Community living skipped a generation. Instead of having me closer to home, my parents exiled me to Cheyenne. There were always miles between wherever I was working and my parents. Despite what my parents thought, I wanted to stick around Laramie. Go to UW. Create a tradition by following in my parents' academic footsteps. I would have worked for Grandma Sally, given the chance. Dad wasn't encouraging. He had ranching in his blood but not on his hands. E.S.

****

Klaus and Marie Steiner had immigrated from Germany in 1918 and settled in New York City, where they shared an apartment with other extended family members. The United States entered World War I, which inspired a nativism movement and xenophobia toward German immigrants. Fearing violence, the Steiners fled for the West.

They were given 160 acres in Wyoming under the Homestead Act that would become the Quiver Mountain Ranch. They built a one-level stucco ranch house nestled at the base of a canyon wall that withstood high winds and fierce blizzards. In 1920, The couple had a son they named Clyde.

The spread eventually comprised over 5,000 acres of deeded land and 35,000 acres of leased state, federal, and tribal land where Klaus ran

Herefords until 1932. Ten years later, Clyde had taken over the day-to-day ranch management and added the exotic *Charolais* breed from France, raised a purebred herds, and crossed some.

The father and son were connectors. They organized the neighbors with small hay fields into a crop-sharing cooperative that eventually became the Wind River Mill in Lander, 17 miles from the Quiver Mountain Ranch.

It was a tall corrugated steel-sided grain storage building next to the tracks where the Northwest rail line ended.

Clyde pulled into the parking lot in his sun-bleached green pickup as balding tires crunched over the loose gravel and slid to a stop in front of the mill. He slammed the truck door and took the two-step landing in one stride.

When the door opened, a cowbell jingle-jangle announced his entrance. Sally Black counted the cash drawer to begin the day.

"Hey, nice lookin'. I got sumpin' cookin'...," he crooned.

"Looks like you're on a mission." Sally recognized Clyde's friendly and booming voice without looking up. "You're my first customer, Mr. Steiner."

"Mr. Steiner? That's my dad! Need a riding halter." Clyde walked over to the horse tack department. "I imagine you've been busy, Miss Sally. I heard you bought a few more horses."

"Dad picked up 10 head from the Bradfords." Sally's father managed the Eagle Crest Ranch, one of the largest Hereford-Angus cattle operations in the state, north of Pennington and next to the Bradford place in west-central Wyoming. "It's been hectic over at Eagle Crest. Dad wants me to come up on weekends. He's desperate for help."

"I've been meaning to see your operation. I can give you a lift. Your dad and me can talk about setting up a labor cooperative."

"Uh, maybe. I'm not too crazy about getting back to ranch life. I'm a city girl now. It's $7.45. On your account?"

Sally pushed the "total" button on the cash register, which opened with a "BING, BING. She put her hand in front of the cash drawer to keep the coins from flying out.

"Nah." Clyde handed her a $10 bill. "You let me know when you need a ride home. I'll keep bugging you about it."

"Eagle Crest is too far away for quick trips. I'm here because Dad wanted me to spread my wings. Go to a bigger high school. Lander's good. It's booming compared to Pennington."

****

When Sally and Clyde first met at the Wind River Mill, their relationship was friendly. They knew each other in high school but hung around with different crowds. Their small talk at the mill developed into a personal connection. The two dated off and on, and in 1940 they were married.

Sally commuted to the Wind River Mill while Clyde ran the expanding cattle operation. She eventually quit her job to help with the administrative ranch chores.

Early in 1942, her two brothers enlisted in the U.S. Navy. Clyde followed by signing up a year later. Before shoving off, he came home after basic training, sporting his tailored dress blues and shiny boots.

Sally was pregnant when Clyde deployed to the South Pacific late that summer. Sally drove him to the train station in Rock Springs.

"You be a good little sailor." Clyde assumed their child would be a boy. He held his hand over Sally's womb. "I'll be back in no time. Your mom will read you the letters I send. You gonna be okay?"

"I talked to my dad about getting me some help while you're away. Your worker coop has been a God send."

"You take good care of our son. I'll keep in touch the best I can. Write me. I gave you the address."

The two embraced. Clyde climbed up the stairs into the passenger car, smiled, and waved at Sally as the Southwest Chief pulled out from the station en route to LA by way of Raton, New Mexico.

From there, he was bussed to basic training at Camp Elliott. After eight weeks, he rode a troop train to the San Francisco Port of Embarkation at the Presidio and was transported by freighter to the Pacific Theater as part of the 3rd Marine Division.

Clyde survived the Battle of Bougainville. His luck ran out in the Battle of Guam. He was one of nine soldiers listed as Missing In Action (MIA).

The two would never see each other again.

Sally kept hoping Clyde would one day walk up the road to the ranch house. Operating the ranch on her own became complicated. When Sally went into labor, two ranch hands helped deliver Gary on Kentucky Derby Day, May 6, 1944.

****

When Gary was a toddler, it became clear Sally needed more help. She hired Marvin Collins to be her head wrangler after his discharge as an Army mechanic in Italy. Before the War, he was the Eagle Crest Ranch Assistant Manager.

"Thanks for helping me out, Marvin. It's been a long time since we were chasing calves at Eagle Crest. You sure you'll be okay here?"

"Most of the men I knew in Pennington enlisted and scattered. It's time for a fresh start."

Fresh start it was. Their work relationship grew into romance. Sally remarried for practical love.

In 1948, Marvin and Sally had a son they named William. Everyone called him Billy. When he was in the 6th grade, his half-brother Gary's job was defending him from a bully who moved from Savannah. The school was small, and everyone knew the outside troublemaker named Lenny. His father was hired to be the Chief of Police.

"Back of the bus," the driver instructed Billy as he boarded the Yellow Dog.

"Back of the bus."

Gary followed. The two slid onto the bench seat about midway.

"I have a newspaper staff meeting after school. Do you think you can stay out of trouble? Mom is picking you up."

"Get in trouble? It's not me. The big kid will leave me alone if I stay inside. Mom says it will be just a matter of time before I'm taller than him."

"I'll be your bodyguard if you keep up with my ranch work."

"Oh, no, you don't. You know your way around the place better than me. And you're big!"

Gary played for the Lander football team on the offensive and defensive lines. As a sophomore, the coach awarded him a "Most Minutes Played" pin.

"Someone will have to take over. It might as well be you, little brother."

****

Despite his aversion to handling livestock, as long as he lived at home, Gary did his fair share of chores. He wrestled the calves after they were roped and held them down to be branded.

"Remember to shovel out the barn," Stepdad Marvin yelled to Gary.

"After I finish this chapter!"

Gary quietly completed his ranching chores with few complaints. Like his natural father, Gary worked well with others and had a calm demeanor. The ranch was a great place for him to be alone but together. Gary pulled on his boots and then rambled down the stairs.

"Unload the oats. Might rain." Marvin handed a hat to Gary on his way out the door. "Must be a good book!"

"It's about the 5th Army in Italy. World War II. You'd like it."

****

Gary preferred to help with administrative duties and hung around the ranch house office. One worker he encountered regularly was his mom's assistant, Becca Pembroke. The two met in passing when she first arrived.

Gary was impressed with her. Most importantly, Becca kept his younger brother out of trouble. She was an astute, fast learner and open to trying just about anything. Gary helped her gain experience with the ranch lifestyle, like taking her on antelope hunts and getting her accustomed to peeing in the woods. Becca felt safe and didn't worry about being alone in the middle of nowhere. Gary invited her along to round up the stray cattle.

"I'm taking Billy to the edge of the ranch looking for Mavericks."

She jumped at the chance. Gary showed her evidence of ancient humans who once roamed the property, like petroglyph designs on sandstone, teepee rings, and a buffalo jump.

"I brought the fishing gear. We have some of the best brookie creeks in the area. We'll fill the creel by noon since we're on private land. No outsiders here."

"You won't get any fish stuffed and hang them over the fireplace?"

"Nope, we eat or smoke the good ones. Release the small fries."

Gary helped Becca develop all her senses and liberate her from East Coast stodginess. At home, she was expected to be quiet, which was more important than any ideas she may have. Becca couldn't face returning to her mother's Cherry Ridge world of high society parties and galas. In Wyoming, she could express herself freely instead of being allowed only to make monotonous small talk.

20

Gladys & Taylor

September 29, 2006—11:30 a.m. CDT: Elizabeth pulled out from the fuel pumps and parked in front of the Deli & Hardware Store. Oklahoma was hot and humid in late September. It took two hands to open the glass door.

An air-conditioned gust of cool air whooshed out of the convenience store stocked with a little bit of everything.

The line at the snack counter moved like the grocery store checkout conveyor belt. The attendant handed the customer ahead of her a pleasant-smelling bag. A few of the fries left oil traces on the white paper.

"Who's ready?" The server pulled a pair of disposable gloves over his massive hands and adjusted his paper cap under which he tucked his medium-length hair-netted locks.

"I heard it's Turtle Taco Day," Elizabeth ordered without looking at the menu on the wall.

"What size? We have large, large, and large."

The server towered over the serving area. He hiked up his Double-D apron and crouched to fetch a white Styrofoam box from under the counter.

"How about that small, large piece?"

Elizabeth pointed at the warming pan.

"I happen to know that's the best one," said the server with a smile while plopping the golden-brown deep-fried dough into the square box. On top, he ladled on a scoop of steaming cumin-infused chili with lots of beans and hamburger. Then he tonged on shredded iceberg lettuce, a dip of diced tomatoes, and garnished it all with grated orange cheese.

The Styrofoam box squeaked when the server clicked the little tabs into the slots. He placed a prepackaged black plastic spork, a matching knife, and a handful of napkins into a paper bag.

"Hot sauces are over there. Grab a pop from the cooler. $6.37."

Elizabeth pawed through her purse.

"Is that the 10 percent off cash price?" The server nodded. "I have the thirty-seven cents."

Elizabeth picked out a Diet Dr. Pepper and tossed a few packets of hot and mild sauces into the bag. She mixed the two for the right spiciness.

She walked quickly outside and checked to see if her car was locked on her way to one of the picnic tables. On second thought, she opted for air conditioning and sat in a booth at the front of the store.

It was noisy because of the adjacent laundromat. Washing machine doors slammed as clothes carts clunked around the linoleum floor with broken wheels. Youngsters charged around like nobody's business while their moms waited for their clothes to dry.

"You're not from around here," observed an older mom sitting in the booth across from Elizabeth. She worked the Word Scramble game in the newspaper's comic section. "Afraid one of us might steal your car?'

"In New Orleans, you can't be too safe. Well, it's the first time I've been around so many, uh, different people."

"You mean people like me?"

"It's all new. I don't want to talk about this."

"Oh, I'm just kiddin' around."

In NOLA, the Triumph Hotel patrons were primarily white and upper class. She had no reason to mingle with the diverse housekeeping staff or enter anywhere near the 7th Ward that Katrina wiped out. Same with her childhood in Wonder Bread Wyoming.

"Wow, this is a lot of food." Elizabeth caught an aromatic blast from the still-steaming Turtle Taco.

"I can't eat all this."

Elizabeth returned to the checkout line for a plate. She cut a chunk off of her taco to share.

"I'm Gladys. My sister works here. Today is her day to supply the fry bread. The best. Not too greasy. Not too doughy."

"It's Elizabeth. This is my first Turtle Taco." Elizabeth pushed the plate over to Gladys, who spoke and munched at the same time.

"The key is fresh oil. She fries them at home and then brings them over. The oil has to be perfect. She makes each piece separate in a cast-iron skillet. Passed down for two generations. These are special."

"It does resemble a turtle. A restaurant in Denver sells them." Elizabeth poked at the tender fry bread with her fork. "I'm now a connoisseur."

"Denver? Aren't you from New Orleans?"

Gladys savored another bite of the chewy fry bread.

"My second job was in Denver. I work in hotel management, er, I did work in hotel management."

"There are many casinos around here. You'd be hired on the spot."

"The dog ate my tribal ID."

"Don't worry. I declare you an honorary Turtle, a TINO."

"TINO?"

"TINO, Turtle in Name Only. Your new name is Taco Tortoise."

Elizabeth let out a chuckle.

"I'm sure that will help me get a foot in the door."

Elizabeth noticed a tattoo design on Gladys's forearm.

"Turtle?"

"That will open doors. Very important to my tribe."

She put down the earring and searched for a box containing henna ink and brushes.

"We are like Turtles. They live anywhere. Water, land. I can paint you a henna turtle tattoo. $5."

"Maybe next time."

Gladys looked over Elizabeth's face. She reached into her tote and pulled out a grocery store sack filled with smaller plastic baggies of beaded earrings.

"You could use some of these. How many? Your mother would like a pair. These will look good on you. Five dollars. Buy 10 for Christmas presents. Four dollars."

Elizabeth sorted through the baggies of beaded earrings. Only wires?"

"The hardware store ran out of posts."

Elizabeth hung a pair with a rainbow design on her earlobes.

"My mother will like these." She handed Gladys a $20 bill. "Thank you."

Gladys waved the money and headed to the cashier.

"Hold on."

"It's okay. Get your granddaughter something."

Gladys nodded, "Thanks," and inserted the bill into her coin purse.

"Where you off to now?"

"Colorado. My parents aren't doing so well. My mom's pretty sick."

Elizabeth took a couple more bites of her fry bread, then packed the rest and handed it to Gladys.

"I'll pray for you. I have a good feeling. You be nice to your mother. We're not around forever! Come back anytime."

"You're more attentive to me than my mom."

"We're close-knit. My oldest needs me to babysit, so I do my laundry on this day at this same time."

****

Elizabeth picked up a brochure on her way out to her car. She read about Route 66, "The Mother Road." During the 1950s and 60s, it was one of the most famous drives between Chicago and Los Angeles.

"'Life was easy back then. Relive your simpler past today ...'" she read while waiting at a stop sign before navigating her Forester onto U.S. Highway 66 west to Amarillo, Texas. "Coulda fooled me."

Six hours later, she stopped in Tucumcari, New Mexico, and entered Johnson's Friendly Table Café, one of many interesting, classic roadside cafés still in business along Route 66. Elizabeth pulled into the diner parking lot, opened the forest green-painted front screen door, and sat at the counter. The server met her with a menu.

"Welcome, I'm Taylor. Coffee?"

"Just water."

The server set down a menu and a glass of water in an amber plastic tumbler. Elizabeth poured the water into her bottle. Most of it dribbled all over the counter.

Taylor daubed up the puddle with a white bar towel from under the counter, filled Elizabeth's water bottle to the brim, flipped her pad to a blank sheet, and took Elizabeth's order in one motion.

"You have good hand-eye coordination."

"I play basketball. Welcome to the 'Gateway to New Mexico.' You're lucky we're open. Most days, we serve breakfast and close at 2. Today, we opened at two and serve breakfast for dinner. What'll it be?"

"I'll try your 'Number 1.' Scrambled with crispy bacon."

Elizabeth took a moment to look up at the specials on the blackboard behind the counter.

"White, Wheat, Rye?"

"Uh, sorry, make it the special, the Omelet Florentine. No toast. Can I get corn tortillas and extra spinach?"

"Allergic to bread? I'm the same way. My dad keeps salad fixings and vegetables around the kitchen to suit me. Hash browns or home fries?"

"Hash browns. Are they fresh or frozen?"

"I come in after school. Grate the potatoes one at a time. I have the scars to prove it, not really. I use a cleat to hold the potato, so I don't add any extra protein."

"Sold."

She closed the menu. Taylor forgot something on her way to the kitchen.

"Do you want two or three eggs?"

"Two should be enough. Remember the side of spinach."

Elizabeth signaled with a hand-washing motion. Taylor motioned towards the back and delivered the order to the service window.

"Small special. Side of spinach for a pickier eater than me!"

Taylor had Elizabeth's food waiting upon her return from the restroom. She was lucky she sat down when she did because all the counter stools and tables were filled with hungry Tucamcarians.

"Well, Miz Popeye, how was your omelet?"

Taylor cleared Elizabeth's dishes.

"I liked the vinegar you added to the spinach. Tangy. My mom likes it like that. Are you one of the Johnsons?"

"Yeah, my Grandfather Johnny took over the place in the 1950s," Taylor smiled and cleared the plates. "It's been good. I think I'm destined to work here. My parents are getting older. None of my cousins are interested. Which direction are you headed?"

"North."

Elizabeth wiped the corners of her mouth with the white paper napkin she folded and put in her shirt pocket for future smudges.

"Colorado? I'm a junior and applied to CU. I want early admission at a few places. New Mexico, too. My parents want me to stay closer to home. Boulder is close. Not too close. I can come back here on weekends … or not."

"Moving away from home is a good thing. When you're young, see the world before life gets complicated. Don't be a stranger at home."

"My coach went to CU and is putting in a good word for me. We'll see. Out-of-state tuition is so expensive. If I can get a scholarship, I can afford it. My mom is a New Mexico State alum. She thinks I'd get to play in Las Cruces. State has a hotel and restaurant management program. 'Come back and run the café,' she says."

"I lucked out and had a career in hotel management. Started out working part-time at a big property but didn't go to college for it. It's a big burn-out. Running a restaurant would be less of a headache."

"I don't know about that. My folks have to do everything themselves. CU doesn't have a hospitality program, though. I want to stay in the dorms. Be around lots of kids. How many bad influences will I have there hanging out with round ballers? Besides, Mom's afraid I might start smoking marijuana. She says there are too many hippies in Boulder."

"Don't believe everything your mom tells you."

"Easier said than done. Where in Colorado are you headed?"

"Boulder. Checking on my hippie mom. She's having a pretty hard time. Health problems. Quite a handful for my dad. He's kind of a hippie, too."

Elizabeth signed the credit card receipt.

"You're a second-generation Boulder hippie?"

"Laramie hippie."

"My mom wants me to check out Wyoming, too. Out-of-state tuition is cheaper than in-state here."

"Not only do you need to play ball, you have to deal with Laramie snow and wind."

"I'm not from Florida. I might make the team there. Have a great visit. My grandmother was sick at home for a month before the mighty Lord took her. It was good for Nana to have all of us around. Better than an old folk's home. Be more positive."

"Well ... Where's a good place to stay?"

"Most tourists want the Route 66 experience. My uncle and aunt own the Dilly' Dillo, like Armadillo?" Taylor pointed down the road. "They'll give you the family discount."

****

A few doors from the Friendly Table, Elizabeth couldn't miss the red, green, and blue neon lights flashing "Dilly' Dillo Motor Inn" and "Direct Dial Phones."

She pulled into the check-in area under a canopy. It was classic 1950s Southwestern architecture with an adobe-like, brownish stucco facade.

Elizabeth opened the door, and a chime sounded. Elizabeth approached the counter and picked up a mayonnaise jar labeled "Change for the Bed."

A matronly woman with her hair tied up into a bun entered from an apartment behind the front desk.

"Evening. How can I make your day better?"

"A room for the night? The restaurant referred me."

"That Taylor's so helpful." The clerk turned around and fetched the key from the pegboard behind her. "Ten percent off."

"I don't need the discount."

Elizabeth filled out the registration card.

"This is a small town. Everyone's family. Cash or charge? I'll also take your check." The motel was classic, down to the manual credit card machine. "You're in 103. If you leave before 9, drop the key in the mailbox."

Elizabeth circled in front of her room and negotiated her Forester into the built-in covered carport. She opened the door, gently smacked it into the sidewall, made her way through the narrow width, and retrieved her overnight bag through the hatchback.

She opened the room door with an actual key that had a diamond-shaped turquoise-colored plastic fob that read, "If found, drop in any mailbox." One of the table lamps was glowing. The lingering odor of mothballs reminded her of Grandma Pembroke's New Jersey basement.

Elizabeth kicked off her shoes and lay down on the firm mattress. She noticed a brown metal box on the bed stand. It dawned on her to return to the motel office. She retrieved a fist full of change from the jar on the check-in counter. Elizabeth plunked two quarters into the "Magic Fingers" coin slot and relaxed to the soothing vibrations. The Englander Mattress Company came out with the mechanical vibrating mattress in 1958.

The Dilly' Dillo differed from the mega-conference and convention center hotels where she used to work.

"I wonder what it would be like running a little place like this?"

21

Buffalo Jump

Idle chat with strangers on my leisurely drive to Boulder was insightful. Those conversations made me realize how much I'd grown tired of myself after playing the same bad memory tapes through my head. I should have rewound them and talked with Mom and Dad more often. My parents shared curiosity as a personality trait. Dad was a journalist, and Mom was a researcher. Both were interested in everything around them except me. E.S.

******

One sunny mid-October Saturday afternoon in 1961, Gary, Becca, and Billy had roamed the ditches, checking to be sure all the irrigation gates were closed. The ranch's native grasses were turning to shades of brown as the days grew shorter.

"How about we ride to the back of the ranch?" Gary suggested.

They saddled up and trotted down the road. Billy opened the wooden gate, allowing the others to pass before swinging it shut.

Gary guided his party to an ancient buffalo jump where hunters harvested bison by coaxing the stampeding animals over the edge. The threesome dismounted and hiked down the ravine. Billy kicked up a few bones at the bottom.

"I bet if we dug down, we'd find all kinds of stuff," Becca guessed. "The entire bison was used for something."

They climbed back to the surface and rode up a hill to some orange, black, and white speckled granite cliff faces, where rock art adorned the walls. They dismounted, and Gary lifted Billy so he could scrutinize the images obscured by the greenish lichen growth.

"There were antelope a long time ago? Those are antelope horns, all right. What are those animals ridden by hunters?"

"See the long necks? Your dad says there used to be llamas around here. Have you learned about llamas?"

"Llamas in Peru."

Gary rubbed his hand on the rock, brushing away some loosened lichens.

"Those critters at one time ranged around western Wyoming along with the antelope. Indians passing through here were nomads. They were efficient since everything had to be packed and hauled. No pottery. No baskets. When the Spaniards introduced the horse, the nomads could accumulate more stuff and move faster."

"Who needed horses if there were llamas?"

"I don't know. They aren't very big. Probably couldn't haul teepee poles."

"Maybe people back then weren't very big."

"There are legends about little people who lived in the mountains near here."

"Don't look at me. All I learned from class was how the colonists stole the land for the good of their civilization," explained Becca. "There were some old books in the library. I helped my mom at the Cherry Ridge Museum. I found stone tool fragments that were displayed and learned about the Lenni-Lenape tribe. They were fishers and farmers. The fish remains were used as fertilizer in their crop fields. Exploring your ranch makes me more curious."

******

School was soon to begin for Becca, and it was time to prepare for winter at the ranch.

"It was good having you around here." Sally's kind words brought a smile to Becca's face since she was the type who liked acknowledgment of her work. "You're welcome back next summer. I liked having another woman around the place."

Becca returned to New Jersey. Near the end of the 1962 spring semester of her junior year, Becca received a detailed letter from Sally asking her to work on the ranch again that included start times and other details about the upcoming summer. Becca wrote to Gary asking about his plans.

"Why can't he write back? Maybe I should send him some self-addressed stamped envelopes."

Her mother showed no interest in any boy Becca liked.

"You're putting too much effort into something that will never happen if I have anything to say about it. That Wyoming boy? He's not like us. You would have a special life with our friend, Jack Middleton. He's from the church."

"Our friend. You're his substitute mother. Stop living in the Dark Ages. It's the 1960s. John Kennedy is president."

"Don't get your hopes up. Face it. Your Wyoming boy doesn't care about you. He's not our kind. Nothing will change that, not even Kennedy."

****

On the other side of the country, Sally tried to set her son straight.

"Why keep avoiding her? Becca likes you. It's not like you two are getting married."

"We work together. I help out around here. That's it."

"Becca could use a little support and encouragement from you, son. She's new to all this hands-on ranching."

"Mom, I admit that she and I are interested in old cultures. Maybe we can write a book. She is a good writer. I've read her letters. I'm not much for long hellos or goodbyes. Girls complicate things."

"How would you know?"

22

Willie Eagle

September 30, 2006—8:32 a.m. MDT: Tucumcari was a quiet town compared to NOLA, or anyplace else, for that matter. Elizabeth slept like a baby, arose at daybreak, and dropped off the key and extra quarters at the Dilly' Dillo office. There wasn't much back road traffic that time of day, except for the occasional semitrailer zooming by trying to make good time.

Elizabeth's mind wandered between fretting about her next line of work and rehearsing how she would face her mother. She slowed, turned off Route 66, and entered the booming metropolis of Santa Rosa. She soon darted past the "Welcome to Colorado" sign on I-25.

"A high schooler from Tucumcari has the next four years planned out. I can't decide which way to drive to Boulder. Shit's getting real," Elizabeth muttered with her eyes forward, tears dribbling down her cheek.

She fiddled with the radio.

"… Thanks for joining the 'Cowpokes Connection' show. I'm Jon Spencer here on Southern Colorado Community Media. I hope you're enjoying this beautiful fall day. Next on the platter is Bobby Smithee's new single *By the Time I Get to Tensleep*."

"Don't remind me?" Elizabeth shook her head as she sipped from her bottle and scowled at the salty New Mexico water.

"For our listeners up north, Bobby's performing next week at the Dog ..."

Elizabeth flicked off the radio.

"Things could be worse. Dad could be in Uganda, and Mom overworked and underpaid in some dead-end office job in Lander," she thought as she neared Trinidad.

A directional road sign pointed to the Granada War Relocation Center.

"What the heck. I have time. We'll have something to talk about."

She pulled over at The Grease Pan for a 10-minute oil change, stopped at a convenience store for a day-old donut and a hot dog for lunch, and cruised through Trinidad to eastbound U.S. 50.

Elizabeth knew about the 10 hastily constructed internment camps, including Granada, where 120,000 Japanese from the West Coast were isolated after Pearl Harbor was attacked by the Empire of Japan in 1941. She rambled up a dusty road and stopped at the site marked by an obscure wooden "Camp Amache" sign.

"Granada? Amache?"

She wandered around, stepping over a concrete foundation on which one of the 300 barracks was constructed. The camp's peak population was about 9,500 internees, making it the tenth-largest city in Colorado during World War II.

Elizabeth's imagination got the best of her, thinking she'd see barracks guarded by soldiers and internees wandering around. Instead, A woman was wandering the property, pulling plant remains from around the compound.

"We're a small but appreciative crowd," she said without looking up from her work. "Sprucing the place up for spring. We have an annual remembrance event before summer."

"I thought you were the ghost of one of the internees," Elizabeth responded.

"This place still brings back bad memories of a dark time in America. What brings you here this time of day?"

"My mom wrote the application for the National Park Service."

"Good for her. Thanks to the designation, we're reconstructing a barrack building. Come back when the weather is nicer."

"I may take you up on that."

She negotiated the rutted road back. At the intersection of U.S. 50 and Colorado 350, Elizabeth saw a sign pointing north to the Sand Creek Massacre site.

"Hm, another hour. Might as well check it out ... as recommended by Miguel." It was getting to be dusk. She punched the location into her GPS Street Pilot III.

When she saw the massacre site information sign, Elizabeth didn't know what to expect. "On November 29, 1864, Colonel John Chivington led 750 soldiers to surprise attack 500 Arapaho and Cheyenne tribal members encamped in southeastern Colorado."

She imagined a peaceful teepee village where families went about their lives before ending up dead on the prairie. Instead, she pulled into a barren, graveled parking area.

A few minutes later, an early model Dodge pickup with temporary Wyoming tags rumbled up the road. The truck with a small sweetgrass braid hung from the rearview mirror parked next to her Forester.

"Nice day for a massacre," observed a middle-aged man as he climbed out of the cab. His wife joined him. "Why are you here?"

Elizabeth was startled by the aggressive remark.

"My mom told me about this place and thought I'd stop."

"What does she know?"

"She used to teach anthropology."

"This is a sacred place, not a place for you or scientists. You tell your mother you met Willie Eagle. This is Teresa. We're headed to Oklahoma for a ceremony. We need some privacy."

Feeling like an intruder, Elizabeth didn't linger.

"Nice meeting you."

****

Traffic was horrendous at 7:15 p.m. The sky was getting dark, and she didn't like driving at night. Where I-270 turned into U.S. 36 didn't come soon enough. Elizabeth hadn't been on that road for years. She was surprised at how the once open prairie was now a sea of concrete strip malls interspersed with housing settlements.

She pulled up in front of the Blue Sky Village Common House in the 15-minute loading zone. The plastic wheels propelled her rolling bag, clicking in rhythm as they passed over the sidewalk cracks. She punched 1501 into the intercom keypad.

"Elizabeth?"

"Land shark."

The latch "buzzed," which unlocked the door.

Elizabeth rode the elevator to the second floor and found the condo door was propped open.

"Is that my destiny?" she asked as she entered. Elizabeth pulled out a chair and joined her father at the kitchen table, where he was sorting his medicine.

"They're over-the-counter except for one prescription. I'm not taking it. Don't tell your mom."

Gary placed a fish oil capsule, a garlic pill, and a green superfood tablet into a compartmentalized plastic box initialed with the days of the week.

"It's a mosaic."

"Add a teaspoon of Hollandaise sauce. You'll have yourself a meal."

Elizabeth picked up a white cylindrical plastic container. "Orange flavored Metamucil? Yum."

"An old guy sits down at the bar. The bartender asks, 'What'll it be, Metamucil and vodka?' The guy answers, 'Yeah, the regular," joked Gary. "You have my permission to use that in your movie."

"Pretty good pick-up line at the senior center, I imagine."

Elizabeth took a sniff from the tall plastic vessel like it was a fine bottle of *Pouilly-Fuissé*.

"Smells like orange with a hint of green roughage."

"I'll have you know, Elizabeth, I have the colon of a 30-year-old! Psyllium has been part of my routine since college. Before it became trendy. Don't knock it until you've tried it!"

She entered the kitchen, mixed up a glass, looked at the grainy mixture, then searched through the cabinets.

"I need the Absolut."

"If you parked in the loading zone, move around to one of the parking spots in the alley. We have a resident parking cop. It gets him riled up, which gets me riled up."

"The same guy who rummages through the recycling bin, reads the address labels, and shames offenders for not breaking down their cardboard boxes?" Elizabeth asked after chugging her straight-up Metamucil slurry.

"The parking cop is a different guy. The recycling monitor now pokes around in the compost bin, looking for those little plastic labels on tomato skins. Just move your car. Save me a headache I don't need right now."

Becca entered from her bedroom to check out the commotion. She made her way over to her fancy chair and plopped down.

"Did you bring whiskey and fresh horses?"

"I should have. You're out of vodka, Mom."

"It's around here someplace. Waiting for you is exhausting."

Elizabeth reached down and gave her mother a standing half-hug.

"How about a Metamucil Screwdriver?"

"Ha, Ha. The regular? There will be plenty of time for us to catch up. Don't get us in trouble with the Blue Sky Parking Police."

Elizabeth moved her car to the alley.

"Can you unlock the back?" yelled Elizabeth into the intercom.

"Becca, get back to bed. Yesterday, after your fall, I called the Sunrise people and told them you get tired more than before. They'll be by at their usual time, maybe sooner."

"Sunrise DID come by. Don't you remember?" Becca was a bit frustrated. "Nurse Riley checked on me today. I have a bump. No concussion. You? Take your medicine!"

Gary had a look of concerned frustration on his face.

"Yeah, yeah, you don't have to keep reminding me!"

"BUZZZZZZZZZ!"

Gary opened the back door to the Common House. He returned to the table and his sorting. Elizabeth trudged up the outer stairs.

"You can help your mother back to her room. It's past my bedtime." Becca commanded in the third person.

She pressed the remote-control button. The hydraulic motor tipped her toward the walker.

"Your chair has all the bells and whistles," Elizabeth said, inspecting the contraption. "It's a new setup since I was last here. When did you move downstairs?"

"I don't know. You should come home more." Becca's sarcastic jab irritated Elizabeth, considering she dropped what she was doing to drive for three days. "It's easier for me to get around."

"*Beyond Sand Creek* is on in a few minutes. Your daughter can help me."

Elizabeth escorted her mom to the bedroom. Becca had her evening routine down pat. She made her way into the bathroom to change into her nightwear. It was a pair of brown and gold UW women's basketball shorts complemented by an oversized orange Alzheimer's Caring Society Walk-a-Thon T-shirt. She climbed up onto the bed.

"Elizabeth, can you gather the towels and put them in the basket? Sunrise does my laundry tomorrow."

"I can do it, Mom. I'm here to help."

"Boy. When I tipped over, what a helpless feeling. My head still throbs!"

Becca shook out the cobwebs as she pointed to the small, blue cooler by the bed. Elizabeth handed her mom one of those frozen gel packs that keep fresh food shipments chilled.

"Better than a bag of peas."

Becca sat with her legs bent and knees together. Elizabeth sat in the bentwood chair and fiddled with the safety railing.

"If it's not down, getting up to pee in the middle of the night is a pain. If I fall out of bed, I fall out of bed. It wouldn't be the first time."

Gary poked his head in the bedroom door to see if all was okay. Becca waved him away, and he went back to his documentary.

"How was your drive?"

"You would be proud of me. Knowing how you want me to take an interest in your interests, I took a detour. I stopped at the Sand Creek Massacre site and Camp Granada."

"Well, what did you think? The National Park Service applications were tedious. I'm surprised either of them was marked. You know the two places are connected."

"I didn't."

"The Granada camp is better known as 'Amache.'"

Becca explained that Amache was the daughter of Cheyenne Chief One Eye and married a rancher named John Prower. The county was named after him.

"The two were taken hostage when the cavalry stormed the ranch during the attack. Amache became a well-known woman in the area. The camp is named for the Amache Post Office."

"Who knew? There wasn't much at either place. A guy scared me off in the parking lot."

"It's a sacred place to the Cheyenne and Arapaho," Becca explained. "I want to take you to Oklahoma. We have some unfinished business there."

"I have some unfinished business here. Remember when we went to Lander? The powwow? Visited Grandma Sally? That was about all I've learned about how you and Dad met. All I know is you knew each other on the ranch."

"That's about it. I went to work for your grandmother when I was in high school. Your dad and I both come from rugged individual stock. How we ended up living in this community? It didn't come naturally to us."

"Gary! Can you get Elizabeth set up on the couch?"

"What about your friends? I met Avery. Who's Jack?"

"How do you know about Jack?"

"The graffiti in the Calamity Club basement."

"Very observant. Enough for now, young lady. Waiting up for you always wears me out."

Gary turned off the TV and led Elizabeth to the living room. He showed her the cedar chest with extra linens, and the wool Hudson Bay blanket she used as a kid on chilly July camping trips were kept. She cast the multi-colored throw pillows crocheted by her Grandma Sally out of view and made up the futon.

23

Princeton University

When I first arrived in Boulder, I wanted to learn more about my parents' histories. I was working in Denver in 1996. Avery and I helped my parents move from my childhood home in Laramie to Boulder. I asked about their friend Jack when I gave Avery a lift to the airport. "Ask your dad" or "Ask your mom" was all I could pry out during our two-hour drive. Back then, I thought stopping to help my parents showed I was willing to participate in their lives. They pushed me to be independent and not to rely on them, despite Mom nagging me to start a family as if that was her first choice. E.S.

****

Becca's personality type would have been classified as being introverted. She had spent her childhood self-isolated.

"Mom, I don't mind being polite around all your church friends. I have my own life. Why don't you trust me? How much trouble can I find in this town? I'm in high school. I don't need a curfew."

"If you picked better friends, I wouldn't have to keep an eye on you. Why can't you spend more time with Jack? At least I know him. He's like us."

"He's like you."

Since his mother died, Jack's primary personal support came from the Pembrokes. Becca and Jack were friends because of their Congregational connection, both being preacher's kids.

Becca and Jack went their separate ways after the 8th grade. She ended up at Garden View County High School. He went to Princeton Prep, where the Harvest Ball happened in October 1960. It was THE event in Cherry Ridge.

Jack always attended the church youth fellowship, hoping Becca would be there.

One night, he walked into the kitchen with a gleam in his eye when he saw Becca mixing up a pitcher of lime Kool-Aid.

"I didn't think you were going to make it."

"You're lucky I showed up. My mom dragged me out of the horse stable. Ugh, I don't drink anything green."

Becca stared at the putrid concoction. The undissolved sugar granules still floating around reminded her of the sewerage discharge into the stream behind the church.

"Have you picked out something nice? If you have your heart set on an outfit, I can buy it for you."

"When is it again? I think my mom has it under control. She wants to go more than me. Besides, you're a junior. I'm a sophomore. Go with someone your own age."

"One year difference? That's close enough. Besides, the man is supposed to be older and wiser.

"More like a wise guy."

The *soiree* at the private school was also a debutante dinner, complete with a three-course meal at the Cherry Ridge Country Club.

"It's next Friday night. Dad's letting me drive the big car."

Jack followed Becca toward the church basement.

"Don't you want to be introduced to society in a proper fashion?"

"My mom has it on her calendar. If you'll excuse me ..."

Becca forced a smile and carefully steadied the Kool-Aid pitcher down the stairs leading to the fellowship hall.

******

The night of the dance, Jack idled a shiny black Mercedes Benz sedan in front of Becca's house.

"HONK, HONK!"

Mrs. Pembroke came out on the porch and waved at Jack to come inside."

"You know better than that," she said with a frown. "Doesn't Becca look elegant?"

"That gown looks familiar," Jack noticed.

"It's mom's. She wore it once as a bridesmaid at your aunt's wedding. Remember? Two summers ago. A hundred and twenty bucks and no pockets."

"You look stunning. You'll debut to society escorted by the latest Princeton man from Cherry Ridge."

"Congratulations. Did your dad buy your way onto the baseball team?"

Jack graduated from Prep and enrolled for the fall semester at Princeton University. He didn't have to worry about his grades and whether or not he'd be admitted because he was a "legacy" since his father and grandfather were also graduates. He forgot to mention that Princeton was the only school that accepted him.

"Can't wait to get out of this town," lamented Jack. "I'm moving into a big house near the campus."

His dad bought the place to entertain his cronies when he came to watch the Tigers play football and basketball. Jack had the place to himself most of the time, except on game days when he was relegated to serving drinks to the good old boys and picking up after them.

"I'll be waiting for you, Becca."

"Princeton doesn't admit women. If Princeton is such a great place, why are you always in Cherry Ridge?"

"Networking. I wish you'd meet some of the people I know. They could help you. Besides, did I say anything about you going to school? I could find you a job on campus or in town. My dad knows the curator at the New Jersey Natural History Museum."

"... and do what, be a secretary? Dust the exhibits?"

24

The Three Musketeers

September 30, 2006—9:28 p.m. MDT: Elizabeth warmed up a cup of day-old coffee in the microwave after setting up the couch. She then joined her father at the kitchen table and shuffled through the mail piled on the table.

"How was your TV show?"

"I'll finish it later. DVRed it. There's a chapter in my book about how Blue Sky Village is trying to get the city of Boulder to return the Fort Chambers land to the Arapahos. *Beyond Sand Creek* is about that. The documentary was made by a local filmmaker named Alyn O'Hara. Used to write for the Lander paper."

"Sounds like a project right up Mom's alley."

"Much of her work is included."

Elizabeth came upon an official-looking letter.

"Do you get Social Security? You're 62."

"My plan was to draw from my pittance of a newspaper pension. Now I'm not so sure that'll be enough."

Gary motioned for Elizabeth to hand him the letter showing his years of working along with his expected monthly payout.

"Live it up while you can, Dad."

Gary moved his finger down the chart.

"Social Security, what the paper owes me, will be enough to get by. Your mom's retirement from teaching should keep us in groceries. I hope you're saving something."

"The hotels where I worked had pretty good benefits. I have a 401K and saved a few bucks."

"Your investments won't do you much good now."

"Because they tanked after 9/11? The politicians figured that desperate people like me would pay the penalties for early withdrawal. More profits for Wall Street. I'll be patient. I'm in for the long haul." Elizabeth stacked up her dad's pill bottles like a pyramid. "I have a long time before I need to think about retirement."

"At the rate you're going, retirement will come sooner than later, especially when you're a famous screenwriter being paid residuals. Make money while you're sleeping."

She got up and looked through the fridge and kitchen cabinets.

"Where do you keep the creamer?"

There was a moment of silence.

"Damn it! You too? I forget a few things. It's nothing," Gary snapped. "Half the people here can't remember where they left their keys," He had a vengeful look. His voice escalated. "Keep looking. I'm taking my medicine if it makes you feel any better."

"What medicine?"

"He rattled a pill from the plastic amber vial and plopped it into the "M" for Monday" compartment.

"Calm down! You don't have to yell."

"The full dose made my bones ache."

"What are you talking about?"

"I had to finish the first draft of my book. I'm taking a half dose. If I go crazy, it's your job to finish it."

"I can edit, Dad. Maybe it will make for a good movie. I'll tell you what didn't happen out of respect for the dead."

"I grant you full poetic license!"

"I'll get your book file before I leave."

Gary waved the typed manuscript.

"Only a hard copy. Take this to Lightning Fast and make two copies. Next time, I'll be able to tell you where to find the creamer."

"Must be in the same place as the vodka."

He shook a pill from the vial, tossed it back, and swallowed.

"How about a Metamucil chaser?"

"Are you taking us up on our offer to live in Laramie?" Gary took a deep breath as the medicine calmed him down. "The place is yours if you want it. Rather than wait until we're on the wrong side of the grass, we can deed the place over to you sooner than later."

"I agree it would be less of a hassle. Relax. You're all over the place, Dad."

"Good move, stopping here first. Stick around. Mom has some news to tell you. Look, run up to Laramie. Check out the Calamity Club. We held off on renting it."

"We should tie up a few loose ends before I go to Laramie or wherever."

Gary pointed toward Becca's bedroom.

"Before you head back anywhere, get back in there. Your mom's stalling as much as you."

****

Elizabeth arose from the table and slinked back into her mother's room.

"I thought you'd be conked out by now. Whatcha reading?"

"*Mother-Daughter Patchwork.*"

"Any good tips?"

"Not to hold back, confront our demons, and quilt our relationship back together."

"How allegorical of you."

"Elizabeth, let's get down to it. What do you think? Are you ever going to settle down? Have kids? Live in a real house? How old are you now, 40? There's still hope. You're the end of the Pembroke line. Someone has to carry on the 'Ball of Twine' tradition."

"Well, all righty then. Marriage? Don't get your hopes up. If I get around to kids, I can adopt. Quit exaggerating. I'm 38. You have

Pembroke cousins. What about Uncle Frank and his daughter? She's a Pembroke. I didn't think this genealogy stuff was important to you," Elizabeth defensively responded.

"It's the end of MY Pembroke line! You're screwing that up."

Gary couldn't stand the bickering and came in to referee.

"Oh, stop, you two. It's the 21st century. We agreed to give her a loose leash, Becca. We raised her not to mess things up like we did."

"Mess up? Okay, I think both of you did a terrific job taking care of me. I've had misgivings about even being alive! How many times did I ever ask for help? Hardly ever. And when I did, you said to handle it myself. My future? Watching after my ungrateful parents."

"I wanted you to ask for help, Elizabeth. Let us know what you're doing. Couldn't you have at least gone through the motions? Dropped by once in a while. Brought somebody home. Anybody. I'm not picky. You bring out the worst in me."

Elizabeth searched through a bowl of fruit on the nightstand.

"You know what they say about one bad Clementine. Stop worrying about my life! Mom, you wrote about rural families in the 1600s. They controlled the number of kids to match the amount of food they ate and the work they finished. Your observations were correct. I'm walking proof. We have a very anthropologically efficient household."

"Here, I thought you didn't care about my interests, Professor Meade. I'm your mother. I didn't want you growing up like I did. We're both free spirits."

"You thought I was unmotivated? Schoolwork came easy for me, is all. I had too much spare time on my hands. You know why my friends liked me? I let them copy my homework. And Dr. Rebecca, you can now call me Dr. Margaret!"

"I put up with your pot smokers and drinkers. Once you got out from under our thumbs, the stakes got higher. I'm not talking out of my hat. I had a mind of my own, too."

"When I got caught with the weed in high school, what would have happened if I went to jail? I would have ruined your reputation. I wanted to get caught for the thrill of it. Oh, now things are making sense. We're both felons. We could have had side-by-side mother-daughter mug shots at the Post Office."

"Felons on paper! You weren't trying to make Department Head."

"Your contrived reputation hasn't done you much good, now has it, Mother. You always pulled me into your guilt trip about how YOU saved my life. My version, I could have died because of ME and YOU!"

"I should have been a better mother."

"You were a wonderful mother. I'm standing here, aren't I?"

I was a little manipulative."

"A little? "You don't have to remind me. I've been going through life thinking I'm a black cat stepping on cracks in the sidewalk and running under a ladder, throwing rocks at mirrors!"

"The guilt trip I laid on you didn't help."

"Oh, now you come clean. You don't think I'm on my own guilt trip? Despite my apprehension, who's here to take care of you now? I imagine it would have been a different story if I had kids. If anything, I saved YOU!"

Gary completed his kitchen chores and walked toward the bathroom.

"It's past Cinderfella's bedtime. I turn into a pumpkin at midnight. Get some sleep. Finish your fight in the morning."

"Gary, we're good. Take your medicine. It's bad enough having one invalid here."

"Make it three when I end up in therapy and on anti-anxiety drugs again!"

"Scratch me off your list. My memory pill refill was in the mail today. They're on the bathroom counter if I forget."

"Here I am, mostly used up. Life matters until it doesn't. You're my legacy, Elizabeth. Can you pass on our family culture if you're not keeping the bloodline flowing?"

"What? I did miss several Decembers. When I lived with Uncle Frank, I came to Laramie over Christmas. There was no tree up. That's when I knew times had changed. If it makes you feel any better, you separated all my Christmas decorations when I helped you move to

Boulder. Wherever I am, I decorate a tree, plastic or otherwise. I still don't open any presents early and have oyster stew on Christmas Eve."

"Even when you were in college, you were around to help out with Christmas. Maybe one day, you can pass those habits along to your spouse. And your kids! Having grandchildren charging around and tearing open presents on Christmas Day was wishful thinking on my part."

"You're one to talk. Didn't you write about cultural celebrations geared to the nuclear family as traditions of the past?"

Elizabeth took the water mug Becca waggled in front of her.

"Well, for other people!"

Elizabeth went to the kitchen and refilled her mom's Flatiron General Hospital insulated container.

"I was in the Intensive Care Unit for a week. My insurance paid $150 for that. If you're ever in the hospital, take everything not tied down. If you need any adult diapers, I have an open pack. How are you on health insurance?"

"I have my policy from the hotel. It runs out in five months."

"This is why you need to settle down!"

Becca took a slurp and banged the mug on the side rail. Elizabeth covered her ears. Water splattered out from the straw.

"Mother, stop."

Gary heard the racket and opened the bathroom door wearing the terrycloth robe Elizabeth had absconded from the Atlantic City Triumph Hotel.

"You two solve the problems of the world?" Gary toweled off his wet hair. "Did you show Elizabeth your notes?"

Becca handed over the handwritten script from her bedside table.

"What's this?"

"I want to get the band back together. Blue Sky Village is turning 10 this year. The Activities Committee is planning some events, including the one I'm producing."

"'Opening remarks by Gary. Remarks by Avery and Jack (?).'

"None of us have spoken for going on 40 years. Jack and Avery sort of stayed friends."

Becca took a deep breath, thinking about their good times together. Gary rolled his eyes, and his superficial temporal frontal artery bulged.

"Jack's YOUR good buddy. I can't believe you put up with his bull crap! You bring him up again, I'm..."

Gary paced back and forth, staring at the floor, and took a seat in the shadows.

"Calm down, Dad. Can you say what you really think? When you lose your mind, maybe you'll forget about your pal, Jack. Okay, 'Music list: *She's Only a Baby* by The Bronco Brothers.'"

"When you were born, I was on tranquilizers for a year. The song's about 'downers.'"

"I was that bad?"

"Popping pills was socially acceptable to handle moms like me. Keeping me drugged up at home? I was just another woman under male control. When men were stressed out, they went on vacation. When I was stressed, I went to the doctor."

"... and this is a song you want to play at a 10th-anniversary party?"

"It's memorable for me and all the women who live here. A social statement. Speaking of drugs, your father hasn't been well for quite some time."

"I gathered."

"Have I put my hearing aids in the microwave yet?"

"You don't have hearing aids."

"It's no big deal. I finished typing up my book."

"You spend all your time in front of a typewriter or computer. You don't talk to people. You cover up your bad memory with small talk. Listen to yourself repeating the same thing over and over."

"Why do you think it's called small talk? When you think about it, most conversation is small talk. 'How are you?' 'Fine.' 'You?' 'Fine.' 'Have a nice day.' 'Looks like rain.' I can hold my own with anybody in the gibberish department."

Gary arose with a yawn and a stretch.

"Talk about me all you want. I'll proofread until it puts me to sleep. You know the routine."

Elizabeth nodded, grabbed the mug, and checked the doors.

"Rail up?"

"I may have to get up in the middle of the night."

Becca watched as Gary fiddled with her bed. The rail clanked down. He picked up his manuscript and a red pen.

"For the sake of the book, your long-term memory is good. Otherwise, I don't know what we're going to do with you."

Elizabeth returned with water. Becca picked up a stack of booklets on her bedside table and held them in front of Gary's face.

"You two don't think I can take care of myself anymore?"

Elizabeth took the flyers from various continuous care residential communities, independent and assisted living places.

"Mother, you make things sound so dire."

"They are dire. Remember the last time you were home, and we went over our trust documents? This water mug will one day be yours. You finally have responsibility. You're our official guardian. In charge of spending our leftover money."

"Wait a minute, you moved into the cohousing because there would be others who could watch after you. You know, the Caring and Sharing Committee?"

Elizabeth nervously shuffled the booklets, sorting them by size.

"Neighbors can be supportive, like when I need help unjamming the disposal. Our friends can also help out, too, for a while."

"We're not asking anyone to change our diapers or, as Nurse Riley calls it, provide 'intimate personal care.'"

"'Intimate personal care.' Sounds like a group therapy for over-the-hill hookers."

Gary grabbed the promotional flyers from Elizabeth.

"If I have to move to one of these places, Grandma Sally'll let you stay at the ranch if you ever need."

Becca pulled the blanket over her shoulder and tucked her arm under the pillow.

"She and your Uncle Billy are about all you have. This wool Pendleton? Grandma gave it to us as a wedding present."

"Your neighbors should adopt the geometric pattern for the community logo."

Elizabeth straightened up the sky-blue blanket.

"Sally sent a small one when you were born. You don't remember when she came to Laramie to help out. 'Hand it down,' she says. It's in the cedar chest. Not that you'll ever need it."

"You don't let up," Elizabeth sighed. Did you tell Grandma Sally about all this?"

Becca closed her eyes but kept up the conversation.

"I'm surprised she hasn't made it down yet. Sally has some business in Boulder."

"Did Uncle Billy take over the ranch since Dad wasn't interested?"

"He did take over, reluctantly. I thought about going back to help. Be closer to the ranch. I was offered a job at the Lander paper. There wasn't any opportunity for your mom except to teach history at Fremont Community College. Even if we stayed at the ranch, the move wouldn't have been worth it."

"What about your people, Mom?"

"My people disowned me. 'Marry Jack. He's your ticket to the good life, your Grandma Pembroke would say."

Becca fumbled around for the remote to raise herself upright.

"I remember going out on the train to New Jersey when I was at East Elementary. You got me excused from school. Grandma took us to the top of the Empire State Building. I liked it when Grandpa introduced us at church, and we were the guests of honor at the social hour."

"They were nice because it was you and me. Neither of us met up with their expectations."

"What's that supposed to mean? I was five."

"Okay, I have to keep going through these sage words of mine. Remember your news?"

Gary went back to his room.

"I didn't go into cultural anthropology for nothing. I have some papers to show you. I want to visit Oklahoma."

"So you've said. I was through there on my way up. We could have met then."

Elizabeth rolled her eyes.

"If you answered your phone, young lady, maybe we could have."

"Your mom's doctors advised against it," Gary said to Becca. "Can't you stop?"

"I don't want to fall asleep angry."

"One day, I hope you'll remember that we had more good than not good that happened between us," said Elizabeth.

"I don't have any regrets. We'll always have Puerto Vallarta."

Becca took a deep breath and reached up with a smile. Elizabeth moved forward, and the two shared a hug.

"I want you and your dad to take care of each other. Are we still the Three Musketeers?"

Becca extended her hand to Elizabeth. Gary joined in the handshake.

"All for one and one for all!" They chanted their trite ritual in unison.

"So this is our big 'talk?'"

Elizabeth placed her palms over her face in frustration.

"Remember Grandma Sally's line, 'What happens, happens. You have to keep moving forward.'"

Becca nodded off. Elizabeth picked up the old photo of her parents posing with Avery and Jack, which was missing the glass.

"I'll get you a new frame."

"You don't have to whisper. Mom sleeps with one eye open."

Gary entered the shared bathroom to his adjoining office/bedroom and closed the door. Light scattered across the floor under the doorsill.

Elizabeth flicked off the light and rechecked the front door before flopping on the couch.

25

Brees Air Field

My talk with Mother had its usual arc, but I'm happy it ended calmly. She was caught between her free spirit when she moved to Wyoming and her structured East Coast upbringing. If Jack and her parents had understood her interests and independence, life would have turned out differently for them and me. Jack rationalized his mission to Wyoming as being more than pursuing my mom. He, too, was running and liked that there were more cattle than people. It seems I'm back for the same reason. E.S.

****

Becca had established residency by attending Lander High School for her senior year. That meant paying in-state tuition when she enrolled at UW for the 1963 fall semester. Jack was in his second year at Princeton and bothered her at the dorm at least once a week, always calling at 7:00 p.m. on the dot.

Jack was exasperated that Becca seldom answered and resorted to mailing letters.

"You're never around. Call collect," he wrote.

She eventually rang him up, hoping to keep her puppy satisfied.

"Hello?"

"Jackie Middleton? Will you accept the charges from Becca Pembroke?" asked the operator.

"Put her on."

"Here you go, ma'am."

"Hello? I didn't get your messages."

"It's about time. Jackie Middleton? You're lucky I accepted the call."

"You know these girls. Always forgetting to tack notes on the bulletin board."

She always told the same tiny fib.

"I want to buy your ticket home for your Christmas break. Dad's having a big party."

"Jackie, I'm spending the holidays with my roommate. You don't have to keep calling me."

He rolled his eyes upon hearing the nickname he despised.

"Roommate? Your mom will be so disappointed if you don't come home. I think you're playing hard to get."

"Maybe our parents should put some effort into coming out to Wyoming."

"They're too busy. We're always entertaining. I'm home most weekends for something or other."

Jack didn't mention that his Ivy League status didn't help him get his laundry done. He returned home mainly to have his dad's housekeeper wash his clothes and iron his shirts.

He's been love-struck since childhood and couldn't get Becca out of his mind. He had a heart-to-heart talk with Mrs. Pembroke, who convinced him it was in their best interest to do whatever it took to win over Becca. With his dad's blessing, he dropped out of Princeton and flew to Laramie for the UW fall semester in 1964.

****

Brees Air Field at the Laramie airport was five miles outside town in the Laramie Basin off the Snowy Range Road. Jack had trepidation about his travel to parts unknown.

When the rich kid from a New Jersey suburb climbed out of the Skystage Airlines twin-prop DC-3 plane, he was shocked by the desolate Laramie airport, a far cry from LaGuardia or Newark.

Jack called a taxi and went outside to wait. It was 30 minutes before the yellow D&D cab rumbled up the access road.

"Sorry for being a little late. I had to drop off my mom at the doctor."

The driver climbed out and unlocked the trunk.

"I'm used to a line of cabs fighting for my fare."

"Not here. Dave Lawrence," the driver said, shaking Jack's hand.

Dave loaded two top-of-the-line gray American Tourister suitcases molded from steel and slammed the trunk lid. It didn't latch. He moved his fishing gear to the back seat to make room.

"In Laramie, we don't have cabs. We have one cab. I'm it. You can sit in the front. Don't touch anything." Dave turned his taxi turned around and headed towards town. "What are you doing in Laramie?"

Dave glanced over at Jack while keeping one eye on the road.

"Good question."

Jack imagined waltzing with Becca while sipping champagne.

"Kind of an odd time to move here." Dave looked around the blue sky with scattered clouds. "You're lucky there isn't a foot of snow on the ground."

"I've heard about the weather. I have a friend here in school. She doesn't seem to mind."

"Where we going?"

"Crane-Hill," read Jack from a scrap of paper he pulled from his shirt pocket.

"There's one of each, Crane Hall and Hill Hall."

Dave pulled up to the front of a doctor's office where his mom was waiting and signaled Jack to crank down the window.

"What did the doctor say about your shoulder?"

Mom slid onto the back seat next to the tackle box.

"No lifting. Can you take over the snow shoveling?"

"Meet my mom. She's a spry one."

"Hello, Mom."

Jack looked up at her in the rear-view mirror.

"It's Diana."

The matron positioned her bifocals on her nose. The gold wire frames hung around her neck on a small chain.

"Diana and Dave? D&D Taxi?" Jack surmised as the cab pulled up at the curb.

He retrieved a wad of bills bound by a rubber band from his front pocket.

"It's Dennis and Diana. Mom and my stepdad had the company before he passed five years ago. I took over when she had to give up her keys."

Dave pulled into the loading zone.

"No charge. I was late to the airport and had the side trip. Have a good time. U-Dub's a party school."

The two retrieved the luggage from the back of the car.

"Good to know. Maybe this is a business opportunity."

Jack stuffed a $10 bill into Dave's pocket and tapped on the passenger-side glass. The window rolled down.

"Nice meeting you, Diana."

Jack nodded thanks to Dave, who held the front glass door open.

"What are you doing for a car? You can't get around the wide-open spaces without a car."

"Hadn't thought about it. I'll borrow one from my dad."

"We have a '61 BMW 1500 sitting under the carport in the back. We'll give you a good price to free up some room for this thing. There's a mechanic in Bosler who keeps her up."

"I have your number."

Jack lugged his bags to the information desk, wandered into the dorm lobby, and waited in line for two students ahead of him.

"You're not from around here."

The desk clerk gave Jack the once-over when he stepped up.

"Paperwork?"

He pulled the slip from his shirt pocket.

"You're a long way from home. Just in time for the semester to start."

"Well, I had to choose Princeton, Carnegie Mellon, or Wharton. You know, the Wharton School of Business at the University of

Pennsylvania. I got a full ride to Princeton." He didn't mention that his scholarship was courtesy of his father's checkbook. "They wanted me more. I was bored, and here I am."

"Things are looking up. You haven't lived until you've dated Western girls."

"Hill Hall 327. It's a single room at the end of the hall in the corner by the stairs. You'll have plenty of privacy. Hill is co-ed."

"I'm not crazy about the dorms. They're so institutional."

"You'll get used to the decor—'Early American Mental Hospital.'"

"I have a big house in Princeton, near campus. Now that's privacy. Do you know of any houses for rent in this town?" Jack stared at the name tag pinned on her blouse. "... Constance Morgan. Constanza! Are we in the same dorm, *mia signorina?*"

Connie rolled her eyes, slightly impressed.

"I'm in Ross Hall. My roommate is from New Jersey."

"Becca Pembroke?" asked Jack. "Did she tell you her mother sent me out to save her? She is my betrothed."

"That's a good one. She mentioned you might drop by," responded Connie.

"'Til death due us part," Jack said while he folded up the paperwork and stuffed it in his pocket.

"That's a little melodramatic."

He grabbed his two bags and headed toward the elevator.

26

Harold Butler

October 2, 2006—8:46 a.m. MDT: The commotion in the condo subsided. Elizabeth was still catching her breath as she sat with her father over Becca's lifeless body while the EMTs packed up. Elizabeth noticed Riley retrieve an empty vial from the floor.

"Samples from one of our suppliers."

Elizabeth got to her feet, grabbed the white plastic bottle, and read the label.

"Don't you mean your drug dealers? 'Narcotic, non-addictive.' what's that supposed to mean?"

"It was her option to take those if the pain became too severe. Taking too many meds affects people in different ways. Just let her be."

Riley handed Elizabeth a magazine flipped to a January 2006 magazine article. Unbeknownst to anyone else, Becca had researched various options to end life on her terms after the U.S. Supreme Court upheld Oregon's assisted suicide law.

******

Elizabeth let out a deep breath.

"Okay. Okay. Where do we go from here?"

She picked up an empty, clear glass pint bottle with the lid screwed on.

144

"So that's what happened to the Absolut."

Gary took the bottle from her.

"She specified the services would be three days after her death. So that makes it Saturday afternoon. You and others from Sunrise are invited. There'll be a big reception."

"Thanks, Gary. I'll mention it. These planned-out hospice deaths are less complicated than random ones. I'm so sorry."

"What? Why didn't you tell me Mom was in hospice?" Elizabeth asked with a frown.

"For starters, she held back about how bad off she was from everyone. The uterine cancer came back fast. Stage 4. The lymphoma was part of all that," Gary said.

"So, all your neighbors knew? You didn't tell me?"

"Mom wanted you to come and see her. Not out of sympathy."

"She pulled that off. If she wanted to keep control of her situation, she accomplished that, too."

Elizabeth held up the empty pain pill vial and handed it to the nurse.

"You three were very organized," complimented Riley.

"If you only knew," added Gary.

"Speak for yourself, Dad."

"I'll leave you and Elizabeth for some alone time."

****

The EMTs followed Riley out the door and down the stairs. A few minutes later, Gary went down to greet Phil and his assistant Bart, who arrived at the Common House in a blue Subaru Outback with "Eco-Haven Events" magnetic signs adhered to the doors.

Susan mustered the Caring and Sharing Committee as Phil and Bart directed the action.

"I'm sorry to hear, Mr. Steiner. I know the neighbors didn't want many disruptions."

"Well, this is all pretty disruptive. We Steiners are historically unorganized when giving up the ghost."

"We'll get all the bases covered. You have enough to worry about."

Phil dispatched Bart to retrieve the mortuary cot.

"It's the second floor. 1501." Gary pointed Phil to the elevator. "My daughter's up there."

Susan followed along with her committee up the outside stairs.

****

Phil, Bart, and Gary lifted Becca's remains onto the cot and raised it until the chrome-plated struts locked into place. The death doulas rolled Becca to the downstairs bathroom, where they gave her a sponge bath. They dressed her in the outfit she prescribed in her funeral planning document.

Susan removed the clothes from a big Berwin's Department Store bag. Who knew the first Berwin's opened in Lander, "The Gateway to Yellowstone," in 1884 to sell dry goods to tourists heading to the first national park?

Her outfit was a white-collared blouse and a plain forest green skirt. A dressy pair of Tony Lamas were pulled onto her feet. The leather soles were like new with few scuffs. The red toes were stitched with yellow thread. The top boot shafts were very supple. The same intricate yellow stitching highlighted the darkish-green leather.

Elizabeth threaded the turtle wires through her mom's earlobes.

Gary and Elizabeth followed the cot down the elevator and into the Common House Exercise Room, where Becca's body would lie for viewing before the funeral service. Harold and the Maintenance Committee arrived to straighten things up.

The cardboard coffin in the Exercise Room was lined with dry ice and covered with a cotton cloth. Gary and Elizabeth helped Phil and Bart lift her from the cot.

"May I RIP" and "Happy 10th" were Becca's contributions to the eclectically designed box.

Gary placed the sky-blue wool blanket over her. All paused for a moment.

"Eco-Haven Events is an odd name for a mortuary," Elizabeth noted as she and Phil walked to the dining area.

"We're an alternative to traditional memorials and funerals. Not everyone wants a spiritually-based ceremony. Eco-Haven can do those if the bereaved party wants sustainable disposal of their loved one's remains. Your mom specified cremation. Not the best choice considering the carbon dioxide."

"Hm. Interesting."

"She asked for my advice about her remote plans. Legal issues."

"Remote plans?"

"Maybe your dad knows about those."

****

Following their caring and sharing duties, Susan and Harold dropped by the Exercise room to offer hugs and well wishes.

"We're so sorry. You know how close I was to Becca."

Gary put up with Susan's mildly irritating demeanor because Harold was his closest friend in the community.

"She's done with the pain. She's here in spirit. Thanks to you and the committee for helping out. Harold, thank you for all your help. You didn't have to clean up our condo."

"Think nothing of it. You and Becca were so with it."

Susan returned home. Harold lingered to help Gary move tables into the Exercise Room.

"Some of us have more certainty about when death rings the doorbell. Becca was flighty yet organized."

"What a wake-up call. Susan's done more death planning than me. About as far as I've gotten is to put my "five wishes" in a baggie stuck in the freezer. The last I checked, it was next to the ice maker in case you need to find it."

"Ha, I'm the last person you should be telling."

"That's right on. The memory is the first to go."

"Eco-Haven emphasizes people and traditions—less on hardware. If we considered burial, the cardboard coffin would have eliminated the need for concrete or plastic vaults. Even with cremation, we avoided the toxic embalming chemicals."

"Strange conversation! When we were young, we discussed the miracle of birth and baby diapers. Now we talk about the reality of death and adult diapers."

Harold picked up one of the framed 8 x 10s on the remembrance table.

"It's Becca and me on the Continental Divide with two of our college classmates, Avery Meadows and Jack Middleton, taken 40 years ago. It's the Libby Flats Observation Point. They're in Wyoming. Avery is up by Devil's Tower. I don't know about Jack."

"You all got along?"

"I dread seeing that SOB, Middleton. We haven't been in touch since September 1967."

"Must be a vivid memory."

"You could say that."

"The three of us bought a house together. The Calamity Club. I still own it."

"Very scenic view. Libby Flats? Never heard of it." Harold pulled up a chair. "Sounds like fun. You have 'resort property' in Laramie! Sell that, and let's chip in on a place in Sun City."

"Maybe. Snowbirds keep a house in the north for summer and winter in the south. Boulder is warmer than Laramie. Elizabeth may move there until she figures out her next steps."

"Who snapped the picture?"

"Self-timer and a tripod. It was during my journalism days. I learned news writing and photography, courtesy of the Navy. When I wasn't protecting you from the Commies, I worked for *Blue Breeze* magazine. After the service, I was with the UW newspaper and had a dark room."

"What happened to your setup? I was a born scrounger. An obsolete darkroom setup would be worth something."

"I don't know about that. When we moved down here, it was purged at a garage sale. If I went to Flo's Flea Market, I wouldn't be surprised to find it there gathering dust."

"Susan forced me to take a class about 'downsizing.' My biggest challenge was cramming 3,000 sq ft of junk into a 1,000 sq ft place. Before we came to Boulder, I went through a pile of clothes at a yard sale. Came across a shirt Susan yanked out of my closet. I draw the line at buying back my old stuff."

"I still have a packed garage in Laramie. Lots of memories in those boxes. Avery stayed with us for a few days in '96 before flying out to climb Everest. Didn't get to the top because of the weather."

"I remember that expedition. A bunch of people died during a blizzard. I watched a movie on TV, *High Altitude Death*. Our oldest had something to do with the production in California, not Tibet."

"Avery's from Jackson. We first met when we were teenagers. My mom permitted a mountaineering school to operate out of our ranch. Avery was the lead instructor."

"Jack? He pissed me off. I pissed him off. I'm still pissed. He's more than pissed. I imagine things between us could have been better. Life happens. Did I mention he pissed me off?"

"I think this is the first time you and I have had a chance to talk since we moved here. It's funny how funerals bring people together." Harold placed the photo back on the table display. "I can replace the frame with frosted glass to cut the glare."

"We've been meaning to fix that since Becca fell."

Gary pulled an envelope from his pocket.

"What's that?" asked Harold.

"It was the only letter I received during basic training after I left home."

He wrapped the letter in the Dodgers do-rag and placed it in the cardboard coffin.

"Your contribution to the time capsule?" Harold asked as he walked out of the room. "I'll get out of your hair."

"I guess you'll miss the Dodgers in the playoffs," Gary said, setting her baseball cap on her lap. "Cheer on 'Dem Bums' from the nosebleed section."

27

Laramie Hardware Store

When Mom died, I had a lot to process. It was ironic that I was raised to be independent from my parents, but it turned out we had a latent dependence on one another. I looked forward to reconnecting with Avery, who also had a family estrangement. Other than being picky eaters, we had a strong bond. Avery was a perfectionist who was always in the right place and time. My timing was a different story. E.S.

****

Avery Meadows had enrolled in an accounting class at the UW College of Commerce & Industry (C&I) and took a seat at the end of a row. A student wiggled past and sat down on the first day of the 1964 fall semester.

"Jack Middleton. Just transferred from Princeton."

"Princeton as in New Jersey? Are you on the lam?" Avery leaned over the desktop to shake hands. "Avery Meadows."

"I'm not concerned about school if that's what you mean. I'm a whiz at accounting if you have questions about debits and credits."

"I'm here just in case I have to move back home and help my folks manage their hotel. I'm not much into numbers."

"Everything useful I learned about life was from the back of a baseball card."

150

"Thanks for the tip. I'll dig out my collection if my mom didn't throw it away. Short sleeve pastel blue polo shirt? You know, this is Wyoming. It snows on the fourth of July."

"I heard about the weather. I have several of these."

Jack untied the wool sweater with Argyle designs from around his neck. Avery and the other students sniffed the air.

"Old Spice?"

"If Dad hadn't worn it, I wouldn't exist," Jack paraphrased the TV commercial tagline.

Avery noticed Jack's blue felt cap.

"Not much baseball out here."

"This hat? My grandfather gave it to me. Christmas 1952. That was the first year he took me into the City for my first Yankees game. I could get a new one. This has memories."

"Laramie's a little less hectic than New York."

"Different kind of hectic. I checked into Hill Hall. Got antsy and ditched the dorm. Mu Nu Upsilon took me at the last minute. I didn't want to go through fall rush. There were some strings, but money talks."

"MNY, the genius house."

"You don't have to be a genius to add and subtract. More like the 'square house.' I have more room there."

"If the frat isn't for you, I have to kick out one of my housemates in November. I'd rather rent to a respectable Ivy Leaguer like you."

"Did you talk to my girlfriend's mother?"

"It would be my luck that you're a deadbeat working for tips at the Stag Point."

"You sound desperate. I'll keep it in mind."

"Let me know soon. I'll hold the room. You have a girl here?"

"The girl's part of it. My dad strongly encouraged me to go to Wyoming. See the world. Return to Jersey and run the family business."

"Sounds like you were exiled. My dad booted me out of his life. I was studying art. To keep him happy, I switched to Wildlife Management.

That's more manly, you know, facing down bull elk is better than drawing them."

"You should wear Old Spice, 'Forged with Nature.'"

"Yeah, smelling fearless and valiant? That'll do it. I've always had an interest in the outdoors, though. Have you ever done any rock climbing? Mountaineering? I'm looking for climbing partners."

"Nah, I'd like to learn how to fish out here. My grandpa took me when I was a kid. We bait-fished Stony Pond from a rowboat."

"What? The Yankees fan wants to be Hemingway. 'The Young Man and the River?'"

"Fishing was serene in Cherry Ridge. Good for a hyper kid like me. Sunfish lurked near the surface, waiting for their next meal of hovering gnats rippling the mirror-like pond surface."

"You are Hemingway."

"Baiting the hooks with slimy worms creeped me out. I didn't want to inflict mental anguish on myself. I felt for those worms."

"That's why you want to fly fish? You're quite the sentimental animal lover."

"Wait until you get to know me."

The professor entered and scrawled his name on the blackboard.

"Sorry I'm late."

The class quieted down.

****

With encouragement from his grandfather, Jack had mustered the nerve to wind the wiggly annelid on the hook without inflicting too much pain on his and the worm's psyche.

"The sun's moved overhead. The fish will head to the bottom," explained Jacob. He navigated to the small dock and moored the boat. They walked home along the pond shore with their catch. Jacob stopped, bent over, and picked a stone from the sand.

"This is an arrowhead chip. Native tribes lived here many years ago. They hunted for their food."

Jack took the flat, hand-tooled stone and skipped it across the still water.

"Take that, you no good Injun!"

"You know better than that. There were many villages near Cherry Ridge well before our ancestors arrived. Be respectful of the people who came before us. What's the Golden Rule?"

"I know, I know."

****

Jack and Avery packed up their books when class was over and walked out of the C&I classroom.

"How's the fly fishing in Jackson Hole? I want to save some worms from mayhem and death. All I know is from a *Roaring River* magazine article about fly fishing the Snake River."

"Fishing's pretty good around there. The running rivers are different. Mostly no tourists in Laramie."

"I'm willing to pay. I bought a bamboo rod, a reel, and a box of lures. Jersey has a few fly-fishing areas."

"Sure. We can go out some afternoon. I'll bring my fish sense. You buy the beer."

The following week, the fall weather was warm. Their class let out at 1:30 p.m. Avery was always ready for an excursion, wearing plaid flannel shirts and broken-in jeans held up by a tooled leather belt accessorized with various buckles.

"Let's stop by the MNY house." Avery gave Jack the once over. "You can get ready."

"I am ready."

"Your Brooks Brothers shirt will scare off the fish."

The two walked from class to Avery's three-bedroom brick house. Jack waited by the passenger door of Avery's 1960 VW SO23 chrome-trimmed Arctic white van parked in front.

"It's open!"

"You don't lock?"

"Wyoming is a pretty safe place. Not many people lock their houses, either. Of course, we all have a gun or two. I have a 12-gauge shotgun for birds. A .30-06 for deer and bigger. My guns are stored under the bed. Don't tell anyone."

They tossed their book bags on the floor.

"Immaculate van," complimented Jack as he slammed the panel door shut and climbed into the passenger seat.

"The van? I call it the 'Silver Steed.' It's good for field trips. I need a place where I can be by myself. It's on a long-term loan from my dad. He figured his only child needed wheels. I think he felt guilty."

"Must be good for wildlife management."

"Most of my department are manly men. Dad and I liked hunting and fishing together. Outdoor activities weren't enough."

"If I were single, I'd hang around with you."

"Oh, you're just saying that, big fella."

"Natch. After you teach me a thing or two about fly fishing, how about showing me how to shoot?"

"I can do that. I keep a .270 under a blanket in the back. Some guys like to show off their rifles mounted in plain sight on their pickup truck rear window gun racks."

"You lock up guns and not your house?"

"Priorities."

Avery adjusted the mirrors, eased out the clutch, gently clunked into the car behind, and pulled onto Arthur Avenue.

"Chester Arthur was the first U.S. President to visit Yellowstone National Park during an 1883 fishing expedition in Western Wyoming," Avery explained while pulling onto Arthur Avenue. "His presence in Yellowstone conserved the park and curtailed massive development."

"Where'd you learn that?"

"I'm a Wildlife Management major."

Jack rubbed his hands together in anticipation.

"Let's go fishing, President Arthur."

"I have an extra rod in the back. Your bamboo caster one won't be good."

At the light, Avery turned north at 14th Street and headed west on Nellie Tayloe Ross Boulevard, the main drag extending from one end of town to the other.

"Nice buckle you have there."

"It's not Cartier if that's what you're asking. My first summer job in high school was at a mountaineering school in Lander. One of the base camps was on a ranch at the foot of the mountains." Avery slowed down and waited for a street construction crew. "It's about time they filled those potholes. Anyway, the guy at the next place over gave it to me in exchange for some work I did. It was more of a favor. He had some cattle killed. Most were mutilated. I fixed the gate to keep the coyotes out."

"Mutilated?" Jack leaned back, impatient with the wait. Traffic began to move.

"Mutilated. The soft tissues were cut, leaving weird patterns. Like around the udders and lips." Avery gave the street crew an index finger wave as he rolled by. "It was in all the papers."

"I like that," Jack observed. "… the pattern on your buckle."

Paying no mind, Avery backed into a parallel parking space.

"What's it supposed to mean?"

"Not sure. Some beatnik thing. I didn't bother to ask."

"I dig it."

Jack climbed down. Avery pulled open the front door. A set of sleigh bells announced their entrance to Laramie Hardware.

******

Mr. Farris, the store owner, greeted them with a smile. He always made the same small talk.

"How's your dad doing? You know, back in '45, me and the Mrs. got snowed in on our way back from Pocatello. Stayed at the Moose Paddle. Nice people. One day, we'll get back up to Jackson."

"I'm sure they'd appreciate seeing you and Mrs. again. My friend Jack is new on campus. Fresh from New Jersey. He needs to look like a fisherman. We're heading up the mountain for a few hours."

Mr. Farris led the two over to the work clothes aisle.

"A good-looking young East Coaster like you? You'll scare the trout with those slacks."

"These? I wear them all the time."

Mr. Farris thumbed through stacks of folded-up jeans.

"Around here, your 'all the time' will be a little different. You look like about a 34. Inseam? Try these. They're 36." Mr. Farris handed him a pair of Levi shrink-to-fit jeans. Next, he pulled a Pendleton plaid wool shirt from the adjacent display table. "I think this will be a good one. It has two pockets. One for your little black book there. One for your money."

Mr. Farris gave a snide grin and pointed to the dressing room where Jack tried on his new Wyoming wear.

****

He and Avery wandered the store.

"Did you decide to carry any climbing equipment?"

"I ordered the rope you thought would sell, Gold Line. I sold a few coils to climbers. Most went to ranchers. They'd never seen anything like it. I was skeptical. They said the Gold Line didn't stretch or fray. You know Pete Martin up by Bosler?"

"Not yet."

"He's young. About your age. His father inherited the place from a long-lost relative. Didn't want anything to do with it except for Pete. Thinks he's a wheat farmer. He bought every one of those oval clips."

"Carabiners."

Avery looked over the small display case filled with climbing protection equipment.

"Carabiners. I had to order more. It was so easy to slip them through a clove hitch knot. Better than those steel ones. They're hard to screw together wearing gloves."

Mr. Farris unclipped a carabiner from the chain of them on a wall hook and rapidly opened and closed the gates.

"They didn't bust when it got real cold."

"You'd get a new batch of customers if you'd carry more outdoor equipment."

Avery smiled when Jack walked out of the dressing room in a stiff pair of Levis and his new fishing shirt.

"I'm getting too old to make big changes. This place could use some young blood. If you run out of things to do, hit me up. It'll give me more time to visit your folks up in Jackson!"

Mr. Farris smiled at Jack, who twirled around and modeled his new get-up.

"Time to go. I want to get us on the river."

"Looks like I don't need to bag anything except those shoes. We have to do something about those tassels." Mr. Farris grinned at Jack's tan loafers. "Try these wool socks and see how they feel in this pair of Red Wings. The fish won't know you're from New Jersey."

Jack sat down and laced up his boots. The socks wadded up in the toe.

"I'll get used to 'em." Jack grimaced and wiggled around his toes the best he could.

"You sure? Nothing worse than ill-fitting boots. You got Band-Aids? You might wear a blister. Here's a belt. It's on me. They're a little baggy now. Those 501s'll shrink up. Wash 'em in hot." Jack did a few knee bends. "Better yet, wear 'em in the tub and let 'em dry on ya. They'll form fit to your legs. Very stylish."

✳✳✳✳✳✳

Avery summoned Jack by shaking the sleigh bells. Jack strutted out of the hardware store like John Wayne and waited at the passenger side.

"I overheard your friend's thinking about selling out, retiring. Ever thought about getting into retail?" Jack's stiff trousers didn't bend well in the knees. "You can sell softer jeans."

"I've thought about it. Laramie could use a sporting goods store. In Wyoming, the definition of 'sport' is guns, ammo, and killing anything that moves. I was thinking about keeping the regular hardware stuff. Add a section for climbers. Carry some ropes, tents. Maybe Little League mitts and bats."

"Excellent location."

Jack looked around at the mix of retail businesses in downtown Laramie.

"I'll take you climbing one of these days. When we don't have time to head to the hills, some routes go up buildings like that rock wall. Mr. Farris thinks climbers on his storefront are good for business."

Jack noticed across the street a red and green neon sign flashing, "Fuji Café," arcing over a bright orange poppy.

"Where's the bucking horse? Like the sign says, 'Best in Wyoming.' Must be the only one in Wyoming."

"It's been here forever. You know Takehiro Fujiyama from our accounting class? Sits in the front? Goes by 'Tak?' He moved to Laramie after World War II. His parents ran a grocery store and restaurant somewhere in Northern California. Do you know about internment camps?"

"Like cemeteries?"

"Internment, not interment. After Pearl Harbor was bombed, Roosevelt relocated Japanese people on the West Coast to camps in the middle of nowhere."

"Sounds familiar. German POWs were locked up in Jersey at Fort Belle Mead, close to Princeton."

"Didn't know that! His dad was a mess hall cook. His mom was a secretary at the hospital. Tak and his mom started out at a camp in California. After the war, they ended up in Denver. He's several years older than us."

Avery waited for a station wagon before backing out.

"I don't know the fuss over a few Japanese. What about his dad?"

"Ask Tak. The story is complicated."

"My grandpa told me the Jersey Shore was turned into a big military bunker. German subs sunk a dozen or more American ships off the Atlantic coast."

"You should feel right at home. Over the hill from where we'll be fishing, German POWs were imprisoned at Ryan Park. Anyway, someone in Denver knew the Laramie Highway Grill needed kitchen help. They packed up and were fish out of water in Wyoming."

"I thought I was crazy moving here. Speaking of moving, I'll think about your extra room. It depends on how Becca likes the MNY house."

****

Soon after Jack had joined the frat, he invited Becca for a visit. Becca used both hands to creak open the heavy wooden door and entered the spacious living room.

"I'm surprised your dad let you move to Wyoming."

"No big deal. Princeton refunded his money. Not really refunded. They gave him credit for his annual endowment donation. I was tired of crowds, and besides, you're a damsel in distress."

"... and you've been watching too much 'Superman.'"

"Your mom thinks I'm faster than a speeding bullet."

"This place is better than the dorms?" Becca gazed at the dusty shelves filled with never-opened books. "It's as big as your dad's place in Cherry Ridge. A little more cluttered. Why didn't you stay in Hill Hall?"

"The cafeteria food was bad."

"No salad forks? Was it as good as that?" Becca pointed at a half-eaten slice of pizza on a napkin.

"Our housemother is kind of lazy. It's so convenient to the fridge. Pop open a beer if I want." Jack picked up an empty Coors bottle from the coffee table. "I can get you one. We have wine, too."

Becca sashayed towards the front door.

"No, thanks. Maybe another time. Besides, I'm a Bud girl."

"I can show you my bedroom. I pay extra for a single. It's more spacious than the room I had in the dorm."

Becca glanced around the living room and sniffed the blended aroma of stale cigar smoke and beer vapors circulating the high ceilings.

"I can picture it."

"It's a few minutes until dinner. We're having roast beef. I hear it's from your Quiver Mountain Ranch."

"I have to get back to the lab. Thanks, anyway."

"I can walk you over there."

Jack leaned on the door.

"You should get cleaned up for your banquet. Thanks for the tour."

"So much for the MNY experiment," Jack thought while the door slowly closed.

28

Avery Meadows

October 4, 2006—1:38 p.m. MDT: Avery Meadows purchased Laramie Hardware with Jack's financial backing in 1965. They changed the name to Laramie Mountaineering after two predatory big-box discount stores moved into town and devoured the hardware business.

Jack funded a cut-and-sew manufacturing branch in the back of the store to produce products for outdoor enthusiasts, including a new line of sleeping bags, tents, and outerwear called Upward.

Their small factory was lucrative. Jack and Avery sold to their employees in 1993 for cash and residuals. Avery bought the Bison Horn Lodge Bed & Breakfast near Devil's Tower in Northeast Wyoming.

President Teddy Roosevelt designated the massive rock resembling a *Jack and the Beanstalk* scale tree stump as the first U.S. National Monument in 1908. Over the years, Avery made over 1,000 ascents of geological anomaly, which protruded 1,267 feet above the Belle Fourche River prairie and surrounding sandstone landscape.

The Oscar-winning *Cosmic Contact* movie production filmed its culminating scenes at Devil's Tower. In 1975, the movie producers and the U.S. National Park Service contacted Laramie Mountaineering, inviting climbers interested in working on the film crew.

Avery and several other outdoorsy people accepted the job offer to camp on-site for two weeks, where they strung cables up Devil's Tower from the parking lot.

****

A *Cosmic Contact* lobby card that pictured Clint Redstone and Roberta Williams hiding from an alien spacecraft was thumb-tacked on the wall above the phone.

Breakfast was over. Avery and B&B manager Madison Ahmad cleared the tables. The Ahmad family owned three motels in Sheridan and Gillette and had a long history in Northeast Wyoming. Madison cleared the dishes, and Avery chatted with the patrons while refilling water glasses.

"I heard you say we're going up the Durrance route this morning." One of the tourist climbers placed his hand over his coffee cup. "I don't want to risk emergency urination up there."

"We'll have a pre-climb meeting. Ahmad will go over everything."

"Is it easy?" a nervous tourist asked from the adjacent table, signaling for more coffee.

"First climbed by Jack Durrance and Harrison Butterworth in September 1938 with a ladder."

"You're kind of, uh ... You don't strike me as the climbing type."

"Why do you think the tour package includes two days for us to teach you basic techniques and then practice?"

"I've been up the Tower with big groups. A few years back, I called my friend Dylan from Gillette. We guided 15 people from the Campbell County Rec Department. I remember it well because it was Halloween. One of the ropes stuck in a crack and delayed us three hours. That night, the moon illuminated our way. Everyone got down safe and sound at the expense of missing a big party."

Manager Madison rang a handbell. It was time to herd the Tower tourists to the equipment room, where the climbing parties assembled. As the autumn days grew shorter, the climbs began earlier when the lower sun kept the rock cool.

****

Avery answered the harvest gold push-button phone amid the breakfast clatter.

"Bison Horn Lodge."

"Hello, Meadows. It's Steiner," Gary enunciated into the receiver.

"Hold on a second." Avery walked into the hallway while unraveling the coiled cord. "That's better. Yeah, it's been a while."

The two exchanged the usual small talk.

"I have some not-so-good news. Becca wasn't doing too well."

"What do you mean, 'wasn't?'" Gary went on to explain. "I'm stunned. Of all of us, I would have put money on me being the first to go."

Avery glanced at a picture hanging askew on the wall under the *Cosmic Contact* lobby card, the same photo Becca had on her nightstand. "Are you holding up, Steiner?"

"I'm good. Can you contact Jack? You might have better luck. He might want to know."

"Do you have anything planned? Anything around the 'Pact?'"

"'The 'Pact?' I've had too much on my mind. I'm organizing a service. Well, Elizabeth is doing most of the work for Saturday afternoon."

"Thanks for the update, Steiner. Keep me in the loop. I'll get an early start on Friday. With or without Middleton, I'll be there."

"If you can't make it, no big deal. It would be good to catch up in person."

"I'm the CEO. I'll leave the cat in charge. It'll be good to see your daughter."

The two college friends hung up. Avery tracked down Madison in the equipment room.

"I see everyone's ready to go. Except for that one." Avery shrugged toward the fellow with a blank expression, staring out the window. "Line him up in the middle someplace so he can't escape."

"I'll keep an eye on him."

"Listen, I have to leave town for a few days. I may be back sooner than later. A college friend of mine died in Boulder. Can you keep an eye on the place?"

"I'll follow your meticulous schedule to the second." Madison continued clearing the breakfast tables. "Bummer about your friend."

"She was the glue that kept our little group stuck together. It'll be a quick trip."

"Plenty of good rock down south. You got Veedauwoo on the way down. I heard your old store is having a climbing festival over the weekend. Make a surprise appearance!"

"My schedule's too tight. Sounds like you're trying to get rid of me."

"The only time you get out of here is when you take the cat to the vet."

"Not true. I go to Sundance for groceries once a week. I'm driving through Laramie. Will miss Veedauwoo. Legend has it that one of my classmates lives in Centennial. He was the guy who backed me when I bought the hardware store."

"Don't let him take all your money."

"He took his share and is bumming around. Must be nice. I wouldn't have this place if it weren't for him."

"We have one party going up the Durrance this morning. Two groups Friday. The rooms are all full through next week. We'll be good here. I'll call Dylan if I need help. Be safe. You know, the Flatirons are south of Boulder. Throw in your shoes."

"You're sure now. I'm not leaving until tomorrow. I'll have my Nokia with me."

"Don't break down before Douglas. No cell service. Go on, git! My two boys have been looking for something to do. I'll see if their aunt can bring them over to clean rooms. Make some Christmas money. The circumstances aren't the best, but take some time before the climbing surge and hunting season."

"The Centennial thing could be a wild goose chase," Avery thought while pacing around the lodge.

29

Happy Angler Tackle Shop

When they were young, Mom complained about Jack flaunting his money on the latest fashions and flamboyant lifestyle. Forty years later, when I met him at the Blue Sky Village full moon party, I thought Jack was a homeless guy from the shelter up the street. Had Mom been there, she would have grumbled about how shabby he looked. Maybe we all get tired of trying to be someone we're not. E.S.

****

Avery had encountered more construction on the way out of West Laramie and downshifted to avoid a bicyclist who cut off the Silver Steed.

"I'll take you to Fuji's one of these days for a plate of insects and raw fish. Speaking of fish and bait, next stop, the Happy Angler Tackle Shop."

Avery hoped they didn't spend too much time outfitting Jack because fishing after dark was against the law.

The store was packed with fishing gear. Nets of all varieties hung from pegs on the wall. A repurposed Coca-Cola cooler full of small containers of worms filled the air with an organic aroma. Jack took a carton from the cooler and held it by the wire bale.

"Pretty good use of Tak's extra 'to-go' boxes. Don't order the soup. Fuji Café brand worms."

Avery eyed the fishing flies of all sizes and colors sorted in clear plastic boxes under the glass countertop while waiting for Ben to finish with another customer.

"Avery Meadows? What are you doing here on a school day?"

"Ben Roberts, meet Jack Middleton. He transferred from Princeton."

Ben sprinkled samples of the finest feathered lures for the season across the counter.

Jack shook Ben's hand.

"How do you two know each other?" asked Jack.

"Our paths crossed in Lander when we both did work for Piedmont Mountaineering. Ben lectured about critters. I was the lead instructor."

"After I retired from the Wyoming Wildlife Department two years ago, I bought the store and moved to Laramie," replied Ben.

"I switched my major because of what I learned, paying attention to your talks during my summers working for Piedmont."

"Your flattery will get you a 10 percent discount today."

"Business is good?" asked Jack while he sorted through the flies on the counter.

"I get a steady flow of customers. Fishers go through fishing lures. The Country Club is across the way. Kids bring me golf balls. I pay them 15 cents a ball and sell them for half a buck. Anglers and golfers are steady customers. When the world ends, scientists will find the waterway bottoms covered by fish hooks and Titleists."

"We're going out for a few hours this afternoon. I read in the paper the brown trout have been hitting at dusk."

"Yup. Water's been pretty low. Some nice pools. Bob from next door pulled this out yesterday." Ben pointed at a Polaroid snapshot of a 13-inch brown trout. "Used one of these."

Ben pawed through the flies on the counter and showed Jack a brown and bristly Muddler Minnow.

Jack pinched the barbed hook, careful not to jab his finger.

"Did you make these? If I'm a fish, I'd eat this. It's a work of art. Even if I weren't a fish, I'd give it a taste."

"My daughter has an eye for tying flies. Can I put a few in a bag?"

"Let me show you what I have." Jack pulled the lure box from his pocket. "I brought these out from home."

Jack pushed his green flatfish with yellow dots next to the Muddler Minnow.

"These are more for deep water lakes. Where did you say you're from?"

"I didn't, but I'm from Jersey."

"Once you figure out Libby Creek, maybe Avery will take you out on Lake Hattie."

"I learned how to fish in my grandfather's rowboat."

"I just got a new trolling motor. Runs real slow and smooth. You two can try fishing from my rig."

"That would be great!"

"How about you, Avery? Do you ever get over to Lander? How's Sally? I haven't been back since I moved to Laramie."

"Can't remember the last time. I don't get to Jackson much, either. Now you're making me feel guilty. You remember Becca?"

At the mention of her name, Jack clenched his fists. He blew off steam at the sunglasses rack while Avery and Ben caught up.

"Didn't she cook for us when we took Piedmont's courses to the woods? She'd whip up a mess of eggs for 20 while keeping all the coffee cups full."

"She could hold her own. I want to say hello to Bob."

Avery went next door.

"You say there was a girl named Becca you knew in Lander?"

"She was from New Jersey, too. Nice girl."

"Hm, toss in a pack of those baseball cards and a Bonkers Bar."

Jack struggled to pull his wallet out of his stiff jeans pocket and paid.

****

Avery returned with a six-pack of Bud and met Jack waiting in the van.

"Bite of Bonkers?" Jack asked through the open window.

"Nah, I don't mix. You owe me!"

Avery slid open the van door and set the beer behind the passenger seat.

"Shades?"

Jack pulled a pair with the tag still on them from his inner coat pocket.

"Where did you get those?"

"They're on loan. I borrow things from stores for stress relief. I'll take them back."

"Yeah, right. There's an opener in the side pocket."

"I'm not much of a Bud man. You know I prefer Coors. It's a delicacy back East. I came out here to bootleg Coors back to Jersey."

"Coors gets a premium price? I'll drive the delivery truck."

Avery precariously balanced a beer in a handmade can holder fashioned from twisted and woven electrical wire.

"I'm a carpetbagger out here. Like after the Civil War, there's nothing wrong with being an opportunist. Buy low, sell high. Buy high, sell higher. You're quite the entrepreneur. If you don't patent that can holder, I will." Jack opened up the wax pack of baseball cards. "I'll trade you this 1964 Lou Brock for a piece of jerky."

Avery examined the card.

"Jerky is worth at least Lou Brock and that Bob Gibson. Do I need to remind you how the Cardinals swept your beloved Yankees last week?"

"We won back-to-back in '61 and '62."

"Yeah, and you lost back-to-back in '63 and '64."

"So, how do you know this, Becca?"

Jack was coy as he munched his strip of jerky.

"Becca? When she was in high school, her parents sent her out. I guess she needed a change."

"Change is good."

"Do you know Gary Steiner? The three of us met on his ranch by Lander."

Jack thumbed through his baseball cards. There was a Mickey Mantle that he carefully caressed into his pocket.

"I've heard of Gary Steiner."

"The quiet type. He knows how to wrestle down a calf, so don't get in his way!"

Avery spurred the Silver Steed, and the VW headed for the hills.

"I've known Becca since we were kids."

"Is she the girlfriend? Becca never mentioned a boyfriend. She talked about a friend who moved to Laramie. That must be you."

"What the hell am I doing here?" Jack pondered while watching the rolling fields pass by on the Snowy Range Road.

30

Pete Martin

October 6, 2006—5:04 a.m. MDT: Avery was a conscientious mountaineer, always arose at daybreak and nervously paced back and forth, hoping the day's guided climbs would go off without incident.

The coffee clicked on at 4:00 a.m. Avery poured the first cup into an insulated mug. The rotating carbo-loaded breakfast menu was set. Yesterday was pancakes, scrambled eggs, and sausage.

Today was a batch of Bison Horn *chilaquiles.* Avery's job was to slosh around a dozen whisked eggs and diced potatoes in a stainless steel bowl and then refrigerate.

After that chore was completed, the early riser fetched an early-model Upward orange nylon backpack with a worn leather bottom from a peg by the door, removed the climbing harness, various pieces of protection, slings, belay devices, and piled the tangled glob of equipment under the bench.

"Maybe Madison's right."

On second thought, all the gear was stuffed back into the bag.

"Thanks for the breakfast prep, partner!"

Madison loaded the bacon into the oven before retrieving the egg slurry from the fridge and opening a bag of tortilla chips. Avery set aside the pack and made the rounds with the coffeepot.

"By the way, I'm sorry I questioned your abilities yesterday," The nervous climber apologized. "It's just that ..."

"It's just that my hands and fingers aren't cracked with busted nails compared to an oilfield worker? I have a pierced ear? Forget about it. You're not the first."

"What's for breakfast? Smells good."

"It's a recipe from a climbing trip to Mexico with the guy I'm trying to track down today if I can ever get out of here." Avery was half paying attention. "Madison, have you seen my 'go-bag?'"

"You pre-packed it, and I stuck it in the closet. Good thing you had it ready. You'd never get out of here. Pack one for me next time so I can go. Let the cat keep everything organized around here."

"It was in case the B&B started on fire. The cat's go-bag is in the pantry next to her food! Do you promise me you'll keep the place from burning down and get the cumin mixed into the eggs the way I like?"

"You should have spiced them yourself."

Avery got back to the nervous climber.

"How was your day on the rock? You look no worse for the wear. Listen, no hard feelings. You can't hold grudges in the mountaineering business."

"I was a little jittery on the hike to the base. I'm sticking around for the day. Taking my time back to Rapid City. My flight leaves later tonight for Omaha. I'm checking out Mt. Rushmore. Where are you going this time of day?"

"To tell you the truth, I don't know. It would be a relief if I couldn't find this guy."

"I thought you had to get out of here."

"Control freaks can't let go!"

"Sounds like you don't want to make the trip."

"I'll spare you the ugly details. I'm not too crazy about finding my old business partner. It's just a matter of time before we meet again. Might as well get it over with. As long as you're looking around the Black Hills, stop by Crazy Horse."

****

It was 10:15 a.m. when Avery stepped out of the B&B and headed out to the 1993 white Eurovan, the *Tiburon Blanco,* aka the White Shark, in the parking lot. A big Calico cat was awakened when Avery opened the door. The loyal feline knew it was time to go and jumped out.

The kitty sat on the boardwalk porch and watched the Eurovan with the Winnebago camper package rumble out toward the highway with Devil's Tower as a backdrop.

Avery's destination was Centennial (population 270), a former lumber-milling town in Southeast Wyoming. The route was west on I-90 to Gillette, then south on Wyoming 59, a treacherous two-lane.

The Interstate drive was a breeze. On any road, the White Shark was taller than passenger cars. That was beneficial in the winter. The downside was that the rig had little power to pass the long tractor-trailers.

Highway 59 was a different story. Massive trucks rumbled down the narrow road with oversized mining equipment. It was weird stuff, like humongous front-end loader tires that crowded the centerline.

A flatbed truck with the extra-wide bulldozer shovel about blew the top-heavy Eurovan off the road with narrow shoulders. Those white-knuckle moments were a big downside to the drive.

Trucks were one thing. Then there were the rock star-sized buses from points south that delivered workers to the mines around Gillette. The bus traffic clogged up the road during rush hour, which seemed like all the time since the shifts changed around the clock.

The Shark emerged from the Highway 59 bottleneck and took it easy through Douglas. There wasn't much traffic on I-25 south of town. Rather than book it to Laramie, it was time for a stretch break in Wheatland at Boomer's Truck Plaza.

****

Avery topped off the tank, backed the White Shark into a spot in front of the restaurant, went inside to pay, and took a stool at the counter. The server, named Harper, brought over a menu and a glass of water.

"Do you need a minute? I'm a little unorganized. I just got out of my creative writing class at the community college. Coffee?" She took a deep breath, pulled back her ponytail, and tied it with a teal scrunchy, accentuating her auburn hair and pink blouse. "You're my first customer!"

Harper poked a pen that wrote in purple ink behind her ear, turned over a cup on the saucer, dribbled coffee from a brownish-copper plastic pot, and set it on the counter.

"I'm ready but can wait until your heart rate drops to normal. There's not much to do on road trips around Wyoming except gas up, wait around, and eat. Nervous eating, you know. Do you cover all the jobs here?"

"All the jobs?" she asked while digging a pad from her back pocket.

"I see your name is Harper Cook. Are you also Harper Server?" Avery quipped. "Harper Cashier?"

"Ha, no. I want to be 'Harper Writer.' I have a column in the local paper about the food scene. This job I stretched into an internship. One thing I want to do is find the best hamburger or best whatever in every county." She noticed Avery's Devil's Tower mug. "You're from Sundance? Have you tried the burger at the Klondike in Beulah? Our Boomer Burger is the best in Platte County. Of course, it's the only burger in Platte County."

"You know your burgers! Not Sundance. I have a B&B by Devil's Tower. We flip a mean one if I do say so myself. We call it the Tulgey Wood. Best in Crook County."

"Tulgey Wood? Sounds like a has-been golfer."

"That's one of the climbing routes. How about something light? This is my first meal this afternoon. I'm stopping in Laramie. My friend owns a restaurant at one of the truck stops."

"I know the place. Try the Tiki Burger. Best in Albany County."

Avery read over the selections scratched in white chalk on the blackboard above the coffee machine behind the counter.

"How about your special?"

"The hot beef comes on white with brown gravy. You can add a small salad for $2.00.

"Okay, bleu cheese, no croutons, and rye. Fries instead of mashed. Gravy on the side."

"Rye? Are you sure you want a hot beef sandwich? It's a dollar extra for changes. We don't have bleu cheese. Just white and orange."

"Code words?"

"White's 'Ranch.' Orange is 'French.'"

"Make it French. A bottle of Bud and gravy on the fries."

"Are you from Wisconsin? I'm from there. We have a dish called *poutine*. I can add cheese if you like."

"How about cheese curds? My dad is from Oconomowoc!"

"Are you kidding? This is Wheatland, Wyoming. The closest thing we have to that squeaky delicacy is nothing."

Harper flashed a smile, one Midwesterner to another on her way to place the order.

"Special on rye, gravy on the fries, croutons on the side, orange!"

The cook shook his head.

"I need some help back here from finicky eaters!" he yelled out from the kitchen with a chuckle.

Avery downed the last swig of Bud and chased it with a gulp of water.

"The afternoon pit stop rush is picking up. I better let you get back to work. I'm stingy with compliments, but you know how to fry stuff. Those potatoes were hot. Not too greasy."

"Thanks! I won't charge for the substitutions. You say you're nervous? We get nervous drivers when the snow blows sideways."

"I was about pushed off 59 by a flatbed hauling a gigantic coal shovel."

"Now, that would make me nervous."

"Not as nervous as my drive to Centennial. Looking for an old friend. We haven't been in touch for 20 years."

Harper retrieved the sawbuck that Avery had tucked under the plate.

"Doesn't sound like a friend. I went to my five-year class reunion. Darned if I didn't run into my arch-enemy from the cheerleading squad. We hated each other in high school. I was amazed at how much she had changed. Married. Has a baby. Very mellowed out. Maybe I'm the one who had an attitude adjustment."

"Jack and me? We had our moments. Nothing like his big falling out with one of our college housemates. It could be scary."

"People are the same at heart. I'm an optimist. They change their actions and don't realize it. I like to think for the better. If you're going 34, there've been deer on the road. They have a sixth sense when it's hunting season. Don't let your mind drift."

"Thanks for the heads up."

****

Avery turned off at Wyoming Highway 34 and cut through the scenic Sybille Creek Canyon. The route was named for a French trapper who established an outpost at the confluence of the Laramie and Platte rivers.

"THUMP, THUMP!"

A coyote on its way across the road greeted the front bumper.

"Shit."

The noise was a reminder of the time a three-point buck jumped out from a Shirley Basin Road borrow ditch and was obliterated by the White Shark. A small animal accident shouldn't be as bad as banging into that deer.

Avery walked over to the carcass, pushed it onto the shoulder, and inspected the now mangled 17-county Campbell County license plate. Since there were 23 counties in the state, figuring out where a driver lived was simple.

A little further along the desolate two-lane, an old boy walked down the shoulder. Avery pulled over and waited for the pedestrian to catch up. The stranger placed his weather-worn, stubby fingers on the door frame as the window powered down.

"Need a lift? Are you AWOL [Absent Without Leave] from the Navy?"

"You mean this cap? Well, sort of. I'm a couple miles up."

The fellow climbed into the cab and strapped in. He popped one of the pearl snaps, securing a breast pocket of his black western-cut shirt, and pulled out a business card.

"Pete Martin. Been another strange day. All of a sudden, I find myself at the turnoff." He pointed his thumb back toward the state Wildlife Lab.

"At least the weather's good. You must have been missed."

"This time, it's close to home. The wife's used to it. Our kids get teased at school." Pete took off his skipper's cap and scratched his balding head. "It's tough enough running a marina in Wyoming without the distractions."

"I know your lake. I learned about it in geology class. It's a remnant of the Western Interior Seaway." It had been ages since Avery thought about the vast lake created by the retreating prehistoric inland sea that dried up 70 million years ago. Its deepest spot was 2,500 feet from the surface and hadn't yet been explored. "Have you seen the Loch Laramidia monster?"

"In a manner of speaking. Like I said, 'distractions.' Where did you start today?"

"I have a B&B over by Devil's Tower. Say, did you ever know Mr. Farris? My former partner and I bought the Laramie Hardware from him."

"See this?" Pete showed a carabiner clipped on his belt loop holding a ring of keys. "Bought him out of these when I was first starting out. Reminds me of what I've learned since then. It's to the right by those mailboxes."

The ancient mariner pointed to the side of the road where Avery turned, navigated over the crest of the single-lane rutted dirt path, and stopped.

"I like that buckle of yours." Avery glanced at the codger with a skeptical grin. "Where'd you get it?"

"Long story. Longer than the time we have right now. Stop by sometime when you're not in a rush. My number's on the card."

"You own this place?"

"My dad inherited three sections from here to Bosler. The folks stayed in Lincoln. I was out of high school with nothing better to do. Came out and decided to give it a go. Me and my brother. I was greener than the wheat when we started. My brother wasn't much help. He fell in love, and last I knew, was back in Nebraska someplace. Holdrege, maybe. My wife's family farmed in Iowa, so that was a big help. We still raise small grains. Low wheat prices killed us. Pumping water uphill is pricey."

"Mr. Farris told me about you when I was in college. Impressive. I haven't been by here since then. This used to be an unmarked road."

"The other way to get here is hiking from the Laramie Peak side." Pete climbed down, hitched up his worn Wrangler jeans, unlocked the gate, and limped back to the passenger window. "The lake was a good fallback. The state paid us a few bucks each year for an access easement and let us use lake water for irrigation. I have to negotiate every year. They agreed to construct the boat ramp and marina. I learned from the Loch Laramidia Monster to wait and see what happens. Most times, problems work themselves out."

"By the way, I'm Avery Meadows. Next time, I'll stay longer."

"I'll give you one of these shirts."

Pete tipped his hat and pulled the gate closed behind the Eurovan, which bounced under a worn wooden "Lake Laramidia Marina–Free Admission" sign spanning the road.

******

Wyoming 34 ended at U.S. 287. Avery turned south to Laramie. On the way through town, an obligatory stop was at a college haunt, the Stag Point. During the day, the Stag served locals. Avery sat at the bar and gazed around the rustic wooden interior. The two-headed calf was still perched on the beam supporting the ceiling. A bullet hole scarred the mirror behind the bar.

"It was 1965. One of the wildlife management grad students got a little out of hand. Pulled out a .22 sidearm and shot the reflection of one of the football players," Avery reminisced to the others.

"You don't say. I've wondered about that," a gray-bearded guy yelled from the other end under the TV hanging on the wall.

Avery gathered a copy of the *Laramie Daily Press,* strewn over the hardwood bar, and flipped to the front page.

"You know Pete Martin? The lead story's about him."

"Kind of an odd cat. I worked out at the lake for a few months. He's not the strangest thing out there."

Avery grinned at a headline.

"I just gave him a ride. I sensed something in my bones about that lake. About that guy. Can't describe it, though."

The Stag Horn shifts were changing, and the daytime bartender was stocking the shelves. He was in his late 40s, maybe early 50s.

"Can you put your hair up," the next-shift bartender held up a long strand of hair she carefully pulled from the orange slices in the drink garnish tray. He walked out from behind the bar, pulled back his graying locks, and secured them with a rubber band, the kind that held a celery bunch together.

"Did you read this?" Avery asked the night shift bartender.

"Kind of weird. There was a TV crew in town. I was in summer school," the bartender recalled while counting the cash drawer. "They came in here. Did some interviews. They wanted to talk with me, but I was too busy serving the other weird people wantin' to be on TV."

"Speaking of weird people, does Jack Middleton ever stop by?"

"Hon, if I had a shot of Old Cabin Still for every oldster who comes in here asking about their college days, I'd be an alcoholic."

The young bartender cleared away the shot glasses from the previous customer and set down a sweaty bottle of Bud. Avery held up the crumpled newspaper section.

"Can I take this?"

"It's from last Sunday. Go for it."

The American League Division Series Game 3 between Detroit and New York was on the TV hanging in the corner. The Tigers at home in Comerica Park were creaming the Yankees.

"Not much of a game," Avery thought, leaving the change on the bar before caroming the cue ball around the pool table rails on the way to the street. There was quite a crowd lining up.

The Stag Point transformed from a local hangout into a college bar after dark. The day-shift bartender was now the night-shift bouncer. Avery helped position the little table next to the front door.

"It's 'Stag Point Beer Night,' $4.00 pitchers. Two bucks off. People line up after class, get stamped, leave and return. It saves time when it gets busy. We have a band upstairs, too. Hey, aren't you from Jackson?" the bouncer asked as the line of partiers began to organize itself. "I'm Wallace."

"Avery Meadows. I remember. The hair threw me."

Wallace retrieved the rubber stamp from his hoodie pouch.

"It's the small Wyoming world."

"Do you get back up to Jackson much?"

"Once in a while, when I need money, which is pretty much all the time." Wallace opened the ink pad on the bouncer stand."

"Your pop used to do odd jobs around the motel. He let me help him."

"See? He paid more attention to you than me. I didn't think I was that lazy. But I didn't meet up with his expectations. Internalized lazyhood. I had no future in Jackson except if I wanted to clear tables. Here I am washing beer glasses in Laramie. He props me a little to keep me from robbing banks."

"I hear you on that. It was a blessing to get away from my old man. Jackson's a tough town."

"Not as tough as our fathers. Stamp?"

"I think I've outgrown Stag Point beer night."

****

Avery drove the back way out of town on the Snowy Range Road and stopped by the Happy Angler Tackle Shop.

"No, I'm Ben's daughter. I took over the store about five years ago. My mom had MS. We took care of her until she passed. Dad still lives behind the Burrito Bob's if you want to go pound on his door. We're about ready to close. I'll give you a deal on day-old worms."

In the late afternoon, heading toward Centennial, there were more antelope grazing along the fences than cars whizzing by. Avery slowed down before the booming Centennial metropolitan area. The White Shark flipped up a cloud of dust from the Old Stage Stop gravel parking lot, one of two bars in town.

The VW Eurovan was out of place next to the Ramcharger pickup truck with oversized tires that dwarfed three All-Terrain Vehicles parked in front of the rough-hewn log cabin-like establishment.

The patrons downed more than a few cold ones while spinning an equal number of yarns. Avery ordered a bottle of the usual and then walked over to the table of hunters.

"Any luck?"

Avery's locks were tucked under a Devil's Tower trucker's cap.

"Take off that *chapeau* and stay awhile. Are you a hippy or a dippy?"

The tall hunter with the orange down vest kicked a chair away from the table. Avery sat down. "We were scouting. Last year, we had pretty good luck in Area 10. Saw some good signs of elk today. You sure you belong in a rough place like this?"

"I haven't been in here since college, young man. I'm looking for Jack Middleton."

Avery took a swig.

"I'll draw you a map if you deliver him a message. Tell him to 'Go to Hell!' I'm bein' polite in mixed company, hippy-dippy. Barkeep, a round of whiskey, and whatever our new friend wants. Cosmo?"

31

Half Acre Gymnasium

After piecing stories together, how Avery and Jack bonded after randomly meeting is a mystery to me. Jack had a strange way of showing affection. He mixed up stubbornness with perseverance. It wasn't Jack's fault that his dad and Grandma Mary sent him to Wyoming on a Wild Becca Chase. Mom was not interested, but Jack didn't take "no" for an answer. I suppose we're all unavailable in some aspect of our lives. E.S.

******

Avery had grown tired of being a landlord. Managing a three-bedroom house in a college town was a full-time job.

"Bad news and worse news, pal o' mine. My dad won't let me quit MNY and eat his prepayments. Worse news, Becca doesn't like the place," lamented Jack.

"Stay in touch if anything changes."

Meanwhile, Gary was honorably discharged from Vietnam in June 1965. Rather than staying at home to help operate the ranch, over his mother's objection, he adjusted to Wyoming life by enrolling at UW for the fall semester. All incoming first-year students were required to live in the dorms.

"I was in a combat zone for two years, and now I have to live with smart-ass teenagers?"

******

Gary filed an appeal with the Dean of Students. His request to live off-campus was denied. He called around for advice.

"Avery, it's Gary Steiner."

"You're back!"

"My mom gave me this number. I thought you'd be in Jackson."

"Nah, things haven't changed on my home front. What a surprise!"

"Just easing back into civilian life."

"I'm surprised your mom didn't lasso and tie you down in that hay field."

"If she could've, she would've."

"Piedmont cut me some slack. Becca and I came down to Laramie two years ago."

"So, I heard. Here's my problem, I enrolled at UW and need a place to stay. Any ideas?"

"Good timing. I'll have one, maybe two rooms open. It'll be like old times at the ranch."

"Can I stay there until I can get into the dorm?"

"Apply to live off campus. Stay for a while."

"I did. They denied me."

"Did your mom send documentation? Your enrollment papers?"

"Those didn't help. I qualified as a nontraditional student. Not nontraditional enough. Having a kid would have helped."

"Stay at my place until the dorms open."

******

Before Thanksgiving break in 1965, the Half Acre Gym doors opened for 1966 spring class registration. It was a mad rush to get inside and sign up for classes. Becca and Gary waited for their turn in the Political Science Department queue.

"What are you two doing here?"

Jack casually eased his way into the line.

"Gary stopped by. We haven't had time to talk much since he was discharged. I don't need a babysitter, Jackie."

"Quit calling me that. I'm not eight."

"It's only because we're family friends. You can always call me Beckie."

"Sure. I came out to be sure you don't hang around with the wrong people."

"Get over yourself. We're at the head of the line. International Relations is a popular class. I need to get this Poli Sci elective out of the way. Plus, with my schedule, I have to take as many independent study classes since my plan is to go to Germany."

"This is upper-level," Jack 'splained to Gary. "You can't enroll. What do you care?"

"Vietnam is ramping up. I want to learn about the politics around the huge waste of taxpayer dollars. I got permission. I'm a freshman on paper. An old one at that, and a vet."

Gary pulled the exception letter from the department head.

"Hey, thanks for saving me a place." Avery did the "chat and cut" into the line. "We can all study together."

"What would I get out of your wildlife perspective? Ditto for anthropology?" berated Jack.

"Illegal international trafficking of big game animals and their valuable byproducts is high finance, Mr. Capone. Smuggling would be a natural tie-in for you," joked Avery. "Besides, now that we're business partners, it'll be a good way for us to bond."

"And it doesn't sound like you've heard about grave robbers scavenging the tombs of ancient civilizations in Central America? The Anthropology Department is deep into recovering stolen artifacts in Germany. I have a grant deadline coming up to fund my field trip there."

"Who needs a grant? My dad will pay for the whole expedition."

"Some things never change. I suppose you want to tag along and carry my bags?"

Becca was studying the Mountain Shoshone, who once wandered the forests where they hunted mountain sheep with reflex bows made from ram's horns. The bow arms curved away from the archer along the full bow's length.

A unique Shoshone bow covered with gold foil was pillaged during the Indian Wars and traded in 1904 by a Wild Wyoming Show member to the Dresden Natural History Museum in Germany. The Nazis looted the collection during World War II and took any artifact that purportedly had spiritual power. After the War, the relics were recovered from a mountain fortress in Bavaria, except the *Arco de Oro*, the Golden Bow.

******

One Friday afternoon, Becca was in the lab repurposing her upcoming cultural anthropology field trip to meet the International Relations class requirement. The door squeaked open and clunked shut with an echo that bounced off the high ceiling.

"I could have surprised you and climbed through the window." Jack's voice resonated through the spacious laboratory. "Now that we're in the same class, I can keep a close eye on you. Show you my attentive side. I didn't appreciate it when you ditched me after I went off to Princeton."

"I don't have to clear anything with you, Jackie."

"You're not allowed to call me that."

"That's part of our history. You want to relate to me? Accept it. Your manners haven't changed since Sunday school. You could have found out that I went missing. You never asked how my summers went. Even if it dawned on you to be slightly curious, it's none of your business," Becca muttered while deep into her proposal writing. "On the other hand, imagine my surprise when you showed up on campus. I found out from gossip."

"Didn't your mom write to give you my arrival information? 'Talk to Becca,' 'Act like a gentleman.'"

"Communication and acting aren't your strong points. You assume I open all my mail. My mom? I didn't hear from her. As for your mother? I didn't know her. She died too soon and couldn't pass on any semblance of decency to you. Did you forget everything you learned from your Grandfather Jacob? He was an honest man. He was a good influence on me. What happened to your father? What happened to you?"

"Keep my mother out of this. How can you pass me up? I'm courteous. Polite. Turned water into wine. You won't find me using the wrong silverware during dinner. Plus, I'm more like you than you think."

"I bet my mom forgot to mention anything to you about her mission to push Gary away from me. She's overreacting. We're friends!"

"She told me to be sure you're okay and not getting homesick," Jack said, gaslighting Becca with a flimsy excuse.

"Homesick? Give me a break. I'm not the one wanting to revisit all our Cherry Ridge memories. You topped out in kindergarten. I don't know how many times I told you we've been good friends for a long time. Please don't overdo it. Let's not mess that up."

"All right. I came across the country. Quite a risk up to this point, considering you've never formally told me, 'Go away.' This is the most straightforward you've been. Are we making progress?"

"We have one class together. I'm trying to finish my project. Don't you have classwork to complete?"

"Classwork? I came with your mom's blessing to rescue you. She thinks my social graces are a good influence."

"My mother has nothing to say about what I think. If not using a salad fork during the entire meal is your redeeming social quality, I'm not impressed. At least Gary understands my interests. He's a friend. You're a friend. My mission in life is to restore some sense of justice to native people. Gary grounds my idealistic cultural awareness. He comes from a practical world. You come from a world that ticks me off."

"Your roots, Becca. You're above these hicks."

"On the ranch, there's no time for excuses or figuring out how to save face. There's no negotiating when it comes time to bring in the cows. Unlike you, Gary never belittles my choices."

"Free spirits made this country great, except it's not a girl's place to be independent."

"That makes no sense. "Go West, Young Woman, Go West' Becca paraphrased Horace Greeley, the newspaperman who ran for President in 1872.

"I don't have limitations. I remember when my mom forced me to attend your hoity-toity private school dances. Do you know how bad you made me feel when you told everyone about my gown being a hand-me-down bridesmaid dress?"

"I was kidding around! I come to your dusty lab. I've given you Injun items. You must like them because you haven't returned any shattered pottery."

"Lay off. We're talking about the cultures of people. While I'm thinking about it, take that extortion box."

"I support your hobby."

"Hobby? I get it. You're charming. Trying to be helpful. I never know if some servant in white gloves will slap my wrist when I reach for the wrong glass. Being in Wyoming gives my life some meaning. I don't want to be handcuffed in your high society torture chamber. This place gives me freedom with no questions asked. It's the 1960s."

"I have plenty to offer. The good life. Where do you see yourself in five years? Getting dirt under your fingernails? Working for wages slinging hay."

"Thanks for asking. Those are the most personal questions you've ever asked me. For your information, I'm going to graduate school. You will call me Dr. Pembroke. I'll be a starving scientist researching stories based on ancient campsites on my roommate's desolate ranch land."

"I can be vulnerable, open with my emotions."

"Open for you means opening your wallet."

Footsteps reverberated through the room.

"You're here kind of late. I heard voices from my office. Is everything okay?"

"No problems here, Professor Wolfe. My friend was just leaving."

32

The Odd Duo

October 6, 2006—5:15 p.m. MDT: Avery hung around the Old Stage Stop for another drink and exchanged a few tales with the locals before continuing the hunt for Jack. According to the directions scribbled on the back of the cardboard beer coaster, access was off the Snowy Range Road toward Laramie.

"Do I turn toward town or head to the hills?"

So far, so good. A dirt road east of Centennial extended a couple of miles to a fence where the trees began. A cattle guard protected the transitional ponderosa to lodgepole pine forest. The next turn on the map was at a big tree. The trouble was all the trees were giant.

The White Shark rumbled down the road to an open gate. The mailbox on a weathered fence post was labeled "Middleton" scribbled onto a strip of duct tape with a black Magic Marker.

The echo of high-powered rifle gunshots sounded in the distance as the Eurovan dodged crevices in the rain-rutted road. Avery slammed the door and walked on a beaten path through the now amber grasses to the cabin. Jack was shooting at a row of Coors beer cans set up on a makeshift firing range steadied against a hill.

"Still remember what I taught you? You're looking a little less elegant than I remember."

"It was too late to rent a tux." Jack removed his noise-canceling earmuffs. "Get out that .270 of yours and blast a few cans back to the Stone Age."

"Are you the Son of Robinson Crusoe hiding in the middle of no-where these days?"

"Not for long." Jack pointed at the slash piles. "The Forest Service is thinning out the beetle kill over the next few years. You can see the railroad track bed now." Jack tossed Avery an AR15 rifle. "What's your business, good looking?"

"I bet you say that to all your ex-partners. So I don't forget, one of your buddies at the Old Stage had a message for you to 'Go to Hell.'"

"That's nice. He must be mellowing out. I must have a way with jerks. Well, I got a little sideways with a few of the regulars over a poker hand."

"Bad news travels fast, Middleton."

"In the end, I got away with it."

Jack turned back to his target practice. Wisps of dry dirt puffed from bullets splattering into the soft soil.

"You're quite the Wyoming guy now." Avery aimed at the targets. "Pretty good for the low bid. I'm on my way to Colorado. Steiner had one of these with the Blaze Bayonet, remember? He called me the other day."

"What does that mother fucker want? Did he die?"

Jack aimed at a target with a stick figure labeled "Steiner."

"Well, not quite. It was Becca."

"She's been dead to me since the 'rip roarin' barbecue. Yeah, I saw her obit in the paper. I heard someone called the bar looking for me."

"Thought maybe you'd want a change of scenery. It'll be a quick trip. Funeral's tomorrow. I'm the messenger and your chauffeur."

"Look, I don't hate the mother fucker. I've been pissed off at him for the past 40 years. It's been a waste of my brainpower. Worth it, though. Here I am, stuck in fucking Centennial, Wyoming." Jack took the AR15 from Avery. "It's not for hunting."

"Get your stuff. You're the main reason we all agreed to our 'Pact.'"

"Fuck the 'Pact.'" Jack refilled the magazine and lobbed the .30-06. "My AR is too much gun for you."

"How much longer are you going to be irritated, frustrated, and otherwise pissed?" Avery aimed at a tin can and pretended to squeeze off a shot. "'Bang.' If you don't mind me saying, you treated Becca like crap. You tried to get me to do your bidding."

"I counted on you to keep things smooth between Becca and me."

"You counted wrong. I did both of you a favor by staying out of your business."

"Meadows, I did you a solid when I left you to run our business without my meddling."

"You were pretty good with the sewing crew. Your charm paid off, business-wise. Kept the machines humming for two shifts a day."

"Money talks, Meadows. We wouldn't have gotten near the price if it wasn't for your Upward clothing and equipment line."

Jack put down his weapon and headed into the cabin. Avery took some target practice. A few shots and ejected shells later, Jack emerged with an early-model Gucci bag with a broken zipper.

"I was half waiting for you."

"Doesn't that fancy bag have a lifetime guarantee?"

"New and nice aren't my style these days."

"Let's take my two children. No babysitters in the wild. Your Kraut-mobile will be a safe place."

Jack checked to ensure the chambers were empty and placed the two firearms under the foam pad that folded into a mattress.

"Where's your .270? I'll trade you some baseball cards for it. I could use something I can hide."

"You should have let me know two years ago. She was a good one. I now keep a .22 long-round pistol in the glove box."

Jack returned to the cabin and carried out a package.

"Thinning out a few things."

"I see you're still driving that puke green BMW."

Avery loaded Jack's bag and box.

"She's made it 280,000. My goal was to drive the distance to the moon, and I'm still counting. Hans' son took over the garage in Bosler and still fixes my vintage piece of crap. What are you waiting for? Let's go. The 'Pact.' Remember the 'Pact.' The 'Pact' awaits. Must not forget the 'Pact.'"

****

The Odd Duo retraced the bumpy route back to the Snowy Range Road.

"After we sold out, what did your beloved father think about you not going back to run your family business?"

"Fred? He's still kicking. We're barely a family, and it's not a business. He knows his friends take advantage, but my Padre gets personal satisfaction from passing out money. Still jogs a mile every day." They lurked through Centennial. Jack stuck his arm out the window and flipped off the Old Stage Stop as they cruised past. "Hits a few on the range. Not bad for 89. Being a Jersey exile ended up good. Wyoming grew on me."

"Based on what I heard from your pals at the bar, you're a legendary con man."

Avery spotted two deer in the barrow pit and turned on the lights.

"Compared to my dad? I'm no conman. We didn't see things the same after I moved to Wyoming. I lost interest in making money. Over the years, I cut a few corners. Card sharking was a new challenge. How much dough does a guy need?"

Avery eased around a slow-moving stake body truck hauling a horse.

"Your dad was more into using the money to do good."

"He could have at least begged me to come home. Dad bought loyalty, not that there was anything wrong with it."

"... and you didn't? Does 'Connie Morgan' ring a bell?"

"Thanks for the reminder, Pavlov. What can I say? We both came from money. Connie was a good backup plan. I wonder if she's still a good kisser. I saw her a few times after the big falling out. Summer of '67?"

"How could I forget? I spent the night at the ER."

"What are you talking about? It was like four stairs. Being a nurse-maid doesn't count. If it makes you feel any better, not a day goes by that I don't think about that barbecue."

"Do you want to drive by the Calamity Club? Remember the good times?"

33

Libby Flats

Avery and Jack were better acquainted with Mom because of their parallel histories. They each knew different sides of her. She was quietly confident and didn't let on about her intelligence. Nor did she shed her unflappable East Coast ways. Mom surprised everyone by removing her "perfect student" mask and could have too much fun with the best of them. When I left the corporate world, the difference between my real jobs and working for myself was no longer having to put on a pretense. E.S.

****

Jack couldn't have picked a worse time to drop in to bother Becca in the lab. On top of grant writing, field trip preparation, and her International Relations class project, she had been studying for a laboratory practical test about identifying arrowhead fragments.

"Look, why don't you come with us tonight? You want to blend in? We're going to the Stag Point later. It's pitcher night. No cover for girls, and we get half-price drinks," Becca suggested.

"What could go wrong? If you invited Steiner, no talk about his goddamn Navy Cross," warned Jack.

"Despite what you think, Gary, Avery, and you are my main support system. There's not much to do here on Friday besides studying and 'The Stag.' It'll be your initiation."

"Right."

"Come to the front of Ross Hall. We'll walk downtown around seven."

Jack was happy about the invitation and took off. Becca packed up after the coast was clear.

"Thanks, Professor Wolfe. I'll make an appointment to discuss the Dresden grant next week."

******

Becca headed back to Ross Hall to relax before the evening events. Jack was the first to arrive a little before 7 p.m.

"You look nice, Becca. 'Pitcher Night' must be a formal event around here. Did you get your project finished?"

"I still have some 'Ts' to cross. Some *umlauts* to place. I'll finish up tomorrow. It has to be postmarked on Monday."

Becca and Jack waited outside the dorm.

"Don't have too much fun if you're working, what, on a Saturday morning?"

Avery walked up and gave Becca and Jack a group hug. Gary approached them from up the street.

Becca exchanged small talk about nightlife in Laramie on their stroll to the bar. They stood in line for a few minutes before each readied to pay the $2.00 cover.

"I got this."

Jack jumped ahead to pay for everyone. Becca pulled two dollars from the bouncer and handed them back to Jack. She forked over her money. The quarrel ended with Avery and Gary stuffing their cash into Jack's shirt pocket.

There was an empty booth by the window across from the bar. Becca had the window seat when Jack moved in next to her.

"Change me places in case I have an emergency."

Jack obliged as the server arrived at the table.

"I'm Gretchen. Hey, Avery. Did you finish your mammalogy lab? It's a real bear."

"Good one! Do they let you wear that in here?" Avery asked about the T-shirt from the Rainbow River Bar, her family's business.

"Nobody's supposed to notice! Dad's always trying to get the word out." Gretchen buttoned up her Nordic shrunken wool sweater halfway to cover the competitor's logo.

"I think you know these two. Gretchen, meet Jack. He came out here from New Jersey."

"Are you running from something? Nobody transfers to Wyoming from New Jersey on purpose. No white after Labor Day."

She noticed Jack's out-of-season slacks.

"Becca and I come from the same town in Jersey. She convinced me to make the big move."

Jack tried to put his arm around her as Becca shoved him away with a smirk.

"Our parents are friends. They think I need a guard dog!" Becca gave a canine snarl.

The four reached for their identification cards.

"It's okay. I know Avery. You're all good. What can I get you, a pitcher, four glasses?"

The table nodded in agreement, except Jack.

"Make it three. I'll have a dirty Bombay Martini. Three olives."

Jack pantomimed that he wanted his drink stirred, not shaken.

"The polo shirt. I pegged you as a bourbon man." Gretchen gave Jack a wink. "No Bombay. Beefeaters."

"If you let me leave my Sapphire behind the bar, I'll be a Stag Point patron for life. When do you get off?"

"You better clear it with your girlfriend. One pitcher. A dirty Beefeaters. Three olives," she repeated back.

Gretchen reached the bar and pointed at Jack. The bartender grinned and shook up his drink. They finished their pitcher, and Jack downed the last sip of his cocktail.

"Another round?"

Gretchen picked up the pitcher and wiped the table.

"I think I'm about done," Becca yelled, covering her ears.

The evening was young. There was more than enough tip money on the table.

"Anyone else ready to go?" The Stag was elbow-to-elbow when the ear-piercing rock and roll band fired up at 9:00 p.m. "I'm getting claustrophobic."

Becca took her last gulp.

"Anything else?" Gretchen stopped at the table one more time. "You should stick around. The music's pretty good. You know Lucas Long from Pinedale? It's his band, the Barn Doors. He thinks he's a country-western Jim Morgenson."

"I don't know if I can handle Luke twirling his T-shirt and letting it fly into the crowd. How about those farmer sunburn lines? We may be back a little later," Becca screamed over the chatter.

"Remember to get stamped on the way out."

Gretchen wiped down the table for the next crowd.

"How about we take Jackie here on a 'Libby Run!'"

"You're ticking me off on purpose."

"Oh, get over it. Remember our 'Jackie - Beckie game?'"

Becca scooted her way out first. They stopped at the door so that the bouncer could stamp their wrists. Jack rolled his eyes.

"'Libby Run'? Is this the cowboy version of a snipe hunt?"

"If you're going to hang around with us, there's a place in the Snowy Range. You'll like the drive. Plenty of light left. There's a band at the Old Stage Stop. Let's go to Libby Flats, then see what happens. The journey is more important than the destination."

Gary got behind the wheel. Avery rode shotgun. Becca and Jack sat in the back. Twilight moved across the valley. They made the 45-minute haul to Centennial, then up the mountain to the Libby Flats Observation Point, named for a 19th-century prospector named George Libby.

Becca was the first one out. She charged up the stone steps to the elevated deck. The prominent southern silhouette of the Colorado Rocky Mountains was breathtaking as the stars became lighted pin-holes on the darkening horizon.

"I'll make it up Longs Peak one of these days," Becca sighed as she gazed at the majestic southern mountain range in Colorado.

Gary and Avery walked below the observation deck and plotted a climbing route up the native stone wall. They scrambled up before pulling themselves over the platform railing. Jack was the last one to the top. He huffed and puffed because the elevation was 10,344 feet higher than Cherry Ridge, New Jersey.

"What a view. The fresh air is invigorating. Are you okay in those loafers? Where are your Red Wings!"

Jack panted as he leaned on the stone wall, reached into his wallet, and pulled out a flattened cannabis joint.

"Anyone need a pick-me-up? Some Rhode Island Red? Big city kids are good for something." Jack reached into his pocket for his sterling silver Ronson lighter with the Princeton coat of arms emblazoned on the side and toked up. "Stick with me. We, Middletons, are connected. My uncle was a bootlegger."

"So this is it? Getting loaded at Libby Flats? All cultures have cere-monies. Our little group is a culture. We need a ritual, something to keep us bound together. A secret pact."

34

Tak Fujiyama

October 6, 2006—6:32 p.m. MDT: Once Avery guided the White Shark back on the smooth pavement toward Laramie, the drive wasn't far to the I-80 exit and the Prairie Schooner Truck Center.

"We're stopping here because ..."

Jack fidgeted in his seat.

"Fuji's."

Avery pulled into the massive parking area and stopped by a gas pump.

"Yeah, I know. Tak Fujiyama's place downtown. I was a regular."

"Too bad. I've had my heart and stomach set on some Japanese since I left the B&B. No *sukiyaki* in Sundance. We won't stay long. You have to be more presentable, Mr. Pig Pen."

They pulled forward and went inside.

"Here's for the gas on '3' and a shower for this dusty dude."

The clerk rang up the sale and handed Jack a towel.

"Toss it in the hamper by the door."

The *Trucker's Guide to America* rated the Prairie Schooner showers five stars because of amenities like shampoo, conditioner, and body wash dispensers in each shower stall.

The Odd Duo headed to the shopping area. Truck stops stocked a little of everything for the bleary-eyed late-night traveler, including clothing racks for all seasons.

"Pick out something nice. Meet me in the café when you're presentable."

While Jack cleaned up, Avery waited in the food line and perused the menu taped to the counter. Along with short order truckstop food like chicken fried steaks and hamburgers, the fare included *sukiyaki*, egg foo young, pork noodles, and chow mein.

"Avery Meadows," Tak bellowed out through the service window with a big grin.

"Go Pokes!" Avery noticed Tak's braid threaded through the back of a brown baseball with a gold bucking bronco embroidered on the crown.

"Laramie Mountaineering makes hats now. The Cowboys are my 'noodles and broth' in the fall and winter."

"What's up with the pickle jar by the register? Your part-time job?"

"In honor of my sister, Keshi."

"I remember that story."

"Every year, I put out the jar for my ceremony fund. We drive to Colorado for a remembrance every Memorial Day."

On his way out to greet Avery, a customer stopped Tak.

"Yes, we're open for breakfast here and downtown. We have rice or potatoes. If you want your eggs Hawaiian style, we have SPAM. Sorry about that."

"It must be busy running two businesses," observed Avery.

"We have a good crew. So far, nobody is stealing from me. I spend most of the time at our downtown place. Laramie Mountaineering is still booming across the street from us. You know Casey? Promoted to Production Manager. We catered a party last week."

"I'll try to stop by on my way back. You've done pretty well for yourself, Tak. Maybe a month ago, I saw your café on one of those morning variety shows."

"We took a chance and expanded out here in 2004 when the Cajun place went out. So far, so good. That TV segment was amazing for business."

"I'll try the *Sukiyaki* Bowl, 'As Seen on TV.'"

Avery's arms spanned across in grandeur.

"'Number 2'!" Tak yelled to the assistant manager, who took over for him at the grill.

"Your Devil's Tower place isn't exactly a two-star dive."

"Not a Michelin rating. We're tops with Goodyear."

"What about your partner, Jack Middleton? He went off the edge there after graduation."

"When we sold out, I bought the B&B. Jack? I dredged him up in the woods by Centennial. You remember Becca Pembroke from school? She passed the other day."

"I heard. My granddaughter had her for a class."

"We're going down for her funeral. Can you add a 'Number 4?'"

"... and a 'Number 4!'" Tak was distracted by a patron. "Napkins and stuff are over there."

"If you can get away, it's tomorrow afternoon."

"Can't make it. Pokes are in Albuquerque. We have a TV for road games. Older fans prefer our place. Not many students. I don't know if you've met my wife, Jennifer." She acknowledged with a wave after hearing her name as she rang up the customer in front of Avery. "How's Gary taking it?"

"I think okay. He's the stoic type. Can you keep Jack's food warm until he gets out of the shower?"

Avery handed Jennifer some cash for the food.

"Nah, Nah, your money's no good here."

Tak motioned for Avery to move out of the line.

"Come up to the B&B. My treat."

Avery retrieved a sleeve of disposal chopsticks and a mustard pack from the condiment table. Meanwhile, Jack picked out a pair of trousers, a flannel shirt, socks, and underwear in the truck stop store.

"Sorry, we don't take Platinum or Gold."

Jack piled his merchandise on the counter and pinched his thumb and index finger together in front of the clerk's face.

"Cinco minutos."

Jack wandered into the restaurant. The clerk moved his clothes aside.

"I need some help over here. Please."

Avery was frustrated by the familiar request, rested the chopsticks on the edge of the thick paper bowl, followed Jack to the checkout clerk, and paid.

"I owe you," Jack said as he toted his new outfit to the showers.

A few minutes later, stroking back his damp hair, the lumberjack in sneakers entered the restaurant. Avery pointed at the service window. Jennifer fetched Jack's meal.

"Hello, Takehiro. How's business? I thought you'd be retired by now." Jack asked on his way to the line.

"Can't afford to stop. I've been catching up since my Dad brought us to Laramie."

"You haven't stopped downtown to see us lately."

"I started doing more banking by telephone. I'm not much for curious people."

"Is my lot in life to always dress you for every occasion?"

Avery pushed a yellow packet across the table.

"Smells good."

Jack unwrapped his sandwich and squished the mustard out on the bottom part of the bun. Tak walked over to their table on his way back to the kitchen.

"It was good seeing you two. Looks to me like you could use one of these, Jack," Tak unfurled a pink T-shirt.

"Thanks. I'll wear it in good health."

"Give my regards to Gary."

"We'll be through at least one more time before it's all said and done. I've heard rave reviews about your Tiki Burger. I talked to a food critic in Wheatland who said it's the best in Albany County."

"You know, the pineapple makes the sandwich." Jack straightened out the slice. "Remember when I first came to town and saw Fuji's?

You took me to Laramie Hardware that time. Geezuss, what was I thinking?"

"Good question." Avery popped three fries from Jack's plate into his mouth. "Pretty good. Hot and not too greasy."

Jack chomped down.

35

The Calamity Club

Blame the Vietnam War for the Odd Trio living in the same house. When Dad was discharged, staying at the ranch didn't make much sense. Disregarding Grandma Sally's wishes, he went AWOL to avoid being drafted into ranch duty. UW was a logical choice since the Veterans Administration paid his tuition, books, and housing. Wyoming was, and still is, a land of opportunity and a good safety net for anyone expanding their horizons or starting out fresh. As for me, moving back home was the last place on my list, but I'm always amazed at what happens when I let life play out. E.S.

****

It was just before spring break in 1966. After International Relations, Avery, Jack, and Gary had cut classes for the rest of the day to shoot a few racks of eight ball during The Stag Point "Hump Day Happy Hour" from 3 to 6 on Wednesdays.

Avery lined up a shot on the eight that nicked the 15.

"My rent goes up 10 percent on July 1st. That won't mean much to 'Deep Pockets Middleton.' Is it worth it? I'll kick out my two housemates. Then move in together?"

Jack chalked up and figured out a shot.

"Makes sense. I don't know what the frat does with my dues money. It's not for cleaning the carpets. I'm about done stepping on Risk game pieces in every room. You're making me run the table, Meadows."

Jack scratched. Gary placed the cue ball, aimed at the six, and pointed his stick at the left corner pocket.

"You think dirty carpets are bad? I get buckets of cold water poured on me when I'm in the shower. Moving in together is a great idea." Gary made a defensive shot and hid the cue ball behind the two. "Better yet, I have this benefit from the Navy. The G.I. Bill. I get a guaranteed loan to buy a house. There's a new development going up east of town. If there's a down payment, it won't be much," he said as the ball rattled around the pocket.

Avery squeezed the cue ball between the two and eleven and nicked the eight into the left side.

"Nice shot. Our housing is paid until the end of the school year. The mortgage payment will be less than rent," explained Gary. "We have some time to get this figured out. I can get a contract together. If one of us moves, the buyout could include our down payment and a percent of each month's house payment. Avery? Jack? We can't miss, right? I graduate next year and have my job at the paper."

"I don't plan on going anyplace. Wyoming Wildlife offered me a job if the Laramie Hardware deal doesn't work out. If I leave, it would be to help my parents in Jackson. I'd be stuck there forever. Count me in."

"The MNY house is finally kicking this freeloader out. It doesn't matter where, but Becca will be moving in with me. Since you're not moving to Jackson, you owe me. Our deal will work out. I didn't back the purchase of our business for nothing. Part of your job description is to be Becca's soft shoulder."

"That's extortion. You sound like your dad!"

"She's planning on grad school, so there's no sense in me returning to Jersey. Fair warning. I'll be the first you'll have to buy out. Start putting cash aside. I'll take the biggest bedroom."

"We're all in? Settled."

The three placed their hands on top of one another like breaking a football huddle.

"The 'Odd Trio,'" Jack proclaimed. The other two were perplexed. "You know the *Odd Couple* Broadway play about two mismatched roommates? We're three!"

"Because our house has military roots? We're now on a last-name basis. Steiner, Gary. Middleton, Jack. Meadows, Avery. Reporting for duty!"

Gary arranged with his Lander bank for the three of them to buy, as tenants in common, a brand-new three-bedroom, split-level house with an oversized two-car garage and an unfinished basement. Their place had a great location in an up-and-coming subdivision named after tamers of the Wyoming frontier.

****

The sale closed in May before school let out. The Odd Trio packed up and began their moves one load at a time. The house address was 3003 Calamity Street, named after Calamity Jane. There was Buffalo Bill Circle and Wild Bill Hickok Court.

Avery pulled the Silver Steed into the driveway.

"Howdy, neighbor. Eugene Billingsley. You can call me Gene." The tall, gray-haired gentleman stuck his hand through the driver's side window.

"Didn't you used to be the Registrar?"

"Been retired for two years. That was my job since before the War, World War II, that is." His gardening shirt was pressed, and his work pants creased. "How does your family like the neighborhood? The school in the next block is pretty new, too. This block is the first one to be built out."

"Meadows, Avery Meadows, from Jackson. We're still living out of boxes. None of us are married. No kids to trample your nice lawn."

"Did you check with the city? There are rules about how many unrelated people can live in one house," Gene warned. "This neighborhood was planned to be a quiet one. We blocked an apartment four-plex on the end of the street the city council wanted to build."

"I appreciate your concern, Mr. Billingsley. Our realtor made sure everything was okay. We don't take up much space." Avery glanced at the RV in Mr. Billingsley's side yard and the boat parked in the driveway. "We call ourselves the Odd Trio."

Avery fetched the brown and gold UW Cowboys flag from the Silver Steed. The standard fluttered in the breeze.

"We dubbed our house 'The Calamity Club.' We're all Pokes' fans." Avery laid claim by tapping the side of the house with the flagstaff and jamming the pole into the ground against the porch enclosure. "We're one happy commune and support the Chamber of Commerce."

"You know, things are pretty quiet around here. The loudest noise here on the weekend is from lawnmowers. You planning on putting in a yard? Too bad these places didn't come with sod."

Gene walked over to the outdoor water spigot and picked up his green garden hose.

"Have you heard of 'dry land farming'? We're planting wheatgrass and native flowers to hold the soil. Not much water needed. Rather than decorative greenery, I'm thinking vegetables."

"No hippie tomatoes in the front yards. You don't want to stand out around here. Are you a house of pot-smoking beatniks?"

"Gary writes for the paper. Jack and I bought Laramie Hardware. We're members of the Chamber of Commerce."

"We like our Kentucky bluegrass. The city has rules on how high the weeds can get."

"The great thing about wheatgrass? You can't smoke it."

"The neighborhood wants you to blend into our subdivision."

"Don't worry. The wildflowers are quite showy. If we plant the right species, there will be blooms year-round." Avery picked a white aster daisy and poked the stem into the end of Gene's hose. "We want to fit into the neighborhood. You'll always get invited to our parties."

"Come the first week in December, the neighbors put up Christmas lights. Let me know if you need any starter strands." Gene removed the flower, opened the water valve, and adjusted his thumb on the end of the hose to provide a gentle spray over his potted geraniums. "There's a neighborhood supply if you're too broke to buy your own."

"You're a mighty good neighbor, Mr. Billingsley."

Avery picked up a crate out of the Silver Steed.

"It's 'Gene.' You can call me Gene."

Mr. Billingsley shot an arc of water onto the sidewalk to wash a few grass clippings off the driveway.

"I still have trouble calling grownups by their first name, Mr. Billingsley."

Avery balanced two stacked boxes and carried them into the new house.

****

The Odd Trio settled into the new digs after several loads. The neighbors were the least of their worries. Sitting next to each other in class and sipping beers at the Stag Point wasn't the same as arguing in the living room about who would get the main bedroom with a three-quarter bath.

"I've never known either of you to go out on any dates. I came out here to save Becca from the hazards of the Wild Frontier and the likes of you two!"

"Becca works for my mom. She's off limits for me."

"Not my type," responded Avery.

Joining the Calamity Club wasn't a high priority on Becca's list. During the summers, her department arranged for her to travel with an archaeological dig crew to faraway places where she was accustomed to sleeping on the ground.

****

Becca liked the dorms because she got along well with her Ross Hall roommate, Connie. The two hit it off in a geology class. Geology was an elective for Becca. She figured it would be helpful for her to learn how to determine the ages of the historic and prehistoric cultures she investigated.

Connie was a geology major, a practical field of study for her. She wanted to manage the black gold pumped from underneath the ranch pastures rather than learn about animal husbandry.

"Becca, you're still coming home with me over Christmas? I'll show you some teepee rings on our land. There's also a ravine filled with bones. There's no telling what you'll find down there. Besides, we can get to know each other better. My parents are country clubbers. My circle was very cliquey. I didn't have many friends growing up."

"My dad's a preacher. I'm supposed to act 'proper.' My friends were all from the church. Let's get our hands dirty. Professor Wolfe might be interested. Getting permission to go onto private land for fieldwork is a problem."

"Don't worry. My parents are big donors to UW. They like the exposure from good projects," Connie assured. "I'll explain to them you roamed around the Steiner Ranch before college and might dig up a *Tyrannosaurus*."

"You know the Steiners?"

"I know of the Steiners. It's the Wyoming Underground Telegraph. They run those big white Charolais. My folks drove over to the Cattlemen's meeting in Lander last summer. I've never been. They raved about the spread they put out."

"I was there, too, and helped Sally, er, Mrs. Steiner, with the cooking. We're a pretty good kitchen team."

"I hear you and Gary are also a pretty good team. There are rumors around campus."

"Gary? We worked together. He helps out his mom. I like him. He has a quiet side. Very accommodating. Maybe too accommodating."

"Jack's from New Jersey. He's in my Econ class. Says you two are an item."

"Jackie? We're childhood church friends. I didn't know he was coming to Laramie until I got an underground telegram."

"What's with the 'Jackie?'"

"We had a Sunday school game. I was Beckie. There was Johnnie, Frannie, and Jackie. He mostly didn't like it because of Jackie Robinson. Couldn't stand him."

"Seems kind of drastic for a wealthy young man about New Jersey to drop out of Princeton and move to Wyoming."

"That would be Jackie's problem."

"Oh, so he's available?" Connie's eyes lit up.

"That would be your problem. Don't say I didn't tell you so. He's the kind of guy who could get you in trouble. He's a sneak."

36

Deputy Maddox

October 6, 2006—8:45 p.m. MDT: The Prairie Schooner Truck Center hopped nonstop for 24 hours. When they left the restaurant, orangish sodium vapor lights reflected off the windshields and chrome in the parking lot.

On the way out, Avery pulled up at a gas pump and sponged off the headlights gunked up with mosquito parts from the drive through Sybille Canyon. There wasn't much traffic when they pulled onto I-80 East and got off at the 3rd Street exit to U.S. 287 South toward Fort Collins.

"Two hours to Boulder should be a cruise this time of night."

The journey was smooth until Tie Siding. The speed limit dropped to 45 for a half-mile when the White Shark cruised through.

"Damnit. Grab the 2006 envelope."

Avery was disappointed by the reflection in the rearview mirror. Jack rummaged through binoculars, a first aid kit, and a handgun in the glove box.

"Put my little friend under everything ... and be sure it latches."

A Sheriff's white-over-brown cruiser appeared out of the darkness, with lights flashing. Avery pulled over and powered down the window.

"I clocked you at 68 in a 45."

"I was just going with the traffic."

The Deputy checked his watch.

"This time of night, you are the traffic."

"What about the pickup that flew by like a bat out of hell? This isn't a hippie van, Deputy L. Maddox," Avery read on the brass nameplate.

"License, registration, proof of insurance. As hard as I try, I don't catch every fish, either. Where you headed?"

"Boulder. For a funeral. We had dinner over at the Schooner."

The Deputy shuffled through Avery's information.

"Have you been drinking? Drowning your sorrows?"

"Fuji's doesn't have a bar."

"Fuji's? Good food. I like the Tiki Burger." Deputy Maddox shined a light around the Eurovan and stopped on Jack.

"Gotta go Tiki. Best in Albany County. I know the owner. Takehiro went to UW with us."

Jack wore a forced grin.

"Any beer back there?"

Jack squeezed behind the two front swivel seats and opened the empty fridge and the cupboard next to the sink.

"We had on our seat belts. Do we get a discount?"

"You look familiar."

"I haven't been anywhere near the county jail," pleaded Jack.

"Stay put."

The Deputy walked back to the cruiser and returned with the completed paperwork.

"Your pal's right. $10 off for wearing your seat belts. How long have you lived in Crook County? I see you moved out of Gillette five years ago. The state law says you must register your car where you live. Those '17' county tags are technically expired."

"I could use a new set of plates after that coyote in Sybille. I'll get right on it."

"You hit an animal? The law says to notify Wyoming Wildlife. There's an office right there in the canyon." Deputy Maddox ripped out the citation. "Here's your court date if you want to appear, or you can send your money to this address. Any questions?"

Jack leaned over toward the driver's side.

"Do you accept Platinum or Gold?"

"We don't. You can enter your Visa or Mastercard here. Mail it or call the office. Next time I see Tak, I'll mention I stopped you."

The Deputy made a U-turn and headed back toward Laramie.

"Remember, we have my darlings in the back there. Drive the limit, no probable cause!"

"... and don't go flinging things around from the glove box, Middleton."

"The same cop arrested me at the Old Stage for being drunk and disorderly. It cost me fifty to get out of that same cruiser."

"Jacks or better?"

****

Jack had become a mysterious recluse around Albany County. When Laramie Mountaineering sold, Jack didn't need the money and messed around Centennial.

His hang-out was the Old Stage Stop. Jack bought a round of drinks for the house, ranging from 10 to 50 patrons depending on the weather and the success of any number of elk hunts.

The weekly Old Stage poker game required a pair of "Jacks or better" to open. The stakes were friendly, with a $2 betting limit.

One late night, three players around the table passed. Jack opened with a $50 bet.

"Hey, can he do that?"

The bartender walked around to the table and was surprised to see Ulysses S. Grant staring up at the dealer.

"He can bet what he wants if the table allows it."

The players agreed to let Jack's bet stand. The wagering continued with the next player tossing in $50 and another $50. The others folded.

"Three for me." Jack contemplated and lowered his Ridge Country Club golf cap bill to shade his eyes. He added a $100 bill to the pot. The remaining player straightened his cards while staring across the table, then matched the $100 and raised it by $50.

Jack saw his $50 and raised $100. His opponent folded and showed two Queens and the Ace of Spades. While raking in his take, one of the suspicious losers turned over Jack's hand.

"Three 10s? You didn't have openers! How many hands have you been cheating?"

"Just lucky, I guess."

Jack stood up. The other players crowded around.

"Leave the money and go," advised the bartender.

"How about you ask me to stay? I leave on my terms."

Jack pulled a hunting knife from his belt sheath and jabbed it into the mess of cards.

"Don't need any trouble. Last call was an hour ago, but you're welcome to play another hand."

"Thanks for the games. I believe I'll be on my way."

Jack retrieved his blade. He was mobbed and sprawled on the floor. Leaving his ill-gotten gains on the table didn't heal the scars of his indiscretions.

******

Since then, Jack didn't show his face much around the Old Stage Stop, except once.

"A few days later, I went back to see if the barkeep would at least give me my ante back. It was my money! Turned out he wasn't around, so I helped myself to the cash box in the office. I recovered it fair and square."

"You're 'Reverse Robin Hood,' steal from the not-so-rich and give to yourself."

Avery checked both ways before pulling onto the road. In Wyoming, semi-trucks appear out of nowhere.

"No probable cause. The AR is a little doctored up. No speeding or mention of dead animals!"

"Great. Breaking and entering, a machine gun, and grand theft."

Avery set the cruise control at 71.

37

Mountaineering School

It was no surprise that Jack and Avery befriended each other. The two didn't miss a beat when they reunited in Centennial on their way to the Boulder. Both were gregarious and shared broad views of the world. That was also why Avery and I clicked during our short time together. Jackson wasn't the biggest town in Wyoming, but the most diverse. Avery hung around the internationally known Piedmont-Carlsen Mountaineering School in nearby Wilson. E.S.

****

Avery met people from all over the world. Being near Grand Teton and Yellowstone national parks, the local economic base revolved around year-long tourism. The Civilian Conservation Corps constructed Snow King Mountain on the outskirts of Jackson during the Great Depression in 1936.

A rope tow first hoisted skiers up the mountain. Avery took to the outdoors as a kindergartener and learned to ski the year an ore car from Colorado's 19th-century gold-mining days was adapted and installed as the area's first chairlift.

The temperate summers and resplendent landscapes attracted the most visitors to Jackson. Avery had finished 9th grade at Moran Junior High School in June. Weather-worn, craggy-looking mountaineering pioneers Joseph Carlsen and Arnold Piedmont needed help when their climbing parties went out and returned from their namesake mountaineering school excursions based in Wilson.

"You're a good kid," a climbing student complimented Avery in an Australian accent. "For a youngster, you act like you run the place."

"Just doing my job. All is good. Everything is here. You have to trust total strangers. Once in a while, a student will take a carabiner as a souvenir."

"You mean one of these?" The Aussie unclipped an aluminum oval from his belt loop. "You remind me of my sib in Sydney when we were young."

"You're a ways from home."

"13,000 kilometers."

"Come back next year. It's a safe way to take a vacation."

A pesky lad flipped the heater switch off and on. Then, the lights in the dingy warehouse flickered. Seconds later, the room went dark.

"Quit goofing around. I let you hang around here if you don't get me in trouble!"

"Want to help?" Avery asked the bored student.

"After you."

Avery grabbed a flashlight to guide their walk through the stacks of backpacks, tents, and random outdoor junk. The beam illuminated the fuse box when they arrived at the utility room.

"Too much on this circuit." Avery shut off the main power. "See here? This is a 20-amp fuse for the fan circuit. The heater and fan overloaded it. The heater is 50 amp. I don't know why the two are wired together. You pop this thing out. Replace it with the same kind."

"Who knew I'd learn something useful? I just graduated from university with no practical skills and schooled by a teenager." They returned to the front room when the commotion died down. "I wouldn't be here except my office paid for this field trip to come out here to get to know each other better."

"Only Wyoming? Have you been to other places?"

"We started in San Francisco and climbed in Yosemite National Park. Now here. I don't look forward to the long bus trip to Arizona. We're floating the Grand Canyon. Back to LA and then home."

"What about Yellowstone?" asked Avery.

"That's tomorrow."

"I wish I could do this all the time. School gets in the way."

"You never know. Put yourself in good situations."

The student handed Avery ten bucks and his assistant a dollar.

****

Everyone else who finished the course had checked in. Avery helped Arnie Piedmont inventory the equipment in the school's storage room.

"Thanks for trouble-shooting the lights. You must have learned something around here."

"I pay more attention than you think. I learned by helping out at our hotel."

"Have you ever wanted to get out of Jackson? See the world?"

"It hadn't crossed my mind." Deep down, Avery was eager for a change of scenery. "Eleven Optimus stoves in their boxes."

"Eleven Optimus stoves." Piedmont verified the count on his list. "I'm setting up some classes in Lander later in the summer. Would you want to help out there?"

"I'll have to ask my parents." Avery showed little emotion.

"I already cleared it with them. Your dad was more than happy. He's letting you drive his VW camper."

"You have no idea how good this is."

"I have a warehouse with an apartment where you'll be staying. You'll be on your own."

"I didn't spend all my spare time at your school because I wanted a job. I'm barely old enough to drive!"

"It's none of my business. Your dad hinted about wanting you out of the house. All that aside, you're a loyal team player. I need a perfection-ist, detail-oriented, not distracted by rowdy guys. I don't get along with too many people right off."

"Consider me your newest mountaineer."

38

Ben Roberts

October 6, 2006—9:31 p.m. MDT: It was late by the time the Odd Duo navigated the White Shark across the state line into Colorado. Compared to the previous 50 miles, it was an uneventful drive south to Fort Collins.

The full moon occurred early this October and illuminated the clear Friday night sky, which was good since the road wasn't very well lit by the swabbed-off Eurovan incandescent headlights.

"Bummer about the speeding ticket." Jack kept an eye out the passenger window for any critters lurking in the shadows. "I'll take care of it. You got dinner. These threads."

"My rule of the road? Whoever drives gets to pay. At this rate, we'll be stuck in the Shark forever until we get it right."

"Very karmic. I'm bummed, too. As much time as we've spent traveling around over the years, I'll be your copilot. This is a blast from the past! I won't charge you a thing." Jack slapped Avery on the shoulder. "You should be honored to have me as company. Your extra set of eyes."

"You the 'hermit,' or you the 'life of the party?'"

"Me the enigma."

Avery turned on the radio and settled on the Northern Colorado Community Radio and the "Western Twilight" show. Jack turned up the sound.

"I like the Barnstormers. Didn't know about this kind of music before moving to Laramie. Wyoming does something to people. At least to me, it did." Remember when I first moved to Laramie? We met your buddy Ben Roberts?"

"Like it was yesterday."

Jack put on the pair of aviator sunglasses with tags.

"I need to drop these off. We could stop when we're through Laramie again, you know, for the 'Pact.'"

"I didn't think you felt guilty about anything."

"I may be a cheat, but I'm a man of my word."

"On my way to find you, I stopped by. The Happy Angler is still there. Ben's daughter owns it now."

"I was surprised you took me fishing the first time. All I got was a pair of boots that were too small."

"It was noble. Becca was impressed with your effort to become more rugged. The string of trout was a good touch."

"I was trying."

"When I first met her, I knew she was something else. One time, we dropped off supplies for one of my mountaineering expeditions. Becca drove the Scout back to the main house and hit a big rut. Flat tire. She crawls underneath. Unbolts the spare. Jacks it up. 'Your job is to be sure the rig doesn't fall over on me,' she says. A one-woman Indy 500 pit crew, that Becca."

"Watch it through here." Jack looked ahead to a stand of trees on a blind curve. Avery slowed down at the LaPorte exit and took another side road.

"This late, we should be good."

"There's Stan's Steak Shack. How about a beer?"

"Ha, DUI? Speeding ticket? Contraband? I think we won't and say we did."

Most nights, the LaPorte Road was quiet. October 6th was the big high school game between Fort Collins and Poudre Valley. The in-town rivals squared off against each other at the CSU football stadium. Cars full of celebratory fans flowed out of the parking lot following the 28-7 victory by the Lambkins.

"So much for this shortcut."

The White Shark was stopped in a line of cars. Jack fidgeted and ready to get out of the Eurovan.

"We should have gone for a beer."

Traffic was slow-moving through Fort Collins until the Eurovan popped out from the traffic jam on the south end of town. Avery chose another shortcut past the car dealerships and ended up on Colorado Highway 66 west to Lyons, then south on U.S. 36.

"There's a marijuana store. Want to browse around? I'm ready for a break."

"I'm pretty sure they don't accept Platinum. Besides, it's medical. Neither of us has a card. Another reason for you to make up with Steiner."

****

The Boulder nightline glowed on the horizon. The GPS Street Pilot guided them to their North Boulder destination. They pulled up to the loading zone parking spot.

"Behave yourself, Middleton."

Avery pounded on the front door. There was no answer. The Odd Duo followed the music and reveling crowd noise that filled the air on their way to the back of the condo complex. The sounds of the party echoed down the street.

"I'll be good. I hope Steiner got rid of his Blaze Blade. I'm leaving my kiddos covered up in the van."

Avery led the way to the courtyard full of neighbors visiting and imbibing. An iPod Hi-Fi stereo speaker blared from a window over-looking the courtyard. A hand-painted sign hung from the balcony, "Long Live Becca!"

39

The Paintbrush Room

When the Odd Trio met up at the full moon celebration, the reunion picked up where it left off in 1967. The three got along reasonably well when they first moved in together. "Three peas in a pod" was an apt cliché. Mild-mannered Dad was at the pea pod stem end, Conniving Jack at the tapered pod point. Avery was in the middle, keeping the other two from mangling each other. Jack mellowed out but couldn't get his crush on Mom out of his head. E.S.

****

July 24th, the Odd Trio had been watching the final round of the 1967 PGA Championship golf tournament at the Columbine Country Club in Denver.

"That was amazing," Jack said as Don January waved at the appreciative crowd after winning an 18-hole playoff over Don Massingill. "Do you play, Meadows?"

"I would have. I'm left-handed. Can't find clubs."

"They're out there. Bob Charles is a leftie. He won the British Open in '63."

"Bob Charles?"

"He's a Kiwi."

"Kiwi? Like the fruit?"

"I thought you were the wildlife biologist. You know, Kiwis? The New Zealand national bird? How do you know about kiwi fruit?"

"Jackson is a very global town. One of the Chinese restaurants has them on the menu. How do you know so much about golf?"

During the commercial, Gary changed the channel to *Bachelor's Choice*.

"My dad got me a summer job caddying at his club. I didn't play much. Being around the game, I was pretty good at reading greens. It was about all I had in common with the arrogant SOB."

"You're a chip off the old block," Gary uttered on his way to the kitchen.

"How about another beer? Get one for yourself while you're up," Jack commanded.

"Okay, Bachelor Number 3, what kind of beer would you bring me on our first date?" Gary hollered, mimicking the show host out of earshot in the kitchen.

"Coors!"

He tucked the wall phone handset between his ear and shoulder while digging around the refrigerator.

"Hello? It's Gary. How's it going? You wanted me to call?" Gary whispered over the phone line. "... Not much, watching golf. I'm wondering if you want to meet us later. We're driving up to Lake Marie ... You have plans. Well, if things change, maybe I'll see you up there. We'll be in Avery's VW behind the lodge."

Gary hung up and juggled the three beers.

"The weather is supposed to be good. Anything happening during Wild West Days?"

"Not by me, for a Monday. Becca wants to watch the rodeo." Jack feigned a lasso twirl around his head. "One of her friends from Lander is barrel racing, Yee Haw! What's barrel racing?"

Jack held up his hand, and Gary tossed a Coors yellow jacket. Avery caught the Bud that knuckle-balled through the air.

"How about you, Steiner?"

"How about me? What?"

"How about camping? Better than sitting around here. How about tomorrow?"

"Tomorrow? I say tonight. We'll get there well before dark. Your Silver Steed is self-contained."

"Throw in your bag. I'll drive. Middleton?"

"Becca says I have to show more interest in her activities. I'll be with you two in spirit."

"Middleton, I gotta hand it to you. You're persistent."

"Help me out here, Meadows. She relates to you."

"Why, because we go to the same haircut place?"

Avery and Gary readied themselves for their excursion. Gary retrieved a small red steel-sided Coca-Cola cooler from the basement.

"Let's come back in the morning. Stop at Fuji's. It's a big mess cooking camp eggs," Gary yelled on his way to the kitchen. He cracked a few ice cubes from the aluminum trays into the cooler, and dropped in a half loaf of bread, some frozen hamburger patties, an open pack of bacon, and the egg carton. He walked out the front door and set the cooler in the van.

Avery followed and opened the rear engine compartment.

"Oil? Check. Generator belt tension? Check. Distributor wires? Check."

They were ready to pull out. Avery rolled the Silver Steed down the driveway, shifted into third, and eased out the clutch. Gary lurched forward when the engine chugged, and the clutch plate grabbed onto the flywheel.

"Isn't that hard on your transmission?"

"Sometimes the starter doesn't work. It's a balancing act. At least the damn thing will start when I park on a slope."

"You Volkswagen people are nuts."

"We're a cult."

****

Jack preened for his rodeo date with Becca. As much as he tried to avoid it, his informal wear was still that of a city slicker. Jack owned a pair of corduroys with patch pockets. He took them to the dry cleaner, who added a crease. His boots with sterling silver-capped toes were pointy enough to kick bugs in the corner.

The phone rang as he tightened his string bolo tie around the collar of his sunflower-yellow shirt.

"It's Becca. Something's come up. Plus, my friend isn't racing until tomorrow or Wednesday."

Becca paced around the dormitory hallway with the phone to her ear. Three of her impatient dorm mates, waiting to use the telephone, bugged her to hang up.

"I made reservations at the Paintbrush Room. I had to pull a few strings. It's Wild West Days!"

Becca turned to the impatient crowd and placed her hand over the transmitter end of the handset.

"Can you wait a few more secs?"

"Sorry. What about later on Sunday? We can show my friend around Laramie."

Jack rolled his eyes and hung up before Becca finished.

"Is that a 'maybe'?"

"This could be a blessing in disguise," Jack thought while admiring himself in front of the bathroom mirror. "I wonder if Becca even has a barrel racer friend."

******

After Becca canceled their dinner plans, Jack wasn't about to give up his reservation at the swankiest place in town.

Ever since he transferred to UW, his tall tales of faraway places on the East Coast have been entertaining, and he hoped his reputation would be good enough to land him a date. He sat on a stool in the kitchen, thumbing through his little black book.

"Hello, Patty? Jack here. You know from finance class? You're still on campus? I know it's the last minute, but ..."

Patty cut him off.

"I'm in summer school. I have a study group tonight. Give me a little more notice next time."

After hanging up, he flipped to another number.

"Is this Connie? It's Jack from Econ 301. "It's going okay. I'm glad I caught you. I never know who's still around. Did you finish your paper on 'marginal propensity to save?'"

"It's about time you called. I didn't think you'd get around to it."

"Uh-huh, uh-huh, you're surprised I remembered? I have a memory like an elephant. Listen, can you join this elephant for dinner tonight? I'd like to know you better. We can talk about economics theory."

"Where are we going?"

"The Paintbrush Room. It was a tough reservation!" replied Jack about the railroad storage building converted into Laramie's finest eatery in 1942. The name was derived from the field of fiery-red Indian Paintbrush, the Wyoming state flower that surrounded the restaurant constructed from sandstone blocks.

"Fancy schmancy. I don't know what to wear."

"You know, it's Laramie. I'll pick you up at seven. Ross Hall? … My car? It's a BMW 1500. Greenish. Only driven by a little old lady on Sundays."

Jack pushed the receiver cradle with a sigh of relief.

On his way back to the living room, he opened the fridge. Gary and Avery had claimed all the beer. He settled on an apple before returning to the couch. He crunched off half the pome and flipped through his economics textbook, cramming for his date.

****

The time neared 6:30. Jack made a final stop in front of the bathroom mirror before heading to Ross Hall. Women stared out the windows on the second floor, watching Jack approach the door. Men were allowed in as far as the lobby. There was Connie. She looked elegant in a white blouse, tan skirt, stockings, and stylish dark brown pumps.

"You look very nice, my dear." Jack helped her with her sweater. "It's Wild West Days. No cowgirl attire for you?"

"I don't get to wear my civilian clothes much."

"No heels to show off those legs of yours?"

Jack opened the passenger door, and Connie swung her legs into the bucket seat.

"Not practical." Her dorm mates tapped on the glass, approving her date choice. "Are you okay with this?"

Connie adjusted the rearview mirror and checked her face. Jack re-adjusted it before pulling out.

"You look great."

"No, this. This date. Word around the dorm is you're chasing Becca Pembroke. My roommate? Is she your girlfriend?"

"Right now, I'm here chasing you. We don't need to mention Becca."

"Just checking."

"Now that we have that out of the way, you know I'm a Jersey boy. I don't know much about you except that you're a whiz at macro-economics."

"Are you getting familiar with Wyoming? I'm from Douglas. Well, Converse County. I went to high school in Douglas. We have a big cattle ranch, the Morgan Livestock Company. We don't like to talk about the oil."

"Oil and cows. You can't go wrong with that combination." Jack parked his car at the far end of the parking area. "The last thing I need is some rowdy cowboy in a big pickup truck dinging my doors."

Jack took Connie by the crook of her arm. The two made their way across the lot to the crunching sound of gravel.

"Aren't you glad you didn't have to fix a broken heel?"

Jack held the solid wooden door open and was greeted at the hostess's desk.

"We have a reservation for around now. It's Middleton."

Jack scanned the list and pointed, relieved to see his name.

"We made special arrangements for you. I have the perfect spot."

The hostess led them to a table for two next to the window.

"Jill will be your waitress tonight."

The hostess took the "Reserved" sign and handed out the menus.

"I hear you come from New Jersey money. Can you imagine a merger between East and West? You're old money?"

"You know, I'm from Pilgrim roots. What kind of merger are you thinking?" Jack was getting a little sweaty under his collar as Connie smiled.

"Depends on what you have to offer. We don't have old or new money. We have money. Don't you think the workers are cute?" observed Connie as the bus boy wearing a coon skin hat and a U.S. Cavalry uniform brought water.

"Very cute. Are you in summer school?"

"I'm taking a physics class. It's easier than during the year. Plus, my parents want me to earn money on my own. I've worked off and on since I've been here. They don't want me to think everything is handed to me."

Jill stopped by with her pad open.

"Are you ready? The buffalo ribs are the dinner special."

Connie kicked off her shoe and rubbed her toe up and down Jack's shin and up his thigh.

"Uh, I'm about ready," said Jack as he felt his forehead warming.

"I just love the prints on the wall. Can you believe Calamity Jane was here?"

"The owner is a collector," explained Jill. "All the knick-knacks are originals."

"I think we need a minute," interrupted Jack as he loosened his collar. "Well, uh, what else do you do on campus?"

"You mean other than this?" Connie asked with a grin. "My mom was a nursing student. She got me a job at the Student Health Clinic. It's the Morgan Student Health Clinic. My parents gave a big donation to renovate it a few years ago. 'It'll broaden your horizons. Nursing will improve your people skills,' she tells me."

Connie leaned closer to Jack and locked eyes while opening her ruby-red lips.

"If you ever need your throat swabbed, I'm your girl."

Jack winked as Jill turned and flung her fringed leather skirt.

"We may need another minute."

The Paintbrush Room was second to none for omnivores. For starters, they split an order of battered mushrooms with a creamy dipping sauce called High Plains Nectar. Connie tried the moose tenderloin. It was a thick filet wrapped in bacon cooked medium-rare. Jack had the buffalo T-Bone. It was something a *Dino Hunter* would have ordered during the Pleistocene.

"Thank you, Jack. What a spur-of-the-moment treat."

The busboy dropped by a bread pudding topped with a scoop of vanilla ice cream. After dessert, they finished off their second bottle of Merlot and chased it with snifters of Hennesey.

****

Jack paid the check with two crisp Benjamin Franklins. They headed back into Laramie.

"We're having a good old time. The night is young. The Stag Point isn't the quietest place to sip a Drambuie. No place in Laramie is quiet during Wild West Days."

"Would you like to come up to see the heart and lung posters in my laboratory?" asked Connie while they stood at a stoplight. She took out a tube of lipstick for a touch-up.

"I don't know. I'm a conservative young Congregationalist."

"Even better! You must have something to prove."

Jack pulled up behind the student health clinic. Connie fumbled with her keys. By feel, she fingered the square one that opened the lock.

The heavy metal door opened with a groan. There wasn't much small talk. Connie caressed Jack's hand and guided him into one of the examination rooms with a window lit by the streetlight outside.

Connie slipped out of her shoes and sniffed Jack's neck.

"This is the other reason I wear quick-to-kick-off pumps. Hmm, I love an Old Spice man. Will you respect me in the morning?"

"Probably, since it's already the morning."

Jack pulled Connie closer and unbuttoned her blouse.

"This may be the start of a very practical friendship."

He ran his hands over her shapely torso. Connie kissed Jack's open lips with passion.

40

Brock 'Blaze' Thompson

October 6, 2006—11:35 p.m. MDT: Avery and Jack dragged up the walk, where Gary greeted them. He gave Avery a hug and then extended his hand, ignored by Jack.

"Well, Middleton. What's the latest?"

Jack was nervous and anxious. He hung back and sat away from the crowd in a lounge chair, glancing around the condominium complex.

Avery and Gary sat at a table under an umbrella.

"Great timing. We have a big celebration every month during the full moon. This month, we're honoring Becca." Gary stood up. "Everybody, meet two of my friends from college. Avery drove from Devil's Tower and found Jack under a rock. I can't remember if I mentioned my daughter. Elizabeth is around here someplace."

The omniscient observer waved at the crowd from the upper deck.

"C'mon down!" Gary yelled.

"I stay behind the scenes."

"We were housemates in Laramie. Called ourselves the Odd Trio. It'll be like old times. I reserved the guest room for them," announced Gary. "I don't know how long they're staying. It depends on how much they can put up with me."

******

Avery wandered away, looking for a beer. Jack saw that Gary was by himself.

"So, Steiner, my friend, how's your life? Everyone's having fun. Reminds me of what I imagined the fun campout you and Avery took."

"As I recall, you didn't sit alone at the Calamity Club that night either, 40 years ago."

"Thirty-nine, but who's counting? All the way down to Boulder, I thought about beating the crap out of you, Steiner," Jack whispered, pointing his finger. "I didn't want to take a chance you'd have a Viet Cong flashback. Dump me in a swamp."

"It was the *Pathet Lao*, and we don't have a pool." Gary blocked out the joy around him. "I thought either you or I would be the first to die. Neither of us would have any reason to be sitting here."

"I still wish I knew what Becca saw in you!" Jack clenched the middle of Gary's T-shirt, oblivious to everyone around staring at the confrontation. "Becca and me? We had a history since childhood. You screwed it all up."

****

The full moon celebration was in full swing. The reveling crowd energy contrasted with the air surrounding Gary and Jack that was as thick as the artichoke dip. Avery returned with three red Solo cups teeming with a thin layer of foam.

"Steiner? I see you're getting reacquainted with our resident recluse, Mr. Havisham. This is a very respectable kegger. Middleton, aren't you exhausted from running from the law?"

"You mean the cop who might have searched your Eurovan?"

Jack pulled Gary up by the shirt.

"Hey, you two, good beer choice. Small breweries are a growth industry in Boulder." Avery tried to de-escalate the confrontation. "Don't forget marijuana. Who would have thought our felonious college activities would now be legal?"

Avery's interruption riled up Jack even more as he let loose of Gary's collar. He stomped around the courtyard on his way to the back alley.

"That was four decades in the making. So much for 'time healing all wounds.'"

Avery unfolded the newspaper section from the Stag Point Bar and handed it to Gary.

"You're quite the peacemaker. I avoid another brain injury, and you want me to read the paper?"

"I've been thinking about it since I picked up this guy in Sybille Canyon. Did you ever run across Pete Martin?"

"In the 1980s. He was big news back then." Gary skimmed over the page. "Martin ran the marina. I went out there with a photographer. "A TV crew from *Mysterious Mysteries* was there. It was strange. The photos didn't turn out. We ran a series about him. He seemed credible."

"I stopped at the Stag. The bartender told me a cable producer was in Laramie during the summer."

Avery chased a pretzel down with a swig of beer.

"Was he wearing that black shirt? He wouldn't let me leave until I took one. Next time, stop and see him. I'll meet you there."

"You and Middleton okay? Did all those squabbles we had at the Calamity Club set you up to live in this place? You were kind of a loner back then."

"I fit in here. Remember the scene in *Chopper Paradise*? Bikers pick up some chicks and ride to a commune. The Calamity Club was more like a commune. We owned the house together. Divvied up the work. Kicked in for expenses. Here, it's cohousing. There are lots of rules about everything. Supposed to force us to get out of our shells, I guess. We own our condos and share in the maintenance. I'm on a committee in charge of fixing the lawn sprinklers."

"Lawn? This is the 21st century. Don't you remember anything I taught you about drought-tolerant plants? The Calamity Club was ahead of its time and good while it lasted."

"ARRGGHH!!!"

The blood-curdling scream echoed off the garages and through the Blue Sky Village courtyard. Avery and the other revelers jumped out of their seats, except for Gary.

"You should feel lucky you didn't meet up to your father's standards, Meadows. A, you weren't draft-eligible, and B, you're still normal. Jack could be dead in the alley. Me? Unless something triggers me, I'm un-phased by murder and mayhem. I'm like Brock 'Blaze'...," Gary made air quotes. "... Thompson. "Shell-shocked. So far, I haven't burned down any major cities. Now, I always look over my shoulder. In exchange for that, all I got was that crummy house. I was 'Gung Ho' about killing Commies. When I was discharged, I came to my senses. Saving Vietnam was a waste of time and bodies."

Jack calmed down and returned with a plate of snacks.

"Got it all out of your system, Middleton?"

Gary fingered a meatball smothered with sticky barbecue sauce.

Jack craned his neck and let out a deep breath.

"I have boundaries. I'm not going to taunt you for the time being."

"I was anti-war and took a piece of your G.I. benefits. I've felt bad about that, Steiner."

"Meadows feels guilty? My dad paid some Army reserve guy to give me a medical deferment, bunions. Couldn't march. I had to take an ROTC class for anti-heroes. A business opportunity for someone. What if rich parents sent big donations to schools for special treatment for their kid, or a place on a sports team, or a draft deferment?"

The party was winding down. Always helpful, Susan was gather-ing the spent cups and plates. Elizabeth made her way down to lend a hand. Working in the background was a throwback to her hotel banquet days.

"Aren't you going to introduce me to your friends?" Susan cleared away Jack's half-eaten plate of snacks. "Over there is my husband, Harold. We live next door to the Steiners. Well, Gary. I understand you all were very close."

"We were at UW together. First time we've seen each other in 40 years. I'm Avery. Great kegger. I haven't been to one since college. Meet Jack. He and I had an action-packed drive down from Wyoming."

"Not a kegger. It's a celebration." Susan handed Avery a trash bag. "You're in charge of the recycling. We have single-stream. No need to sort."

Avery followed orders, scraped the food scraps into the compost container, and bagged the rest.

"Action-packed? I'm glad Meadows found out where you were hiding. You look good."

Gary filled the silent pause.

"To tell you the truth, I'm not good." Jack frowned at Gary six inches from his mug. "When I moved to Wyoming, my father disowned me. Did Becca tell you her mother abandoned her after you broke up the Calamity Club?"

"I hoped you would have mellowed, Middleton. Filing your bogus lien against our ranch was low. My mom still hasn't gotten over it."

"I'm lucky I didn't end up in prison for longer. It was worth it."

"Lucky your father brought in those high-powered mob lawyers from Rock Springs."

"I paid your mom back. I did my time in a prison cell. I wore orange coveralls and picked up beer cans and Bonkers Bar wrappers from the highway ditches. I can't vote. Look, man, I'm the innocent bystander here. I didn't ask you to mess things up between Becca and me."

The other residents saw the brewing storm that cleared the court-yard.

"There was nothing to mess up. How about your fling with Becca's best friend, Connie? You would have been a great threesome, Connie, Clyde, and your cash."

"Okay, boys, let's call it a draw. Becca's DEAD. We're not far behind. She always reminded us about our 'Pact' when one of you got too worked up." Avery broke up the brawl as Jack rolled his eyes. "Get over yourself, Middleton."

Jack turned around and walked away. After a few moments of contemplation, he returned and extended his hand.

""Damnit. I'm too old for this." Steiner, this doesn't mean I'm over it. Blaze Thompson didn't get away with burning that town to ashes."

"This isn't a movie. If I wanted, my Blaze Blade's in the hall closet." Gary and Jack shook. Avery's hand topped the grasp. "Party's over. Harold, can you show these friends of mine to the guest room?"

******

Avery and Jack walked downstairs. The motion-sensor lights illuminated the hallway.

"Most cohousing communities have a space for overflow lodging," explained Harold.

The room was small and efficient enough for a trundle bed to be configured into two singles. Avery straightened a picture next to the window.

"That? Susan painted it. She copied my Post Office mug shot. We have an Art Room if you get ambitious. You, too, can create non-representational portraits."

Harold pointed them down the hall to the bathroom.

"Towels are on the rack. Use the rug. Unless you bring your preferred brand, there are various shampoos and soaps. Susan is a vacation hoarder. She takes those little bottles from hotels. You may not have stayed at the Plaza, but you can say you washed your hair with shampoo from the Plaza."

"Tight quarters, Middleton. Reminds me of the time we stayed in the *hostel casita* in Sombrerete. We flew into Mazatlán. That local bus ride over the mountains was wild," Avery reminisced.

"How could I forget? Meadows got singled out by the *Federales* looking for gringos with drugs. You didn't grab that chicken flapping around the bus to blend in with the locals."

"They pulled Middleton, six other climbers, and me out of the bus at machine gunpoint and tossed our bags. We repacked, and then they searched us again. It didn't help that we had tourist visas from Mazatlán and no work permits. The climbing was pretty good at Sierra de Organos Park except for the cactus."

Jack plopped down on one of the beds.

"We had to share a mattress about this size. You keep your hands to yourself."

"That's easy for you to say, Middleton. Okay, Harold. I think we should be good."

"You have the run of the place. There's a full kitchen upstairs. Use the small guest refrigerator."

Harold handed Avery a card with numbers for neighborhood restaurants and the keys.

"The round one is for the room. This unlocks the Common House. The building is battened down all the time. As a heads-up, tomorrow, I guess it's already tomorrow, we're hosting the funeral service. There will be commotion upstairs. It's also game day. The Buffs play Baylor. "The town gets pretty clogged up starting in the morning when the hard-core tailgaters set up."

Harold kicked down the doorstop. The Odd Duo followed Harold up the stairs. As they retrieved their stuff from the Eurovan, a junk mail envelope with a hand-written message slipped under the windshield wiper caught Avery's eye.

"Please move your vehicle. It is a 15-minute limit," the note read.

"What the … ? Can anything else go wrong? Take the bags down."

****

Jack worked his way through the front door and saw lights illuminating the hallway in the otherwise dark building. He dropped the luggage by the stairs and walked to the doorway, where he saw the colorful cardboard coffin bearing Becca's body awaiting the funeral service.

Jack entered and sat in one of the dining room chairs in front of the coffin.

"Well, Becca, it was a long haul for you and me. We had history. Not the exact history I would have liked. Do you know this? I've been in love with you since we first met as kids. Would things have turned out better if I stayed in Jersey? After 39 years of being separated?

"I've thought about you every day." Jack took a deep breath. "Do you think this is easy being so thoughtful? Things didn't turn out so great for me. Self-inflicted, though. I ended up alone. Nobody to treat to dinner or share a vacation."

Avery parked in one of the parking spaces in the alley, returned to the Common House, and heard Jack's voice echo out of the lighted room.

"I've thought about that picture." Jack retrieved the photo of the group on Libby Flats. "I couldn't go back to what I was or what was expected of me. I wish you knew that. When I saw your piece of crap husband tonight, I came close to knocking off his block.

"I couldn't imagine you two together. Still can't. Your mom and my dad ignoring Steiner's existence didn't help. It reinforced my hatred of him. Not 'hate.' I don't think our families ever got over the Civil War. I showed up tonight because of your ridiculous 'Pact.'"

Avery peeked through the doorway.

41

Site 37

I didn't realize Jack and Dad carried so much angst over the years. Back in July 1967, Jack was oblivious when Dad took a big chance setting up Avery for the overnight trip to Lake Marie. Avery was a planner and would have wanted a few days to go shopping and service the half-reliable VW. Dad was a man of circumstances. That trait rubbed off on me. The circumstances I set up for myself weren't that great. I kept making mistakes as fast as I could. E.S.

****

Gary was happy that Avery had decided to take a break from Monday night TV and miss the final episode of *The Dino Hunters*. Besides, Jack got on their nerves. On the way up to the Snowy Range, Avery stopped at the gas station next to the Happy Angler.

"By the way, I invited Becca to have a burger with us. It was last minute. I hope that's okay, Meadows."

"You know, Middleton has a hot date with her tonight."

Avery dug around for the stove fuel can. Rather than built-in burners, the 1960 Type II van came with a German-made Ender portable stove. Both went inside.

"You're now a home wrecker?"

"She's the one who wanted me to call. Didn't know if her plans were solid or not. She won't make it."

236 | ALAN O'HASHI

Gary looked over the candy selection by the cash register and settled on a Bonkers Bar.

"Well, it's too late to turn her back. Grab a bundle of wood."

Avery paid for everything, and the two got back on the road.

"It was an innocent invitation. We seldom have a chance to visit since Middleton takes up all her time."

"I get it. Strictly platonic. Becca can take care of herself. Intent is one thing, but appearances can cause problems."

"Now that you mention it ..."

****

After Becca gave Jack the brush, she changed into her walking boots and dusted off her Levis before grabbing a light jacket from the hook. She ambled to the ground floor as her key ring jingle echoed through the Ross Hall stairwell.

Becca didn't drive her Ford Falcon much and espied the red roof in the dorm parking lot.

Before classes started her first year at UW, Becca had earned enough money to buy a used compact car in Lander.

Sally's husband, Marvin, helped her pick out the 1960 two-door Falcon sedan with a peppy inline six-cylinder engine with four speeds on the column. She learned how to drive a stick shift on the ranch by handling the Allis-Chalmers tractor in the hayfield.

****

When Becca first came to Wyoming, her parents helped her buy a used Ford Falcon. After Becca pulled out from the dealership parking lot, onto a straightaway, and opened up the throttle south of Lander, she fish-tailed onto the ranch entrance road with a squeal.

Sally heard the Falcon roll up to the ranch house.

"Six cylinders give you a little extra when you're driving those hills to Laramie. Four-speed? Automatics are no good in Wyoming."

****

Becca managed to avoid speeding tickets while driving around Laramie. In third gear, the Falcon could pick up some speed. She liked pushing it through a yellow light on a clear stretch of Nellie Tayloe Ross Boulevard, formerly Equality State Boulevard.

The Laramie City Council renamed the street after Nellie in 1955, commemorating the 30th anniversary of her election as the first woman governor in the country. Her husband, William B. Ross, was governor from 1923 until he died a year later. Nellie succeeded his appointed successor, Frank Lucas when she won a special 1925 election. She lost re-election to a full term in 1926.

Becca whizzed through the intersection and veered left into the Rancher Bar package liquor drive-thru window.

"Six-pack of Bud."

"Need a bag? One for the road?"

"No thanks. A box and a bag of ice would be nice."

The clerk pushed the beer carton across the stainless-steel window counter. Becca got out and hoisted her cargo onto the backseat, which she covered with an army blanket as insulation.

"Honk, Honk!"

She smiled at the impatient driver and gave a friendly wave.

The road was dry until a late afternoon thundershower gently moistened the asphalt in the Laramie Basin. Stands of aspen trees broke up the bristled lodgepole pines, blanketing the foothills. The aspen leaves lighted by the sun quaked in the breeze and contrasted with the black clouds casting shadows on the road.

The Falcon was peppy and moved up the steep and narrow highway. One problem was the slow windshield wipers. Driving on the ranch was challenging when she bounced over the dirt roads. The rain splattered on the windshield and turned the dust into mud.

On the way to Centennial, she expected hail to follow the nickel-sized drops smacking against the glass as she drove toward the mountains.

Traffic crept through Centennial, except for the locals who knew it was okay to pick it up through town. Since there was no police force, clever citizens painted a junk car black and white. The local vigilantes bolted two red Hills Bros. coffee cans across the top of the would-be cruiser.

A dummy dressed as a cop sat on the driver's side and monitored the traffic. Tourists would stop at the edge of town to take pictures with Officer DeCoy. Every first-timer through Centennial got a laugh from the makeshift sting operation.

Becca could have bought beer at a bar in Centennial. She opted against it because she'd have to go inside. Even during broad daylight, rude razzing from the patrons wasn't worth the convenience. She cruised the 10 miles to Lake Marie Lodge, named in 1879 by Charles Bellamy in honor of his wife, Mary. She was later the first woman elected to the Wyoming State Legislature in 1910.

Gary and Avery stood up to welcome the red Falcon that rolled into Lower Loop Campground Site 37.

"How was your drive? We got some sprinkles here. Did you get much in town?" Avery asked while busily organizing the evening meal.

"You know, summertime in Laramie. Nice outfit, Avery. We're twins!"

"Oh, this old thing? What are you talking about? Everyone wears jeans and flannel shirts."

"Not McDougald plaid! Can one of you get this?"

Becca pushed the front seat forward.

"Allow me." Gary fetched the beer and noticed some straggler ice cubes in the bag, which he poured into the cooler. "I didn't realize you broke other plans to come up here."

Gary handed Becca a cold one.

"You mean with Jackie? Nothing is ever set with him." Becca took a swig from the red, white, and blue can. "I hope he got a better offer. I feel sorry for him."

"Jackie?"

"He doesn't like the name. It's a throwback to when we were kids. It's a term of endearment. I only call him that in mixed company to irritate him."

"Sounds like an identity crisis," observed Gary.

"You nailed it. I should stop tormenting him. We've been friends since we were kids. He's like a puppy dog tugging at my cuff. His constant attention bugs the crap out of me. Anyway, how's your mom?"

Becca retrieved the bundle of wood from the Silver Steed.

"She's good. Billy's good. She keeps hoping I'll come back. Take over the ranch, 'Keep it in the family.' Billy is family. Life will be different by the time he takes over. It's been hard enough for Mom and Marvin."

"I hope so. I heard President Kennedy is coming to Laramie when school starts, 'The New Frontier.' Civil rights? Man on the moon?" Becca wandered around looking for pine tree twigs for kindling. "You're on the newspaper staff. Will you get to do an interview?"

"I'll get a press pass. The national papers will get first dibs. Other than school, how have you been? You keep saying your parents are venturing out from New Jersey."

"I don't know. For them, this is the 'Old Frontier.' They always have some excuse, 'Oh, there's thus-and-so happening at the church,' or 'I'm hosting Historical Society.'" Becca stacked the wood like teepee poles. "Maybe I'll tell them I'm pregnant. They'll board the next plane out here, especially if it were Jackie's. That would be my worst-case nightmare."

Becca signaled the 'striking-a-match' motion. Gary rose to the occasion and lit the fire.

There was a pleasant "sizzle" after Avery flipped each burger in the cast iron skillet.

"How do you like yours? These are sounding 'medium'"

The mixed aromas of crackling grease and pine smoke filled the air.

"Helps build strong bodies eight different ways," said Gary as he opened the white bread bag with red, yellow, and blue balloons printed on the wrapper.

Becca placed six slices on three camp plates.

"How do you three handle the cooking?"

"On a rotation. Meadows on Monday and Friday. Me on Tuesdays and Thursdays. Middleton on Wednesday and Saturday. We're on our own for Sunday."

"You tricked Jack into cooking. That's a good one. He thinks chocolate milk comes from brown cows."

"Middleton's idea of cooking is Beefaroni off the shelf and out of the can."

"Do you two rotate as his maid?"

"You'd fit in with our household. He's been on my case to talk you into joining the Calamity Club," said Avery.

"He thinks you telling me would be more believable? Because we like the same plaid? 'You'll save on dorm rent,' he says. 'You'll have your own bathroom.' Fat chance. I can't think of anything more disgusting than dried-up toothpaste in the sink, except maybe that Bonkers Bar over there covered with ants. Since you're his agent, Avery, tell Jackie not to get his hopes up."

42

Lyndon Johnson

October 7, 2006—2:32 a.m. MDT: Gary's heart raced from his argument with Jack after the full moon party ended. He wandered around the condo, getting organized for the funeral set for the afternoon. The day would be busy, and the last things he needed were distractions and bad memories.

Gary set the timer on the coffeemaker. Rather than hitting the hay, he flipped through his closet.

"Becca, you're not around to make fun of my clothes. I miss that already."

He was restless and headed down to the Common House. He saw the light casting out from the Exercise Room, where he joined Avery at the doorway and sat next to Jack in front of Becca's cardboard box.

"I remember when my family picked me up after' Nam. I put the war far back in my mind. No matter how hard I try to forget, the memories are always there. You're lucky I didn't 'Blaze' on you," Gary stared straight ahead. "I was pretty messed up when I got back—combat fatigue like Blaze Thompson, my alter ego. I still feel it today."

"Being a draft dodger, I'm not much into PTSD and war hero movies. Steiner? You returned as some elite Special Ops war hero and hung your framed Navy Cross and Purple Heart on the wall with the citations bestowed by President Lyndon Baines Johnson in all his war-mongering glory. Those medals were things my money couldn't buy."

"It was the Secretary of the Navy."

"Him, too, for going along with it all."

"When I was in junior high school, I was on a mission. My dad was killed in World War II. Well, I don't know if he died. Reading about the war in pulp fiction novels motivated me. My uncles served in the Pacific. I imagined what happened to my father when he went missing. We never met. I felt like I needed to enlist. A rite of passage."

"Ha, you're a war hero."

"Did LBJ get after you for dropping out of the ROTC program?"

"I avoided the draft and came out here chasing Becca. The school lost track. Like all my unpaid parking tickets. She came out here to get away from me. I should have figured."

"No need to get sentimental. You had it made with Becca. Me? I'm surprised we even met. I was focused on getting ready for the service. She stayed in touch. I ignored her. You had all kinds of chances, Middleton."

Gary sat emotionless. Jack was restless and scratched his head in frustration.

"You're one lucky stiff, Steiner."

"It's not like you didn't have your chances, Middleton. You still don't realize how much she liked you."

Gary sat back and kicked his legs forward.

"Here we are, 40 years of gray hairs later. Plus, I'll have you know, I was thrilled when LBJ decided not to run for reelection."

"Nixon wasn't much better. How about that goofy 'Pact' of hers?" asked Jack.

Gary sat oblivious as Avery observed from the door.

"We made it on account of you, Middleton. Our 'Pact' isn't goofy. How about you, Steiner? Think you'll be with it enough?"

43

Veedauwoo

VW rides were an Odd Trio trademark. The action-packed White Shark trek to Boulder was uneventful compared to Avery and Dad's drive in the Silver Steed to Lake Marie in '67. Dad wasn't much of a planner, so journalism was a good fit. The news didn't happen on a timetable. Planning or no planning is bad planning if you consider life as one interconnected disaster. I needed a change but didn't know how to make that happen. From the get-go, I had no control over my destiny. E.S.

****

Plenty of daylight remained in the early evening at the Lake Marie Lodge campground. The three diners had finished their burgers amid the other campers' faint conversations, chuckles, and clanking as the sun set, casting a glow from behind the majestic peaks.

"You cooked. Becca and I can clean up."

"I'll take care of it. I like to use my onboard sink. This is make-up for the meal you made the other night. You simmer up a pretty good venison chili."

"Wasn't because of me. Mom shot and cut up the deer." Gary put the bread away. "She knows how to keep the meat mild-tasting."

Becca recapped the ketchup.

"I know she can handle a knife. First I heard about her hunting."

243

Gary stacked up the camp plates and sorted the silverware.

"The way she grew up on the Eagle Crest Ranch, the women supervised the butchering." Gary tossed the paper napkins on the fire. "Any critter, pheasant, deer, steer." The vaporized hot grease flared up, sending the napkin soot swirling. "There's an antelope hunting contest in Lander. Men only. She usually guides one of the teams, but Marvin would stand in for her at any of the hunt ceremonies."

"That's not right."

"You know her view. The destination isn't important. It's the thrill of the hunt."

"Thanks for cooking. The burger was perfect," complimented Becca

"Anything tastes better when someone else cooks it," Avery humbly responded.

Becca handed the plates to Avery.

"The moon will almost be full tonight, according to the star chart in my lab. You and Gary want to head over to Libby Flats? Look around the horizon?"

Becca gingerly picked up the candy bar by the wrapper that had dropped in the dirt and plopped it, ants and all, in the beer box trash container.

"I need some time by myself." Avery tossed another log on the fire. "Nothing's more peaceful than a messy picnic table."

"Gary?"

He searched around the Silver Steed for his jean jacket.

"I'm ready. Wanna walk?"

"It's four miles. Let's take the Falcon. It gets cold after dark." Becca checked for her keys in her back pocket. "You'll be okay by yourself? We'll get out of the cook's hair."

******

Becca cranked the wheel into the Libby Flats parking area.

"My geology class came out here on a field trip. Connie showed me some fossils in those limestone rocks."

The castle turret-like structure was constructed from native stones. At timberline, the trees were sparse. The winter winds were so harsh that there were no boughs on one side of the tall, narrow trunks that resembled flag poles.

"Ever been here before?" Becca asked with a shiver. On this warm summer evening, the wind had a chill with a breeze flowing through the basin. "I think it's very spiritual."

"The only other time I've been here was when you brought us up here for Middleton's first time. I drive by. Haven't stopped since then. Now I know why. It's freezing!" Gary covered his ears to warm them up. "Have you been to Veedauwoo? Now that's a spiritual place. A big rock formation on the plains east of Laramie. I sometimes stop when coming back from Cheyenne. It's a BLM Recreation Area."

"BLM? Sounds tasty. Bacon Lettuce and Meatloaf?"

"Ha! Bureau of Land Management. Part of the Quiver Mountain is BLM land."

Becca restarted the engine and flipped on the heater.

"What's in Cheyenne?" Becca squeezed Gary's thigh and reached over his lap to find the stocking cap she kept in the glove box.

"Meetings. Mom and Marvin can't make the drive, so I go. You might be interested in this. Last week, I went to a hearing about brucellosis." Gary moved Becca's hand aside. "Our herd is brucellosis-free. The state Ag Department is considering changes around vaccinations."

"I read about brucellosis in my Wyoming History 1858 to 1958 class. It's supposedly passed from bison to cattle. Causes cows to abort their calves."

Becca put her arm around Gary's shoulders and caressed his neck.

"No verified cases. All signs point to elk as the culprits. Bison get the bad rap. Meadows was working on an epidemiology paper about that and came out to the ranch. That was a good trip. We went to Jackson and stayed at the Moose Paddle Inn."

"I know veedauwoo is an Arapaho word. Means 'earth-born.' You can take me on a field trip for a personal tour. Maybe I'll find petroglyphs. Are there any secluded campsites?"

"I go climbing there with Middleton and Meadows when we have extra time."

"You trust your life to Jackie? Is he any good?"

"He's an eager learner. I think he wants to impress you with his new-found Wyoming skills. Besides, he likes the best climbing gear money can buy. Always has the latest. That's why we bring him along."

"Where did you learn? I don't remember you climbing around at the ranch."

"The Navy."

"Are there Pacific Ocean mountains?"

"Mountains in jungles. Jumping out of helicopters. Can we talk about something else as a preventive measure?" Gary grabbed his jacket from the back.

Becca had a curious look.

"Talk of the tropics does warm me up. More like revs me up. You don't have to lock. I hope someone steals this bucket of bolts. The transmission is starting to go."

Becca slipped her coat over her shoulders and stuffed the keys into her back pocket.

"Could be it needs a clutch adjustment. Why don't you come to the ranch for Thanksgiving? My stepdad can take a look."

"Let's hope it's not the gearbox." An alluring smile came to Becca's face. "I could use a good excursion with no school involved."

Gary couldn't get out of the Falcon fast enough. Becca took his hand and led the way across the parking area and up the stone steps.

"The moon will rise in the south." She pointed toward Colorado. "Tribes have ceremonies in July based on the moon cycle. This cycle is making me a little warm."

Gary went to one of the fixed brass tubes that swiveled south toward the Colorado Rockies, east to Laramie Peak, west toward the Sierra Madre Mountains, and north at Medicine Bow Peak.

"Did I show you the ceremonial stone arrow and medicine wheel on the ranch?"

"Several times on our way to the big hay field. Are you trying to impress me with anthropology small talk?"

Becca looked through the brass tube pointing toward Rocky Mountain National Park. Gary took a turn looking through the tube.

"The Arapaho had names for all those mountains. That one? Longs Peak is *neńiisótoyóú'u*," Becca said, standing close and warming her hands in his front pockets.

The sparse pine boughs swayed and whistled in the breeze when the night quieted. Occasional nocturnal animals scurried through the brush to give life to the darkness.

44

Pam Middleton

October 7, 2006—7:36 a.m. MDT: Blue Sky Village was abuzz beginning at first light. Eco-Haven Events director Phil inspected the cardboard box in the Exercise Room.

"Do you want this here or in the main room?"

"The main room," said Gary. Phil added a few more pieces of dry ice.

"This is it, my Dear." Gary stroked Becca's lifeless cheek. "I'll do my best to carry on your work. I saw Professor Hanlon is offering Arapaho language classes. I'll sign up."

Gary nodded, signaling Phil to cover the box.

The ever-present busybody, Susan, paced around, trying to find something to do while waiting for carry-in dishes to arrive.

This was the most activity in the Common House since the green water deluged the place during the St. Patrick's Day ice-making machine fiasco.

Albert was set up for the pancake breakfast in the courtyard.

"Thanks for doing this, Albert." Becca requested red, white, and blue flapjacks for her last meal. She hoped to partake rather than being there in spirit. Gary brought down a big jug of maple syrup.

"One of the last conversations Becca and I had was about your griddle. My mom swore by hers."

Albert held up the plug, enshrouded with deteriorating Bakelite, and stuck it in the socket.

"They don't make 'em like this anymore. It's something about how the aluminum conducts the heat." He turned up the cooking temperature dial to the hottest setting. "I picked this up for a buck at the Red Oak Acres yard sale."

"So you mention every 4th of July. The last thing the Maintenance Committee needs is a 10th-anniversary fire."

Gary poured maple syrup into a gravy boat to be heated. Becca, being from the Northeast, was accustomed to the pure stuff. A little-known fact about New Jersey, the Garden State was home to an obscure maple syrup industry. The Congregational Youth Club took annual field trips to the Great Swamp Maple Products Cooperative. Becca and the other kids were given a bottle of syrup as a souvenir. She special-ordered a quart every syrup season since living in the West.

"Save me two pancakes and an egg, over easy."

Albert spread a layer of corn oil over the flat surface with an equally ancient metal spatula.

"It'll be my pleasure!"

Gary returned to the Common House. Jack was in the TV room.

"Get off your butt. It's my turn to civilize you."

"Can't it wait until the commercial?" Jack tore away from his *Morning A.M. Show*. He got up from the couch with a shrug. "You're spoiling me with all this electronic stimulation."

Jack poured a cup of coffee. He and Gary returned to the condo.

"Our little visit last night was a long time coming," Gary observed, walking a few steps ahead of Jack. "I've been dreading it for 40 years. Much has changed."

"… and much has not. Don't think you're off the hook, Steiner. I'm still pissed. Since I've been out here, you've reignited my inferiority complex. My Pilgrim ancestors would be no match for you rugged Westerners. No lie, my ancestors were part of the first Thanksgiving."

"Ha, Ha. 'How the West Was Lost.'"

Gary sorted through his closet and pulled out two shirts.

"My Mom used to pick out my clothes," Jack recalled.

"You never mentioned your mom much, even when we did along."

"Dad married his high school sweetheart, Pamela Barry. She kept his spending habits under control. I didn't know her very well. She died in 1951 from polio when I was just a lad. After that, he spent money like it came out of the tap. I followed his lead."

"Your mom getting sick must been tough on your dad."

"Which made it tough on me. I always thought he had a thing for Mrs. Pembroke, Becca's mom. I doubt anything came of it other than some flirting behind the church. They spent a lot of time together when Pastor Jere was out of town."

"Some things are best left taken to the grave. Try these.

"Who are you, my new mother?"

"If they don't fit, tough."

"You sound like my mom!"

"I figure making up with you, Steiner, will be a rehearsal for changing things with my dad. Maybe I can get him out on the course. Talk it out between holes." Jack shook out a pair of slacks and placed them next to the shirts on the bed. "He left me for dead when I moved out here. Becca's mom is in an assisted living home. I wonder if she even knows about all this."

"Becca called several times to tell her about the relapse. Couldn't get through. The calls weren't returned either. I tried a few times. I doubted she would've talked to me even if she was there."

"It was my doing, ol' pal. We're different back East. Conservative, to put it politely. Even the liberals are conservative."

"That's your view."

"It's my excuse. Not a good one, mind you."

"See how these shirts fit. If you don't like them, you're on your own."

"Gee, thanks, Mom."

Gary wandered down to the Common House. Jack modeled his duds in front of the full-length mirror. The khaki pants and a blue button-down collar shirt were throwbacks to his youth.

"The sneakers are a nice touch," thought Jack.

He took a backswing with an imaginary seven iron and grimaced after he thrust his clenched hand with anger and fury into the solid wood closet door, bruising his ego more than his fist.

45

Backseat

It was a good thing that Jack didn't know about my parent's rite of passage. We took an annual July trip that included a stop at Libby Flats. I turned 19 following my first year at community college. Dad broke out a bottle of champagne and three crystal flutes. He and Mom made a toast to me for reaching the age of maturity, at least on paper. I didn't realize the toast also celebrated the big secret they'd kept from me. E.S.

******

Avery didn't let anyone help put things away in the Silver Steed. Like repacking a parachute, everything fitted just so. Avery had cleaned up after the delicious chuckwagon dinner and stretched out on the picnic table, listening to the sounds of the great outdoors, like the distant sound of chatty campers and the late afternoon birds chirping through the faint odor of smoldering pinewood.

The noises stopped when the campground curfew began at 9:00 p.m.

******

Gary and Becca leaned back against the Libby Flats observation deck wall.

"This getaway was like the good old days. On the ranch, we had white bread with everything. Hamburgers, hotdogs, peanut butter." Gary filled the conversation with small talk. "Buns are a little too classy for me. At the Pistol Pete Bistro the other day, I ordered the Cowboy Doggie and asked for two sliced-up hotdogs on white bread. The guy doing the sandwiches thought I was nuts. I should have asked for a discount."

"He should have charged you double."

"When I was a kid, anything but a roll was uncivilized in Cherry Ridge. Bread makes me queasy, anyway. 'I'll have the sliced turkey sandwich on lettuce.'"

"Turkey sandwich salad."

"I go through a lot of napkins."

"You thrive on cultural oddities. Have you wondered why a layer of water forms on the surface of ketchup? I call it 'cat-slurp.'"

"What about pickle juice?"

"I like the flavor of 'cat-slurp' blended with pickle juice on a soggy piece of white bread. Billy makes a sandwich by piling on a layer of potato chips and slathering peanut butter on the facing slice."

"I didn't know Billy was a vegetarian. We never had pickles in the fridge. I think they gave my dad gas. Not good for a respectable preacher. Sally always had a gallon bottle of pickles in the refrigerator. That's a lot of pickles!"

"Mom reused pickle juice. Remember? She diced up vegetables and let them soak. She pickled everything."

Both had a good chuckle about their conversation about nothing while settling their tasty burgers by wandering around the observation area.

"According to my cultural ecology professor, some tribes refer to the moon in July as the 'Buck Moon.' Bucks grow new antlers around now." Becca gazed around the 360-degree view from the nearby Medicine Bow Range to the Colorado Rockies. "Is the full moon rising affecting your horns?"

Gary turned to face Becca, took her hand, and massaged her breast with his other.

They gazed into each other's eyes before Becca pushed back.

"It was also called Thunder Moon because heavy rains happen in July."

The two viewed the southern sky from the observation deck stone wall.

"You're now a weatherwoman? Sounds to me like the Wild West Days committee should consult you about controlling the monsoons during the rodeos."

The evening sky darkened as the sun slid behind the mountains.

"It's common knowledge from the *Farmer's Almanac*. A hundred seventy years of pioneer weather predictions can't all be wrong!"

Becca cooed into Gary's ear.

"What will your mother think?"

Becca scooted closer to him.

"My mom? What will your Pilgrim mother think? This isn't good for her Revolutionary Sisters image."

Gary pushed her away with his hip.

"It's Sisterhood of the American Revolution. My mom won't find out. Even if she did, she'd pretend like she didn't hear."

Gary reached under Becca's jacket and shirt, fingering her bra hooks.

"Maybe we need to amend that 'Pact' of yours. Include other rites."

Becca turned and nuzzled Gary's neck.

"Like what?"

"Isn't it about time you headed back to Laramie?" Gary nervously grinned as Becca moved behind him, gliding her hands into his front pockets. "Connie will worry about you."

"She's a big girl. I imagine she found something to do tonight." Becca became more aggressive and pulled Gary toward her. "You've always been way too practical. Your mom's been encouraging me to see if I could get your attention."

"She insisted to me you're not as shy as you seem. Especially when you're at attention."

Becca sensed Gary's arousal.

"Me shy? I made out with three hookers in Vietnam."

"One for each year of duty?" Becca stroked his swelling jeans. Her tongue made its way between his lips. She caressed his inner thigh. Gary relaxed and kissed back. "How was that compared to your hooker smooches? Tell me about them. I like that kind of talk. Have you ever inspected the fine upholstery of the back seat of the elegant Ford Falcon?"

"You want to hear about my time in Vietnam? I can't talk about it."

"Oh, knock it off. I don't want to hear about camo and ammo."

"This is all a little new to me."

"Now you're stalling. No sense in learning by listening."

"I might need a little coaching."

Becca rotated herself against Gary's loins.

"Should we even be talking about this?"

"Would you rather me tell you about my first period, or how about you tell me about your top-secret missions? Rest at ease, Sailor. I'm a prim but worldly Jersey girl. Maybe I'll award you a Silver Star to go on that Navy Cross. Our mission will be accomplished if you have to haul me out of here on a stretcher."

They awkwardly walked down the stone steps and continued to make out across the parking lot. Becca opened the door, and Gary followed her into the back seat.

"I won that Navy Cross after almost being left for dead in the jungle."

Becca struggled out of her jacket, unbuckled Gary's belt, and unbuttoned his jeans.

"Tell me about it when we're done."

The windows soon steamed up on the inside as the full moon rose.

46

Fred Middleton

October 7, 2006—12:45 p.m. MDT: Phil propped open the Blue Sky Village Common House front door and placed the "Steiner Service" Eco-Haven Events sandwich board on the sidewalk.

Neighbors and friends streamed into the Common House. Well-wishers set cards in a basket on a counter by the door. Blue Sky Villagers placed items in remembrance of Becca on the cardboard coffin lid. Susan organized the covered dishes on the kitchen center island. Elizabeth put the perishables in the fridge.

A big metallic blue Ford F-150 pickup pulled up in front. Gary's stepbrother Billy climbed down and doffed his black felt hat with a woven horsehair hat band. Sally lowered the passenger window. Gary came out to greet his mom and Billy with a smile.

"You're looking good in your 'goin' to church' jeans. The starched shirt's a nice touch, little brother."

"Only the best for my sister-in-law."

Gary gave his brother a firm handshake.

"Long drive? Where's your dad?"

Billy lifted Sally's wheelchair out of the truck bed and unfolded it.

"Arthritis. Marvin's not up to doing much of anything," Sally replied while she straightened out her flowing navy-blue dress and then eased into her wheelchair.

The extended cab door swung open. Gary and Billy steadied Reverend Perez as he climbed out of the back seat.

"The first thing I need to do is visit my mother, Madre Nature."

"Down the hall. first door."

Gary set up his walker and guided him into the Common House.

"Everyone, meet my mother, Sally, and brother Billy. Reverend Perez will join us in a minute. They got an early start from Wyoming today."

Billy replaced the chair from the end of the first row and positioned Sally and her wheels. Reverend Perez sat in a folding chair next to her. Billy folded up the walker and leaned it up against the wall.

"Welcome to Blue Sky Village." Susan knelt at eye level. "We're all looking forward to your speech at the Columbus Day protest."

Before long, a tank-size, midnight black SUV pulled up to the front. The driver was Jack's dad, Fred Middleton. He walked around to the side door. Who stepped out? It was Becca's mother, Mary. Fred handed over her bamboo cane.

Before taking Fred's arm, he retrieved a lint roller to pick up the fibers attracted by Mary's black mid-length cotton-blend mid-length dress. She took the roller and brushed off his black silk suit and tie. They were a bit out of place dressed in traditional funeral garb. Jack greeted them at the door.

"I'm surprised you made it. You're still driving Mercedes, I see."

"It's 'M Class.' The best they had," Fred said, ignoring Jack's extended hand.

"Mrs. Pembroke, it is good to see you, too. It's been years."

"Where are you two staying?" asked Jack.

"The Triumph Towers by the airport. We have to get right back, son. I have a board meeting on Monday. Mary has a dinner with a big donor she can't miss."

"Grandma?" Elizabeth interrupted Mr. Middleton. "I hope you remembered."

"Oh, Dear. How long has it been since we last met at the concert in Atlantic City? That Roscoe Tanner show was the best."

Mary handed Elizabeth a brown paper bag she hauled on the plane.

"The Tanner show? It was 1997. Please don't remind me. You weren't in the Green Room."

"Then, poof. You took off for New Orleans on me."

"Five years later. My bad luck timing has been impeccable. I don't know what was worse. Leaving New Jersey after 9/11 or stuck in my apartment by the wrath of Katrina."

"Dad, Mrs. Pembroke, I think there's someone you should meet." Jack tapped Gary on the shoulder. "Gary Steiner? This is Becca's mom. Meet my dad, Fred, Fred Middleton."

Jack waved at Sally and Billy. Elizabeth escorted them to the conversation. A surprised Gary hugged his mother-in-law.

"I wasn't sure you got Becca's phone calls, Mrs. Pembroke."

"... and her cards. I read them all. Please, call me Mary. We're always too late with everything. I dragged Fred along. He wasn't crazy about making the trip, either."

Fred offered Mary the crook of his arm for added stability.

"Oh, I can't very well let you fly alone. Those airport people would have abandoned you at the curb."

Fred and Gary shook hands.

"Meet my mother, Sally Steiner, and brother Billy. Apparently, you know Elizabeth."

Jack spotted a woman and a younger man turning the corner on the sidewalk and then entered the Common House.

"Connie Morgan?" Jack asked with a surprised tone in his voice.

"Morgan-Richfield now. Jack Middleton, you're the last person I expected to see here."

"How'd you find out about the funeral?"

"Becca was very well known." Connie gave Jack the once over. "What happened to the white polo shirts?"

"I remembered, 'No white after Labor Day.'"

"You still look great! I felt terrible because we drifted apart after, you know. Then all that happened between you and Gary."

"Yeah, well ... It was an unstable time."

"I couldn't face my parents back then. Went to California. Stayed with my cousin in Modesto. Worked odd jobs. I got involved with a nice guy named Bob, Bob Richfield. We ended up eloping."

"Are you still on the ranch?"

"Hasn't been the best of times. Bob died in a freak accident three years ago in one of our pastures. He was driving in a post and hit a power line. Died instantly."

"It's been hard on Jacob to lose his stepdad."

"You know, my given name is Jacob, after my grandfather."

"I decided to name our son after his father."

47

Laos

Dad's war heroics were seldom discussed. Nobody at the funeral mentioned the Navy Cross. The medal was a negative remembrance that his courage was a Vietnam casualty. If there were a name for it back then, it would have been Post Traumatic Stress Disorder (PTSD). Thinking back to my youth, Dad was withdrawn. I took it as indifference. That forced Mom to shoulder the burden of caring for my emotional needs, which wasn't helpful. I noticed a big change in Dad's behavior when I arrived in Boulder and realized my destiny was to be his eyes and ears. E.S.

******

Gary joined the Navy after graduating high school in 1962. Gary took basic training at Camp Elliott near San Diego, like his father. Ever since the recruitment officer gave him a pep talk at career day, he and the other Seaman Recruits looked forward to the intense, eight-week training to build their physical and mental endurance and receive hands-on experience.

Basic training wasn't anything like he expected, especially the downtime. Mail calls and mealtimes were the highlights of the day.

"All those guys waiting for letters, what's the big deal?"

Gary didn't socialize much in the barracks and spent his time on the lower bunk napping and reading. Every morning, a Petty Officer lugging a mailbag opened the door.

The other Seaman Recruits were eager for each mail call, hoping to receive a letter from their wife or girlfriend with news about their kid's birthday party or the latest Little League game summary.

"Steiner!"

His eyes opened with surprise. He retrieved the envelope and noticed the return address was the ranch. He stuck the unopened letter into his pocket.

****

In addition to the standard basic training, Gary was assigned to one of two 13-man Seabee Technical Assistance Teams (STAT) that supported CIA-funded Civilian Irregular Defense Groups (CIDGs).

"Are there mountains in the jungle?" Gary didn't know why he learned skills like rappelling and how to set up belays. "I thought we were helping the locals to defend themselves."

"Your job is not to wonder why," his Recruit Division Commander ordered. "Are you ready for tomorrow?"

"I'm afraid of heights!"

"Then you'll be in for a surprise."

Surprise was an understatement. He and the other recruits trained alongside the 173rd Airborne Brigade and practiced jumps from UH-1 Huey helicopters. Gary was freaked out and relieved that a static line would, in theory, deploy his parachute since he thought he might freeze up on the way to the ground.

Following basic training, Gary remained at Camp Elliott with the other 12 members of his STAT team. They took additional classes and were sent to Vietnam in January 1963. The Military Sea Transportation Service (MSTS) carried helicopter units to South Vietnam. The STAT teams were given additional coursework during the 21-day voyage.

"I took three history and math classes, and now I'm qualified to be an adult in the real world? One day, I'm a ranch kid, and here I am, seasick, puking my guts out."

****

Soon after arriving at the Danang airbase, Gary's STAT team spent the next few months learning about their construction assignments supporting the Special Operations Navy Division (SOND).

Gary led a crew of Laotian construction workers setting fences. His team took a water break from their work in the hot and humid air.

"Steiner, Gary?" a voice asked from behind the team.

Gary stood, turned around, and gave a nod.

"Captain Sombat, RLA."

Khampheng Sombat and his mother immigrated to Fresno from Laos in 1945 when he was eight, fleeing political unrest. After graduating high school, he continued his education at the University of California in Berkeley. He was summoned back to Laos, where he was commissioned as a Royal Lao Army (RLA) officer in 1963.

Gary saluted and motioned for his crew to get back to work.

"Sir, did we do something wrong? I know it's not exactly Navy spec but on the ranch ..."

The Captain led Gary to a bench under a palm tree.

"Our leadership team has been observing you. We like how you relate to our soldiers. You blend in well."

Gary wasn't told that after his team completed work at the outpost near the Laotian border, he would be ordered to stay and provide covert technical assistance to pro-democracy CDIG insurgents in their guerrilla fight against *Pathet Lao* Communist sympathizers across the border in Laos.

****

The picture was clearer. Paratroopers were last deployed during the Korean War. He was pioneering low-altitude jumps over jungles. Gary was restless on his way in a helicopter to palm trees unknown. Hearing the radio chatter, the missions weren't what he imagined based on the books he was obsessed with reading in junior high school.

He opened the letter he received before leaving Camp Elliott.

"Dear Gary,

"I hope you are doing okay. I was disappointed when your mom told me you enlisted. Guess what? I decided to move to Wyoming. I'm working at the ranch again. Your mom let me stay so I could establish residency. I'll be graduating from Lander High. We'll both be Tigers! I'll be going to UW. Would you mind writing back? Your mom wants to know if you are eating right.

"That's all for now,

"Becca

"P.S. Enclosed is a photo of all of us before the July 4th parade."

Gary sighed and became homesick.

"Steiner, Gary. We'll be over the drop zone at 1300 hours."

Gary glanced at his watch.

"Another hour?"

He looked up and nodded at the guy next to him. There was no unnecessary chatter. Gary was uncomfortable starting up random conversations, anyway.

"Check around you for any belongings you may have left aboard and that your seatback and tray table are full and upright, locked. Mainly, be sure your chute is on your back."

"It would be strange if I saw Dad in the POW camp," Gary thought while looking out the Huey at the occasional flicker of light from villages in the jungle below. "I wonder if he looks like his pictures?"

"Drop zone, NEXT! Steiner! You're first." The pilot's voice crackled through Gary's headset. "Make your way to the starboard door."

Captain Sombat smiled and winked with his right eye. A black leather patch covered his left.

"Remember to tuck-and-roll."

Sombat grabbed his shoulder. Gary nervously smiled back. Gary was the first to push himself off, followed by the others. The static lines and "D" bags dangled in the wind, billowing through the black sky.

The navigation crew didn't expect crosswinds. The team floated off course in the silence of the humid air over a forested area two kilometers from the planned drop zone. Gary dangled from a palm tree.

He positioned his night-vision goggles, released from the parachute rig, and dropped 15 feet to the marshy ground. As instructed, he tucked and rolled to minimize the impact on his knees.

Sombat didn't say a word. He signaled with his arms to creep in a prone position toward the tree line, where they would be out of harm's way, at least for the moment. He reoriented his map toward the north.

They faced a cliff covered with vegetation, requiring a belay to be set up.

"Can't we go around?" Gary whispered.

"Add another two hours? We have to get to the objective before sunrise," Sombat responded. "Tie the rope around the tree trunk over there. Wrap it around your butt. It'll be a 'set-your-mind-at-ease' belay. The rock is slick. The last thing I need is to haul you out of here with a sprained ankle or a snake bite."

"Where did you learn how to climb, Captain?" asked Gary as Sombat tied a rope around his waist.

"Wyoming."

"We should talk. On belay," Gary directed, hoping the climb was more straightforward than it looked.

"Belay on."

"Climb."

"Climbing." The wiry Sombat began his ascent. He set a protection point by stringing the rope between two tree branches before reaching the top. Gary kept the rope taut. "Off belay."

"Belay off."

Gary detached from the rope he wrapped around a tree trunk while Sombat set up a top rope. The three remaining team members ascended to the top. They left the rope behind and padded over the hill. Ahead 100 meters, a flickering light signaled the objective location.

The tower searchlight illuminated the perimeter where the teams were hiding. They advanced with care when the light moved away from their position until the four were near the compound gate.

"Our intel says there's a Navy pilot somewhere in there. Sole surviving son."

Sombat pointed toward the guard tower and signaled Tag Team 2 to make its way to the opposite side of the compound, cut a hole in the fence, and wait.

Gary and Sombat cut through the wire. They made their way behind the prison office. Their movements were covered by inaudible Laotian party noise inside the officers' quarters.

Just as Tag Team 1 sneaked past the back door, a woman ran out in a cloud of cigarette smoke, chased by a *Pathet Lao* officer. Over the jocularity and commotion, the officer heard a stick crack in the rustling grass. He became quiet, pushed the woman aside as he drew his side-arm, and slowly walked toward the stoop.

Gary crouched below the porch and latched onto a black combat boot. The officer crashed into the brush, and with his blade drawn, Gary silenced him with a quick slicing motion.

"All this to get one guy?"

Gary took a deep breath and stealthily moved away. There was no turning back from the most stressful situation he'd experienced in his 19 years.

All hell broke loose. The woman hurried back into the office to alert the other reveling soldiers who stumbled onto the porch in various stages of half-dress as they pulled on their uniform shirts. Shots rang out. Meanwhile, Sombat ran to the prisoner cages through a hail of gunfire.

Tag Team 2 tossed a grenade into the jungle as a diversion. The *Pathet Lao* pursuers took off toward the blast and flash.

The makeshift prison cell was a giant cage fashioned out of bamboo poles lashed together with rope. The emaciated barefoot pilot with a scroungy beard crouched in the corner.

The cage door was chained shut and padlocked to the frame. Gary broke down the door with his M16 butt. The pilot could not stand or walk. Sombat tossed the skin and bones over his shoulder while Gary provided cover. The three jogged as fast as they could.

Sombat, carrying the pilot, and Tag Team 2 entered the open field. Gary lagged and was grabbed by a *Pathet Lao* officer lurking in the shadows. He struggled to get behind his assailant and sent him slumping to the ground with a swift swipe of his blade. He picked up the service revolver and pistol-whipped an enlisted soldier running toward him.

The Huey waiting outside the prison compound came under close-range mortar fire and was peppered from the jungle by a *Pathet Lao* Degtyaryov machine gun placement. The chopper pulled up and away as the door gunner returned fire.

"What the hell? You might as well be my little brother."

The dazed *Pathet Lao* assailant rolled into the fetal position. In slow motion, the soldier turned over with a look of vengeance and pointed a Makarov PM handgun at Gary's heart.

48

Amadeus Mozart

October 7, 2006—1:05 p.m. MDT: Phil clipped on his Eco-Haven name badge. He and Elizabeth gathered the well-wishers and prodded them to take their seats. Phil left the front door ajar so latecomers could enter quietly.

Elizabeth managed her mom's funeral production script from a perch in the back of the room. She cued up her iPod with the country blues prelude to, *There's Nothin' You Can Do* by Roscoe Tanner.

Gary took the floor in front of a table with Becca's coffin flanked by photos and flowers.

"Hello, everyone. Elizabeth and I appreciate you celebrating with us on this lovely Saturday. The Buffs have lost five in a row, so I'm glad you came rather than being disappointed at the game. What a way to begin Blue Sky Village's 10th anniversary.

"I'd like to introduce some guests who came a long way to be here. This is my mother, Sally, and uh. You can introduce yourself again."

"I'm William, Gary's brother. I manage the Quiver Mountain Ranch by Lander, Wyoming."

Billy gave a quick wave.

"Becca's mother, uh, is here from Cherry Ridge, New Jersey. She came out with …" Gary began when Jack piped up.

"Becca's mother? Meet Mary Pembroke. This is my dad, Fred Middleton. I came down from Laramie with our classmate, Avery Meadows, over there guarding the beer."

The crowd laughed.

"Be sure you all introduce yourselves after the services," Gary read from the script. "We have many desserts and finger food prepared by my neighbors here at Blue Sky Village. Susan's dates wrapped in turkey bacon and stuffed with low-fat cream cheese are the best and good for you."

Elizabeth cued up the twangy country ballad, *She's Only a Baby*, by The Bronco Brothers. When the song ended, Gary returned to the front and flipped to the next page.

"This is also the opening event for the Blue Sky Village 10th anniversary celebration. It was Becca's idea for her cardboard box to do double duty as a time capsule. She wants this to be a time when we can all share stories that the Becca baubles will conjure up.

"She's been preparing for today since her first cancer diagnosis five years ago. If you want a copy, we had her script bound up at Lightning Fast.

"Becca always liked the movie *Our Conference*, about a group of college pals from a small town getting together at the funeral of one of their mutual friends. I know she wants this to be when we can all share stories. Before I call on my mom ..."

Felix emerged from the basement stairwell, stood next to Gary, and took a bow.

"I see we have a change which will give me a few minutes to lower my heart rate. Welcome my downstairs neighbors ..."

"Thanks, Gary. I'm Felix, and in honor of Becca, I'd like to play the third movement of Mozart's *Oboe Concerto in C*." There was a murmur around the room because the performance wasn't on the program. "I'll be accompanied by my partner, Sandra."

She entered and nodded at the crowd before sitting at the upright piano on one of the dining room chairs. She screeched around, getting herself comfortable.

"Sorry about that. The piano bench is over there under the rhododendron."

Sandra placed her sheet music on the piano's music desk.

"We're winging it here, Solieri."

She cued Felix with a nod before he flawlessly completed the performance to the audience's wild applause. Gary returned to the front.

"Wow, what an unexpected treat. I'm glad you canceled your travel to San Antonio."

"Just don't open that coffin!" Sandra ordered after she and Felix took a closing bow and left the room.

"I want to introduce my mother, Sally. Sally Steiner."

49

La Comida Buena

Grandma Sally was the head of the Quiver Mountain Ranch household. Dad was amiable and did what he was asked. Living among others on the ranch and in the Navy were preludes to life at the Calamity Club and Blue Sky Village. On the other hand, I was expected to get along on my own. My parents assumed I'd go with the flow because they said so. Instead, I questioned everything. No wonder I argued with Mom and was fired from every job I worked. E.S.

******

When Gary had completed his third tour of duty in 1965, he could have reenlisted again and stayed in Danang. He was in line for a promotion but was passed over twice. Instead, he chose to head back stateside. He returned on an MSTS transport ship to San Diego and took a commuter train to Union Station in Los Angeles.

Upon his arrival and reintegration into the American hustle and bustle, Gary was culture-shocked after three years away in a foreign land, having lived alongside other 18 to 20-year-old guys who only knew high school and the realities of war.

It was a pleasant spring day in 1965, quite a relief from the heat and humidity of Vietnam. He had a full-day layover before departing on the Coast Starlight train from LA to San Francisco.

He searched through his duffle, retrieved two small blue velveteen-covered boxes, and then checked the bag to Rock Springs before walking outside and taking a deep breath.

"Can't say I miss the smell of diesel fuel and heavy artillery explosions," he said to himself.

Instead, there was the odor of street tacos and the upbeat sound of live *mariachi* music across from the train station on Olvera Street. The tunes performed by the family house band enticed him to a small café called La Comida Buena.

Gary sat at a small table to watch and listen. The violin player put down her instrument.

"Good afternoon. I'm Isabella. Lunch for you?"

"Can I sit for a few more songs? I haven't heard music like that before, nor the food I smell being cooked."

"Ah! The cumin and garlic will get you every time. You being here was our cue to get to work. If you're around, we play a set before dinner time. He's my father." Isabella pointed at the standup bass player, leaning his instrument against the wall. "We've owned this place for two generations. I'm the third. There's my mom in the kitchen getting ready to cook your lunch."

"I don't want to be a home wrecker."

Gary perused the menu as the band members tied aprons around their waists.

"I've never been to Los Angeles or tried Mexican food."

"How about the special? It has a little of everything. Two tacos, two cheese enchiladas, and chili relleno casserole." Isabella pointed at the menu with photos of each of the dishes. "The casserole is my favorite. Cheese stuffed peppers baked in batter.

"One 'Number 1.'" Gary handed back the menu. "Tap water will be a treat."

"LA water isn't exactly Perrier."

"Not as bad as over-chlorinated river sludge."

Isabella delivered a glass and a pitcher.

"Ice? I haven't had ice for three years. Can't wait to drink from our Wyoming well."

She set down another glass filled to the top with ice cubes.

"Wyoming? Are you a cowboy or Indian?"

"I'm sort of both. My dad's family was from Germany. They were cattle ranchers. He was the cowboy." Gary pretended like he was riding a horse. "My mom's Arapaho. We're a matrilineal tribe, so that makes me Arapaho."

"You don't look like a cowboy or an Indian."

Isabella glanced at the dark blue beret he wore with his civilian T-shirt, Levis, and black Converse All-Star low-top sneakers.

"The hat? I was just discharged from the Navy."

Isabella picked up one of his boxes and looked inside at the Purple Heart with a Bronze Star.

"Are you a war hero?"

"Just doing my job. The Navy gave it to me for flying around in a helicopter and peeling potatoes in my spare time. Keeping you safe from the bad guys."

He opened the second jewelry box and showed Isabella the silver Navy cross attached to a blue ribbon.

"What did you do to deserve that?"

"It was my first mission. I didn't know what I got myself into. I don't like to talk about it. When I get home, I'm displaying them next to the 'Most Minutes Played' pin my football coach gave me."

"*Felicidades!* Tomas, chips and *pico de gallo* for our warrior!" Isabella called out to her cousin in Spanish.

"*Pico de Gallo?*"

Gary dipped a chip in the mild concoction of fresh diced tomatoes, jalapeno pepper, and cilantro.

"'Beak of the rooster.' I don't know why it's called that. *Picar* means to chop. *Pico* is peppery. Maybe spicy vegetable scraps chopped up for chicken feed."

Gary snarfed down his food. Isabella refilled his water and brought the check.

"Dessert? How about a raspberry *empanada*? They are similar to turnovers."

"No thanks. I have some time to spare. I want to walk around. Learn about Mexico."

"This is El Pueblo. It's the birthplace of Los Angeles. 1781. Our neighborhood is a big community. See these tiles and the furniture? All from the neighborhood."

The restaurant walls were adorned with ornate blue, white, and yellow tiles hand-painted and fired by an *azulejero* in the next block. A *mueblero* across the street made the tables and chairs.

The café filled up with a steady flow of customers. Isabella escorted a party of three to a table across from Gary and wiped down the adjacent table.

"More like the American version of Mexico that attracts tourists like you."

"We have the same problem. Tourists expect to see us wearing feathered headdresses. They think we live in teepees. Hunt bison. There are powwows with dancing competitions. Tourists get a taste of what's left of our tribal culture before the government wiped us out."

"Olvera Street is a big tourist trap. Nobody around here wears those big sombreros and serapes draped over their shoulders."

"Back in the day, businesses in the reservation border towns hung signs like 'No Dogs or Indians Allowed.'"

"My grandfather has similar stories about Latinos. He was a *traquero*. Crossed to work on the railroad." Gary handed her a twenty and took a final swig of LA ice water. "If you change your mind about dessert, stop at the bakery down the way. They provide us with our pastries."

"I'll look around on my way back to the train."

He settled up and wandered the narrow streets. Unlike Wyoming, the *calles* were alive with shopkeepers chattering with the many locals and visitors browsing around.

Gary stopped at the *pandaria* for a fruit-filled *empanada* and looped back to Union Station.

****

He didn't have to wait long to board the northbound Coast Starlight. As the train rumbled over the tracks, the dark sky out the window was broken up when the train made frequent stops on over-lit platforms, like a local bus. The rhythmic evening ride was calming and a welcome change from sleeping through explosions and fighter jet sonic booms.

The moon lit up the Pacific coastline. Occasionally, as the train rounded a bend, he saw the crashing waves against the shore splashing a mist that caught the lunar glow.

The train pulled into Emeryville, where he transferred to the California Zephyr. The train ride east was long. He could stretch out across two seats, which was a luxury. Riding on the rambling train that bounced down the tracks was a snap compared to sleeping on the ground with one eye open.

The scenic and forested route between the Sierra Madre Mountains and Reno was much too short compared to the monotonous ride across the deserts of Nevada, Utah, and western Wyoming. He woke up every few hours, hoping to see a herd of wild horses gallop by in the distance before morning greeted the train.

At sunrise, just before Evanston, he walked to the snack bar in the dome car.

"I'll have a plain glazed and a chocolate glazed."

"You can buy the Meal Deal that includes a drink."

Gary gave the thumbs up. The Steward used a wax paper tissue and placed the two donuts on a plate.

"Where you headed?"

The Steward poured coffee into a Union Pacific cup and set it on a saucer.

"Back home. Three years is a long time to be away."

"Where you headed? Closest Chinatown is in Chicago."

"Another case of mistaken identity. I get off in Rock Springs. Thanks for your morning delicacies. Way better than my C-Rats."

50

Mary Pembroke

October 7, 2006—1:46 p.m. MDT: Billy helped his mom to her feet and assisted her to the front, where she steadied herself on the table edge. The decorative red and white ribbons on her dress gently fluttered when a sudden breeze flowed through the open front door.

"What a hard act to follow. It was beautiful. Thank you, son. Gary asked me to speak to you in Arapaho. It's not too good."

Sally unfolded a handwritten piece of paper.

"When Becca was in high school, her parents sent her to Wyoming to be disciplined.

"She didn't need that as much as she needed a place where she would be spared from judgment. She worked on my ranch. Was my right-hand man and woman. I say man because she was better than any of the men. She could ride and cook. Drive the tractor. Fix fence. Took good care of Billy."

Sally pulled an old leather item from her skirt pocket.

"You might have read Becca's obituary about her work returning tribal things from museums. Reverend Perez got all that started by helping Becca get this medicine bag from the museum in Lander. It belonged to my great-grandmother. Becca reunited us with our past."

****

Sally returned the artifact to her pocket and then got off-script.

"The big Jameson Collection is for sale again. Thirty years ago, they wanted a lot of money. Today, they want more. Last time, a few elders from the Arapahos. Others from the Dakotas, Montana, looked over everything and blessed it all."

"Mrs. Steiner, how did he get all those things?" Jack blurted out from his seat. "Are they traded like baseball cards?"

"Young man, if you're interested, we're talking about building an Arapaho Cultural Center on land owned by Boulder. I learned yesterday, before we drove down here, that the city government is sponsoring us. We can set up for some of our ceremonies.

"The meeting is Wednesday right here. Good if you could make it. Undoing the past is good. I'm also sorry about what happened with our history. I may not remember your actions, but nothing will change the bad feelings you caused."

Jack was contemplative.

"Prison must have been agreeable with you, Jack Middleton. You were lucky. I have a good feeling about you, anyway. Next Sunday, after all our meetings, we're holding the first sweat on the Fort Chambers site. You better be there."

Gary stood and got the service under control.

"Mom, you're on a roll, but this can wait until later."

Sally turned to Jack.

"You had nothing to do with the Indian Wars. You do have to acknowledge your ancestors left our culture for dead, and your government was set up for you, not us or anyone unlike you. We were herded to reservations. Forced to be farmers. We didn't need money until then.

"We were forced to sell our things, beadwork, shoes, clothes, weapons, anything Indian so that we could buy food. Back in the 1970s, Becca did all she could. Same with Reverend Perez."

"Thank you, Mother. Is there anyone else who has a few words?"

Fred and Jack helped Becca's mom make her way to the front.

"I'm Mary Pembroke from Cherry Ridge, Cherry Ridge, New Jersey. Since we're letting it 'all hang out.' I'd lost touch with Becca ever since I pushed her to Wyoming. I always hoped she'd come to her senses. It was me. I needed to come to my senses. Her dad and I had plans for her. Well, I had plans for her. I took advantage of Jack.

"Gary, I know this is the first time we've met. I can't tell you how sorry I am for being so ignorant. I'm from a different universe. I thought I was in the center of it."

Mary caught Elizabeth in the corner of her eye.

"It's been good to know you as a grown woman. You were just a child when your mom first brought you to our home. You should have stayed working in Atlantic City. I'm glad I could do a little something and add to today's celebration.

"I read all the letters Becca sent me over the years. I was too full of myself to answer any of them. She wrote about one wish. Becca found stone tools around her riding stable when she was a child. We had them on display at the Cherry Ridge Museum."

Mary presented a package to Gary.

"Please see that these are returned."

Gary invited others to give any words of remembrance before the end of the service. Billy reached under his chair and raised his hand.

"My mom gave me permission to leave this with Elizabeth."

She made her way to the front. Billy handed her the blue coffee can. She pried it open, then retrieved one of the stone tool shards collected on the Quiver Mountain Ranch. A smile came to Sally's face.

"Thanks, Billy. Lots of memories here," Elizabeth replaced the lid. "I'm glad I didn't swallow any of these when I first met you, Grandma! This will be our donation to the Arapaho Cultural Center. If that ever happens."

"Hold on."

Jack ran downstairs. While waiting for him, several others spoke, including neighbors and colleagues from the universities of Wyoming and Colorado.

******

"Thank you, Susan, for your kind words. I also appreciate the support we've received from Blue Sky Village."

Jack bounded up the stairs and handed a box to Sally. She inspected the contents.

"I have no need for this. It's for you to decide."

She handed the package to Jack as he returned to his seat. Gary took the floor.

"Next is Reverend Perez from the St. Alban's Mission. He married Becca and me. Baptized Elizabeth. Can you give us a few closing words?"

Gary motioned him to the front of the room.

"On behalf of the Steiners, extended and not-so-extended, thank you for attending to remember Becca."

Reverend Perez led the attendees in prayer.

"O, God, whose mercies cannot be numbered. Accept our prayers on behalf of thy servant Becca Steiner, and grant her an entrance into the land of light and joy, in the fellowship of thy saints; through Jesus Christ thy Son our Lord, who liveth and reigneth with thee and the Holy Spirit, one God, now and forever. Amen."

51

Coal Car Truckerama

I feared that Dad would lapse into one of his PTSD moments when Jack started talking during the funeral service. When I was young, I asked him about Vietnam. Mom immediately changed the subject. He would walk away when we would get into it, sometimes mid-sentence. Mom tried to cover for him. That would lead to a fight with her. Defeating Communism and PTSD upon his discharge was complicated by a more menacing foe at home. E.S.

****

The Zephyr had chugged into the Rock Springs station. There wasn't much hoopla surrounding the return of Vietnam War veterans. Gary was the lone serviceman to disembark. Sally, stepdad Marvin, and Billy greeted him. On their way out of town, Marvin pulled his International Harvester pickup into the Coal Car Truckerama.

"I've been telling everyone we were picking you up today. Nobody pushes me around anymore. I'm in high school now. Trying out for football. The school is thinking about an ROTC program. I want to be a Navy officer."

"Don't be so quick about going to Vietnam. It wasn't the war I wanted to fight."

Gary's heart raced. He opened his eyes wide before covering his face with his palms.

******

Specks of orange sunlight had appeared through the overgrown Laotian canopy. Gary hesitated when he saw the gun barrel pointed at him. The jittery young soldier pulled the trigger. One shot rang out and blasted cleanly through Gary's shoulder. He wrestled away the handgun and fired one shot into the ground, sparing the young soldier's life.

His hands trembled as he made his way through a hole in the perimeter fence. Gary was relieved for the moment, only to find that the evacuation helicopter was nowhere to be seen. Loud Laotian voices and foot stomps through the marshy grass drew nearer.

******

"Gary, are you with us?"

"Sorry. Just daydreaming."

"I'm glad to have you back, son. Thanks for the *Blue Breeze* subscription. We could keep up with your writing. Son, are you okay?"

"I'm okay, Mom. Tired."

"Don't forget me! I learned how to drive the John Deere. Tell him, Dad!"

"Your little brother's a born a rancher. It's about time you came home. Join in the fun."

"I'll help when I can, Marvin. New tractor? That's progress! You're looking good, Billy. A tough guy now. Some of what I taught you must have rubbed off. Your confidence has grown."

Gary was on the scene when Billy was bullied in school. He was one of the few Arapaho students in his grade. When Billy's classmates taunted him, Gary's towering presence was enough to send the bullies running.

"We expect you to take more responsibility around the ranch. Your mom and I could use your help. Summer will soon be in full swing."

"Oh, Marvin, can you stop talking business? We're having a party for you, Son. I've been getting a menu together with some of the other mothers." Sally was head of the VFW Wind River Auxiliary. "All the vets are organizing a ceremony. The Buffalo Drum will be there. You're a war hero."

"No big deal. We were training the local army."

Marvin looked at Gary with incredulity.

"When I was in Italy, Indian guys like you and me were given the dangerous duty. We were expendable. Army commanders watched too many movies. They thought Indians shot straighter, were sneakier, braver. We were all Tonto, always the sidekick."

"Marvin, I'm happy to be back home. Life in uniform wouldn't be the best for Billy. It's getting worse over there."

The war escalated in 1964 when a North Vietnamese patrol boat reportedly attacked the U.S.S. Maddox and the C. Turner Joy in the Gulf of Tonkin, resulting in massive American military expansion in South Vietnam.

"It's time you came to your senses. Your mom and me? We aren't getting any younger. How's a typewriter gonna provide enough money for you? A desk job is no place for a decorated veteran. Navy training built up your strength. You were around all kinds of fancy equipment like helicopters, tanks. Fixing the tractors will be a snap. Your little brother needs your help."

"Not interested. I learned how to write stories and climb mountains. That's good enough for me. I'm going to college."

"Marvin lay off. We have a party to plan!" The server came by with more coffee. Gary signaled he'd like a warm-up. "Becca asks about you. When are you going to come to your senses? You knew she stayed with us for her senior year? She was a real help."

"... and smart. I don't know if I would have figured out how to diagram sentences without her. She brought some of Mom's sourdough starter and showed the 4-H club how to bake bread with no yeast."

"Be practical. Listen to Marvin. Ranching is part of us. It's stressful to hire new workers. The young hands are different now. No work ethic, even at the Eagle Crest. Our young men would rather work in town. The Arapahos have owned it for two generations."

Gary glanced up from his coffee.

"Your great-grandfather kept the old ways alive there. Once, he came to Eagle Crest in his full regalia. My dad fixed him up with a horse. He chased a yearling around the corral and imagined shooting him with a bow and arrow. He got one last hunt out of his system."

"You and Marvin taught me to stand in two worlds."

"Not out of choice, the government banned our religion. Said it was evil. One year in BIA [Bureau of Indian Affairs] boarding school was enough for your mom and me."

"Especially women." Sally showed Gary her disfigured fingers from being smacked with a yardstick by one of her teachers. "You lead by example. No matter where your life takes you, be good and do no harm."

"I don't speak Arapaho. Our ceremonies are a mystery to me. I'll do what I can to respect our traditions while I'm studying journalism. If it makes you feel any better, I'll keep track of Becca and be sure she's okay."

52

Connie Morgan

October 7, 2006—2:49 p.m. MDT: Gary thanked each mourner as they exited the funeral service. Sure enough, Susan's yummy dates were the first to go in the appetizer department, followed by the artichoke-parmesan cheese dip and pita crackers.

"Did the airline give you any trouble, Grandma?"

"My assisted living place has a bus. We go to the store once a week. No problem there. I didn't have to check it as long as it was cooked and vacuum-packed."

"Good choice." Jack was on his second pork roll sandwich. "How did you know about these, Elizabeth? They are exclusive to Jersey. Taylor pork roll. It's the original. The Kaiser rolls. Nice touch for us connoisseurs."

"It was in Mom's script. You didn't know I was in the hotel food service business. I can source obscure food. The sandwiches were the hit of the party. Thanks, Grandma!"

"You're welcome. Not because I'm a big pork roll fan. You visiting Jere and me when you worked in Atlantic City was our little secret. I hope you and your dad will feel welcome coming to New Jersey. I sold the Pembroke home when your Grandpa Jere died. Maybe you can bring Jack with you. He can get you in trouble. I know Fred still has plenty of room. I should have listened to your advice back then. Today might have been different."

"Different 'good' or different 'bad?' Thinking about the past stresses me out."

****

Albert was cleaning up his vintage griddle. Elizabeth walked over to the counter in the back of the kitchen.

"You did double duty today."

"Forget about it, Elizabeth. Today was payback time. Your folks gave me a hand up when I was sick." Albert scraped the shards of pork roll and fried eggs into the compost can. "The first time I went to the hospital, your dad was 'Gary on the Spot.' He drove me at two in the morning. When I was rehabbing in Lakewood, your mom gathered donations from the neighbors to defray my wife's gas cost."

Avery and Jack retreated to the kitchen, where they helped the Caring and Sharing Committee members pick up the mess.

"Middleton, it was good to meet your dad. I didn't think he was the pompous ass you make him out to be."

"Fred's mellowed in his old age. Started getting rid of stuff. The guy only needs one golf cart." Mrs. Pembroke delivered a stack of used plates to be loaded into the dishwasher. "Ever since I was a kid, you always liked me, Mrs. Pembroke."

"You were such a good boy, Jack."

Jack shook his head as Mary returned to clearing the tables.

"She's the main reason things got so screwed up between Becca and me. 'Buy Becca nice things, make her happy.'"

"Well, you were a jerk," said Avery. "I've wondered why I even hung around with you."

"Low self-esteem. I didn't come to grips with myself until the big blowout in '67."

"We were a good rock-climbing team, Middleton."

"If I couldn't trust good ol' Avery with my butt, why would I trust you with my money? We did okay when we sold out. I was right. The recession in '93? Not bad for two slouches. I got personal satisfaction keeping my share far away from Dad's meddling fingers."

****

Billy, Jacob, and his mom delivered dirty dishes from the courtyard.

"How about you bend Billy's ear about trading for a few head of his Charolais?"

The two excused themselves to the courtyard.

"Jack, it's so good to see you. You too, Avery. Can you two help me with the recycling?" asked Connie.

"I drove by Douglas on our way down. I heard Converse County has been booming," observed Avery.

"I sold some of the ranch. I couldn't afford not to. The town is expanding the parks. Adding nine holes. Could use some help designing it, Jack."

"I haven't picked up my sticks since 1966. Jacob can't help you with that?"

"He manages the oil and gas. There's a well on the 12th hole."

"Only in Wyoming. That would be a challenging hazard. 'Mickelsen's lining up his shot from the sand and eyeing a slight fade around the pump.' Like a miniature golf hole."

"We're thinking about how to pass the cattle operation to our ranch manager. I gave him a piece of land next to Jacob." He and Billy set up a beer pong court on one of the Courtyard tables. "I better check to be sure those two aren't getting in trouble out there."

****

"Looks like you and Connie still have it," Avery mentioned while scraping off the small plates.

"She was a little too laid back for me during our college days. Of course, everyone in Wyoming was too laid back. I wonder if she's still a good kisser."

"Too laid back? This coming from Jack, jilted lover living alone in his ruin of a mansion in the woods?"

"I had an attitude adjustment."

Elizabeth gathered the remaining tableware around the Common House and stacked them in the sink for the next load. Her dad continued his visit with the stragglers. Sally joined Avery and Jack.

"You three sticking around? Our spiritual elders are organizing a sweat. Be there. It will do you all some good."

"Don't worry, Mrs. Steiner." Jack wasn't about to test the wrath of Sally. "We have a quick trip to Laramie. We'll be back in plenty of time."

Sally was pulled aside by some of the Blue Sky Village neighbors. Elizabeth returned with more dishes.

"My dad's having fun. I'm glad you two came down to support him. Did you notice he was having trouble getting through his part of the service? He skipped you two."

"I was tapping the keg and didn't realize there was a lapse in the service. Besides, it was best because everyone liked listening to Gary's mom."

"Are you going to start this thing up, Jack?" Elizabeth located the detergent under the sink and powered up the heavy-duty wash cycle. "My dad was diagnosed with early-onset Alzheimer's, and you two going after it last night didn't help."

"I figured. Must have been the full moon."

"He seemed okay all day before you lit into him."

"I have a way with people." Jack glanced over at Gary, chatting it up with some of the lingering well-wishers. "That Come-to-Jesus talk was a long time coming. We're still not done."

The kitchen clean-up was finished. Elizabeth put down the dish towel. She, Jack, and Avery joined the conversation at the big dining table.

"I'm glad Fred invited me along. For a son-in-law, you're not as bad as I imagined," Mrs. Pembroke said with a laugh.

"Son-in-law has a nice ring to it," Gary responded.

"'We can't be enemies,' Pastor Jere would say. He was a conscientious objector in World War II."

"I should have gone Jere's route."

"Jere was stationed close to home at Fort Belle Mead. He ministered to the German prisoners there."

"Be careful with your war stories," Elizabeth warned. "Dad can get erratic. His long-term memory is solid. Short term? Different story. Dad would be better off if I weren't here. I'm bad luck."

"Don't be so hard on yourself. Being ridiculed by Middleton about sent me to a psychiatrist permanently!" said Avery. "That's more accurate than funny."

Phil and Brad wheeled the Eco-Haven cart into the Common House great room. Phil slid the cardboard coffin onto the frame, wheeled Becca's remains, and loaded the box into the station wagon for transport to the crematorium.

Sally was still energized, even after a seven-hour drive and two hours on her feet.

"Mrs. Steiner, it was so nice to meet you finally. Do you still host the Cattlemen's Association barbecue?" asked Connie.

"Not for a long time. Now it's your turn."

Jack escorted Connie and Jacob to their car.

"Reverend Perez, Sally? You're welcome to stay with Harold and me," offered Susan. "We have extra room."

"Thanks for the offer. I'm staying here with my kids."

"I made arrangements at the Rectory. After the meeting on Wednesday, I'm the guest entertainment at two services on Sunday. Billy, are you about ready?"

Reverend Perez excused himself.

"I'm looking forward to your Indigenous People's Day meeting with the City next week," said Susan. "I've heard so much about your work on the reservation."

"One day, I was young, working on a ranch. Didn't know much. Now I talk to myself more and have all the answers, according to me! I'm old and still don't know much. You know what that means? I'm an elder because I outlived everyone. Don't get too excited. Others are coming down tomorrow. Getting out of town is a treat. A motel is an even better treat."

Susan and the Caring and Sharing Committee moved the dining room tables and chairs back into place. Gary and Elizabeth placed all the smaller flower arrangements on each table as centerpieces. Gary set aside the large bouquet from the community for his condo.

"Where are your two pals? Maybe we should take them out for dinner. What's the place you like, Dad?"

"It depends. There are many good places around here. I like the one down the street. Excellent service. Whatever they have will be okay by me."

"It's the Tibetan Peak. We went there for lunch yesterday? You frustrate me."

"I was testing you."

"What? I was testing YOU, Dad. Why not say you can't remember? Your guessing game is a strain on my already paranoid mind."

The Odd Duo sat in the courtyard, sipping leftover beer from the weekend activities.

"Gary seems out of it. I don't know if he remembers the 'Pact.'"

Elizabeth made her way over to their table in the courtyard.

"What 'Pact?'"

53

Vintage Automotive

Considering their history, I hoped Avery would talk Jack out of pulling anything dangerous with Dad. The funeral ended without incident. I'm surprised that long-lost friends, estranged or not, feel obliged to get together at all, let alone at emotional events like funerals. I wasn't the only one who let too much time lapse between the past and present. The quarrels are the same as we grow older, but the stakes get higher. E.S.

****

The Odd Trio poked a written Calamity Club party invitation into the neighborhood mailboxes. Some dropped by to see if the legends were true or to grab a free beer. Most planned to do something else. Next door, Mr. Billingsley was none too crazy about the reveling.

It was the second Saturday in August 1967 and Gary's turn to host the Calamity Club's monthly grand opening. The guest list included Gary's newspaper office reporters, Avery's rock-climbing buddies, and tolerant Wildlife Managers. Jack invited a few nerds from the C&I Accounting Department.

Before the party, Jack stopped by Becca's anthropology lab.

"We're having our August grand opening party next week. You are always welcome. It'll be the usual crowd."

He handed her an invitation.

"In that case, only if I can bring Connie."

"Maybe she has friends. 'Our Grand Opening was so successful last month, we decided to open again!'"

******

Gary was in the kitchen hand squishing hamburger patties with his back turned toward the party in the rest of the house. Becca observed from the doorway.

"Your mom taught me how to fix food for all those Okies the two summers I worked for her."

Gary handed Becca a potato and a peeler.

"Mom likes to put out a spread." Gary concentrated on his barbecue project. "She always asks about you when we talk. Billy misses you, too."

Becca stood close to Gary.

"She invited me to help her with a big community barbecue in September. You invited me to the ranch over Thanksgiving. Don't you and your high school buddies get together around Labor Day? If you're going home then, can I catch a ride? We can get to know each other even better."

"Things have changed. I've been meaning to talk to you about that. Do you need new tires?"

"If that's how you're going to be, it needs two in the rear and an oil change. I could use some help. Maybe you could come with me to Hans's garage."

"Vintage Automotive is in Bosler."

"Hans can give us a ride back to Laramie. Have lunch at Fuji's. We can decide when we should head to the ranch."

"It doesn't matter when we go."

"Look, don't be upset. We can't change the past. Let's make the best of it." Becca put her arm around his waist. "There isn't anything wrong with having a little fun. The drive will do you good."

Jack overheard Becca's voice and stood at the kitchen entry.

"I told you I'd pay to change your oil. I checked your tires. They're good. The last time I talked to your mom, she was upset about you taking a fancy to Little Beaver here. Did you fight the Commies by peeling potatoes, Cochise?" Jack moved closer. "You won the Navy Cross by scalping roaches on kitchen patrol?"

Gary turned around, stepped in front of Becca, and was in Jack's face.

"That's out of line, Middleton. You're usually such a polite jerk."

Becca pushed Jack away.

"I'm just fooling around." Jack apologized with a forced smile. "I should know better with all these knives lying around." Jack turned to Becca. "Remember, your parents and I have, let's call it, an understanding."

The tension was as thick as the hamburger patties on the cutting board.

"I don't care what you have going with Becca and her mom." Gary gave Jack a stern look and raised his greasy fist. "I left what fight I had in Vietnam. Don't push me."

Jack sneered as Gary glared back and returned to his potato peeling.

"Or what, you're going to burn my covered wagon?"

"Let's get back to the party before you get hurt." Becca pushed Jack out of the kitchen. "I think you know my roommate, Connie."

"She's the first person I met when I checked into the dorms. We've had a few study sessions together. She's interested in corporate mergers."

Jack winked at Connie with a smile.

54

Herb Perry

October 8, 2006—1:52 p.m. MDT: The Odd Trio decompressed after the funeral in the Common House TV room. Jack and Avery sat on the couch watching old reruns of *The Dino Hunters* show on the GoldieOldie Channel. Gary napped across from them in the vibrator chair and was startled awake.

"YAAAHHH! AARGAAHH!" Gary came out of his seat and charged toward Avery with evil in his eyes.

****

Seaman Steiner had hidden himself in the marsh, alone and out of breath at the extraction point. He barely noticed the pain in his shoulder from the bullet wound. He knew enough to apply a compress he fashioned from his handkerchief.

His heart raced faster when a *Pathet Lao* squad charged out of the jungle at dawn. Gary screamed out of fear and sprayed his M16 across the landscape, shooting at nothing with reckless abandon. Birds of all varieties burst out from their perches, squawking and flapping.

A Huey rose over the forestation and provided machine gun cover fire. The *Pathet Lao* scattered as the chopper settled. Gary stumbled toward the hovering craft.

****

Jack jumped out of reflex.

"Damn!"

He restrained Gary and moved him to the couch.

"I'm okay."

He shook out of it and relaxed. Gary had sweat beading on his forehead and panted like a blacksmith's bellows.

Avery took a deep breath.

"Relax, Steiner. You had a nap terror. We're waiting for our painting class to start. Why don't you join us? We paint serene landscapes."

The Blue Sky Village community rented out space to earn additional money to keep their Homeowners Association dues lower. An instructor from the Senior Citizen Center taught weekly Herb Perry painting classes. Herb Perry was an eccentric artist who entertained his students on a successful community-access TV show. The workshop was rescheduled for Sunday because of the Saturday funeral. Artists from around town attended the class.

"C'mon. It'll be fun. Elizabeth will be there."

"It's best if I'm alone when I get like this."

Gary took the remote from Jack and surfed through the channels.

****

The Boulder Herb Perry disciple was a retired high school art teacher who wore loud Hawaiian shirts. His gray hair straggled out from under a black béret, Herb Perry's trademark. Most of Perry's certified teachers wore one.

Budding impressionists Monet and Manet sat with their easels next to an aspiring Elizabeth Morisot. Their works were of the same landscape, with a mountain in the background and a lake in the foreground.

"I started as an art major. Ended up in wildlife management to keep my Battle of the Bulge father happy, recalled Avery. "'Act like you're from Wyoming,' he'd tell me."

"Very relatable. My mom wanted me to be a nurse!" said Elizabeth. "Let's get our creative juices flowing. Take a step on the wild side, Jack."

"Neither of you two are my type!"

"You don't have to sit next to us, big fella," she winked.

"We all did time in Laramie, including you." Jack pointed his brush at Elizabeth. "Reminds me of Medicine Bow Peak and Lake Marie. We go to Laramie on Friday. We can paint on location."

"Laramie? I want to tag along. Check out the Calamity Club. Drop off some of my stuff. I may be living there," replied Elizabeth. "Will the Eurovan make it 75 miles?"

"Exploring the back roads while finding Middleton didn't do much for the struts. For you, Elizabeth, I'll get the rig checked out. I don't know about you, but the Calamity Club would be a blast from the past."

"That would be a negatory for me," retorted Jack.

"I've heard stories about YOUR Calamity Club." Elizabeth mixed some titanium white and cadmium green paint to accent the foreground. "There's still a hole in the basement wall. MY Calamity Club? I have stories from when I grew up there. As a kid, one of my chores was to keep the mice out of the pile of boxes and suitcases in the garage. It was a shrine."

"I haven't been in there since I crashed on the couch on my way to Tibet. Thank you, Elizabeth, for the ride to the airport if I forgot to say anything."

"Me?" Jack stuck his finger down his throat, pretending he was barfing. "Back in the day, I added a bathroom in the basement and moved into my den of serenity and iniquity."

"When I was in junior high, we redid the basement. There's an arrow pointing to 'Jack Was Here' graffiti. There must be a good story because someone hung a frame around it."

"Middleton advises me to plead the fifth."

"What do you have to say about the ultraviolet lights hanging in the furnace room? My friends and I used to crawl around in there. We found pot seeds and tried to plant them."

"Meadows advises me to plead the fifth. Speaking of furnaces, do you know when the funeral parlor is delivering your mom?"

"Phil is supposed to drop everything off later today or tomorrow." The instructor walked by and shushed them. "We're good. A little distracted is all."

Not much paint made it onto the canvases. Jack packed up his stuff.

"Have you ever climbed down here?"

Avery finished scraping details into his trees with a putty knife and moved his work to the back of the room.

"The department came to an elk management conference at CU. No time for climbing. Sat in lectures. I was long gone from school but was invited to present my paper about how elk were responsible for passing brucellosis to cattle. That was '69."

Jack rinsed the acrylic paint out of his brushes.

"It'll be like old times. What about Steiner?"

Avery joined Jack at the wash basin.

"I don't know how safe it would be to have Mr. Memorex along."

Elizabeth set her work on the back counter.

"I'll go. I can set up a belay. Keep an eye on my dad."

"We don't need him flipping out on the rock. How about you keep track of your dad here? Meadows and I need to catch up some."

Elizabeth returned to the TV room and sat with her dozing dad.

****

Downstairs in the guest room, Avery dug out a tattered copy of *Rock Climbing the Flatirons* guidebook from his pack.

"We can try something on the First Flatiron. Figure it out once we get there."

They loaded into the Eurovan and sharked toward Baseline and Broadway.

"How about we drive through University Hill? Turn here. There's the Pine Box Saloon. Appropriate for this trip. Beer? Shoot the breeze?" The Eurovan about tipped over after the quick left. "Watch it, Meadows. Do you want to be the next Pact honoree?"

"Remember the Stonewall riot? The cops assaulted a bar full of gay people in New York? Based on rumors, the Pine Box was raided when I was at the elk conference," Avery recalled. "We'll be here for a few more days. Let's spread out the sightseeing."

Avery pulled into the Chautauqua parking area.

"Well, Mr. Griz Guy, something on your mind."

They hiked up to the information kiosk to find out if there was anything they needed to know about before hiking to the trailhead.

"When I saw Dad and Mrs. Pembroke at the funeral, I had this moment of clarity. It must have been miserable for them to go through life pissed off about how they screwed up as parents. They wanted to live guilt-free after I bailed them out."

"Don't you think they've realized times have changed?" The ranger handed Avery a map. "It's the 21st century."

"They're both pushing 90 and just now coming to grips with Becca's choices, my bad choices." Jack led the way on the trail. "It wasn't all bad. I became more independent. I didn't realize how messed up it was to please my dad. I was so close-minded. Gary wasn't different. I was the different one."

"Jackie Boy? Join the club." Avery stuck the map in his pocket.

"You don't get to call me that, either."

"Becca called you 'Jackie.' You should have embraced that. Get over yourself, Middleton. That's nothing. A few years ago, my folks hired out the motel management. Jackson is a hot market. I've had zero contact with them since my dad disowned me when I was 15. That's been a tough one. I felt like I let them down when I bought the B&B instead of helping them run the Moose Paddle. There's no heir apparent beyond me."

"Not much you can do about your macho dad or yourself. It's not like you didn't try to be the good son he didn't have. You ditched the art major. Join the club—the Society of Lonely Only Persons. We're SLOPs, 'SLOP 'til we Drop.' My dad SLOP-ped on me when I decided to stick with you in Laramie. Maybe the old man cut me out of the will."

They arrived at the base of the First Flatiron. Jack readjusted his laces.

"These boots are not made for climbing!"

"That would make for a good song title."

"Since we got to Boulder, I've been frustrated. Over the past 40 years, I think about how things could have differed between Becca and me."

"You kept pushing her away! We all have freedom of choice. That means having to live with consequences. Don't beat yourself up. Becca's gone. Do me a favor. Patch things up with Steiner. That means a quieter life for all of us. That's all you got?"

"All right, all right. Let's get climbing."

"Remember when we scrambled around at Veedauwoo?

"Not since college. I don't get out much. Since we sold the store, I've been hiding in Centennial, cheating my neighbors. No climbing there except when I went up a drainpipe and broke into the Old Stage Stop through the skylight."

"Practical urban climbing skills. Lucky for the statute of limitations. I won't have to testify against you."

"Cut the crap. You were pretty good at 'scaling tall buildings in a single bound,'" Jack did some stretches and cracked his knuckles. "Felonious climbing was a good challenge. You wrote the guidebook, Meadows."

****

The Odd Trio had always driven to Veedauwoo to mess around on the boulders whenever they had an afternoon to kill. If time was short, they challenged themselves with "buildering," a malaprop of "bouldering," the term for climbing short routes on large rocks or small outcroppings near the ground.

Jack and Avery sat around their Laramie Mountaineering office.

"I bought a new rope. It was more than I like to pay."

"I find that hard to believe, Senor Denaro Mucho."

"Ever hear of the OGC?"

"The Outdoor Gear Coop is our competition. It's a nonprofit, so the prices are way lower."

"You're our marketing guy. Get them to carry our Upward tents and bags, Meadows. How about a few boulders? I want to uncoil this rope."

"We don't have enough time to get to Veedauwoo and back. On top of that, the shift is about to change."

"I've imagined a route up Ross Hall. We can impress the girls. I'll call Steiner. He should be out of class by now."

The three urban mountaineers met at the limestone block dorm for their buildering expedition.

"See there. It's a friction climb up by the window, then make a lunge move to where the south meets the east wall."

Avery pointed at the route.

"Steiner, go inside, get on the roof."

Jack handed him his new rope. Inside the dorm, a small crowd gathered in front of the window.

"Looky here, Becca. Your friends are trying to break in."

"Jackie's always making a scene. One time, he jumped off the church balcony onto the pews. Broke his ankle. I still feel bad about not visiting him in the hospital."

Becca glanced out at Jack and Avery, assessing the climb from their dorm room window.

Gary wandered down the hall and tapped on a door.

"Can't get on the roof unless one of you daring women sneaks me up there."

"Since when did you become a common criminal?" asked Becca.

"The last time. We had to pay a $10 fine. It was fun, though."

Connie and Becca led him to the trap door to the roof. Gary climbed up a retractable wrought iron ladder. The high-angled pitch was awkward to negotiate. The shingles were smooth after years of wear. He tied the rope to a vent pipe and then tossed it.

"Rope!" yelled Gary.

"I'll be surprised if we can make it between the two windows," said Avery as the rope uncoiled from above.

"You think it's a friction climb? It's a 90-degree pitch." Jack studied the route. "There are some pretty good nubs I can grip on either side."

Later in the afternoon, the sun was lower in the sky. The walls were cooled down. Jack was the first to rope up and ascend to the top of the first-floor windows before falling off and dangling above the flower garden.

Next, Avery took a little different route. He gripped the corner and leaned back on his way up to the same spot as Jack before he plummeted off the wall and was caught by Gary's belay.

"You boys peeping at the girls? It would be best if you called to make a proper date," a voice yelled out to them from the street.

Jack turned around.

"Helping the ladies with a stuck window, officer."

Gary gathered up some of the rope slack from his rooftop perch.

"Lock 'em up!" Becca wailed out the window.

She put on her sweater and lugged a stack of books for a quick getaway to the Anthropology Lab before meeting Gary in the hallway. The two shuffled down the stairs and out the door.

****

"That was the day I bugged Becca in her lab. Wanted me out of her hair. She invited me to go along with you two for cheap drinks. I knew I shouldn't have made fun of her busted-up petunia pots."

Avery checked out the guidebook.

"How about Freeway? It's 5.0. Should be doable. We can turn back if it gets too late. I'm okay with no ropes."

"Sounds good. We'll have time for that Pine Box pilsner."

55

Morgan Student Health Center

Jack and Avery were hiding something from me, and I didn't understand why. Whatever it was, if Dad was included, they had to go through me. As bad as I thought my life was, when I was in my 20s, I didn't face the responsibilities my parents did. Thinking back to my last conversation with Mom, she was mum about her love triangle. She made it sound like Jack was a platonic friend. For Jack, it was unrequited love. Dad fit in accidentally. Maybe both were forbidden loves. E.S.

****

The summer of '67 had flown by. Before the fall semester, Becca stopped at the student health center, where Connie worked at the front desk and was busy organizing the previous week's paperwork.

"Miss me, roomie? I'm done at 3. I'll buy you a Coke."

Tears ran down Becca's cheek.

"Are you okay?"

"Things got a little out of control."

"Becca?"

"I'm not aggressive about much of anything."

"You're not making sense."

"Maybe I got a little overconfident," Becca sobbed. "During Wild West Days, I ditched Jack. Went on a campout with Avery and Gary. Well, it turned out I camped with Gary. He can be so nice. He's so humble."

"Huh. When you went off camping, guess who called me that night?"

"Not a chance."

"Chance."

"A spite date? I hope he treated you to a nice restaurant. Jackie can be quite the romantic."

"In a sense. If you're worried, I'll be here all day Thursday. I can schedule an appointment for you around then."

****

Two weeks later, as usual, Becca waited for Gary by his newspaper office in the Union after her last class. They walked to Ross Hall, where they usually parted ways.

"Do you have a minute to talk?"

"Don't you have a lab?"

"I'll be late." They lingered on the steps in front of the dorm. "You know we have a history together. I've become pretty good friends with your mom and Billy. I'm not sorry for what happened on our camping trip. I like you, Gary Steiner."

Becca was stalling.

"I like you, too. So …?"

"Remember after Lake Marie, the barbecue at the Calamity Club in August? I tried to talk to you then. Jack picked that fight in the kitchen. I'll get to the point. I'm pregnant."

"Wow!" Gary's eyes beamed. "How did you find out? "

"The rabbit died."

"What are you going to do? I share responsibility. What a surprise, a good surprise."

"Your mom's been trying to get us together since I first came to the ranch." Becca closed her eyes and let out a sigh. "Are you sure you're okay with this? You don't want to take some time to think about it? Are you man enough?"

"There's no turning back. I don't know what more thinking will accomplish. We have to work on this together. Like you say, we have a history nobody else has."

"Are you sure? How can you decide on a whim?"

"I've dreamed about starting a family. Dreams come true when you least expect it."

Becca was sheepishly skeptical.

"One reason I joined the Navy was to keep Mom from bugging me about taking over the ranch. I should have listened to her."

"I don't know how that would have changed things. Did you want to get away from me?"

"Get that out of your head. I just had other things on my mind. We could have done more planning compared to no planning."

"There's more to becoming parents than how we got here."

"No better time than the present. Like my mom says, 'One day at a time.' We don't have many options."

"I may not want to keep it."

"Adoption?"

"That's too complicated."

"Colorado just changed its state law."

"The adoption law?"

"No, the other law. It hasn't been 21 weeks."

Gary handed her his handkerchief.

"Where did you learn about this?

"It was in the Denver paper. Colorado was the first state."

"Have you talked to your parents?"

"This is no time for joking around. What they don't know will be a blessing."

"The timing is right for us. I have a job at the paper. You have your assistantship. Soon, you'll be a well-respected college professor saving the world!"

"I'm no Wonder Woman. We could live at the Calamity Club. Having a house would make things a little easier. My instability is my stability."

"If it's a choice of keeping our baby or not, I'll put whatever effort it takes to make a family with you. I'm man enough."

56

Charles Jameson

October 11, 2006—10:07 a.m. MDT: Wednesday following Becca's funeral, Sally and Gary hosted the meeting to debrief the Monday morning Columbus Day protest with Boulder community advocates from the Social Justice Society.

Susan and Harold busily rearranged the Common House dining room. Elizabeth returned with a box of pastries from the Cedar Tree bakery up the street and fired up the drip coffee maker in the kitchen.

Jack and Avery sat in the back in case they had to make a quick getaway. The front door was propped open. People filled up the tables. Sally soon arrived. Billy and Reverend Perez helped her to the head table, where she was joined by two other Arapaho tribal elders and convener, CU linguistics professor Kelly Hanlon.

"Young lady, you were at Sand Creek last week. Willie Eagle."

"I remember," Elizabeth cautiously responded.

"Why are you here?"

" Becca was my mom."

"Hm, that makes you Sally's granddaughter! You should have said. She's my cousin!"

"It's a small Arapaho world," welcomed Professor Hanlon. "We'll open the meeting with a prayer by elder Mr. William Eagle."

Mr. Eagle recited a prayer in Arapaho and returned the program to the Professor.

"Welcome especially to our guests from Wyoming, Sally, Billy, the Eagles, Reverend Perez. Before we debrief the rally, Sally wants to discuss the Jameson Collection. For those unfamiliar, these are Native American relics owned by Charles Jameson in Tulsa. Sally? Can you provide us with some background?"

"Becca came to visit me, maybe 35 years ago. She first met with Reverend Perez and thought the Episcopal church might be interested. The idea was to purchase the collection and return everything to the tribes. Pedro, Becca, and her anthropology department helped Mr. Jameson inventory his things. He didn't know what he had."

"Sounds like this Jameson wasn't a collector." Jack piped in from the back of the room. "He was a hoarder with too much money on his hands."

"The St. Alban's Mission was involved back then. I think it was the early '70s when Becca returned a second time when she was in graduate school.'

"The Mission displayed around 100 Arapaho items at our little museum," explained Reverend Perez. "Over the years, Arapaho elders helped us monitor the collection."

"What kind of money are we talking about?" asked Susan. "We want to be helpful. I'm frustrated by the growing size of the project."

"It's big. In the 1970s, Mr. Jameson turned down $1 million," Professor Hanlon reported. "Now that he's out of the picture, his estate is motivated to sell. There's a tribe in Oklahoma opening a casino. I believe they are putting a bid together. The Arapaho effort is far ahead of others because UW recorded the stories about the objects."

"Churches are pushing back because of the price, but I think there's quite a bit of guilt around missionaries destroying tribal life," added Reverend Perez.

Professor Hanlon asked for other comments and recognized Sally.

"If anything, it would be good to have Wind River things returned. Arapaho and Shoshone things. I don't know what the other tribes think. That's another stumbling block. All the tribes have a say in this."

"Let's get back to this after lunch. How about the Columbus Day protest? For the first time, it went okay. What do you think, Sally?"

"We need to focus on how to get land back where the cultural center could be built. I know many tribes went through here, but this is Arapaho land. Boulder owns a park. Ideal spot for the cultural center between Wyoming and Oklahoma."

"Thanks, Sally. For starters, we can work with the Episcopalians. Move the St. Alban's exhibit. Gary, you've been sitting there quietly. Is there anything in your book about any of this?" asked Professor Hanlon.

"My mom is the brains behind it all. Check Becca's files. My book? If there's anything to add, Elizabeth is the editor."

Jack raised his hand.

"The city is allowing ceremonies? This is all very interesting, Professor. I didn't realize how connected all the tribes were back then. I'm curious about the cultural center."

"We're still connected through ceremonies. The Center is still a pipe dream," Sally sternly interrupted. "You're one reason we're behind, Middleton. I still haven't recovered from your little prank."

"Thanks, everyone. I think this would be a good time for our lunch break," Professor Hanlon said. "Let's be back here in an hour."

****

The Odd Duo went back through the sandwich buffet line.

"Do you two have some time to talk today?" Elizabeth asked as she ladled out Sally's macaroni-hamburger soup.

"Keep putting out the pork roll," said Jack. "It's better after aging for four days. Never goes bad."

Avery built a sandwich from the usual fixings like lunch meats, cheeses, veggies, and condiments.

"How about when you finish and we return from the Post Office? Meet you at the puzzle table."

Jack and Avery joined Gary, Sally, and Reverend Perez.

"Did you get Becca's mom and your dad out of here, okay?" asked Gary.

Jack dunked a slab of pork roll in a splotch of mustard on a small plate. He signaled that his mouth was full.

"I saw them off on Tuesday. They had to get back for their very important meetings. When they were younger, Wyoming wasn't their cup of tea. Too quiet. Anyplace west of New Jersey was their cup of gruel."

Gary set down his soup spoon, closed his eyes, and breathed deeply. He thought loneliness was living on the Quiver Mountain Ranch in the middle of nowhere until he stood alone in a Laotian marsh 7,800 miles from Wyoming.

****

The Huey circled and hovered three feet above the waving sedges. The *Pathet Lao* mortar fire continued from the jungle. The door gunner continued to provide cover. Gary bled profusely from the gunshot wound to his shoulder. It seemed like it took him forever to reach the helicopter. Captain Sombat dragged Gary aboard as the chopper lifted off.

"Danang Airfield, NEXT!" The pilot announced as the Huey disappeared into the dark of night.

****

Jack looked into Gary's blank stare.

"Are you with us?"

"I have a dream. In this part, I finally get extracted. I snap back to normal like nothing happened and relive it again."

"I'm lucky you didn't flashback on me Friday night."

"You're lucky I didn't flashback to the middle of the dream when I was wielding my Blaze Blade. My counselor at the VA says I need to eliminate stress. This week hasn't helped."

After dunking a half-sandwich in the soup that dribbled over the table, Avery went to find a napkin. Professor Hanlon sat down.

"Jack, right? Kelly Hanlon."

Jack exchanged a nod across the table. He was naturally wary but didn't engage because he was swallowing another mouthful of pork roll.

"This culture preservation work grows on you. I get the impression you've been at this for a while." Jack managed to answer after finishing his swallow.

"I've worked with the Arapaho tribe since the '90s. Helped them publish a language book. We've been working on this land repatriation thing for quite some time. Your friend Becca was a colleague of mine at CU. How do you know the Steiners?"

"Becca was a childhood friend." Jack's life passed before his eyes. "I got to know Gary through her and Avery here."

"She was thinking about this Arapaho thing up until the day she died. It's beyond me why she was passed over for leadership jobs at UW and CU."

"My take? Becca had a mind of her own, strong-willed. Wyoming reminded me of Jersey. At least in my circles. Socially conservative. You can interpret that how you want."

"Why did you ask about the Arapaho Cultural Center? It was Becca's labor of love."

"I had an interest mostly because she had an interest. I've been trying to figure out what to do with my life. All this Arapaho stuff now has me curious."

"It was good meeting you two," Avery interrupted and pointed toward the alley.

Professor Hanlon joined Sally, Gary, and the Eagles at another table.

"Thanks for the updates, everyone," said Jack as he ran down to the guest room and returned with a package. "Post Office?"

The Odd Duo waved at the crowd on their way to the Eurovan.

"I don't pay for parking. Too much traffic downtown. There's a branch by that little bakery."

Avery pulled into the strip mall loading zone and put on the emergency flashers. There was no line when Jack stepped up to the window. The postal clerk motioned for him to place his box onto the scale.

"Anything fragile or flammable?"

"Looks fragile," the clerk observed after inspecting the contents.

"I need some tape and a zip code."

"Let's see here, 'San Ildefonso Pueblo Historic Preservation Office; P.O. Box 2007, Santa Fe, New Mexico.'" The clerk scrolled through a list. "87506. Any insurance?"

"I trust you."

Jack readjusted the bubble wrap and sealed the box with an industrial packing tape dispenser. He didn't know that two pots similar to those he acquired in the 1960s appraised on the Corner Cupboard TV show for $26,000 each.

" We don't accept Gold or Platinum."

Avery waited in the drugstore check-out line and bought a tube of toothpaste and a Bonkers Bar.

"Meadows? I think you can buy your stuff over here!"

****

The Odd Duo returned to Blue Sky Village.

"Is this my purpose in life, cleaning up the Common House kitchen after meetings?"

"I thought there was a committee for that. Get used to it, anyway. You'll have to make up for when it's your dad's turn for Kitchen Patrol."

"Don't remind me. Do you have time to talk now?" The three sat down. "You two have some sort of plan. Remember, my dad has Alzheimer's. During the time I've been here, he's been getting worse."

"Our quest has been in the works for over 40 years. Your parents didn't tell you anything about it? It'll be less complicated if you keep an eye on your dad."

57

Sodom & Gomorrah

The Odd Trio left the full moon party yelling match in the past. The second Jack walked into the courtyard. I could feel the air pressure rise. That blowup was a child's spat compared to what happened in September 1967. Mom didn't burn bridges, and that caused hard feelings. I've never been stuck on anyone, as bad as Jack was stuck on Mom, but then again, I'm a bridge burner. E.S.

****

Jack pulled a hundred-dollar bill from his pocket.

"I'll buy, you fly. Get us something real tasty."

Gary soon returned from the store, unloaded, and fired up the sturdy BBQ kettle, a smaller version of the industrial-size smoker his stepdad, Marvin, welded together from a 55-gallon drum.

The meal was planned out perfectly. Gary grilled the thick bone-in rib steaks medium-rare, the baked potatoes wrapped in aluminum foil came out piping hot, and the roasted ears of corn in the husk were perfectly tender. Nothing whetted an appetite like the mixed aromas of a barbecue.

"Hey, you got a bonfire going on out here!" Avery said, cowering from the flames, jumping out of the grill as black smoke circled around the backyard.

"The steaks were a little more marbled than usual. Plus, I tossed on some hamburgers we had to use up. We'll have plenty of leftovers."

"You know," I never ate leftovers until I moved to Wyoming," observed Jack.

"Hearty appetites around your dinner table?" Gary asked as he turned the meat with a pair of tongs.

"Anything that wasn't eaten was for the kitchen staff."

"Waste not want not," said Gary.

"More like waste lots and waste more at the next meal."

Gary's eyes burned as he wafted the smoke away.

Mr. Billingsley, from next door, called the cops because there was so much smoke. Two fire trucks showed up in front of the Calamity Club. The neighbors gathered in front of the house, envisioning the burning of Sodom & Gomorrah. Avery walked to the front yard to check on the crowd.

"You are all invited. We have plenty of food to go around."

"Just a barbecue out of control," the police officer on the scene advised Mr. Billingsley.

"I can be a wishful thinker."

After the commotion subsided, the Odd Trio sat on the deck enjoying their meal, washed down with cold beers. Gary went into the house to check on the apple pie baking in the oven. Avery and Jack talked business while waiting for the dessert.

****

"Are these financial statements correct? Compared to last year, we have a lot of summer inventory going into the fall. You're the cash flow expert, Meadows."

"I talked to the crew about having a sale. All the Downtown Merchants are in the same boat as us. We can organize a sidewalk sale around Homecoming. The football team's so good. There will be lots of action around town."

"The others are old fashioned, except Tak down at Fuji's," observed Jack. "It's the '60s. We're white-collar hippies. We're members of the Chamber of Commerce. Peace, Love, Dove, and Capitalism."

"There's still plenty of climbing. I thought of teaching a series of mountaineering classes. Maybe Veedauwoo. The Snowy Range. Discounts on winter stuff. Deep discounts on summer."

Gary returned with the pie he carried with two oven mitts and placed it on their outdoor table.

"That should free up some cash, Middleton. As long as you don't gamble it away."

The pastry was delicious. Avery returned to the house and retrieved the community stash box from under the couch. After sorting out a few buds and cleaning them on a Buffalo Brothers double album, the seeds tumbled gently down the album crease back into the box.

Avery's fingers were the most agile and was the best joint roller. Step 1: Hold the rolling paper. Step 2: Sprinkle on the pot. Step 3: Roll the perfect cigarette with one flick. Step 4: Give it a lick to seal up the edge.

The Odd Trio sat in the folding chairs and engaged in giddy small talk.

"How about those Pokes? They better live up to the year they had," Avery asked and answered, took a toke, and passed the joint to Jack.

"Too bad they lost to CSU," Jack held in the smoke, exhaled, and groaned about the '66 team going 10-1 and defeating Florida State in the Sun Bowl. "We should have made a road trip to El Paso."

They argued about the merits of a business degree compared to a science degree. Both were important. Jack was the financial brains, and Avery knew about the ecology of mountaineering.

"Time for a Calamity Club meeting," Gary announced.

"What gives?" Jack was uneasy. "You know how to kill a good buzz!"

"How long have we lived here? We paid rent to ourselves. We've stayed out of trouble. It's been fun. Maybe it's time to mix things up." Gary hesitated. "I want to buy you two out."

"Mixed up is right. Could be a good idea. We could use a little cash to put into the business. Right, Meadows? Prop us up for a few months until we liquidate some inventory."

"We could move into the apartment above the store," Avery took another toke.

"Becca is moving in with me," Gary declared.

There was dead silence. Jack was enraged and approached Gary with a glare of vengeance.

"So, Connie was right. I thought you were a noble savage! I thought you respected me."

"What are you talking about? Becca doesn't give a damn about you. What's this about you and Connie? Doesn't seem to me you're so respectful of yourself or Becca."

Jack cocked his arm, readying for a right cross. Avery intervened but wasn't strong enough to stop him. The unexpected punch sent Gary down four steps to the sidewalk below the deck. His face and the side of his head bounced off the concrete.

"I'm out of here! Put my stuff in the garage," an enraged Jack screamed. "I know where you live. I know where your family lives. And fuck Becca and her goddamn 'Pact.' The only reason I agreed to that shit was to keep her happy."

Jack stormed into the house. Gary was unconscious. His blood dribbled onto the concrete.

"I didn't think he'd take it so hard." Gary shook his head and regained his wits.

Avery hurried inside and retrieved a dish towel to daub the blood flowing down Gary's face as Jack slammed the front door behind him.

"I didn't realize Middleton was a mean drunk. Probably not the best way to break the news. Figure out how much you owe us. I'll deal with our Mohammad Ali. By the way, I'm good with moving out by the end of the month. Congratulations, I think."

"Remember our campout? Lake Marie?" Gary asked while shaking out the cobwebs.

"Yeah, and you and Becca didn't return to camp until the next morning. I thought you two abandoned me."

"Take me to the hospital. I feel like I'm gonna throw up."

"Ohh, so Becca + Gary equals three"

314 | ALAN O'HASHI

"Are you getting married? When's the big event?"

"Which one? I think the baby's due in the middle of April. Peace, Love, Dove, and Diapers!"

Avery loaded Gary in the Silver Steed and drove to the Emergency Room. He was diagnosed with a moderate concussion and whiplash.

****

Being pregnant during the winter was good since Becca wasn't much into cold weather and winter recreation.

The two were married in December before Christmas 1967. After a big bachelor bash at the Post Office Club, Reverend Perez officiated a small wedding at the Episcopal Church in Laramie, attended by Billy and Sally. Stepdad, Marvin, stayed behind to tend to the ranch.

The highlight was a nice dinner at the Fuji Café.

Becca phoned her family in New Jersey. The calls went unanswered. She received one card from Uncle Frank in California, who sent a $50 savings bond, which was appreciated.

58

Queen of Spades

October 12, 2006—7:08 p.m. MDT: Gary and Elizabeth were still exhausted six days after the funeral. Glassy-eyed or not, they continued sorting through Becca's boxes and files. A document in a folder Elizabeth was leafing through caught Gary's attention.

He retrieved his manuscript, flipped to a chapter marked by a sticky note, compared what he saw in the file, and then scribbled some notes with a red pen.

"I have to make edits when I think of them."

"Good idea. I can't read your mind, or lack of it."

"Did you entertain your new pals today? I hope they aren't bored. It seems they're blending into Blue Sky. Pretty good for Jack since I don't think he's had much contact with people."

"You should let them read the draft. They'll help you recall memories for your book. Is there anything in your story about a mission you three have been plotting?"

"Is this a test? I know what happened 30 years ago. 30 minutes ago? Forget it."

"I noticed. Take your medicine. I don't want to find you wandering in the street muttering to yourself!"

"If there is a mission, Avery's in charge."

Gary returned to his story. Elizabeth went downstairs to the Common House. The Odd Duo was playing cards in the dining room with Harold.

"Mind if I sit in?

Elizabeth walked over to the table as Sandra walked by the picture window and waved inside.

"That's my cue. You can take my spot." Harold slid her the deck. "I told Susan I'd get out of her hair while her book club was meeting."

Elizabeth took Harold's seat and shuffled the cards a couple of times. It was Avery's cut.

"No matter how pretty the dealer looks, always cut 'em thin, always win."

Avery shifted the deck back to Elizabeth.

"The game is Spades. I like to shoot the moon every hand," Elizabeth warned while she flicked the cards with a spin.

"Shoot the moon?"

Jack was coy about some players' risky strategy by taking tricks with all the trump cards, including the Queen of Spades, the object card.

Avery signaled the table by tipping back an imaginary bottle and went to the fridge.

"I hope you like *Hefeweizen.*"

"No thanks, wheat beer makes me sneeze." Elizabeth sorted her cards. "I think I saw some fizzy water. So, tell me about this 'Pact' you're always talking about."

"The old picture on the table at the funeral service?"

Avery handed Elizabeth her beverage.

"I've seen it. Before you get too far, Mom and I discussed selling the condo and moving Dad into an assisted living place. As it stands, I'm staying in Boulder for the time being to help him get his affairs in order."

"The 'Pact' is harmless."

Jack discarded the three of diamonds and picked up the 10 of hearts from the discard pile.

Elizabeth won three out of six hands, two by shooting the moon, and returned to the condo. Gary was watching *After Hours* with Tom Gering, which had its moments, but overall, he was funny but not hilarious. She continued sorting through more of her mom's boxes in the living room.

"Were you hanging around with your two chaperones?"

"Chaperones? Right. Are you asking because you know or don't know? We played some cards. Your friend Jack is competitive."

"Competitive? He's a cheater. I hope you weren't playing for money. You were messing around instead of working on the next Oscar-winning screenplay?

"My life's a screenplay. First, Mom's cancer, now your Alzheimer's. Do I get a real job or jump off the cliff and be a writer? My unemployment runs out soon. No jobs around here."

"Now that's a movie plot. It's a good time for a change while you have safety nets. Live in Laramie for cheap. Go back to school. Get student loans. Fall back on your nursing. Mom's not here to bug you about that."

"Who's going to be sure you don't trip down the stairs or forget to take your medicine? Give you CPR? Keeping track of you would be better than sitting in the classroom again. Rinsing out your bedpan has to be less stressful than studying."

"I'd be more alarmed if Alzheimer's gave me black sores on my legs or blurry vision. Give me a sign!" Gary pleaded as he looked toward the heavens.

"You want a sign? Take your medicine! If you want me to hang around."

"I'm not as sharp as I once was. Nobody around here is. The doctor says I'm in the late-moderate stage. I have three, maybe five years left. Why do you think I'm trying to get this book done?"

"Let's keep going through Mom's stuff while you still have your wits about you. I've found some good story fodder in those papers."

"Have you run across anything about your Mom's big secret?"

"Speaking of secrets, let's get back to your 'Pact.'"

"Libby Flats. Remember? We went there when you were a kid."

"How could I forget? Every summer, you promised to tell me about Libby Flats when I was older. Well ..."

"I turn into a pumpkin at 11."

"Don't you mean midnight?"

"Eleven Pacific Time." Gary wandered into the bedroom. "Check the house. I'll see you in the morning."

Elizabeth opened a file box dated 1994. She set the box on the floor between her extended legs and flipped through the manilla folders. She stopped at one labeled "OK etc." In the file was a letter on company letterhead.

"Dear Becca:

Thank you for being a part of the Genotype Inc. focus group. We relied heavily on the input and expertise of anthropologists, geneticists, and historians to test our massive databases. In exchange for your work, we hope you and your loved ones will enjoy the enclosed.

Sincerely,

Molly Jordan, CEO

Genotype Inc."

Elizabeth logged into her mom's Genotype.com account on her dad's computer. Becca's subscription had expired, so Elizabeth updated the password. She entered her mom's birth name, birthday, and place of birth, then hit the SEARCH button.

Records popped up. She was printing a copy of the massive document when it stopped midway through.

"Dad? I need more paper!"

"It's somewhere in the desk, maybe?"

Elizabeth completed the print job, walked to the living room, and saw the red light blinking on the answering machine.

"This is Phil from Eco-Haven. Sorry to be calling so late. I'll bring over Becca's ashes first thing in the morning."

59

St Alban's Mission - Ethete

I was preoccupied figuring out what the Odd Duo was planning when the Arapaho Cultural Center and Fort Chambers meeting ended. While they were out messing around, Grandma Sally helped me clean up the Common House kitchen and filled me in about the first time we met. Mom's visits to the ranch were working social calls. I've been entertaining myself since the first time I was dragged along. E.S.

******

Becca and Sally had become a good kitchen team and looked for any excuse to prepare a feed. In early November 1970, Becca was nearing the end of her doctoral work when she drove to the Quiver Mountain Ranch, which wasn't the wisest time for a long, middle-of-the-week drive. She bounced the beat-up Scout up the road in a cloud of dust. Becca opened the car door with a squeak. Sally came out to help her unload.

"The Scout. No Gary?"

The sunshine took the edge off the temperature in the 30s. The dry feel of an impending storm was in the air. Becca opened the passenger door.

"This must be Elizabeth. "She looks like you."

Becca picked up her daughter and followed Sally to the front porch.

"There's supposed to be a foot of snow. Gary insisted I take his 4x4. It has a great heater. Mileage isn't as good. Had to fill up in Rawlins and Lander to get here."

"Billy can top you off with ranch gas when you leave."

Sally put out her arms. Becca allowed her Mother-in-Law to cradle her granddaughter. They sat on the wicker couch. "Sun feels good. Take it in while you can. How old is she now?"

"Three in May. I think she has your eyes! Thanks for sending the quilt. She is so calm when I wrap her in it. I think she feels your heart."

"My cousin, Marge. She sews blankets of all types." Sally reached for the placemat on the table between the two chairs. "As small as this. As big as the queen-sized turquoise one I gave you for a wedding present. I'm surprised Gary let you go it alone."

"You know how the newspaper office can be, too hectic to tend to his daughter's demands. We could use the break."

Elizabeth squirmed around. Sally helped her down to the throw rug on the porch floor. She shuffled back to her mom.

"Are you two okay?"

"My field trips, his work, and Elizabeth. It's a big balancing act. We're both 'cowboying up,' as Gary says."

"You're always welcome here. "Sally signaled it was time to go inside. "You know Luna comes in and out."

Sally headed to the kitchen as the Coon Cat crept toward Elizabeth. Neither of them knew what to make of the other.

"She'll be fine. We want her to explore around. She takes after you, a mind of her own!"

Becca laid Elizabeth on the couch. She was soon fast asleep for her afternoon nap, cuddling with her stuffed black and white panda, Tim.

The remaining summer crew moved the cattle herd down from the mountains. Sally was planning out the dinner menu. The main course was roasted chicken.

Sally thawed two birds in the refrigerator before seasoning them in black enameled roasting pans with a dry rub. She preheated the oven, placed the lid, then slid the pans into the gas oven.

"When you showed me how to do in an old hen my first summer, that was enough to make me buy chickens from the store."

"That was a rite of passage. You've taken to city life now. Two hours ought to do it." Sally closed the oven door, set the timer, went to the wall phone, and clicked the hook switch. "We don't want to undercook. The last thing I need is sick men."

Besides introducing Elizabeth to her grandmother, Becca's other purpose for the visit was to meet with Reverend Perez again so they could update each other about their tribal artifact repatriation project.

"Good. A dial tone." The phone buzzed a few times. "Hello, Pedro? Sally Steiner, here."

"Sally! Whew, I was resting my eyes. I don't move as fast these days. It's been a few weeks since we've seen you in church."

"We've been down six hands since Columbus Day. I've had to help move the last of the cattle down myself. Snow's supposed to fly tomorrow."

"What can I do for you?"

"You remember Becca Pembroke? She's Steiner now."

"Did you forget? I married them in Laramie. We had the fancy dinner at the Japanese place."

"She's now a professor in Laramie. I'll let her tell you directly."

Sally passed the handset to Becca.

"Hello? Reverend Perez? Not a professor yet. It's been a few years since we last talked when I was an undergrad. The Anthropology Department still has an eye on the Jameson Collection. Your help has brought us to where we are now. I've wanted to meet with the elders."

"My schedule is filling up. I have some time tomorrow after lunch." Reverend Perez glanced at his pocket calendar. "If there's snow, I don't want to slow you down."

"Tomorrow afternoon is perfect."

Becca hopped up and down with delight.

"How about you meet me at the Mission, say 1:30? I'll see if anyone is around. No guarantees. There's a funeral tomorrow."

Sally and Becca caught up with each other while the chickens roasted. Around 5:30, the kitchen aromas meant it was time to set the table for dinner.

Billy was the first worker to arrive and rang the bell on the back porch, hailing the other crew members. Not an ort remained on the platters. Becca and Sally sat at the "kid's table" with Elizabeth. The crew finished dinner and was pretty good at taking their plates to the sink.

"Let's get you in the mood for your meeting. Billy, find the coffee can. It's on the shelf next to the buffalo skull."

Becca walked into the front room and sat Elizabeth on the floor with a basket of her favorite toys. The curious, long-haired beast with tufted ears and a ringed tail came right up to Elizabeth.

"Looks like my new niece is an animal lover," observed Billy

"They're about the same size. Why with the name?"

The big critter rubbed against Becca's ankle.

"She walked right up to the backdoor. Wanted to come inside. It was during a Blue Moon. She liked to walk under our feet at dinner. One of the men from Chihuahua said, 'Let's call her Luna.' It's Spanish for 'Moon.'"

Billy scattered arrowheads, stone chips, and hide scraper shards on the coffee table.

"Lots of memories in that can."

Billy shooed the cat off the couch.

"These are what you and Billy collected over those two summers," said Sally, sliding the stones around the table. "It seems like a long time ago."

Elizabeth climbed off her mom's lap, eyes peeking above table level. Elizabeth was fascinated by the stone chips. Becca kept her from sticking the small ones in her mouth.

"Go ahead, pick out a few. You found many of those."

"I feel bad we took them. Like the people who stole all this land." Young Elizabeth moved the stones around the table. Becca handed her one of the large scrapers, which wasn't a choking hazard. "These rocks are like trash from a campsite. Even trash has traces of the people who left it behind."

Becca moved Elizabeth's curious hand away from the pile of stones. Billy showed her a flat, sharp rock.

"Magic Mountain Side notch. If you're skinning a bison today, it would still work." Becca retrieved her daughter, tangled up underfoot. "What do you think about your Uncle Billy?"

Elizabeth was more content sitting on the floor, banging the stones on the wooden planks. Billy selected another one.

"That's a piece of a plains knife used by bison hunters. It's new, maybe seven or eight hundred years old." Becca selected an arrowhead from the pile. "This is a good one. There's no telling how many people passed through your ranch. Some of these are four or five thousand years old."

"It's a little strange thinking about the stories of people. Maybe we should put all this back." Billy picked out a piece of tooled quartzite. "Tell me this. Do you call them bison or buffalo?"

"There's no rule. The scientific name is *Bison bison*. I call the live animal 'bison.' *Boeff* is the French word for meat, so I call Bison by-products like the meat, capes, bones as 'buffalo'- buffalo horns, buffalo hooves ..." Becca examined the tool Billy had in his hand. "That was used to clean a buffalo hide. This dark, glassy thing? It's obsidian used to make sharp razor cuts. It's an odd color. Normally, I'd expect black obsidian from Yellowstone. I've seen examples of this type from Guatemala. Weird. This quartzite scraper was duller and used to clean off the flesh."

"You've learned a thing or two at college!"

Billy plunked the stones into the coffee can.

****

By morning, six inches of snow had blanketed the ranch. Becca and Sally bundled Elizabeth. She sat on Sally's lap in the Scout. The snow-packed roads made for a slower-than-usual drive to St. Alban's Mission, a few miles from Ethete. They pulled into the gravel parking lot next to a 1960 Dodge Dart, a sensible, downsized car, perfect for a frugal priest.

Becca tugged on the handle and pounded on the massive wooden door. Reverend Perez's footsteps echoed through the darkish sanctuary.

"Get out of the weather!" He grabbed the snow shovel and cleared the porch. "Who do we have here?"

"This is my daughter, Elizabeth."

Reverend Perez led them into the dank, shadowy church foyer.

"I knew of you when your mom was getting married," he said to toddler Elizabeth. "You're such a modern woman, Becca."

"It's the 1960s. My self-imposed obstacles are the mothers of Elizabeth's near misses, not to mention mine," Becca philosophized. "I hope she'll remember all the trouble she's been causing."

"I'm sure she'll appreciate all you do for her. Life is more complicated these days. How about some coffee?"

"I'm okay. Sally?"

Reverend Perez led them into his office.

"Black, about half."

Sally picked the soft dining room chair in front of the desk. Reverend Perez poured coffee from a percolator into a ceramic mug. A few framed religious prints adorned the once-white walls, discolored from the unshaded sunlight.

Elizabeth was attracted to a colorful blanket with geometric patterns tacked on the wall behind the desk.

"A church in Farmington, New Mexico, presented it to me. One of the tribal elders there told me the patterns represent pyramids from Central America."

"That's interesting," Becca observed as she picked up Elizabeth, ready to tug down the wall hanging.

"When will you be taking over your department from Dr. Wolfe? Not many women in top positions."

"Not anytime soon. I'm still a Ph.D. student."

"You're a natural fit. Tribal culture is written on your heart."

"When I was a kid, I found stone tools in the woods. My mom had them on display at the local museum. All things tribal are connected."

"We have a small collection. Mostly Arapaho. Let's take a look." Reverend Perez led his tour into the next room. "Not the best way to store them." He flipped on the flickering fluorescent lights. "What do you need from me this go around?"

"We talked about Charles Jameson and his collection the last time I was here. He's still alive and kicking, but his family wants to sell. Over the years, he's accumulated over 1,000 pieces and doesn't know what he has. My department received a grant to inventory his stuff. We can add the St. Alban's collection into the mix."

60

Bobby Smithee

October 13, 2006—5:15 a.m. MDT: Elizabeth didn't sleep very well after reading through the paperwork she sorted out from her mother's files the night before. She sat at the breakfast table with her dad. He stabbed a grapefruit section. A squirt of juice went flying into Elizabeth's lower eyelid.

"Watch it!"

Elizabeth wiped away the acidic fluid before it blinded her.

"If you wore reading glasses, you'd be protected from citrus shrapnel."

Gary could keep his specs miraculously propped on his forehead.

"Did you know about this?"

She handed him the pile of papers. Gary pulled his glasses down.

"I don't know. It was your mom's project."

Elizabeth placed the documentation on the table.

"This stuff goes back to 1862."

Gary's eyes wandered.

"You aren't paying attention. Take your Friday medicine. The bill box compartment labeled 'F'? I'm going out for a jog. Stay put. I'll walk you through it after my run."

She placed the file in her Louis Vuitton briefcase for safekeeping.

******

After Elizabeth took off, Gary flicked on the *Morning A.M.* TV show with the sound turned down so he could listen to the radio. Avery was up and joined Gary for a bowl of granola when the intercom beeped.

"It's Phil from Eco-Haven."

Avery walked downstairs.

"We'll take good care of her."

"I can arrange for her final resting place. That's covered under her policy."

"Becca had other plans. You've done enough. We got this."

Avery retrieved the square cardboard cube and set it on the kitchen table before moving the Eurovan to the Common House loading zone, turning on the emergency flashers to warn the community parking cops, and returning to the condo.

"Good Friday the 13th, Meadows. Did you get an unlucky cup of coffee?"

"It's time to go." Avery handed Becca to Jack. "Throw in your camera stuff, Steiner."

Gary found his bag. Jack grabbed the tripod. The Odd Trio loaded up. Gary rode shotgun. Jack and Becca-in-a-Box had the back all to themselves.

They were off.

****

Elizabeth returned two hours later from her run and leisurely breakfast at the Cedar Tree. She arrived at an unlocked house, the coffee pot still brewing, the radio music blaring over an infomercial on TV about Medicare open enrollment, and her father was missing.

She looked around and scanned out the window to the parking area in the alley. The Eurovan was gone.

"Probably went for breakfast," Elizabeth guessed.

It was lunchtime, and still no Eurovan. She ran to the guest room to find Jack and Avery's stuff still strewn across the floor.

Elizabeth couldn't resist sitting down with Harold and his jigsaw puzzle.

"*Im Blau.* 2,000-piece Kandinsky. Very subtle."

She slid the puzzle pieces around, separating the blue background from the angular colors.

"Did you see my dad come through here?"

"It was a couple hours ago, maybe three. He was with his two buddies."

"Very challenging."

"The puzzle or your father?"

"Did they say where they're going?"

"One of them yelled, 'Wyoming or Bust.'"

"Ah, shit."

Elizabeth rolled her eyes and went back upstairs to her dad's bathroom. She grabbed his unopened Alzheimer's medicine vial next to the sink.

****

The White Shark had a head start as it cruised north on U.S. 287 toward the northern edge of Fort Collins.

"Hey, Middleton. Remember that dive bar?" Avery leaned over the steering wheel and drove by a few familiar haunts. "I'm surprised we weren't thrown in jail the night we dined and dashed."

"That was the least of our problems, considering what was happening in the back room. I wonder how much they had to pay the cops? It was the Dog House by the old train depot. Slow down. There it is."

The pitched, green-shingled roof over a concrete block building painted white was open at 10:30 a.m. on a sunny fall morning. Avery turned into the parking lot jammed with motorcycles from all over the region lined up in every spot for the fall biker rally.

There were no windows. A sunlight stream filled the entryway when the Odd Trio opened the door. It might as well have been 10:30 at night since the lit beer signs covering the walls and the fluorescent lights over the three pool tables were all that illuminated the room. They bellied up to the crowded bar.

"The clientele sure has changed. Looks like they closed the restaurant part," yelled Avery.

"...and the peep show cubicles," Jack hollered back.

The bartender made eye contact with the Odd Trio.

"Bud, Bud, Coors!" Avery barked over the heavy metal rock music blaring around the room.

The bartender was the youngest person in the house. She wore the same fire engine red Dog House T-shirt for sale behind the bar for fifteen bucks. Jack flipped his Platinum card onto the bar.

"Cash! No tabs!" She poured their tap beers while flicking her long blond French braided hair. "ATM's in the corner."

Avery pulled a wad of money and took a stool at the end of the bar.

"Too much testosterone for me. It's not even noon!"

"If you get hassled, I'll be keeping track of Quick Wit over at the pool tables."

Jack and Gary placed quarters on the rail and awaited their turn. A big guy pulled down a gray felt cowboy hat to shade his eyes. He unfastened the bottom button of his black leather vest and pushed up the long gray shirt sleeves covering his muscular forearms before banging the eight-ball into the left side pocket. He picked up the two dollars on the table rail, wadded them up, stuck them in the front pocket of his Wrangler jeans, and awaited the next game.

"I'll be darned." Gary had to look twice. It was Bobby Smithee. "How come I run into you in bars? Where are your guys?"

"Couldn't afford to keep the Barnstormers around. I just can't get strummin' and pickin' out of my blood," Bobby explained while Jack pushed two quarters into the coin slot. "Booking gigs is now on the internet. I use the library computer. There's too much competition with iPods. All the local stations are being bought up and play preprogrammed music. It's a different world, Cuz."

"Now's the time to get after it. The world needs old-schoolers like us. Besides, we're not getting any younger. I hope you're still writing music. Becca going like she did was a wake-up call."

"Yeah, your mom called me."

Jack pulled out the black plastic triangle and placed the 15 balls into the rack. His racking style started with the yellow one-ball and alternating the solids and stripes with the eight-ball in the middle and on the spot.

"Your break."

Bobby cued up his big stick between two knuckles and stroked the cue ball that smacked into the rack with so much force that he sank the maroon five, the blue-striped eleven, and eased the eight-ball toward the right corner that plopped into the pocket.

"Nice shot." Jack shook his head.

Two beers later, he and Gary found Avery. The morning coffee and cereal weren't enough. The Dog House food selection was limited. The bartender unwrapped a frozen pepperoni on thin crust and popped it into a custom oven specially made for the bar brand Growl Pizza with a cartoon tiger wearing a cowboy hat logo.

Bobby leaned on the bar next to them.

"Sorry about the game. Too bad we weren't playing for twenty bucks. The lucky breaks happen when I got nothing at stake. Why'd you stop here, Cuz?"

Gary lapsed into a daze.

"Traveling through a few old memories. Did you know Becca? We're in Boulder for her funeral, which was last week. On our way to Wyoming. Avery Meadows from Jackson."

"I met Becca once when my Auntie Sally and Uncle Marvin had that big cookout when we were sophomores. That was my first paid gig. Remember, Cuz?" Gary was still out of it.

"We were all classmates. This guy, Jack. He's a misfit from New Jersey," said Avery.

Jack showed off the pink Fuji T-shirt he picked up at the truck stop before the funeral.

"I spent a week in New Jersey one night. We played the Bull City rodeo. Then, loaded up at midnight, had a flat in Elmer, no jack, stalled an hour, and drove to a fancy casino in Atlantic City. The hotel rented out our rooms. We slept in the parking lot. All that? So me and the Barnstormers could open for Roscoe Tanner. That crowd booed us out of the house. The only good things about that show were the sliced kiwis and peeled grapes in the Green Room. I can't forget to mention the full-service gas stations. Tanner is a class A jerk weed."

Bobby unfolded a flyer he had in his vest pocket.

"I'm playing here tonight and tomorrow if you run out of things to do."

"We'll be in Wyoming for the next two days. You got any weed?" Jack whispered over the background clatter.

"Aren't you all kind of old for that?"

****

The Odd Trio followed Bobby out the fire exit to a limited edition 2000 Harley motorcycle parked by the door. The afternoon sun, low in the sky, hurt their eyes.

Bobby rummaged through one of his saddlebags and took out an old Band-Aid box.

"Take my last ones. I'm stopping by the store to resupply before they close at six."

"What? How long have we been here?"

"Time flies when you're shooting pool and drinking beer."

"What do I owe you?" Jack asked as Bobby handed him the two joints.

"Just pay it forward. Weed's legal. It's no big deal. I have a medical marijuana card, glaucoma, you know. Let's call it atonement for me bad-mouthing New Jersey."

"What's with the bike?"

Jack walked around Bobby's ride.

"I gave up the pickup when I moved here. Ended up with this foofy thing. I had a girlfriend. Need I say more? I've been trying to get rid of it. A little too pink for me. It matches your shirt!"

"Your girlfriend had good taste. If I had motorcycles, I'd buy it from you on the spot," Avery said. "Whatcha have there is a chick magnet."

"Ha! It's yours. But depends on the chicks!" Bobby chuckled.

"If you have a bad crowd, we'll be in Laramie tonight." Jack slipped the weed into his shirt pocket. "You know that place by Tie Siding?"

"Speaking of Jackson, Cuz, whatever happened to your daughter, Elizabeth? Remember, we all met at the Rainbow? You two were staying at your motel." Bobby pointed at Avery.

"I was still in Laramie running the store. Thought about going up and showing those two around. There's no telling how things would have turned out had I been there. The possibility of seeing my dad, even after 20 years, held me back."

61

Moose Paddle Inn

Dad's cousin, Bobby Smithee, popped in and out of my life over the years. The first time was when Dad took me on a college graduation trip in 1988. If life is too slow-moving for you, hang around with me. There's never a dull moment whenever I'm around. I can't imagine life with no obstacles. I'm suspicious when life goes too smoothly. My bond with Dad grew stronger with each stumble we encountered. E.S.

******

The summer drive from Laramie to Jackson had been a long one in the clunky Scout. The blue sky was shrouded by a gray haze from a forest fire that ignited in June 1988. It was late afternoon when Gary and Elizabeth pulled under the Moose Paddle Inn guest registration canopy.

"Can I help you?" a voice resonated from the apartment behind the front desk.

"I think Avery arranged a room for us."

"Welcome to Jackson. Say again? Shot too many clay pigeons without earmuffs."

"WE HAVE A RESERVATION! AVERY TALKED TO YOUR WIFE!"

"My wife is at the store picking up cleaning supplies."

"NO, SHE RESERVED A ROOM!"

Terry Meadows returned to the apartment and fetched his hearing aids.

"I'm in denial about my hearing," he said while adjusting them. "I had to rent a lot of rooms to pay for these. Much better. Happy to have you." He pulled his black horn-rimmed reading glasses from his pocket protector and read over the paperwork.

"We're checking in. Avery made a reservation."

"I see it here. Plenty of space tonight. All the *touristas* are heading out after the big July 4th weekend," Mr. Meadows acknowledged while scratching his crew-cut head with the eraser end of a pencil. "It's been smoky. Those Easterners must watch too much TV news. We were at capacity, then 30 percent canceled."

"It wasn't bad on the way up. Driving past the Tetons, at dusk, the sun was bright red."

"You must have come from Casper."

"We'll go back through Lander. My mom ranches down there."

"I hear you used to be crazy in Laramie. You and Avery were inseparable in school." Mr. Meadows pulled out a registration card. "Complete the top part."

"I think you're mixing me up with Jack. He and Avery were partners. We all owned a house together."

"That must have been cozy."

"We were one big hovel of happy hippies. Meet my daughter Elizabeth."

"License plate?"

Elizabeth went outside to look.

"5-5487."

Gary took the pen tethered to the counter by a chain and signed the card."

"You're in 217. Let's see, three nights. Tonight, Tuesday, Wednesday."

"Happy graduation!" exclaimed Gary.

"Great. What are we going to do? Hike around Jenny Lake? I don't know if this geezer can keep up with me," Elizabeth boasted to Mr. Meadows.

"I knew that we'd met before. Avery brought you home one long weekend. Doesn't get back home much anymore."

"So, I've heard. That trip? We came here after Avery finished researching cattle disease in our herd over by Lander. Their Laramie Mountaineering store is booming. This Upward jacket is new from there. Stuffed with high-tech filling. I'll report back when we're in Laramie. Expect a call!"

"I'm not holding my breath. Me and the wife? We're slowing down. Could use some help around here."

"I know the feeling."

"Take those coats with you. I have a couple extra if you need 'em. It gets cold at altitude. Check out's 11. If you're early, drop the key in the mail slot. Ice is around the corner by the stairs."

"Sounds like it's time you talked with that 'son you never had.'"

"Is that what you heard? Nothin' wrong with being a little old-fashioned. I suggest you mind your own business."

"Take life moment by moment, is what my mom says."

Gary and Elizabeth hauled their stuff to the second floor. Elizabeth flipped on the light, exposing a rustic room with knotty pinewood wainscoting. The furniture was also made of interesting gnarled pine logs. After getting settled, the two kicked around Jackson.

****

Every place was walkable from the Moose Paddle Inn. The Rabbit Hutch was a well-known Chinese restaurant and always hopping. Since their first working vacation to Jackson after the powwow in Ethete, the Hutch was a traditional meal stop. Elizabeth's usual was the Crab Yangon. She ordered the appetizer for her dinner because eight were on the plate.

After dinner, a mandatory stop on this trip was the Rainbow River Bar, which has been in business since 1937. The swiveling barstools were unique. Each had a six-gun mounted on one of the chair arms.

The Wyoming drinking age was 19 until 1988, when the limit was increased to 21.

This time around, Elizabeth was old enough to enter. She and her dad saddled up on the six-shooter stools. The band was on break.

"Well, Cousin Gary. It's been how many years?" Bobby Smithee walked over to greet him. "How's Auntie Sally been doing?"

"She's good. We're stopping by the ranch on our way back. She appreciated your dad loaning her the tractor last summer. Meet my daughter Elizabeth. We're in Jackson for her graduation present."

"Congratulations!

"I'm a diploma-carrying Southeast Wyoming College graduate."

"You look like your mom."

"So, I've heard. I like your band. It's all we listened to on the way up here. Dad has one tape, and we wore it out."

Bobby dug into his lambskin vest pocket and fished a new cassette still in the wrapper. "For your listening pleasure, Elizabeth. It's our latest. There are a couple on here with Jerry LeClair. God rest his soul. Bartender, get my friends anything they want. Be safe and happy graduation."

Gary ordered a Bud and Elizabeth a Manhattan.

"We don't have cherries or rye. Will bourbon and an orange twist do?"

They finished their drinks and listened to the band for a set.

****

The late-night stop was next door for a hamburger at the '57 Chevy Grille. You guessed it. The chromed grille from a 1957 Chevy, complete with the cone-shaped rubber bumpers, hung above the window facing Togwotee Street. The hole-in-the-wall was steamy from the sizzling burgers and abuzz with inaudible small talk.

"Those wontons were a good start. Carbo up. Did I mention we're checking out the Grand? 'Classic' with American. The works," Gary ordered over the restaurant din.

"How about the 'Best in Jackson?' 'Teton Special' with mushrooms and spinach. Bacon on the side. No bun, extra spinach!" Elizabeth yelled to the cook.

"If your mother were with us, we wouldn't have picked this place. Enjoy it while you can."

Gary dug into his sandwich.

"So, this is my graduation trip?"

Elizabeth placed her fixings on the bed of spinach leaves and crumbled the bacon strips so they covered every square centimeter of the burger patty. Then she topped it with more spinach. For the fries, she made a ketchup puddle for dunking.

"When did you start eating your sandwich with a fork?"

"Hamburger salad. I eat all my sandwiches like a salad. No bread. And where'd you learn that bad habit?" Elizabeth grimaced as her father slathered ketchup over his fries, picking through the mess with his fingers. "You're barbaric."

"Never been much of a fry dunker. Carbo up. The next two days will be epic."

"What's this about the Grand?" asked Elizabeth.

62

Roscoe Tanner

October 13, 2006—12:17 p.m. MDT: Elizabeth was always ready to go on a moment's notice. She checked her briefcase to be sure her overnight clutch was in there, tossed in her father's medicine, grabbed her Upward fiber-filled jacket, and was on her way.

She didn't have any idea where the Odd Trio was headed. The three college mates had a few hours on her. She thought about when she drove her helpless father from Jackson to Laramie after her college graduation trip.

"Kidnapping my oblivious dad? What were they thinking?"

Elizabeth turned on the GPS clipped to the dashboard. The way to Cheyenne on I-25 to I-80 was longer, distance-wise, but faster than driving slower through Fort Collins.

Boulder was a centrally isolated place, even though there were several ways to get out of town. She decided to travel up the Diagonal Highway and then turned east on Colorado 52 to I-25.

Before the interchange, she gassed up her Forester and drove across the lot to a fast-food drive-thru for her standard meal—two regular cheeseburgers, small fries, and small Coke.

An incorrect food order delayed the waiting cars. She was the last one in line, backed out, parked, and went inside.

"Welcome to Dine 'n Go," the clerk cheerily greeted, then punched some buttons on the register.

"'Number 3' with a Coke."

Elizabeth impatiently looked at her watch every few seconds.

"Fryer's down. It'll take a few minutes."

"Scratch the fries."

The clerk rang up Elizabeth's order and handed her a paper cup, which she refused, and waited for her order while dispensing the drink into her water bottle, which seemed like it would never fill.

"137!" Becca's order resonated out of the speaker system.

She looked in the bag.

"I ordered two cheeseburgers."

The clerk checked the order, went to the kitchen, and returned with a second sandwich. Elizabeth sat in the Forester waiting for traffic.

She wrapped the bottom of the sandwich with a napkin to keep the secret sauce from dribbling on her lap before speeding across two lanes of traffic, cutting off a U-Haul van. The driver flipped her off when she pulled onto I-25.

While keeping her eyes forward, she searched further in the bag. An order of large fries was hidden under the napkins.

"Maybe this will be a good day after all."

****

The Odd Trio toked up on Bobby's mellow weed in the Dog House parking lot and snarfed down the last of the pizza they boxed up.

"No probable cause!" shouted Jack as they crept out of Fort Collins.

"Mr. Clean, those clothes have seen better days," observed Avery while making a face upon sniffing the odor.

"Can't be too bad. Gary loaned me these pants for the funeral. The shirt's from Tak at the truck stop," Jack mumbled with his mouth full of pepperoni.

"Grand Mart doesn't close until eight."

Avery swung the White Shark into the big box store parking lot. The Odd Trio stumbled through the automatic doors and made a bee-line to the clothing department. Jack had a New Jersey throwback moment when he entered the dressing room with khaki slacks and a long-sleeved powder yellow button-down collared dress shirt.

Meanwhile, Gary was nowhere to be seen. Avery walked around the store and found him in the electronics department, watching the three rows of TV sets playing the same Grand Mart commercial.

"Stay close."

Upon their return, Jack sat in the snack bar at a table with an order of nachos covered with pickled peppers and a vending machine iced tea.

"Take a load off. The snack bar had leftover *hors d'oeuvres* they were going to trash."

The Odd Trio cleared the table and headed back to the Eurovan.

"BEEEEEEP!"

The store alarm sounded and set off a flashing red light. Two guards swarmed the door.

"Come with us."

The senior Rent-a-Cop escorted them to the security office, where several TV monitors were hooked up to the surveillance cameras positioned around the store.

"Rewind it." The Assistant Manager sat down at the playback machine as the security guard gave Jack the third degree like he was TV Private Investigator John Hendrix. "There you are in the dressing room. Why did you leave your street clothes?"

"If those threads could talk!"

"We couldn't hear 'em. Sure could smell 'em."

"There we are in the snack area. I was waiting to escort our friend to the van. He has Alzheimer's. I'm elderly. I forgot. He forgot!"

The guard looked over the Odd Trio and shook his head.

"My grandmother's your age. She always says she's old and confused. I'm letting you off with that as your criminal defense. I'll take you through the check-out. Pay for the clothes. Get out of here." The guard rolled his eyes. "Besides, my shift is about over. I don't want to deal with the paperwork over thirty bucks."

******

Avery climbed into the Eurovan and parked in a rest area a few miles from town. Gary sat in the middle of the bench in the back.

"Why are we stopping?"

"Avoiding another felony in Wyoming, Middleton. Here." Avery passed the half-smoked joint.

"Good thinking. I don't need to be a two-time loser."

"You're pretty good at getting away with petty crimes. Why didn't you work over your Deputy friend like that?"

"I'm not as bold when I'm straight. Anyone still stressed out?"

Jack pulled the second joint out of his shirt pocket. He pushed in the cigarette lighter on the dashboard. The coil turned orange-hot. Jack fired up the joint and passed it.

Avery French inhaled the smoke, glanced at the rearview mirror, and offered the weed to Gary.

"You've been quiet. You either have lots or nothing on your mind. Quite the stunt our friend Middleton pulled back there."

Gary was glassy-eyed and unaware.

"Say again. 10-9, over," Gary slurred military radio code. Jack swiveled his seat around.

"Turn this helicopter around? Captain Meadows?"

"Then what? He's safe as long as we keep track of him. Give him the weed. I heard it's good for Alzheimer's." Avery looked at the odometer. "I figure it's about 20 miles."

****

Jack pointed at a flashing neon sign on the highway's right-hand side.

"Am I the only one? I need to stretch my legs. Buy some stamps."

It was the old Tie Siding Post Office. The historic building was transformed into the legendary Post Office Club. According to local lore, a one-legged stripper was the talk of the town back in the '50s.

"Laramie can wait," said Avery while slowing down.

It wasn't too late on Friday night, just late enough to keep three oldsters feeling young again.

"Before Gary got married, the Turtle Club organized a bachelor party there in December '67," reminisced Avery. "You weren't anywhere to be found, Middleton."

"I was around."

"Hm. So it was you who took the ignition cable!"

"Lucky for you, the engine compartment was unlocked. My fallback was to slit your tires."

"Now that pisses me off. Here's your chance to make up."

The UW Turtle Club back in the 1960s was a legitimate campus group. There was a yearbook picture, after all. Drinking mass quantities of hard liquor was a show of masculinity.

"How's Becca?"

The parking lot was packed. The White Shark found a resting place at the back next to the big trucks.

"She's cool," Jack confirmed and closed the refrigerator.

The Odd Trio stumbled towards the club. They stood at the front door where a tall, muscular guy, maybe a former football player, pointed to the "$20 Cover, 2-Drink Minimum" sign on the bouncer kiosk.

"Do we get the senior discount?"

The bouncer looked at his watch and hung an "Express Line Special $10" sign. Jack pulled out his Platinum card.

"Cash only, sir."

Jack stood aside. Avery was again disgusted and reeled off thirty to the towering fellow.

"All drinks 15 bucks. Enjoy yourselves. We have a special guest emcee tonight. Ever hear of Roscoe Tanner?"

The Odd Trio looked at each other in amazement upon hearing the name of the Country-Western has-been.

"We should have dragged Bobby and his pool stick with us."

Avery led the way into the club. The scantily clad hostess led them to a place to sit. Avery slipped her a twenty. She moved them to a row back from the stage in the non-smoking section.

The room seemed more spacious than it was because of the mirrors on the stage floor and ceiling. High-octane music with heavy bass pounded through the otherwise smoky room.

"What can I get you?" The long-legged server's high-pitched voice was barely audible over the background music. She placed cocktail napkins from the tray she held over her head. "Want to start a tab?" Need some folding money for our entertainers?"

She accepted Jack's Platinum card.

"Finally, a first-class joint! How about two Buds, a Coors, three shots of your worst whiskey, and sixty in cash, 20 each!"

They ordered just in time for the dancing set to end.

Roscoe Tanner took to the bright stage wearing black wrap-around sunglasses. He was dressed in a flashy, brown polyester-yoked western suit, a black shirt, a bolo tie with a jade slide, and a black Stetson accented by a pair of shiny black cowboy boots. It was Wyoming.

"Get the bum outta here!" Jack howled.

Roscoe swooned into the microphone as he pushed his shades down his nose.

"We'll be right back. Don't nobody go nowhere. While you're waiting for the next flock of chicks, get a load of my latest album, *Nasty Newark Night.*"

"You bad-mouthing Jersey?"

Roscoe stepped off the stage, plopped into a chair next to Jack, pulled a CD out of his tacky jacket pocket, and slapped it on the table.

"It'll grow on you, man. Missy? Bring my fans whatever they want. Top shelf."

By the time the Odd Trio finished their second round and shared a few laughs about sliced kiwis, peeled grapes, and legendary strippers, the next set began.

No one was in any shape to drive. Jack tossed a fistful of cash, fluttering to the stage. They tripped over their feet and made it as far as the White Shark.

63

Owen Chimney

It would be the next day when I found out about the Odd Trio's run to the Post Office. I realized my new job was to be the grownup in the room. I gained plenty of experience in the guardian department. When Dad and I took off for my college graduation trip to Jackson, Mom was teaching summer school again and needed some time to herself. We could have used her support. E.S.

****

It was Tuesday. The sun had peeked over the foothills. Elizabeth and Gary were early risers preparing for their second day around Jackson Hole. Gary found parking in front of the Nordic Chalet restaurant.

Despite the fires, the line of patrons waiting to be seated was long. The Nordic Chalet had the same log cabin feel as the Moose Paddle, which wasn't surprising since the Meadows family first owned it.

The wait was over. The hostess snaked Gary and Elizabeth through the maze of tables.

"I'm Emilie. Do you know what you want or need a minute?"

Emilie carried two glass pots. One had a brown handle filled with caf-coffee, and the other with an orange handle was full of steaming decaf.

"Plain for me."

They both perused the menu.

"I'm surprised we had to wait," observed Elizabeth.

"Mostly our regulars. The tourists have been streaming out of here. There are fires every summer. Last month, there was a lightning strike over by Shoshone Lake. Another by Lewis Lake just before the 4th. I don't know why those fires would be any different from the usual."

"It was hazy driving up from Laramie. Nothing like when Mount St. Helens blew," said Gary about the 1980 volcano explosion in Washington. "I think we're ready. I'll have eggs over easy with hash browns. A raisin round instead of toast."

"I'll have the raisin rounds. The picture looks good." Elizabeth handed back the menu. "I may regret it. Dad, you can finish mine if they give me indigestion … and a side of bacon."

"We use European flour. Some customers are unaffected."

"Let's hope so. We're carbo-ing up today," Gary explained to Emilie and turned back to Elizabeth. "You're not starving?"

"The burger from last night is still a lump in my stomach."

"You mean spinach burger salad. Emilie, can you add a side of hash browns for Olive Oyl?"

****

After breakfast, the two climbed into the Scout for some sightseeing. They stopped at the scenic outlook toward the Glacier Turnout off U.S. 191.

"Great view." Gary gazed around at Grand Teton Peak. "When we get closer, it won't seem as spectacular. On the rock, you can't see the mountains for the boulders."

"On the rock?"

Elizabeth looked through her dad's camera with a telephoto lens.

They toured around the national park and viewed the Teton Mountains, majestically extending from the valley floor. During the graduation outing, they ate lunch on the Grand Teton Lodge patio overlooking a big meadow starting to bloom.

They took a side road on the return to Jackson and stopped at the Chapel of the Transfiguration. It was a log cabin church constructed in 1925 and was featured in the 1964 movie *Josiah Johnson*. Roberta Williams had an uncredited role as Josiah's daughter.

"It's different. I like the altar window framing the Tetons. Aren't you and Mom Episcopalians?"

"Because of Reverend Perez. You were baptized in the Laramie Episcopal Church. As long as we're here, put out some good thoughts. You're my lucky charm. We can't be too safe in case our luck runs out. What do you think about getting up close and personal with the Grand?"

"This is your real surprise? Climbing the Grand? Here, I thought you'd take me up Longs Peak. I hinted about that every time we were at Libby Flats!"

"The destination isn't as important as the journey. One of these days, you can try Longs when you're on your own." Elizabeth beamed at the news. "You're a Wyoming girl. Getting up the Grand is a feat of strength!"

That night, they had dinner at the Rabbit Hutch. The two adventurers carbo-loaded on Crab Yangon, Snake River Lomein, and Buffalo Fried Rice before the next day's trek.

****

The two alpinists checked out from the Moose Paddle Inn and began their Thursday morning excursion at 6:20 a.m. They drove to the Lupine Meadows Trailhead parking area, where a Ranger checked their paperwork.

"The Owen-Spalding route was popular until a few days ago. Everything looks good. Put the permit stub on your dash. Be safe. The fires are under control," the Ranger said about the National Park Service policy to let lightning fires burn themselves out. "Seems the only ones worried are the visitors."

"Fewer tourists for the bison to gore?"

Gary led the way up nine steep switchbacks and finished the 13-mile day hike to the Lower Saddle, where they bivouacked for the night.

They arose to a band of light glowing on the horizon at 4:45 a.m., signaling the Friday morning graduation trek. Elizabeth added water to two packs of freeze-dried beef stroganoff and cooked them with her Primus backpacking stove. She chased every glutenous meal with antacid tablets. Cleanup was a breeze.

"Elizabeth, you packed the First Aid kit, right? The altitude is getting to me."

She unzipped the small bag and fetched a packet of Tylenol.

"Chase these with plenty of water, Dad. You need to keep hydrating. Here are some extras. I read in your guidebook there's a natural spring on the way."

Gary helped Elizabeth bear-proof their camp by hoisting their belongings up a tree and made the final push to the Upper Saddle.

"How's your breathing? We're at 13,000."

"Me? You're the light-headed one taking Tylenol."

"There's Valhalla Canyon. Very exposed." They traversed along the western wall. Elizabeth uncoiled the rope Avery provided. "That's the Belly Crawl. I'm a little too wide to squeeze under the overhang. The *verglas* is melting. Be careful of water and ice."

Elizabeth set up a standing belay. Gary negotiated the rock face by laying back on the ledge, grasping bomber handholds. Elizabeth followed, and the two made it to the Owen Chimney, which was the crux of the route.

"We could free climb it. The rock is icy and wet. It's a 2,500-foot drop. There's no rush. I don't think any weather will move in on us today."

"Is that smoke or fog?" Elizabeth asked while setting up a belay.

"Double-check my anchors, Dad. You don't want me flying out of here."

Gary gave each protection point a couple of firm tugs. She checked her harness, looped the rope into her belaying device, and helped her dad clip in.

"On belay."

"Belay on.

"Climb."

"Climbing."

Elizabeth tightened the rope as Gary made his way up the chimney. He set his first protection point about 10 feet up the crack. He ascended another 15 feet and clipped the taut rope into a second carabiner. Gary tugged to get some slack and glanced down at the expansive valley below.

His view started to spin.

Vertigo.

The crack spit him out.

Elizabeth's face was ablaze, and her heart beat like a hammer pounding a hot horseshoe on an anvil. Gary plummeted toward her fast in what seemed like slow motion. He whacked his head, shattering his helmet. His ankle hit a crag, slowing him down enough to send his torso over his foot.

Gary's rapid descent yanked one of Elizabeth's belay anchors out that entangled in the first protection point. Even though his fall was slowed, it created so much friction that the rope burned through her leather gloves, leaving second and third-degree burns on her raw palms.

"Off belay. Dad, can you hear me?"

Elizabeth was frantic. Gary was knocked out.

"Is this our routine?" Elizabeth panted from the excitement. "Lie on this." She pulled an Upward fleece from her bag for her dad to insulate his torso from the cold surface. She elevated his legs. Gary opened his eyes. Elizabeth checked to see if her penlight dilated his irises. "Remember when you crashed below Medicine Bow Peak? The doctor said to keep your mind active. Keep blabbering. We'll be okay. It's July, not February."

"It snows in Laramie on the 4th," Gary recollected as a few flecks of snow fluttered through the chill.

"Well, then there's that."

Elizabeth bundled up her dad the best she could with two emergency space blankets.

"Hand me my glove shells. I didn't think I'd need those."

"Welcome to the party, Dad."

"Speaking of parties, when you go down, if you run into a Carlsen group, they may have a radio."

****

On her descent, Elizabeth didn't bump into anyone coming or going. Upon her arrival at the Lower Saddle, she encountered two Backcountry Rangers on routine patrol.

"My dad fell out of the Owen Chimney. He's pretty banged up."

"When did it happen? What kind of gear do you have?"

"Was around seven? Maybe a little later. A rope, a light rack, day packs. Running low on water."

"Teton Rescue should be able to get him down before dark," according to one of the Rangers. "No telling about the weather, though."

Late morning storm clouds were forming.

****

Gary was losing feeling in his toes. He wiggled his extremities to keep the blood flowing. There was a temperature inversion pushing down the fog and smoke. He pulled his baklava around his face and was disappointed that the layer of smoke and clouds obscured his view of the valley. The sun shining in the clear blue sky felt good, warming his frigid face.

A Jackson Cooperative helicopter hovered overhead at the Lower Saddle and lowered six outfitted Teton Mountain Rangers.

"You can come with us or stay. One of the Rangers can help you hike down."

"I want to help. I'm an LPN."

"You'll be a good hand compared to some people we get up here. Can you carry the litter? It folds up. Wear it like a pack."

"If it's not too heavy."

"15 pounds, give or take."

The six Rangers led the way. Elizabeth surprised herself when she free-climbed the Belly Crawl. Half the party reached the base of Owen Chimney.

"Are you okay, sir?"

"My ankle's seen better days," Gary stuttered from hypothermic delirium.

"You get to ride in this. It's like a mummy bag," one Ranger explained. We'll keep you as level as we can. Your daughter's been a great help!"

"She brings good luck."

The Rangers checked to be sure he didn't have a spinal injury, then set Gary's bum ankle and cinched him onto the evacuation litter.

Elizabeth and three Rangers steadied the head-end. Three on the other side negotiated the tricky Belly Crawl traverse wall with a pulley system. The team used the fixed ropes to descend the Upper Saddle. The helicopter returned and hovered 150 feet above when the party reached the meadow.

"Can I go with my dad?" Elizabeth yelled into the Ranger's ear.

"Yeah. When they lower the harness seat."

"My stuff!"

"We have a crew that will pack it out."

Elizabeth secured herself, and a winch hauled her up to the helicopter. When the cable lowered, the Ranger unzipped the bag so Gary could see out.

"When I was in 'Nam, I made low altitude jumps and was airlifted out after every mission."

"You don't say, but not in a bag. I was a pilot on a Huey, 173rd Airborne out of Danang!" the Ranger replied over the chopper blade noise. "I get to fly once in a while. Keep moving your toes and fingers."

"Hey, you're Dickie. Shoshone guy! Steiner, Gary, Special Ops - Navy."

Gary shook Dickie's gloved hand.

"Small chopper world. You were one of those bad-ass top-secret mother fuckers. I remember. Early on. '63? You be so bad, you be good!" Dickie attached the litter to the hoist line. "Jackson Hospital, NEXT!" he yelled and waved at the chopper crew, hauling Gary through the helicopter doorway.

Elizabeth held onto her hat as the copilot handed her a set of headphones.

"Strap in!" the pilot barked through the intercom headset.

"Welcome back!" Elizabeth gave her dad the "Thumb's Up."

****

Six orderlies waited to lift Gary onto a hospital gurney when the copter landed on the helipad.

"Lucky for your boot. It would have been a compound break," reported the ER doc. "You have a bad concussion from the blunt-force trauma. No subdural hematoma. Lucky for the helmet."

"Alas, poor helmet. I knew you well."

"Mr. Shakespeare, you get to dine on Jackson Hole's finest unsalted hospital food tonight. Tomorrow, we'll fix your ankle when the swelling goes down, and you'll be on your way."

Elizabeth admitted her father for the night and stopped by the cafeteria for coffee.

"Weren't you in our place yesterday?" asked Emilie from the Nordic Chalet.

"... and the raisin rounds were the best I've had. Of course, they were my first."

"Any raisin rounds you find in the valley, we made them, including here. It can't be the food that brought you."

"My dad fell off the Grand. I just checked him in."

"Yikes! Do you need a ride someplace?"

Elizabeth nodded and followed Emilie to the kitchen, dropping off two pink boxes of raisin rounds.

****

Emilie drove Elizabeth back to the Lupine Meadows parking lot. A Ranger making her rounds met Elizabeth and walked her to the Scout.

"I heard your dad will be okay."

"We'll see."

Elizabeth retrieved the spare key from the magnetic holder under the left front wheel well, returned to Jackson, and pulled into the Moose Paddle parking lot. Mr. Meadows comped her a room for the night. The following day, she stopped at the Nordic Chalet for a raisin round to go before returning to the hospital, where she waited around in the lobby until her dad emerged riding a wheelchair.

"So much for stopping by to see Grandma Sally," Gary said in a daze. "You turned out to be a pretty good nurse."

"Don't tell Mom."

Elizabeth headed back to Laramie through Casper. Her dad was on mild painkillers and slept for six straight hours.

They pulled up in the Calamity Club driveway. Gary hobbled out on a pair of crutches. Elizabeth held the door. Her mom was sitting in the front room with her nose in a book.

"How was your graduation present?"

"Dad fell off the Grand! Nearly was a newspaper headline."

"Broke my ankle, is all. I'll be back to work tomorrow. I'll write about it."

"Are you a screamer or a flapper?" Becca deadpanned and glanced up from her reading with a smile.

64

Cowboy Joe

October 14, 2006—5:32 a.m. MDT: The sun hadn't yet broken the horizon.

"Tap, Tap, Tap."

All Avery could make out was a flashlight knocking on the glass before powering down the window and yawning.

"Deputy L. Maddox. Don't you ever sleep?"

"Looks like you've been having more than enough fun since I pulled you over last week. You can't park here. We got a call from the manager." Deputy Maddox looked around the belly of the White Shark and stopped on Gary. "Is he okay?"

"Sleeping it off," Jack nervously responded. "Just doing everyone a favor. Staying off the road."

"Good for you. How about getting on the road? It's Homecoming, so you'll be ahead of any traffic." Deputy Maddox was suspicious and made a second glance around the camper area. "Are you sure your friend's okay?"

"Thanks, officer. We won't stop until the Prairie Schooner."

"Tak at the truck stop? He says, 'Hello.' You know they open at six for breakfast. If you need to piss, the Tie Siding Store is open. I don't want to arrest you for indecent exposure."

Avery bounced across the parking lot and waited for a semi to whiz by before taking the back road to the Prairie Schooner.

"Shit, Meadows. Remember, I have Otto Matic hiding back there under the mattress. He's juiced up and in no mood to have us arrested."

"Yeah, yeah. Forget about it! It's no big deal. You think this is the only AR15 in Albany County?"

"Not one that can blast an entire elk herd or anything else to smithereens."

****

Avery parked, and the Odd Trio staggered through the front doors.

"Tak and Jennifer are downtown on Saturdays. They'll be here Monday, off and on," the assistant manager said. "What'll it be?"

They ordered SPAM and eggs, stacks of pancakes, and downed gallons of coffee and water. After their monstrous morning pick-me-up, they were held up in traffic backed up from the Homecoming parade.

An MNY frat member monitoring traffic waved the renegade VW onto the route before returning to his flirting session with several Chi Kappa Sigma sorority members.

"... TALK ABOUT YER COWBOY, RAGTIME COWBOY JOE-OE-OE!" Jack sang the UW fight song out the open side door.

Gary was oblivious. The parade ended on Sorority Row, where Avery looked around for a spot to park the Shark. The Odd Trio walked to a cordoned-off area by the stadium and came upon a C&I-sponsored tailgate party, where they reminisced with Turtle Club classmates about their college days, loves won, and loves lost.

Jack returned from the beer truck with a case of cold Coors. The Odd Trio didn't make it to the football game. It was the middle of the afternoon and half a case later before they headed for Centennial.

****

When the revelers pulled into town, Avery opted for a restaurant across the road from the Old Stage Stop, knowing Jack's card-sharking history. The Ore House was a friendly establishment rebuilt after an unexplained explosion leveled the place 20 years before.

The Odd Trio saw the ghost of Becca and stopped in their tracks. The apparition turned around. It was Elizabeth. Jack went for drinks and returned to their table with beers and tomato juice.

"It's about time. I've been here for two hours. I expected you all to show up at the Calamity Club last night. Did my mother make the trip?"

"We took her on a sightseeing tour. She's safe and sound under our watchful eyes." Jack glanced at the box under Gary's chair. "Had her on ice in the Eurovan fridge. Brought her in here for a change of scenery. Fresh air."

"Forget something?" Elizabeth set a medicine bottle that contained her father's Alzheimer's prescription on the table. "I'm pretty sure he could have used one of these before you ditched me. Dad gets loony pretty quick when he misses a dose."

"He snapped out of it when we gave him a few drags of a dementia-altering drug."

"I hope you were in Colorado for that."

Avery opened the vial and handed Gary his pills.

"Remember these moments because they will be good material for your movie, Elizabeth. This is good timing. Did your dad ever tell you about your not-so-humble beginning?"

"I've heard legends."

65

Ross Hospital

When I met the Odd Trio in Centennial after their joy ride, the last thing I expected to hear was their version of my origin story. I can't imagine waking up in the morning with a surprise pregnancy when I was in college. I should have been more empathetic and nicer to my parents. We could have shared rather than argued. Mom's dead, and Dad's losing his memory. Drastic changes are better than the stability I've been scared to face. E.S.

****

Gary and Becca took their entrance into parentdom in stride. All they wanted was a healthy baby. Two weeks had lapsed from the original mid-April 1968 due date.

"We'll give it a little more time," Dr. Fredericks, Becca's obstetrician, said.

The adjusted due date came and went. Another week passed. Late one afternoon, Becca was in excruciating pain that ebbed and flowed. Then, at 1:30 a.m., she blared a horrific scream that startled Gary to bolt up from his sleep.

He dialed up the doctor.

"Your baby is being stubborn. I'll meet you at the hospital. Driving will be faster than an ambulance."

Gary helped Becca get into the back seat. She was writhing in pain. The lights soon illuminated the front room at the Billingsley place.

"It's five minutes to the hospital." His heart felt like a jackhammer in his chest. "Dr. Fredericks is letting the admissions desk know we're on our way. I don't know anything about birthing no babies, Miss Becca. I know about birthing a calf."

"HOT DANG MOTHER FLIPPIN' POOPIN' ... !"

"I'm driving as fast as I can!" Gary and the Scout shot down Nellie Tayloe Ross Boulevard and whizzed past Ross Hall towards Ross Memorial Hospital. "I'm pretty sure you don't want me reaching around in there and straightening everything out."

"Thank you, dear." Becca gasped and writhed in pain. "I'll leave the birthing up to the doctor."

They pulled up to the emergency room door. Gary hurried to the admissions desk as a nurse wheeled Becca into the Obstetrics Department.

"Gary can be here with you. No busybody administrators around this time of night, so consider it approved."

"Thanks," was all Becca could dribble out.

"We're all on a team to help you. I'm recommending we perform a Cesarian section [C-section.] There are risks, potential infections, hemorrhages, blood clots, and minimal uterine cancer risk down the road. There could be issues if you decide to have another child. The main benefit for right now is if there are problems, we'll know about them at the beginning."

"Whatever!"

Becca and Gary agreed to the surgery involving abdominal and uterine incisions through which the baby would be removed.

The C-section was successful.

****

Young Elizabeth was born in the wee hours of May 4, 1968, which happened to be Kentucky Derby Saturday. Coincidentally, the 70th Run for the Roses was Gary's birthday.

"Today, the 11th race will be the best one ever!"

The first-time father was gleeful with a pink bubble gum cigar dangling from his mouth. Gary celebrated Elizabeth's blessed day by watching the Churchill Downs spectacle on TV, which was a bit controversial, like Elizabeth's birth. The original winner, Dancer's Image, was disqualified after a banned drug was evident in the horse's postrace urine test. The placer, Forward Pass, was the declared winner.

The phone rang.

"Steiner residence," answered Gary.

"This is Jayne from the Albany County Cattlettes. I'm pleased to inform you that your daughter, Elizabeth, was the first baby born at Ross Hospital in May!"

"What a surprise! You say we can pick up our standing rib roast at Fiddler's Market tomorrow ... Yes, I work at the paper and can arrange for a photographer to meet us. Thanks for calling!"

"Elizabeth is our good luck charm!"

A few minutes later, the phone rang again. Gary answered.

"Mom! Yes, Elizabeth and her mother are fine. Here's Becca."

"Sally, she's beautiful ... Me? I'm happy most of the time."

"You let me know if your mood swings, and I'll be right down."

"You're welcome anytime. Gary's been very supportive. The paper is letting him do his writing from home. Friends from the anthro department drop by. It's good to have company around to keep me focused. I'm not going anywhere."

"I'll visit anyway."

"You can stay as long as you want. We'll make room. Gary won't mind a few days on the couch."

******

On all of Elizabeth's birthdays, Becca celebrated by baking a celebratory Kentucky Derby Pie. It was a favorite from her days on the ranch.

"Where did you learn how to make that?" asked Gary.

"New Jersey. Cherry Ridge was a very horsey place. At least at the Stony Pond Stable, the Derby was a big deal." Becca savored a bite of the buttery filling. "Mixing up the menu. You didn't know about Derby

Pie until I arrived on the scene. The ranch hands liked it, too, even on non-Derby Days. I called it Rodeo Pie."

"We didn't get out much in Wyoming." Gary poured another round of virgin Mint Juleps. "I enlisted in the Navy around then. No Derby Pie in our C-Rats."

The complimentary roast more than made up for the lack of response from New Jersey.

66

Sunset

October 14, 2006—5:07 p.m. MDT: By the time Gary left the Ore House, the fast-acting Alzheimer's medicine brought him back to his new normal, at least for the moment. Avery slid open the Eurovan's side panel. Elizabeth and her father climbed onto the bench seat in the belly of the beast. Jack rode shotgun. Elizabeth slammed the sliding door shut.

Avery checked to see if everyone was buckled up, adjusted the rear-view mirror, backed out, and slammed on the brakes, sending gravel flying.

"Where do you think you are, New York City?" Avery yelled out the window.

The aggressive four-wheeler flipped off the White Shark.

"Very clever, Dad. I was conceived at Libby Flats during a one-night stand and survived a C-section. The Steiner story is starting to make some sense."

"Your mom and me? Our courtship was more romantic than it seemed. Several years in the making. Mostly on your mom's part."

"Did you love each other?"

"We were going to celebrate our 39th anniversary on Christmas."

"But did you love Mom?"

"I kept the oil in the car. Watched after you when she had a work activity or presented at a conference. She picked you up when I had City Council meetings."

"What about romance?"

"Our romance wasn't like in the movies. Up until you were born, you were our passion. As you grew up, life wasn't perfect, but we made the best of it. Our romance began when you left home. You were always a part of it even when you were gone."

"You were never 'lovestruck?'"

"It was forbidden love. Your mom worked for Grandma Sally. I was focused on joining the Navy."

"Life happens. It's random. I don't know if we would have lasted had we made hay in the barn."

"Now I get why you didn't give Mom the time of day when you two were working on the ranch."

"Uncle Frank was head over heels when he met your aunt. He was looking for Ms. Right. Turned out she was Ms. Right Now. He went through several Ms. Right Nows."

"Mom had no practical application to your life until I dropped onto the scene. Would you have ended up together otherwise?"

"It was complicated with Middleton around. At the time, our lives were rocky. You were the one who added stability."

Elizabeth handed him another dose of his medicine.

"Nah, I'm good. Still buzzed up from the excitement."

"Take another for the good of the rest of us."

Instead of the pill, he took a swig of warm Coors.

"Are all mothers alike? I ignored your Grandma Sally's not-so-subtle hints for me to settle down. Your mom didn't cut you any slack."

"Don't remind me."

"I thought' Nam was tough until you were born."

"Unbelievable, if you ask me. You agreed to make a go of it with Mom based on a lapse in judgment. On a whim? That's a stretch," doubted Elizabeth. "You pretty much ignored her, and you decided to get married. Have a kid? I know, Grandma Sally's way, figure it out on the go."

"It's worked so far."

Elizabeth cuddled up next to her father.

"I love you, Dad."

"I love you, too."

"Meadows and I love you both!"

******

The drive out of Centennial was steep. The top-heavy White Shark reached elevation. Avery handled the curves up to Libby Flats in low gear with ease.

"Back then, you being born wasn't accepted by society. Grandma Sally was happy. Grandma Pembroke, not so much. You forced your Mom and me to grow up in a hurry. It was a struggle. We both worked. The Calamity Club added some stability."

"Little did anyone know how a bastard child would bring her closer together with her parents," Elizabeth mused. "The tagline for my movie."

"...and a chapter for my book. Did you jot that down?"

"I've been jotting down lots of stuff. My origin story is pretty good. Why didn't you call me Libby?"

"We named you Elizabeth and called you Libby until we took you to see *Imperial Lily*."

"How could I forget? Starring Elizabeth Turner. It was her first movie. I thought I could tame wild horses like Lily."

"After that, you insisted on Elizabeth. I brought you to the Wild West Days rodeo when I was taking pictures for the paper. You scared the crap out of me when you reached down to pet one of the bucking broncs."

"You got us press passes to sit over the chutes." Elizabeth stretched out her legs. "I remember wearing boots and a brown straw cowgirl hat with a drawstring under my chin, just like *Imperial Iris*. Thinking about it now, it wasn't very safe, those horses slamming against the metal bucking chute gate."

Gary pretended like he was aiming his camera while uttering the photo cutline.

"A nervous Libby Steiner anxiously sits atop the never-ridden bronc called Dyn-O-Myt for the chute to open and still be aboard eight seconds later. 'Click.'"

"I remember Grandma lifting me onto an old mare. She led me around the corral. I wasn't impressed. I didn't see the purpose of it. My interest would have been greater if I got to break horses. I at least wanted to try!"

"You were always fascinated by your mom's steeplechase stories when she was growing up in New Jersey." Gary stared out the window. "She showed up those Okies."

"I was willing to work at the ranch. Be a barrel racer."

"Your mother wouldn't have it."

"I want the buckles Mom won."

"They're in her jewelry box." Gary jolted forward as Avery downshifted. "Help yourself to my beaded buckle while you're at it."

The White Shark eased around a series of switchbacks.

"You know what messed me up? Mom saying how I caused her cancer because of the C-section."

"I should have been more forceful with your mom if I knew that bothered you."

"Bothered me? It was all I thought about. When you moved to Boulder, that's when I decided to move out of Denver to take the merchandising job at Triumph Towers in New Jersey."

"I didn't realize she controlled you with that. My style is laid back. I shouldn't have been so dismissive of you two fighting about everything," Gary reflected.

"I've been in therapy since my job in Colorado on account of all that."

"Meeting Mom and Uncle Frank at their conference in Mexico didn't help with your PTSD."

"That trip turned out better than it could have, but here we are, Dad."

"Yeah, here we are."

"Now, I can get rid of all those books about C-sections and difficult pregnancies piled on my bedside table. 'From my mother's womb and untimely ripped.'"

"*Macbeth*? Shakespeare would have been proud of you."

"At least you can remember what happened in your college lit class."

"You better pick my brain while I still have a brain. There should be enough in there for another book or your movie."

****

"Okay. You have it together right now compared to last night." Elizabeth retrieved the Delaware file and flipped to where they left off.

"Look here. Rebecca Swataney was married to a guy named B. Tamarend in Kansas. I searched for 'Swataney' and 'Tamanend' in Genotype. Rebecca Tamanend would be my Great-Great-Great Grandma. Tamarend was related to a chief. You named me after her.

"Rebecca's daughter was Gladys. Here she is on the 1894 Delaware Agency roster. It doesn't name her father."

Elizabeth explained that the Lenni Lenape were called Delaware because some tribal members lived on their namesake river. Over time, a combination of European colonization, conflicts, and subsequent displacement led to their migration westward.

She skated her finger across the ledger book line to the column "Anadarko."

"Mom said she wanted to meet me in New Orleans and visit the Delaware people. Not in Delaware. Anadarko, Oklahoma!"

"You weren't too crazy about that idea."

"Well, that was before I got more involved in the family business. Check out this entry. 'Gladys was sent to an orphanage in New Jersey, where the Simmons family adopted her.' Family scandal. Parents shielded the adoption of children born out of wedlock.

"'Gladys married Robert Wilkinson and had sons named Harry and James, and a daughter, Mary.' That's Grandma Mary. Here's Jeremiah Pembroke, occupation pastor, and one daughter, Rebecca - Mom. Uncle Frank must have descended from Harry or James."

****

Avery neared Libby Flats and slowed for a pickup truck hauling a horse trailer. The aspen leaves were beginning to turn. Stands of yellow splotched out from the dead trees that bristled like Irish Wolfhound dog hair.

"Middleton, remember your glissade down the snowfield next to the Diamond?"

Avery pointed toward the steep slope next to the squarish-shaped rock face above Lake Marie.

"My ice ax slowed me down at the end of my runway."

"When I graduated high school, Dad and I were on a hike up to the same snow patch. He tumbled down the boulder field on our approach. It was the first time we fell together."

"That was in the paper. I posted the clipping on the store bulletin board."

A dual-axel truck hitched to a trailer and cruised down the hill in high gear, followed by a line of cars. Avery gunned it and cranked the wheel into the Libby Flats parking area.

Elizabeth reorganized the files, snapped her briefcase shut, and gazed around the vast horizon as the sun began to set through the clear sky behind the western mountains.

"Can one of you give me a hint? Why are we here?" Elizabeth was still in the dark.

Jack pulled the folded-up picture of them posing with Becca from his pocket and handed it to Elizabeth.

"I've seen it."

It hadn't been an hour before Gary's memory started to fade in and out.

"So what's happening now?"

"You and me, both."

Jack shoved the picture in front of Gary's face.

"Remember our college days? The 'Libby Run?' My Wyoming initiation? Initiation to what, I don't know. Twilight joint? Bodily remains?"

"What do you mean 'twilight joint?'" asked Elizabeth.

"Your mom dragged us up here. My first 'Libby Run.' We were having a good old time. We smoked some stale East Coast Cannabis. I think your dad swallowing his memory pills will be as close as we get to the mind-altering part of the 'Pact,' at least this time around."

Avery unloaded the camera equipment and hauled it up to the observation platform.

"Let's get organized before the sun goes down."

"'Bodily remains?'"

Jack led the way out of the White Shark.

"Observe and learn, Elizabeth."

Gary was still in a daze.

"What's in the box? I can carry it."

"You don't remember? Mom's ashes from last week?"

"My mom lives by Lander. I don't know about any ashes. Let me tell you about my friend named Becca. We met on a ranch. She's one helluva woman."

Gary's eyes were in another world. Elizabeth handed her da a dose of his medicine that he dry-swallowed.

"Earth to Dad!"

The Libby Flats faithful made it to the observation deck.

"Over here. Out of the backlight. Bunch up a little bit more." Avery positioned the camera, framed the shot, engaged the timer, and hurried over to a spot in front. "Say, 'GO POKES!'"

The shutter released.

Jack led Elizabeth and her dad to the stone wall, motioning them to open the box and pour the ashes over the edge. The two stood, facing the horizon, as a gust of mountain wind scattered a puff of dust into the late afternoon sunlight.

****

Following the scattering of Becca's remains, the Pact Party turned around upon hearing a voice ascending the stone steps.

"I thought I recognized that white van."

Avery stepped forward.

"Well, well, well. Deputy L. Maddox. Are you stalking us?"

"You were going 45 in a 30 when you left Laramie. Cut off that ATV in Centennial. Crossed a double line on the switchbacks and didn't signal when you pulled in here."

"Are you counting *coup* [coo] on us?" asked Gary about the tribal battle tactic to taunt their enemy rather than harm them.

"No *coup*. Maybe cooped up in the county jail."

Gary read the Deputy's nameplate.

"Are you from Lander?"

"Was. I was dragged there when I was a kid."

"You're Lenny Maddox. Your dad was the Lander Police Chief. Didn't like Indians. I had to shove you around a time or two when you bullied my little brother."

"Don't know what you're talking about." The Deputy unsnapped his holster. "Stand down before I have to call for backup. What are you people doing here? What else are you transporting?"

The Deputy shined his flashlight around the observation area.

"Isn't this out of your jurisdiction?" asked Jack.

"The Albany County Sheriff has a Mutual Aid agreement with Centennial and the Forest Service. Young lady, are you here by your choice? Transporting minors across state lines is a felony."

"I'm flattered. Sounds like you know my dad. These two? They're my bodyguards! You must be Officer DeCoy's partner."

"Did you dump human ashes? Stay where you are. This is a cultural site. That's against regulations."

The Odd Quartet packed the camera gear and returned to the parking area. Elizabeth handed Deputy Maddox the dusty, empty box.

"Can you recycle this? If you're not arresting us, we have dinner plans."

"Avery, can you drop me at my car? Or maybe I can catch a ride with Deputy Maddox."

Jack put his arm around Elizabeth.

"Welcome to the 'Pact.' We're now the Odd Quartet."

67

New Dawn

October 14, 2006—7:27 p.m. MDT: The Odd Quartet cruised into Laramie and rendezvoused at Fuji's. The place was packed. Win or lose, downtown rocked when the Cowboys were in town. Wyoming defeated arch-rival Utah for the first time since 1999, 31-15.

"I can get you over to that booth."

Tak pointed toward his granddaughter, giving the table a quick wipe.

"Who might this be?"

"I might be Elizabeth, Gary, and Becca's daughter."

Tak grabbed a stack of menus next to the register.

"You look just like your mom."

"So I've heard."

"How about you bring us something special? Everything cooked, and no bugs. Is that okay, Meadows?"

Jack closed his menu.

"*Haole* [Howlie - Non-Native Hawaiian] Bento Box for four," Tak howled to the kitchen.

"... and an extra *Sukiyaki Bowl* to go," added Avery.

"What's next for you guys? You're welcome to stay over at the Calamity Club," Elizabeth offered. "Thanks to you all being so late, the place is straightened up. I'm sure you know your way around."

368

****

Tak brought the check and four fortune cookies.

"We serve chow mein, why not these? I got a very good deal. We're 'All-Asian-All the Time.'"

Jack pulled out a wad of bills and reeled off a C-note. Jennifer brought over Avery's to-go order in a white cardboard carton.

"No arguments."

"We should return to Steiner's pad for the sweat lodge tomorrow. Sally was pretty insistent."

Avery cracked open one of the cookies and read the paper slip, "'It's not nice to let down Arapaho elders.' I don't know if there's anything to it. Can't hurt."

The Odd Duo returned to Blue Sky Village. Gary rode back with Elizabeth.

****

October 15, 2006—10:20 a.m. MDT: The Odd Quartet was up and getting ready to ride with Sally to Fort Chambers in East Boulder. Billy camped with Willie the night before.

"You all ready to take a journey back through your lives?" asked Sally as she walked down the stairs. "You're overdressed. By the time we get over there, it'll be in the 50s. Put on some shorts. Skivvies will do. Bring a towel."

Avery brought the Eurovan around. Sally rode in the front, and the others loaded into the back for the short ride to East Boulder.

"While you were in Wyoming, I came out here yesterday. The park manager helped Willie and Billy set up the lodge in the back near Valmont Creek. She monitored where we cut willow branches for the frame. The wood was a little dry but was supple enough. It's a perfect place." Sally gently shook the padlock key in front of Avery.

Avery pulled up, climbed out, and unlocked the gate. Sally hopped down and secured the chain after the White Shark rolled through. They rumbled down a dirt road and parked away from the dome-shaped lodge.

"My grandmother told me this represents Mother Earth's womb. In the past, the arced willow branches were covered with animal hides," explained Sally. "Modern lodges like this are covered with blankets and tarps. Willie's been inside getting it all organized."

He greeted the group in Arapaho. Teresa acknowledged from the campfire where she was boiling water.

Before the ceremony, Billy gathered river rocks and heated them. He used a shovel to heft the heavy, hot stones and drop them into the center pit.

Willie opened the lodge door and invited the quartet to enter.

"Sweating today, Sally?"

"Oh, no. Not this time. How many rounds you going?"

"Four. One for each of them. You can join us."

"I'm helping Teresa cook."

"Billy?"

"Someone has to be sure the place doesn't burn down."

Willie entered and took his place on the floor covered with blankets and throw rugs.

"We are here in honor of this place. After 150 years, we are closer to regaining land taken from us. We're also here for you four. Ask for advice, healing, hope, forgiveness. Be open to new thoughts. They will lead you back to yourself."

Willie tossed cedar wood chips on the rocks. Aromatic cedar smoke filled the room. He recited a prayer and wafted the scented air over his body. The others followed.

He ladled special water over the stones, filling the lodge with steam infused with cedar.

"Don't worry, we'll take a water break after each round. Billy!"

He folded the flap over the opening and returned to tending the fire. The interior was black as a starless night at the ranch. Willie guided the participants in thought. The mix of chanting, singing, and speaking droned through the lodge.

After the fourth round, Willie dismissed the participants. They crawled out and were greeted by Sally and Teresa. All sat and cooled down, pondering their common experience by dipping frybread into their mid-afternoon macaroni and hamburger soup.

****

After the sweat, Sally and Billy were eager to get on the road to Wyoming.

"Why don't you stay over, Grandma? Get a fresh start in the morning?"

"It's six hours with a quick stop in Rawlins."

Billy and Gary lugged the suitcases to the street and loaded them into the awaiting truck bed.

"We'll be back at the ranch by my bedtime. Billy is a night owl, anyway."

A St. James Episcopal van pulled up.

"It's been a good visit. The Boulder church is on board. Things are coming together for Becca's project. We'll get it done for her yet," assured Reverend Perez.

"Thanks for your help and support, all of you," said Elizabeth. "As much as I hate to admit it, I think I've changed my outlook. Life is weaving the old with the new. I've outgrown my past."

Gary wheeled Reverend Perez's suitcase and loaded it into the truck bed.

"Watch out for deer."

October 16, 2006—9:08 a.m. MDT: The Odd Duo also took off after the sweat and stayed over at the Calamity Club. They spent the next day sorting out the garage. Jack's papers and disgusting clothes were bagged up for the trash truck. Avery arranged for the good stuff to be hauled to Flo's Flea Market. A big "Free" sign marked the pile of remaining junk on the driveway. Mr. Billingsley was long gone but was smiling from above.

It was a slow drive back to Centennial with a mattress strapped to the top of the White Shark packed full of "can't live without" stuff.

Avery dropped Jack at his Henry David Thoreau cabin.

****

There was a spare key on a hook under the porch stoop. The photovoltaic solar panels on the roof kept the batteries charged. Jack went inside and flipped on the switch.

He toted his two rifles inside and checked the bullet chambers to be sure they were unloaded, then placed them on the gun rack made from deer antlers hung on the wall.

He unpacked the clothes from his Gucci bag, some Coors beer boxes filled with books, and his American Tourister suitcases.

"Finally, a little quiet time."

Jack went to the cupboard for his bottle of Bombay Sapphire and poured two fingers of gin into a pint Mason jar.

"I wonder who tossed this out of the train?" Jack wondered before taking a sip. He fingered the raised "Patent 1858" lettering on the aqua glass. "I should have been a cultural anthropologist or a trash collector. Cultural garbologist."

Jack relaxed in the chair he scrounged from a dumpster behind the Old Stage Stop. His desk doubled as the kitchen table. He pulled a spiral notebook and a Laramie Mountaineering pen from a side drawer.

****

The next day, Jack placed his two weapons in the trunk. On top of those, he piled trash bags stuffed with wearable clothes. He slammed the lid and loaded a large package into the back seat.

Jack's beat-up BMW was in tip-top running condition, including new tires. You wouldn't know it because of the rusted-out fenders. He filled up at the gas station in Centennial before heading to Laramie, where he dropped the clothes at the laundromat.

"I'll be back next week. Put it on my account."

His next stop was down the block to the Lightning Fast Printing and Delivery Service.

Jack headed north on U.S. 287 to Wyoming 34 and by the Lake Laramidia Marina. On I-25, he passed the Boomer's Truck Stop sign by Wheatland before turning at Exit 153 to the Natural Bridge.

He navigated to an access road and turned under a big wooden sign. The letters were routed into the weathered lumber, "Morgan Livestock Company."

****

October 16, 2006—4:33 p.m. MDT: After dropping off Jack and helping him unload the mattress, Avery continued on the Snowy Range Scenic Byway and found a lovely campsite with an electrical hook-up at the Grand Encampment RV Park.

"The perfect spot."

Avery plopped down next to a tall cottonwood tree overlooking the Platte River, taking in the slow-moving water lapping against the river rocks. October was a great time to break out the fishing tackle and make a few casts into some of the deep pools. Catching fish wasn't as important as fishing.

Avery unpacked the *Sukiyaki* Bowl from the refrigerator, warmed it in the onsite store's microwave, and paid for a Bonkers Bar for dessert.

The following morning, a hot campground shower felt good. There was no telling what microscopic critters lurked in Jack's laundry.

After checking out, the White Shark stopped in Saratoga for a well-deserved soak at the free Hobo Hot Springs at the town swimming pool.

"Where you headed?" a soaker asked.

"Nowhere yet. I'm letting the wind guide me. You?"

"I'm a music producer. Heading home to Fort Collins. I was in Jackson, Alpine, actually, for a family reunion. It was my dad's 70th. I usually can't stand to be around my parents. This time was more enjoyable. My mom's mellowed out over the years."

"I just spent a week the other night in Fort Collins."

"Yeah? Ever listen to Bobby Smithee? He was big 20, 30 years ago. He called me up out of the blue a couple weeks ago. Says he was getting too old to play the bar scene. He had a wake-up call and confronted his past."

"Is that so?"

"Said he started writing again. Sold his Harley and hired me to re-invent his career."

"That's quite a story."

******

Avery drove from Saratoga to Walcott Junction, took I-80 to Rock Springs, and then turned north. Beyond Pinedale was a lonely and desolate stretch until reaching the scenic Hoback Canyon to Jackson.

The Moose Paddle Inn front desk bell clanged.

"What the ... What are you doing here?"

Mr. Meadows was at first confused when he saw the long-haired stranger. He turned up the volume on his hearing aids.

"Just taking the scenic route to Devil's Tower, Dad."

"Sit. I'll get your mother. She's helping with the rooms."

Avery settled into the same couch that's been in the apartment for 60 years. Mrs. Meadows soon arrived and took off her cleaning smock.

"You remember the sofa? It was your favorite place to plop when you were young. We're so glad you stopped by. I'll put on some water. Terry, you stay put and get reacquainted with Avery."

"I couldn't stand retirement and took the motel back from the management company. It was 15 percent that I wasn't making."

Mrs. Meadows brought out a tea service.

"All you ever talk about is business. Your dad's trying to say that he's sorry he disowned you when you moved to Lander. We want you to stay in Jackson and help us turn around the Moose Paddle."

"You must have read my mind. I went to a funeral in Boulder. You remember Gary Steiner? I brought him home when we were in college. Well, his wife died. Being around all that, I had an attitude adjustment talking with a random guy in Saratoga."

"Timing's everything. Look, I know I was tough on you when you were young," Mr. Meadows lamented. "I wanted a real boy, not you.

"Tough? How about emotional abuse? "I did my best to meet your expectations."

"I was wrong about that. It was me. I needed to be more accepting."

"Mom was a girl. She turned out pretty well!"

"Thank you, Dear. It doesn't matter now. We need your help. The management company almost drove this place into the ground. We're too old to do this by ourselves. Can Madison keep the Devil's Tower place going?"

"How'd you know about Madison?"

"I heard you have a very capable partner and as good a climber as you! Mothers have a sixth sense."

"You mean a sixth nose."

"The overflow room is clean. Terry, can you get your daughter the key to 217?"

****

Before Thanksgiving, Avery and her father heard a car backfire under the front door canopy. They greeted a dented 1998 Mazda 626 station wagon.

"I'm glad you could get up here on short notice," Avery said.

Mrs. Meadows joined the group carrying an armful of bath towels.

"Mom, Dad? I think you know Wallace Carlsen."

"It's been a few years. You'll be the second generation to help us keep up the Moose Paddle."

"I remember your dad teaching me how to rewire the room lamps without electrocuting myself," Avery recalled.

"We can get started right now. You will be such a help," said Mrs. Meadows. "I'm getting too stiff to pull on fitted sheets in 32 rooms."

"Avery got us a grant with the local employment office. You'll be training our new crew. Housekeeping. Maintenance," said Mr. Meadows.

"Thanks for the opportunity. This is better than picking up after drunk college kids. I've come full circle. Your daughter was my first boss who paid me when she let me hang around my grandpa's warehouse."

"Paid you to stay out of the way."

By spring, Avery and Wallace helped stabilize the Moose Paddle Inn for a successful summer season. She returned to the Bison Horn B&B just in time for the climbing season.

The Calico cat waited on the front porch when Avery and her White Shark rambled down the access road.

****

October 16, 2006—10:15 p.m. MDT: Sally was happy to return to the ranch. She liked sleeping in her own bed with no traffic noise or street light pollution. They also needed to return because the fall round-up was in full swing.

Billy had to join the rest of his hands in the mountains the following morning. Gathering up the cattle was taking longer this fall. Some cows and calves managed to get stranded in the old buffalo jump pit.

Sally was busy with her vegetable garden. Marvin didn't ride anymore. Instead, he helped her with the watering. She sat on a stool and harvested the carrots.

Part of their herd was driven down to the small pasture where a few hands separated the calves. Most of the crew camped in the mountains. He had faith in his foreman and came down to the ranch house every afternoon.

"You wash up. While we were out back, the delivery man left this notice."

"It can wait 'til tomorrow. I'll stop by when I go to the feed store."

He stuck the slip in his shirt pocket.

****

The following day, Billy loaded up the truck bed with a few bags of oats from the Wind River Mill. On his way back, he stopped by Lightning Fast and handed the clerk the notice, who slid a box over the counter. Billy lugged the package into the house. Sally cut open the parcel with a paring knife.

Inside was a small American Tourister suitcase. She snapped open the latches exposing four White Owl cigar boxes full of baseball cards neatly organized in envelopes by team name. A letter was taped to a paper bag filled with banded $100 bills and a jewelry box.

"Mrs. Steiner - The cash is my split from when Avery and I sold our business in Laramie. It isn't much. I hope the bank will take it!

I brought all my cigar boxes to Wyoming, so my mom wouldn't get rid of my stuff. I can't take any of this with me. Even if I could, I heard St. Peter is a Dodgers fan. The 23 Mantle cards in the small box are from 1952 and turned out to be the "holy grail" of baseball cards. They should get around $200,000 each. Who knew? Send them to Manny at the Midnight Sports Auction House in Hackensack, NJ.

Tell them you got them from me. He'll know what to do. The rest of my collection is from 1952 to 1964. Most of those cards have value. I know that card 1, Andy Pafko is worth $5,000, and Jackie Robinson should fetch at least $12,000. I can help you go through them after I get back to Laramie.

Please accept all this for the Arapaho Cultural Center you want to build in Boulder.

Jack Middleton

PS–Next time you see Avery, give her this 1964 Mickey. It will bring back memories of our first fishing trip."

"Billy? Add that up!"

****

October 19, 2006–6:20 a.m. MDT: Gary and Elizabeth took a few days to finish sorting the household stuff after Billy and Sally took off for Wyoming. Elizabeth hired an auction company specializing in estate sales to thin out her parent's things that didn't spark joy.

"What's my future, Dad? I have no close friends. I've been too self-absorbed and flighty. Who's going to scatter my ashes? I'll end up stuck in Boulder. Move to Laramie? Why go before the winter holidays? Before you know it, winter becomes spring, which is very addictive."

"Yeah, the summers are the best around here. No college kids. No wonder the Arapaho stayed around the Boulder Valley. Go out to California? Your cousin could use your mentorship."

"Drop in out of the blue on Uncle Frank? It would be pretty obvious I was desperate."

"Things have a way of working out," her father consoled.

"I know. Like Grandma Sally says …"

****

Blue Sky Village was a good place for Gary to stick around. After all, the idea behind cohousing was the neighborly support the residents provided to one another.

The community's Maintenance Committee volunteered to update Gary's condo to be handicap accessible. Harold stopped by to show Gary the planned improvements.

"I hear you're heading to New Orleans during the renovation."

"Tagging along with Elizabeth. She has some unfinished business down there."

"As a heads up, our friends Sandra and Felix have been talking around the community. They're trying to get enough of us to ask you to 'strongly consider' moving out," Harold made air quotes. "Our resident participation cops. They think you'd be useless."

"We have 95 percent participation around here, and they want to come after me? This place would be more caring and sharing if those two spent as much time worrying about their neuroses as they did causing trouble for others."

"Right, Dad. Maybe someone will pound on their door. Tell them they should move out for excessive meddling."

"It could be worse. They could be mean and angry."

"No more cohousing gossip. Remember our sweat lodge 'aha' moments."

****

The weather was forecast to be cold and clear. Elizabeth and Gary loaded up her Forester one overcast morning.

"This road trip is a blast from the past. Remember whenever we took a vacation? We aimed to make it to the World's Largest Ball of Twine. When we piled into the Scout, you always said, 'Whether we get there or not isn't important. It's all about the journey.'"

Their road trips took them to Yellowstone as part of the visit to the Wind River Reservation for the Ethete Powwow, to the Grand Canyon, Disneyland, and the Smithsonian.

The drive was uneventful until they entered Kansas.

"As long as we're near, next stop 'Twine Town.'"

Elizabeth punched the directions into her GPS Street Pilot III stuck on the dashboard.

Before they knew it, the "Welcome to Cawker City" sign was in front of them. Elizabeth half expected the back of it would read, "Now Leaving Cawker City."

Then there it was on Wisconsin Street, like when Dorothy and her three companions stumbled through the poppy field, awe-stricken by the sparkling Emerald City in the Land of Oz. The main attraction was the ball of eight million feet of hay-baling twine. It was spectacular.

She parked in front of the shrine to twine. The keepers of the big ball constructed a covering to protect the monstrous flat-bottomed sphere from the elements, although it may not have been tornado-proof in Kansas. Gary took in the grandeur of what was purported to be the most sisal fiber on display in one place.

In the middle of the afternoon, Elizabeth and her dad didn't have to share the view because they were the lone sojourners onsite. She snapped a Palm Treo picture of her dad dwarfed beside the 11-ft tall oblong globe.

"We made it." Elizabeth unwrapped a roll of twine she had picked up at the Grand Mart store before they left Boulder. She tied one end into the twine and handed the spool to her dad.

"Shall we?" They walked around the monstrous ball 40 feet in circumference several times before connecting the end to one of the other strands. "It's in honor of Mom. Didn't you tell me she used to load twine in the hay baling machine on your ranch?"

They strolled a Cawker City sidewalk following a golden strand of twine painted on the sidewalk like the "Yellow Brick Road." Elizabeth was amused by masterworks like the Mona Lisa holding a ball of twine exhibited in vacant storefront windows.

The main downtown attraction across from the enormous ball was an adobe-like structure called the Twine Peaks Hotel. From there, she made a room reservation at the Good Fortune Casino, five hours away, owned by the Cheyenne and Arapaho Tribes.

The two got back on the road.

"Well, Libby, mark this off my list of things to do."

"Libby? Are there any fall rodeos around?"

Elizabeth smiled.

****

Upon their arrival in Concho, Oklahoma, they elbowed their way through the casino slot machines and Black Jack tables to the check-in desk. How could they walk by the loud music blaring from the Mega Millions progressive slot machine without being distracted by the flashing lights?

"Well, Dad, here goes."

Elizabeth inserted a $20 bill into the money slot, made the $5.00 bet, and pushed the button. No luck on three spins.

"Fourth time's a charm. Some guy won $40 million in Vegas a few years ago on a three-dollar spin. It is possible!" Elizabeth rubbed her hands together. The 7s and fruits revolved around and came to a stop.

7, 7, 7, Cherry.

"Oh well, gotta support the tribe!" Elizabeth rationalized.

They wandered through the casino, looking for a bite, and settled on the hotel coffee shop.

"Remember the burger place in Jackson when we got stuck on the Grand? Those were some tasty burgers."

The server making up place settings at a back table met them at the front.

"As I recall, that Grand outing was quite an adventure, at least what I can remember. You ate a Popeye load of spinach."

"You remember spinach? You don't remember about killing yourself?"

The server sat them down at a booth, handed them menus, and grabbed place settings from the red apron adorned with geometric tribal designs.

"I hope you have Good Fortune. I'm Joey. We've been busy tonight. The strip sirloin is tonight's special. Last I checked, we have two left."

Gary and Elizabeth quickly perused their menus.

"I think we're ready. I'll try your turkey Rueben with Thousand Island on the side. No bread."

"No bread? I'll make something up for you."

"I'll have the special, medium rare." Gary popped open the pill bottle Elizabeth placed in front of him. "… and a Bud bottle. Spinach if you have it."

"Is draft okay?" Gary nodded.

"You have spinach on tap?" Elizabeth mused.

Joey smiled.

"Just passing through town? Tomorrow, we have a Texas Hold 'Em tournament. Special room rates if you're a player."

"We're not gamblers. My dad might be. I've been picking up bits and pieces about him I didn't know before."

"Always hit 'Soft 17.'"

"Yeah, right. My dad, the Cincinnati Kid."

Elizabeth shook her dad's memory medicine out of the vial.

"Are you sure you should be mixing? I'll bring you water."

"I didn't read any warning labels. We've made it this far."

Joey brought out their meals. To Elizabeth's surprise, her Rueben was transformed into a tasty salad.

"Where you from?"

"Wyoming. Dad's Northern Arapaho."

"I get up to Wind River once in a while. My bunch drives to Ethete in the summer for Sundance. My dad has family up there. Some of us go along to help with the driving."

"Is one of your relatives named Miguel?"

"How do you know Miguel?"

"Lucky guess."

"Miguel's my uncle. Not a blood uncle. His dad married into my family."

****

The following day, Elizabeth checked them out of the room. She made the short drive to Anadark and pulled up in front of the Delaware Tribal Complex in Anadarko. Elizabeth and her dad entered through a door labeled Enrollment Committee. Kelly, the Office Manager, sat down with a cup of steaming coffee from a maroon University of Oklahoma ceramic mug.

"Good morning. What can we do for you?"

"I want to apply for citizenship," responded Elizabeth.

"Did you fill out the forms? They've changed a little if you used one from a year ago."

Kelly flipped to the citizenship application.

"Boulder? New Orleans? I think I know about you. My mom said she met a woman at the laundromat on her way to see her parents in Colorado. Maybe a month ago."

"That would have been me."

"Very impressive." Kelly leafed through the paperwork. "You go way back, before the Lenni-Lenape exile. The BIA changed our name to Delaware.

"Much to my surprise, I'm one-eighth Delaware."

"Fill out this new form. Everything else looks complete. We'll be in touch if we have questions. Need more information. Otherwise, our Enrollment Committee meets on the first Wednesday. They forward a recommendation to the Tribal Executive Committee. If you don't hear from us in a few weeks, give us a call. Here's the receipt for your paperwork."

"Is this your father? What about him?"

"He's enrolled Northern Arapaho. I'm one-quarter from his side. That makes me three-eighths tribal."

"Very good. Any questions?"

"Not yet."

Elizabeth smiled with a sparkle in her eye.

****

Elizabeth and her father filled up at the Deli & Hardware Store station.

"Hey, Miguel. Remember me? I just met your niece, Joey, at the casino in Concho. Seems there's a big road trip to Lander."

"I let Joey invest my money in the slots. That's how I pay my way. Joey's very lucky. Has a feel for it. The only gambler I know who can make a parking meter pay off."

"Guess who now has a tribal ID?"

"What? Welcome to Delaware West! You get a legit discount."

Elizabeth nodded, and Miguel started the pump.

"I'll pay inside."

She and her father pulled in front of the deli to pay for the gas. There was Gladys waiting for her laundry to dry while keeping an eye on her granddaughter. Like always, she was working on the word puzzles in the newspaper.

"I remember you," Gladys said with a puzzled look.

"It's Elizabeth."

"Yes, Elizabeth. How was your drive to Colorado before?"

"Good and not so good. We're now heading to New Orleans."

"Meet my dad, Gary."

"How does your mother like the earrings."

"She wore them the day she died."

"Sorry to hear."

Elizabeth acknowledged the condolence.

"But you won't believe this."

Elizabeth recounted the story about running across her mom's files from Genotype Inc.

"*nëwinkhatènami*, I'm happy," exclaimed Gladys in her first language. "

"Are you related to Gladys Wilkinson?"

"In a sense. She was my mother, but my father is unknown."

"Her records were in my mom's files. I think my Uncle Frank and my Mom were your cousins."

"What? Welcome to the clan!" Gladys proclaimed with delight as her granddaughter crawled around under Elizabeth's feet.

"You're also related to Miguel?"

"Miguel's also my cousin, but he's much younger than me. He's having a sweat after work. You should come. It will be good for you. Pray for your mother."

"It would be good to sweat. We have to keep moving, maybe on our way back. Speaking of my mom, I think she wanted the tribe to have these back." Gary handed over the box Grandma Mary brought to Becca's funeral. "These are things Mom found as a child in New Jersey."

"wanìshi. I will turn all this over to the Historic Preservation Office. Now you say, 'yuh.'"

"Okay, yuh. I'll take you up on one of your henna tattoos. How about a turtle, a Lenni-Lenape turtle on my forearm like yours? It now has meaning."

"How about after lunch? We came for a Turtle Taco. Today isn't Tuesday."

"Every day is Tuesday on the Rez."

****

As for Elizabeth's business in NOLA, she and her father were there for parts of two uneventful days. Elizabeth was released from her lease with no penalty fees because Hurricane Katrina disrupted everything.

She and her dad sorted through clothes and household items, then loaded anything with meaning into the Subaru. A second-hand store truck picked up the rest. The people who lost everything in the hurricane needed her stuff more than she did.

Gary and Elizabeth returned from their road trip to their renovated condo now with that "new car smell." They didn't have much to unload except some good stories. "Now that I'm a card-carrying Delaware tribal member, I may start an authentic Turtle Taco truck. Take a tour on the Powwow Highway."

"Why not stay in Boulder? It's been nice having you around."

"That's a deal. Not staying here forever."

"Famous last words."

"My biggest revelation? Come to find out, there are four World's Largest Balls of Twine. There ought to be a law."

******

October 31, 2006—5:30 p.m. MDT: Susan and Harold invited their neighbors for a Halloween-themed dinner. Elizabeth still had her henna turtle tattoo and sported the yellow, green, and red ribbons stitched on the blouse her long-lost relative Gladys gave her.

Gary wore his black yoked shirt with pearl snaps and a pair of bug antennae on his head. They walked across the upper deck a few feet. Gary tapped on the window. Harold greeted them at the door.

"Steiners! Happy Halloween! How was your trip? Do you like your new place?"

"The condo looks great," exclaimed Gary. "Better than new!"

"The maintenance guys also slapped some paint in the bathroom. What about the step-in bathtub with water jets?"

"I can't wait to soak and take in the waters," replied Gary.

"I assume the trip was good?"

"It was a good drive. Long, but lots happened. We made a stop in Oklahoma." Elizabeth told the story about how she sleuthed out some ancestral history Becca would have taken with her to the grave.

"Mom didn't get a chance to tell us she was a member of the Lenni-Lenape."

"Good news!" congratulated Susan.

Elizabeth modeled her new hand-sewn shirt.

"I'm a new tribal member."

"This will be quite a celebration," Susan assured.

"There's someone you should meet. This is our oldest and only. Payton, these are our neighbors, Gary and his daughter Elizabeth. You might be interested to know that our Payton writes for Galaxy Gate Studios."

"Galaxy Gate? Impressive! Movies and TV. The big time""

Susan made a big sigh.

"Not that it matters. You disappointed your father."

"Interesting, Mom. Since Dad was the one who talked me into moving to Boulder."

Susan and Harold excused themselves to find a bottle of wine. Susan motioned for Gary to join them.

"I've been a screenwriter in California. The studio let me do my work here. Plus, Boulder's social life is more like LA. I can write any place."

"I had the same experience when I lived in Santa Monica."

"The brass wants me to keep my ear to the ground about projects here."

"… and New Mexico. New Mexico has a pretty good film incentive program," added Elizabeth.

She knew the importance of strong government support for movie production as an economic diversification tool.

"Colorado is very supportive compared to Wyoming. At first, I was going to move into our rental house in Laramie. Wyoming is trying to compete in the movie industry."

"I was on a Wyoming project over the summer. Jackson. What a nightmare. The problem with tourist towns in the summer is competition for rooms and just about everything else. We finished the shoot. It was for an episode of *Alien Invasions*. The production schedule was a few days."

"*Alien Invasions*? Like flying saucers."

"The supernatural market is a huge niche. It's a cable TV show. Weird stories about UFOs, Bigfoot, Bermuda Triangle. I was the local producer getting B-Roll. The story is about a guy by Laramie who says space invaders abducted him. We couldn't get onto the property, so we shot reenactments in Jackson at the big lake there. Better scenery, anyway."

Gary returned from the kitchen with wine stems.

"When I was the editor of the Laramie paper, we did a story about the guy, Pete Martin, and his UFOs over by Lake Laramidia."

"That's the same story. My crew interviewed people in a Laramie bar."

"By the way, the mountains in southern Wyoming are as scenic as the Tetons. Laramie is closer to the Denver airport," Elizabeth mentioned as her father distributed the wine stems.

"Too bad the slowest times to make movies in Wyoming are also the snowiest."

"You should work for the Wyoming Film Office."

"Funny you should mention that. I put in to work there. Did you go to film school?"

"The opposite. You know my dad was an eye doctor. When I graduated high school in 1986, I was supposed to attend college, then medical school, and would be ready to take over his practice. A job after college? What a setup. It didn't help that I avoided science classes. I took screenwriting at UCLA. Pre-med wasn't for me."

"Sounds familiar. I graduated the same year. Got my associate's in nursing. I worked in hotel management for 20 years. I was laid off and now a starving writer."

Susan and Harold returned with a bottle of Cabernet.

"Oh, this is a mother talking. Payton was so bright. Could handle anything." Susan handed the corkscrew and bottle to Payton. "Why don't you finish your degree?"

"What do you mean 'was'? Maybe someday, Mother. Long story short, Elizabeth, I was in the student union. There was a job fair. TV stations and movie studios sponsored tables in the media employment area."

Payton muscled the cork from the bottle and placed it on the table.

"Louisiana has a film incentive program. I couldn't get on with any of the studios unless I sold my soul that lurked between my legs."

"That's a problem. Unspoken in LA like in your LA. I lucked out. I signed up to be a production assistant on a movie. They picked me. It was called *Shortest Night into Day*. Nominated for Best Picture. Being around a studio movie crew was it for me. I dropped out of college. Haven't looked back. Now I'm in the WGA [Writers Guild of America]."

Susan poured wine. They all raised their glasses.

"To newly discovered roots! To Payton and Elizabeth," Harold toasted.

"May this be the start of a beautiful friendship," Gary said as he noticed Payton's belt buckle. "I have a beaded one with the same design. Mine is an heirloom from the 1900s."

"I was in a tourist shop in Jackson. The store clerk would not let me leave until I bought this buckle. He gave me a 75 percent discount. When I went back to LA, my yoga teacher saw it. She said it's Sanskrit. It's *aum.*"

Elizabeth inspected the design. "*Ahhooommm* as in *namaste?*"

Gary moved his head from side to side, causing the antennae to bobble and wobble on two springs. He pulled back the lapel of his sheepskin-lined vest, exposing the same Lake Laramidia Marina *aum* logo embroidered on his vintage black pearl-snap shirt.

"We should compare notes. Looks like this story continues. Road trip! I'm driving!"

Elizabeth jangled the beaded key holder from Oklahoma in front of Gary's smile.

"Who's hungry? We can talk after dinner!"

-30-

68

Libby Flats Recipe Box

Much of *Libby Flats* revolves around home-cooked meals and road food. I started out in the hotel food service industry. I couldn't help but include recipes for the dishes mentioned in the book. Dad was the one who suggested adding the recipes. Libby Flats is also tops on the cookbook bestseller list.

I decided to give my dad a hand and stayed with him at Blue Sky Village rather than move to Laramie. He ended up being my muse while editing *Libby Flats*. Boulder grew on me, and we sold the legendary Calamity Club.

Dad was able to remain in the cohousing community for five years before moving into the Goose Creek Continuous Care long-term care facility. I attribute his longevity to living in an intentional community and interacting with others. He beat the odds and passed away in 2021.

Dad's neighbors, Susan and Harold Butler, sold their condo and relocated to Goose Creek independent living apartments. Payton moved in with me after we signed our book and movie deals. Even though we weren't "seniors," Blue Sky Village allowed us to stay as long as we were active community participants.

After the success of *Libby Flats*, Payton and I pitched a literary cooking show to the Home and Food Network. Recipes arc meaningful ways to bring the characters, settings, and culture to life and provide tangible sensory experiences for the readers. Recipes are also reminders of the comfort food characters shared during their time together, allowing readers to recreate the experience.

******

Bon Appétit

Quiver Mountain Ranch

- Savory Beef Brisket
- Roasted Rooster
- Becca's Rodeo Pie
- Macaroni Burger Stew
- Sally's Potato Salad

Food on the Road

- Fuji Café: Pork Noodle Bowl
- Carl's Czech Café: Holubky
- Deli & Hardware Store: Turtle Tacos
- La Comida Buena: Chile Relleno Casserole
- Piggy's: Famous Jersey Pork Roll
- Dugout Soda Shoppe: Yankee Egg Cream
- Paintbrush Room: Paintbrush Battered Mushrooms
- Friendly Table Café: Omelet Florentine
- '56 Chevy Grille: Teton Special
- Nordic Chalet: Raisin Rounds
- Rabbit Hutch: Crab Yangon
- Bison Horn B&B: Chilaquiles
- Good Fortune Casino: Reuben Salad

******

Quiver Mountain Ranch - Lander, Wyoming

We feed anywhere from 30 to 40 men, so I hope you know a little bit about the kitchen. – Sally Steiner

Savory Beef Brisket

Sally's smoked brisket was a ranch favorite any season of the year. It made for a great main dish in the kitchen or on the mountain when moving the cattle to the high pastures in the spring and back during the fall.

The hay crew couldn't wait for the brisket sandwiches Becca brought them during the summer. The smoker was so big that two or three briskets could be cooked simultaneously, perfect for the Cattleman's Association barbecues the ranch sponsored on the Fourth of July.

Ingredients

- Beef Brisket: 5 lbs
- Wet Rub: Worcestershire Sauce - 2 tbsp to taste, Beef bouillon - 6 to 7 tsp
- Dry Rub: Oregano, black pepper, paprika, salt, sugar, onion powder, garlic powder, etc., at least ½ tbsp of each to taste
- Water: ¼ cup or so to dissolve the bouillon, ½ cup to moisten the brisket

Directions

Place a double or triple-folded piece of aluminum foil onto a cookie sheet large enough to eventually wrap the brisket. Place the brisket on the foil, fat side up. Mix the wet rub bouillon and Worcestershire Sauce and brush the brisket. Mix the dry rub ingredients and coat the brisket's top, bottom, and sides. Curl up the foil to form a vessel to catch the drippings.

Ignite the charcoal, wood chips, or your chosen smoke source. Preheat the smoker to 225 to 250 degrees F. Using indirect heat, place the brisket with the fat side up in the smoker. Cook for 5 to 6 hours until the brisket's internal temperature reaches 160 to 170 degrees F. Add more wood chips during cooking to increase the smoke flavor if desired.

Pour ½ cup of water, more or less, over the brisket. Tightly wrap the entire brisket with the foil, and cook it for 90 minutes. The internal temperature should be around 175 to 185 degrees F.

The brisket should rest for 1 to 2 hours before unwrapping. Place the brisket on a good cutting surface and slice across the grain. Collect the drippings from the foil to moisten the brisket slices.

****

Roasted Rooster

Sally tended a chicken coop out back. Each day, Becca collected the eggs for the household. Others were available to the neighbors who traded them for milk, cheese, and vegetables. Sally named her birds and cared for them as if her coop was a nursery. Becca was surprised when Sally asked her to invite George for a Sunday dinner.

Sally didn't keep her chickens as pets but knew which ones were older than the others. There were two roosters. George was getting a little cranky in his old age.

Doing in the poor fellow was a rite of passage for Becca. She could barely stand fishing and was even more queasy about preparing her first bird for roasting. Sally caught the rooster and quickly put him out of his misery by swinging him by the neck.

Becca's job was to immerse the bird in boiling water, making feather plucking easier. She was in tears as she watched Sally place George's neck on a chopping block, remove the head, and clean the carcass.

Older birds were less tender, and most had a thicker layer of fat, preserving moisture while roasting. Becca made a brine and soaked the bird overnight.

Ingredients

- Rooster or Hen: 1 whole, plucked, and cleaned
- Brine Water: 2 qt of water, ½ cup of salt
- Herbs and Spices: Garlic, Onion, Bay Leaves, Parsley, Sage, Rosemary, Thyme, Salt, Pepper, etc.
- Vegetable Oil: Enough to rub down the bird
- Vegetables: Potatoes, Carrots, Celery, Turnips, etc.

Directions

Make a brine by dissolving salt into the water. Soak the bird at least overnight. As an option, remove the bird from the brine, then wrap it loosely in butcher paper and let it refrigerate for a few days. Aging will improve tenderness.

Preheat the oven to 250 to 300 degrees F. Oil the bird and rub in the herbs and spices of your choice, then place in a roasting pan. Add enough water to cover the bottom of the pan to catch the drippings and keep them moist.

Cut up the vegetables and place them around the bird. Cover and roast low and slow for as long as it takes, eight hours or more.

Continually check the temperature in the deepest part of the breast toward the thigh without touching the bone. The internal temperature should reach 165 to 175 degrees F.

You may want to debone the chicken before serving. The carcass and drippings can be repurposed for soup stock.

****

Becca's Rodeo Pie

When Becca learned that Gary was born on Kentucky Derby Day, she modified a classic Derby Pie recipe. Pinion pines grew in southwest Wyoming. They were sold at a roadside stand by an elderly fellow named Ping Chen. Ping was a child when his parents were killed in the Rock Springs Coal Miner Massacre.

On September 2, 1885, a mob of white miners attacked and killed 28 Chinese coworkers at the Union Pacific Coal Mine near Rock Springs. The massacre culminated years of tensions over wages and working conditions.

Union Pacific paid the Chinese miners less than the prevailing wage to save on costs. The pay disparity resulted in violence based on racial prejudice. The white miners didn't want to work for less and claimed the Chinese took their jobs.

Becca and Sally drove to the Rock Springs train station to pick up their crew members for the hay-cutting and branding seasons. They always stopped at Ping's roadside stand and picked up a bag or two of the tasty pine nuts on their back to the ranch.

Another one of Becca's jobs was tending to the ranch apiary. She and the bees were comfortable being around each other, and she harvested and bottled the alfalfa honey, which had a delicate taste.

The pine nuts and honey added a unique flavor to the filling. Regarding the pie crust, Becca leaned on Sally for instruction. It took Becca a few tries to get the lard proportions right for a flakey crust.

After Elizabeth was born, Becca opted for the frozen crusts in the refrigerated dairy section for convenience. Premade pie crusts and flour tortillas were among humanity's worst inventions.

Ingredients

- Pie crust: 1 (9-inch, from scratch or the store)
- Honey: 1 cup (Quiver Mountain Ranch honey)
- White Sugar: 1 cup (or less)
- Eggs: 4 (room temperature)
- Chocolate chips: 1½ cups (or less)
- Pinion Pine Nuts: 1 cup (can be substituted with pecans or walnuts)
- Butter: ½ cup (melted, not separated)
- Bourbon Whiskey: 4 tbsp (more, less, none)
- Vanilla Extract: 1 tsp

Directions

Prepare or purchase your favorite crust and press the dough into a 9-inch pie plate. Preheat the oven to 350 degrees F.

Use a low-speed electric mixer or manual beater to combine the honey, eggs, sugar, and eggs in a bowl until smooth. Stir in chocolate chips, nuts, butter, bourbon, and vanilla extract. Pour the filling into the pie crust. Create a geometric design on the top with the nuts as an option.

Bake for 45 minutes or so until set. Remove the pie and let it rest for 20 to 30 minutes. Top each serving with whipped cream, if desired.

****

Macaroni Burger Stew

Behind the Quiver Mountain ranch house was a ceremonial sweat lodge made of young willows from the banks of Canyon Creek woven together and covered with blankets and tarps.

Before each sweat, Marvin and Willie Eagle led weekly Sunday afternoon ceremonies. He stoked a fire and added smooth river rocks to the red-hot embers.

There was a hole in the lodge floor where the heated stones were placed. Marvin explained the reason for the ceremony and then sprinkled cedar wood chips on the rocks.

After the lodge participants covered themselves with smoke, he created a steam room by ladling on water. Sally prepared stew and bread for after the sweat.

Ingredients

- Ground Beef: 1 lb
- Diced Onion: ½ to 1cup
- Beef bouillon: 8 cups
- Diced Tomatoes: 1 can, 14 oz
- Tomato Sauce: 1 can, 14 oz
- Oregano, basil: ½ tsp, each
- Bay Leaf: 1 or 2 to taste
- Elbow Macaroni: 1½ cups, uncooked (any macaroni will do)
- Mixed Vegetables: As desired (canned, frozen, or fresh)

Directions

Brown the hamburger in a large soup pot. Depending on your taste, drain off the fat first. Add the onion and dense vegetables like turnips, carrots, and celery and cook until tender.

Bring the soup to a hard boil, then simmer for 5 or 10 minutes. Add the bouillon, tomatoes, tomato sauce, and seasonings. Stir in macaroni and vegetables, then simmer until the macaroni is tender.

****

Sally's Potato Salad

If there was any dish Gary could eat at any meal. It was his mother's potato salad. Sally organized a huge potluck meal when the neighboring ranches worked together to bring down the herds in the fall. There were many versions of potato salad depending on the number of ranches. Some were hot, others with large potato pieces, and a few were too sweet or too sour. Sally had a secret ingredient.

Ingredients

- Potatoes: 6 medium Russet potatoes
- Eggs: 4 (hard-boiled)
- Celery: 3 stalks
- Onion: ½ white onion
- Pickles: 4 medium kosher dills and a splash of brine
- Mayonnaise: 1 cup
- Yellow Mustard: A few tbsp to add tang and color
- Soy Sauce: 2 to 3 tbsp (not too much, so the salad doesn't turn brown)
- Salt: 1 to 2 tbsp

Directions

Prepare the potatoes and eggs ahead of time so they cool before mixing everything. Dice celery, onion, and pickles into ½-inch pieces and set aside.

Potatoes: Peeling the potatoes is optional. Cut them into quarters and place them in a pot. Fill with enough water to cover them. Add the salt, more or less, to taste. Bring the pot to a boil for 5 to 10 minutes, then turn it down to simmer until a fork easily penetrates the potatoes. It's important not to overcook them so they don't become mush when dicing them. Undercooking results in crunchy potatoes.

Drain, rinse with cold water, and allow the pieces to cool. If you have time, refrigerate them to make dicing the potatoes into ½ to ¾ - inch pieces much easier.

Eggs: Remove the eggs from the refrigerator and allow them to warm up. Place them in a saucepan and cover them with water. When

Gary and Becca were married in Laramie. Ichiro Fujiyama hosted the rehearsal dinner at his restaurant. Sally learned to add a tsp of salt and a splash of vinegar to the egg water. The eggs were easier to peel.

Rinse and place the eggs back in the carton. To save time and confusion, mark each egg with an "H" and let them cool or refrigerate until the next day. Peel and dice them with an egg slicer, once horizontally, then flip and slice vertically.

Salad preparation: Place the potatoes, egg, mayonnaise, and a splash of pickle brine into a large bowl, then mix with a spoon until the mayonnaise has coated the potatoes and egg yolks are dissolved. Mix in onion, celery, pickles, soy sauce, and mustard.

Cover and refrigerate.

******

Food on the Move

There's not much to do on road trips around Wyoming except gas up and eat. – Avery Meadows

Fuji Café - Laramie, Wyoming

Tak was young when he moved with his mom and dad to Laramie after World War II. As he grew older, he helped at the café. When Tak was 14, one after-school job was making the next day's *udon* noodles. He learned to boil them so the noodles wouldn't stick together after they were drained and cooled in a big stainless-steel bowl in the large refrigerator.

He also was in charge of boiling eggs and, through trial and error, learned to make them to perfection. Tak followed his father's tip and added vinegar and salt to the water. When he was younger, science classes were his favorite. He learned salt added to the water permeates the shell, and a splash of vinegar breaks down the calcium, making boiled eggs easier to peel.

Another lesson Tak learned in science class was about boiling chips. When unevenly shaped stones are added, the water boils more calmly and minimizes egg breakage.

Ichiro passed down the recipe for pork belly passed down for at least four generations. In Japan, the Fujiyamas harvested wild boar as a source of protein.

****

Pork Noodle Bowl

The pig is represented in the Eastern Zodiac and symbolizes wealth, good fortune, honesty, diligence, and generosity.

Ingredients

Pork Belly

- Pork Belly: 6 to 7 oz (cut into thin to medium slices)
- White onion: ¼ (cut into wedge-shaped pieces)
- *Shoyu* (soy sauce): 1 tbsp
- Ginger: ½ tsp (grated, dry, or paste)
- Water: 6 oz

- Vegetable Oil: Enough to keep the pork from sticking when cooked

Soup

- *Dashi* (fish stock): 1 quart

- Green onions: 1 bunch (chopped for garnish)

- Eggs: 1 hard-boiled (place egg in a pan with enough tap water to cover the eggs. Add a splash of vinegar, a dash of salt, and a pebble. Bring to a boil for two minutes. Turn down the heat, and cover for 15 minutes. Run cold water over the eggs and let them cool)

- *Shoyu:* To taste

Udon (Japanese noodles): depends on the number of servings

Directions

Marinade: Place the sliced pork belly in a bowl or sealable bag with water, *shoyu*, a little vegetable oil, onion, and ginger, then marinate for 20 minutes or so.

Egg: Hard boil an egg cut in half for garnish.

Broth: Fill a pot with a quart of *dashi,* pre-prepared or from powder, and shoyu. Bring the broth to a boil and let simmer.

Udon: In a separate pot, prepare the udon using the instructions of the type you choose. Drain the noodles through a colander and rinse off the starch.

Pork Belly: Add vegetable oil and heat a skillet on medium. You may not need to add oil if your pan is non-stick. Once hot, add the pork belly, pour over the marinade, and cook until browned.

Soup: Place udon into bowls and pour on broth. Place the pork and onions on top. You can also add the pan drippings to improve the flavor. Garnish each bowl with chopped green onion and half a hard-boiled egg. Spice with Japanese pepper, if desired.

****

Carl's Czech Café - Ennis, Texas

The availability of land in central Texas and European political unrest were determinants for Czech immigration to the United States. In the 1840s, Czechoslovakian territories were parts of Austria ruled by a feudal system.

Western European democratic thought began to spread to Eastern Europe, which led to various revolutions. Despite political reforms, peasants struggled to accumulate wealth, resulting in immigration to the United States in 1852.

Karel Adamcik immigrated from Priluky, Moravia, in 1891 and Americanized his name to Carl. He ventured west and settled in Ennis, Texas, where he established Carl's Czech Café. He soon sent for his wife to help with the restaurant. Carl's grandson is the third generation to own and manage the downtown landmark.

****

Holubky

Ingredients
- Cabbage: 1 head, 2 to 3 lbs
- Cooked White Rice: ½ cup
- Onion: 1 chopped
- Ground Beef: 1 lb, more or less
- Ground pork: ¼ to ½ lb
- Egg: 1
- Garlic, Paprika: 1 tsp, each
- Sauerkraut: 1 can, 14 oz
- Tomato Sauce: 1 can, 15 oz
- Crushed Tomatoes: 1 can, 15 oz

Directions

The quantity of *holubky* depends on the number of cabbage leaves. Cut the stem end of the head to make a flat bottom. Place the cabbage in a pan large enough to hold and cover it. Add water and bring it to a boil. Let the blanched cabbage head cool, carefully peel the leaves, and set them aside.

While you're in preparation, make a pot of white rice. Drain the sauerkraut and save the juice. Using half of the sauerkraut and crushed tomatoes, add a layer of each on the bottom of a 12" x 12" casserole dish. Depending on the size of the cabbage, you may need a larger one or make multiple batches.

When leaves have cooled down, use a small knife or a pair of scissors to make a V-shaped notch in the thick end of the leaf. This will enable each leaf to be more malleable.

Remove the thick stem-end core. Chop up the remaining cabbage and add a layer to the casserole dish on top of the sauerkraut and crushed tomatoes.

Use a fork to mix the beef, pork, cooled rice, sauerkraut juice, half the tomato sauce, egg, garlic, and paprika.

Preheat the oven to 350 degrees F.

Depending on the size of the cabbage leaf, hand-form a suitable elongated amount of the filling and place it in the center of the leaf. Fold the thick end, then the thin end of the leaf over the filling toward the center, and then fold the sides to the middle. Optionally, bind each *holubky* with a piece of cotton string.

Place each *holubky*, folded side down, into the casserole dish on top of the chipped cabbage, sauerkraut, and crushed tomato layers. Depending on the number, it's okay to stack them up.

Add the remaining sauerkraut, tomato sauce, and crushed tomatoes over the rolls when the dish is full.

Tent the dish with aluminum foil, shiny side down, then bake in the preheated oven for 2 hours. Remove and cool for 15 minutes.

****

Deli & Hardware Store - Anadarko, Oklahoma

Over the years, many tribes have adopted fry bread as a traditional starch source. The *Diné* (Navajo) tribe perfected the fry bread recipe. In 1993, the Delaware Tribe in Anadarko, Oklahoma, organized the tribe's first National Fry Bread competition.

During the mid-1840s, many White pioneers protected by the U.S. Army entered *Diné* country. The intruders caused problems by their presence. *Diné* leader Narbona and a few hundred warriors met on August 31, 1849, with U.S. Colonel John M. Washington to discuss peace. Later in the day, an agreement was reached, but not before Narbona was killed following a skirmish.

The U.S. Army sent frontier scout Kit Carson to negotiate a *Diné* surrender in September 1863. No *Diné* came to meet with him. Carson scorched the land and cut off the tribe from its food sources. Hundreds of *Diné* prisoners starved on the Long Walk, and eventually, the survivors were placed on the overcrowded Mescalero Apache Reservation.

****

Turtle Tacos

Fry bread was a survival food concocted during four years of imprisonment from government-provided staple supplies like flour, lard, salt, sugar, and dried milk. Since then, many tribes have offered fry bread as popular fare on the powwow trail.

Ingredients

Fry Bread

- Flour: 1 cup
- Salt: ¼ tsp
- Milk: ½ cup
- Baking Powder: 1 tsp
- Vegetable Oil: Enough to deep fry in a skillet

Toppings

- Ground beef: 1 lb, any meat will do
- Onion: ½ cup, diced
- Iceberg Lettuce: ½ head, shredded- Tomatoes: 2 large, diced

- Cheddar Cheese: 1 cup, grated- Sour cream: optional
- Salsa: optional

Directions

Ahead of time, if desired, you can grate the cheese, dice the onion, shred the lettuce, and cook the meat, beans, and chili.

Fry Bread: Sift the flour and mix it with salt and baking powder in a mixing bowl. Pour the milk over the dry ingredients and stir the dough with a fork to form a big lump.

With floured hands, form the dough ball while not kneading. The dough ball should be sticky inside, and the outside will be well-floured. Cut the dough into 4 to 6 pieces, depending on your desired size. Keep your hands floured and form roundish dough disks 5 to 6 inches in diameter.

Pour enough oil to fill a large skillet 1 inch deep. Determine if the oil is hot enough by placing a small piece of dough into the skillet to see if it fries.

When the oil is hot, carefully place each piece of dough into the oil to minimize splattering. Submerse the dough with a wooden spoon as it fries. Fry until golden brown, and then flip over. Each side should take 3 to 4 minutes to cook. Remove the cooked fry bread pieces and set them on paper towels to drain. The oil may need to be changed if your fry bread is dark brown.

Keep your fry bread warm for an hour or so in a 200-degree F. oven. Fry bread refrigerates well for future use and can be reheated in a 350-degree F oven for 10 to 15 minutes.

Indian Tacos are a participatory meal. Put the fry bread and toppings out so your guests can add ingredients on top of the fry bread to their liking.

****

La Comida Buena - Los Angeles, California

La Comida Buena was on Olvera Street in the El Pueblo de Los Angeles Historical Monument. The 44-acre area was saved from bulldozers by a Los Angeles socialite who helped preserve the neighborhood's cultural roots.

According to the restaurant's self-appointed assistant manager, Isabella, the City of Los Angeles had its roots in that neighborhood. Her Great-Great Grandfather Augustine Olvera was the first judge in the county.

Isabella's father came up with the Chili Relleno Casserole as a modern shortcut and a way to "repackage" the classic dish.

****

Chili Relleno Casserole

Traditional Chili Rellenos are on the menu. Roasted Anaheim peppers filled with cheese are battered and either steamed or fried. The casserole is a different way to prepare a traditional dish.

Ingredients

- Anaheim peppers: 6 to 8, relatively straight and similar in length
- Eggs: 4 any size
- Flour: 4 to 5 tbsp
- Milk: 5 to 6 oz
- Garlic, Onion, Cumin: ½ tbsp, each
- Cheese (your choice): ½ lb or more
- Mozzarella Cheese Sticks: As many peppers as you have

Directions

Preheat the oven to 425 degrees F. Grate ½ pound or so of cheese.

Slice off the pepper stems, slit them open, and remove the seeds. Coat the baking sheet with cooking oil. Place the peppers slit side down on the sheet, then brush or spray on oil and roast until cooked. The peppers soften up and shrink.

While the peppers roast, mix 4 eggs, 4 to 5-ish tbsp flour, and 5 to 6-ish oz milk. The batter should be thick enough to adhere to the peppers. Use a fork or spoon to stir in the garlic powder, onion powder, cumin, and salt to taste (The spice granules stick to a whisk's wires).

Check the peppers, and when the skins brown, let them cool, then peel them. This is tedious if you haven't peeled peppers before, mainly if the peppers are under-roasted. It's essential to remove as much skin as possible. Otherwise, your guests will encounter bites that seem like they bit into a scrap of cellophane. Snuggly line up the peppers slit side up in a greased 9" x 13" baking dish or similar. They should scrunch up against each other and fill the dish on all sides.

Fill each pepper stem end to tip with torn mozzarella sticks to your liking. Close up the peppers the best you can. Sprinkle a layer of grated cheese, then evenly add the batter. The slurry should be a little thicker than runny. The mixture will disperse itself between and under the peppers.

Sprinkle the rest of the grated cheese over the peppers and batter. Don't be shy about using too much cheese. It will ooze between the peppers and flavor the casserole.

Bake at 425 for 30 minutes or so. The batter should rise and turn golden brown. Remove from the oven and let cool. Cut the casserole into squares and then serve.

****

Piggy's - Atlantic City, New Jersey

Pork roll is most associated with New Jersey and is typically served at casual restaurants and diners like Piggy's. Pork roll was a favorite of Jack. Even though Becca liked the urban meat, she ordered it as a passive-aggressive way to irritate her mother.

Taylor Ham was initially produced by a Trenton, New Jersey company called Taylor Provisions, Inc. in 1856 and advertised as "prepared ham." In 1906, the descriptor no longer met federal labeling requirements for ham.

****

Famous Jersey Pork Roll Sandwich

Taylor changed the name from ham to "pork roll," a generic term for any "pork roll."

Ingredients

- Pork Roll: 4 slices (6 to 8 oz) such as Taylor
- Butter: 2 to 4 tbsp
- Kaiser Rolls: 4 sliced in half and toasted
- Eggs: 4
- American Cheese: 4 slices

Directions

Before starting, score the edges of the pork roll slices in 3 or 4 places to minimize them from curling while grilling. Brown the pork roll slices on both sides, which should take 5 to 6 minutes. Melt the butter in a skillet over medium-high heat and toast the rolls. Place a slice of pork roll on each toasted roll bottom.

Lower the heat and crack the eggs into the same skillet. Break each yolk and salt and pepper to taste. Fry them over medium or hard. Place a slice of cheese on top of each egg. The heat of the egg should soften the cheese. You can place a cover over the skillet, being careful to be sure the cheese doesn't melt too much.

Using a spatula, place an egg and cheese on top of each browned pork roll slice. If you like other condiments, add mayonnaise, mustard, or ketchup to the top half of the roll.

Dugout Soda Shoppe - Bronx, New York City, New York

The Dugout Soda Shoppe was a favorite stop near Yankee Stadium, baseball season or not. It was opened in 1933 by an enterprising Yankees fan and Jacob Middleton's cousin from Brooklyn. The soda shop struggled during the Great Depression. Jacob agreed to help keep the business from going under if egg creams were on the menu.

Yankee Egg Cream

Egg creams were said to be invented in Brooklyn and popularized during the 1920s. Despite the name, the drink contains no egg or cream.

Ingredients

- Chocolate flavor syrup: 3 tbsp
- Cold milk: 4 oz
- Seltzer water: 8 - 9 oz

Directions

Pour seltzer water into a 16 oz glass. Separately, with a fork, dissolve the chocolate syrup into the ice-cold milk, then slowly add the mixture to the seltzer water.

****

Paintbrush Room - Laramie, Wyoming

The Paintbrush Room, named for the Wyoming state flower, has been a Laramie culinary staple since 1932. The restaurant building was once part of a U.S. Army outpost that protected the transcontinental railroad. Buffalo Bill Cody and Calamity Club namesake Calamity Jane supposedly stayed there.

Cody was a bounty hunter and was dispatched to kill bison that herded up over the tracks and caused delays. Besides the buffalo steaks, the appetizer of choice was beer-battered mushrooms.

****

Paintbrush Battered Mushrooms

Truth be told, Jack tipped the Paintbrush Room manager $100 to guarantee a primo Friday night reservation for his impromptu date with Connie Morgan during Wild West Days.

Ingredients

Mushrooms

- Button Mushrooms: 1 to 2 lbs, fresh and medium
- Flour: 1 cup and set aside 2 to 3 tbsp
- Salt: 1 tsp to taste
- Milk: ½ cup
- Yogurt: ¼ cup, plain (Sour Cream can be substituted)
- Beer: ¾ cup, dark or medium
- Egg: 1
- Vegetable oil: Enough to fill the frying pan to cover the mushrooms

High Plains Nectar

- Ranch Dressing: ½ cup
- Yogurt: ¼ cup (Sour Cream can be substituted)
- Thousand Island Dressing: ¼ cup

Directions

Wash the mushrooms, pat them dry, and trim the stems. Make the High Plains Nectar by combining Ranch dressing, yogurt, and Thousand Island dressing.

Sift the flour and mix with salt in a bowl. Whisk the milk, yogurt, beer, and egg together in a separate bowl. Pour the liquids into the dry mixture and combine by stirring.

Add enough oil to a heavy-bottomed skillet to cover the mushrooms. Heat to 350 degrees F. Cover a baking sheet with paper towels or a draining rack. Toss the mushrooms with the flour and set aside until coated.

Separate the mushrooms into 3 or 4 batches. Stir the batter and dip each mushroom, let the excess drip off, and then add to the hot oil. Stir with a slotted spoon until golden and crisp, which should be 2 to 4 minutes.

Transfer the mushrooms to the baking sheet to drain. Serve with High Plains Nectar on the side.

****

Friendly Table Café - Tucumcari, New Mexico

Johnny Johnson was a math whiz and studied civil engineering at the University of Chicago. In 1951, he was bored and dropped out. He quit school and decided to take to the road.

Johnny rolled into Amarillo, Texas, in his Ford coupe convertible. Johnny looked for odd jobs and came across a construction crew building a restaurant on U.S. Highway 66. He noticed they were having problems getting the crossbeams positioned correctly and gave them a few suggestions. Soon, Johnny was the project foreman.

In the spring of 1952, the Amarillo Chow House opened for business. The owner took a liking to Johnny and taught him the restaurant business, from washing dishes to daily accounting. The Chow House was soon very profitable and was sold. The new owners brought in their own management team, meaning Johnny was out of a job.

He headed west and broke down in Tucumcari, New Mexico. While waiting three weeks for his car radiator to be repaired, he stayed at the Roadrunner Motor Lodge owned by the Smiths. He did odd jobs around the Roadrunner in exchange for room and board, like painting and plumbing.

****

Omelet Florentine

Johnny later learned the Smiths owned a restaurant in town called the Friendly Table Café that wasn't doing very well. Based on his experience in Amarillo, he made a deal and partnered with the Smiths to operate the Friendly Table in 1953.

Ingredients

- Eggs: 4
- Salt and Pepper: Coarsely Ground
- Swiss Cheese: 4 oz, grated
- Butter: 2 to 3 tbsp
- Garlic: 2 tsp, minced or dry
- Spinach: ½ lb, fresh or 10 oz, frozen
- Vegetable Oil: For trying the omelet

Directions

Preheat a skillet or pan to medium. Season the eggs with salt and pepper and set aside. Place the cheese in a medium bowl and set aside. Thoroughly rinse fresh spinach, then drain and set aside. If frozen, measure the preferred amount, allow it to thaw, and set aside.

Line a plate with two or three paper towels.

In the pan or skillet, sauté the garlic in 1 to 2 tbsp of butter for about 30 seconds.

Fresh or Frozen Spinach: Prepare spinach as you like it. Add salt and pepper and 1 to 2 tbsp butter. Transfer cooked spinach to the paper towel-lined plate. Remove excess moisture by rolling up the spinach and squeezing. Place the cooked spinach in the bowl with grated cheese.

Reuse the paper towels and wipe the residual spinach pieces from the pan. Add enough vegetable oil to coat the bottom and heat to medium. Re-whisk the eggs, then add to the pan. Use a spatula to push the edges towards the center, then tilt the pan to spread the uncooked eggs underneath the cooked egg. Continue this until the egg is nearly cooked.

Sprinkle spinach and cheese mixture over half of the omelet. Remove from heat, cover, and allow the omelet to rest until fully cooked.

Loosen the omelet from the pan and fold it in half to cover the filling. Slide it onto a plate and serve.

****

'57 Chevy Grille - Jackson, Wyoming

Downtown Jackson was a very walkable area. The '57 Chevy Grille across the street from the Rainbow River Bar was a block away from the Moose Paddle Inn. The Grille was one of those places open 24 hours, but not always in a row, and busy when the bars closed after 2 a.m.

Teton Special

The cooks didn't write anything down and had uncanny memories, which must have been a job requirement.

Hamburgers and cheeseburgers were the only items on the menu. The "Teton Special" was voted "Best in Jackson" three years running.

The burgers were cooked while you watched, plated, and in front of you in second's flat. Elizabeth and Gary sat at two green-vinyl-covered stools at the horseshoe-shaped counter and yelled out their orders.

Ingredients

- Ground beef: 1½ lb
- Salt and Pepper: To Taste
- Butter: 2 to 3 tsp
- Mushrooms: 2 cans, 4 oz, or fresh, ¼ lb
- Bacon: 4 to 6 strips
- Spinach: for garnish
- Soy Sauce: 2 to 3 tbsp
- Swiss Cheese: 4 to 6 slices
- Buns: 4 to 6, toasted, optional

Directions

Preheat the stove to medium heat. If grilling, oil the grate.

Form the hamburger into 4 to 6 patties; season with salt and pepper and set them aside. Drain the canned mushrooms or wash and slice the fresh ones, then set aside.

Prepare the bacon crispy as you are accustomed–fry, bake, microwave. Drain, pat the strips dry, then set aside. Sauté the mushrooms and soy sauce in the bacon pan until browned. Set aside and keep warm.

As an option, toast the buns on the grill, stove, or other means. Since the heat is so variable, you'll have to plan this out if you use the grill.

Grill patties until cooked through. If you're curious, insert a ther-mometer until the center temperature is at least 160 degrees F, which should be five or six minutes per side.

Spoon mushrooms on top of patties; place a slice of Swiss Cheese on each. Cover or close the grill for a minute or so until the cheese melts. Serve on buns and spinach leaves as garnish.

****

Nordic Chalet - Jackson, Wyoming

During the Great Depression, Jackson, Wyoming, had a tourism growth spurt. In 1937, Avery Meadow's grandparents opened the Moose Paddle Café by converting a blacksmith storefront connected to a livery stable. Food was served in the front, and poker games were dealt in the back room. Slot machines lined each side wall.

The café up for sale in 1942, and Terry Meadows built the Moose Paddle Inn as an affordable option for the upscale Moraine Hotel. The café was purchased by a little-known Norwegian skier named Bjarne Nilsen. He made the 1940 national ski team and trained in Jackson at the Antler Mountain Resort.

The 1940 and 1944 Olympic Games were postponed because of World War II. Rather than return to Norway, Nilsen convinced his uncle to help him buy the café so he could remain in Jackson. He became a business partner with an American skier named Inge Johansen. She was the daughter of Norwegian immigrants who came to Sun Valley, Idaho. She was also training in Jackson. Inger and Bjarne changed the name to the Nordic Chalet and added a Scandinavian menu, including raisin rounds.

The two eventually married in Jackson and had a son named Lars.

Both qualified for the 1948 Games. Inger won a cross-country skiing bronze medal. Bjarne placed 12th in the inaugural year of the alpine skiing event.

****

Raisin Rounds

Inger and Bjarne retired from skiing and led a quiet life. They turned over the Nordic Chalet to Lars and his daughter, Emilie.

Ingredients

Rounds

- Flour: 1 lb
- Baking Powder: 1 tsp
- White Sugar: 1½ cups
- Raisins: ½ cup

- Vanilla Extract: 1 tsp
- Butter: 1 lb
- Cream: 3 oz

Icing

- Cream Cheese: 1 package, 8 oz
- Butter: ½ cup
- Powdered Sugar: 1 cup
- Vanilla Extract: ½ tsp
- Hazelnuts: ¼ cup, chopped

Directions

Icing: Combine the butter, cream cheese, vanilla, and confectioner's sugar with a mixer on low until fluffy. Fold in the hazelnuts. Set aside. Preheat the oven to 400 degrees F.

Rounds: Mix the dry ingredients and the raisins in a medium bowl. Dice the butter and mix it into the flour mixture to a crumby consistency. Preheat the oven to 400 degrees F.

Pour the sugar onto a greased baking sheet or covered with parchment paper. Work the cream into a dough and refrigerate for at least 1 hour. Divide the dough and shape each half into a roll about 2 to 2 ½ inches in diameter. Cut the rolls into ½-inch slices.

Place the dough slices on the sugar and lightly roll or pat them to 4 to 5 inches in diameter. Flip the rounds over to coat both sides. Place the rounds on a parchment-lined baking sheet with space between each. Bake for 7 minutes or until evenly golden brown. Remove and cool. Spread the icing.

****

Rabbit Hutch - Jackson, Wyoming

The Jackson, Wyoming Rabbit Hutch was billed as Chinese with its weathered barn wood storefront on the downtown boardwalk. The restaurant was owned by a couple from Burma who emigrated amid political unrest in 1982.

Elizabeth wondered why the crab and cream cheese wontons were called "Crab Rangoon" in other restaurants.

When the British gave up control of Burma, the Anglicized names of places were changed back to the original names. The country's name became Myanmar, which the United States did not recognize.

****

Crab Yangon

A real estate development company in China hired a Wyoming architect to create a resort community near Shanghai modeled after Jackson Hole called Teton Trail. The stylized Rabbit inspired one restaurant in the project, completed in 2005.

Ingredients

Wontons

- Cream Cheese: 2 units, 8 oz, softened to room temperature
- Crab Meat: crab meat, 6 oz, fresh, frozen, canned, imitation
- Soy Sauce: 2 tbsp
- Sesame Oil: 2 tsp
- Minced Garlic: 1 tbsp, dry or fresh, to taste
- Green Onions: 1 bunch, finely chopped, to taste
- Wonton Wrappers: 1 package, 14 oz
- Egg Whites: from 1 egg
- Vegetable Oil: for deep frying

Sweet and Sour Sauce

- White sugar: 1 cup
- Water: 1 cup
- White vinegar: ½ cup
- Soy sauce: ¼ cup
- Cornstarch: 2 tbsp

- Asian hot sauce 2 tbsp, to taste

- Ketchup 2 tbsp (to taste)

Directions

Wontons: Add enough oil to submerge the wontons in a heavy-bottomed pan or Dutch oven. Heat to 375 degrees F. On a baking sheet, place paper towels for draining.

Mix cream cheese, crabmeat, soy sauce, sesame oil, garlic, and green onions in a medium bowl. Place egg whites in a small bowl.

Depending on the size of the wonton wrappers, drop 1 tsp, more or less of the filling, onto the middle of each wrapper.

Spread egg white on two edges of the wonton wrappers with your fingers. Fold diagonally into triangles and press together to seal the edges.

Divide the wontons into small batches and deep fry until golden brown, which should take 2 to 4 minutes. Remove wontons with a slotted spoon or chopsticks and drain them on the covered baking sheet.

Sweet and Sour Sauce: Place sugar, water, vinegar, soy sauce, hot sauce, ketchup, and cornstarch in a medium saucepan and boil. Stir until the sauce thickens.

****

Bison Horn Lodge B&B - Devil's Tower, Wyoming

Laramie Mountaineering sponsored a climbing trip to the Sierra de Organos National Park in a small town called Sombrerete in the state of Zacatecas. There wasn't much air service to Mexico. After the Calamity Club blow-up, Jack became a recluse and more focused on the business.

The partners chose Zacatecas for their tour of eight climbers because it was a relatively close bus ride from Laramie to Denver, where they caught a bus to El Paso. The climbing party cleared customs there and continued to Sombrerete.

The 18-hour, 700-mile bus ride stopped in every town along the way. Outside Vicente Guerrero, the federal police had set up a roadblock. Officers with machine guns boarded. The Laramie group was picked out of the crowd and searched for drugs.

It was late when they finally arrived at the Hostel Domingo in Sombrerete. The room reserved for Jack and Avery had been rented out. The last room available was one with one twin bed.

The fair-weather climbing was pretty good. The routes were short and made for leisurely days, leaving plenty of time to explore the 500-year-old sights and sounds of out-of-the-way Mexico.

Jack was interested in a small museum down the street from the hostel that displayed an exhibit claiming New Jersey inventor Thomas Edison was born in Sombrerete.

Their favorite breakfast place was on the rooftop of their hostel, where they drank bottomless glasses of fresh-squeezed fruit juice, Mexican hot chocolate, and *chilaquiles* baked with tortillas made from locally grown corn *masa*.

Chilaquiles

Avery adapted the Hostel Domingo recipe with ingredients available in Sundance, Wyoming.

Ingredients

- White Onion: 1 coarsely chopped
- Tomatillos: 6 to 8 (depending on size) Husks removed

- Anaheim pepper: 1 to 2 roasted, peeled, and seeded
- Jalapeno pepper: 0 to 1 or 2 roasted and seeded (omit if spiciness is a factor)
- Cilantro: ¾ cup chopped (or dried to taste)
- Garlic: 4 cloves coarsely chopped
- Chicken: 3 cups cooked and shredded
- Salt: To taste
- Cooking oil: ¼ cup (or an amount to cover the tortilla strips in the pan)
- Corn tortillas: A dozen 6", cut into three strips (or a like amount of tortilla chips)
- Cheese: 2 to 3 cups shredded (any white or orange will do)

Directions

Preheat the oven to 375 degrees F. Line a plate or surface with paper towels. Cut the tortillas into three strips. Roast Anaheim and Jalapeno peppers, peel and seed as necessary. Shred the chicken, and chop the onion and garlic.

Blend the tomatillos, onion, peppers, cilantro, garlic, and salt until smooth. Bring the mixture to a gentle boil in a saucepan. Reduce the heat and simmer. Stir the sauce often for about 10 minutes until thickened. Add the chicken to the sauce and simmer for another 5 minutes until the chicken is heated.

Add the oil to a large skillet over medium heat. Fry the tortilla strips in batches for 5 to 6 minutes until crisp. Place the strips on the paper towel-lined plate or surface to drain. You can substitute a similar amount of tortilla chips.

Place half of the tortilla strips in a 2-quart baking dish. Evenly spread half of the chicken sauce over the tortillas. Sprinkle half the grated cheese over the chicken sauce and repeat the layering.

Bake in the preheated oven for 30 to 40 or until the cheese is golden. Remove the chilaquiles from the oven and let them cool for a few minutes.

******

Good Fortune Casino - Concho, Oklahoma

Elizabeth spent most of her adult life in the hospitality industry. She consumed more than her fair share of restaurant cuisines from around the country. Gluten intolerance was her main source of misery in a job that offered fine dining experiences as an informal benefit.

The month she spent moving from New Orleans to points West was the most road food she'd ordered since the week it took her to relocate by car from Atlantic City to NOLA in 2004.

Reuben Salad

When Elizabeth and her father drove from Boulder to NOLA, the most creative food adaptation she encountered was the Reuben Salad concocted at the Good Fortune Casino. She informed the server about her gluten intolerance and feasted on a Reuben Salad. Out of curiosity, she tried a bite with a rye bread crouton and dealt with the consequences. Her indigestion was mild.

Ingredients

- Lettuce: Various types, torn
- Sauerkraut: To taste, drained and prepared
- Swiss cheese: Sliced and cut into strips or grated
- Pastrami: Precooked, sliced, and cut into strips
- Turkey: Precooked, sliced, and cut into strips
- Rye Bread: 1 or 2 slices diced into cubes for croutons
- Butter: 1 to 2 tbsp, depending on how rich you like your croutons
- Thousand Island Dressing: Enough for the side salad

Directions

Tear a variety of lettuce types into an adequately sized bowl and refrigerate. Slice and cut cheese, pastrami, and turkey, and set aside.

Dice the rye bread into cubes. Melt the butter, toast the rye bread cubes in a skillet, and set aside.

Spread the sauerkraut around the top of each salad bowl. Cover the sauerkraut with the cheese, pastrami, and turkey strips.

Serve Thousand Island Dressing and the rye bread croutons on the side.

Alan O'Hashi and Boulder Community Media (BCM) work with community-based media producers, organizations, and socially responsible businesses to develop their content in a culturally competent manner. His work through BCM seeks to capture the nuance and complexity of self-identity and expands the wider community's understanding of our pluralistic world.

Libby Flats is Alan's first novel. He writes books and makes movies that are not only important and meaningful but also entertaining and inspiring.

Through his books and movies, Alan wants audiences to experience the world from multiple angles, challenge their assumptions through stories, and gain a deeper understanding of individual self-identities and those different than our own.

His writing and movie-making explore the complexities of identity through his personal experiences with other people. Alan's works are powerful explorations of the intersections of race, ethnicity, culture, nationality, and gender and how these facets of identity shape our lives. He complicates the notion of what it means to be a non-white person living in the modern world and challenges the assumptions of others by sharing his experiences and perspectives.

By telling his stories on silver screens and the written page, Alan invites readers and viewers to reflect on their lives and grapple with the complexities of self-identity, not only in the present but also in the past. "I hope to create a more equitable and just society where people from all backgrounds can be seen and heard."

****

Alan hopes his friend and colleague Chris is out there someplace. If *Libby Flats* is made into a movie, Chris is invited to help write the screenplay!

Printed in the USA
CPSIA information can be obtained
at www.ICGtesting.com
CBHW080041060524
7981CB00003B/5